THE NAIL
AND THE ORACLE

Photo by Mark Zicree

Theodore Sturgeon circa 1962.

THE NAIL AND THE ORACLE

Volume XI:

The Complete Stories of

Theodore Sturgeon

Edited by
Paul Williams

Foreword by
Harlan Ellison®

North Atlantic Books
Berkeley, California

Published by
North Atlantic Books
P.O. Box 12327
Berkeley, California 94712

Cover photo collage and book design by Paula Morrison
Printed in the United States of America

The Nail and the Oracle is sponsored by the Society for the Study of Native Arts and Sciences, a nonprofit educational corporation whose goals are to develop an educational and cross-cultural perspective linking various scientific, social, and artistic fields; to nurture a holistic view of arts, sciences, humanities, and healing; and to publish and distribute literature on the relationship of mind, body, and nature.

North Atlantic Books' publications are available through most bookstores. For further information, visit our website at www.northatlanticbooks.com or call 800-733-3000.

Library of Congress Cataloging-in-Publication Data

Sturgeon, Theodore.

The nail and the oracle / by Theodore Sturgeon; edited by Paul Williams; foreword by Harlan Ellison.

p. cm.— (The complete stories of Theodore Sturgeon ; v. 11)

Summary: "The eleventh volume of the series by science-fiction author Theodore Sturgeon contains stories written between 1960 and 1969, including "How To Forget Baseball," a hitherto unanthologized short story"—Provided by publisher.

Includes bibliographical references and index.

ISBN-13: 978-1-55643-661-1 (hc : alk. paper)

ISBN-10: 1-55643-661-0 (hc : alk. paper)

1. Science fiction, American. I. Williams, Paul, 1948– II. Title.

PS3569.T875 A6 2006 vol. 11

813'.54—dc22

2007000769

2 3 4 5 6 7 8 9 SHERIDAN 19 18 17 16 15 14 13

Printed on recycled paper

EDITOR'S NOTE

THEODORE HAMILTON STURGEON was born February 26, 1918, and died May 8, 1985. This is the eleventh in a series of volumes that will collect all of his short fiction. The volumes and the stories within the volumes are organized chronologically by order of composition (insofar as it can be determined). This eleventh volume contains stories written between 1960 and 1969. "How to Forget Baseball," a story about a thrilling, horrifying future sport called Quoit, is anthologized here for the first time. A story co-authored with Harlan Ellison, "Runesmith," is also included.

Preparation of each of these volumes would not be possible without the hard work and invaluable participation of Noël Sturgeon, Debbie Notkin, and our publishers, Lindy Hough and Richard Grossinger. I would also like to thank, for their significant assistance with this volume, Harlan Ellison, Tina Krauss, Marc Zicree, Hart Sturgeon-Reed, Elizabeth Kennedy, Shannon Kelly, Eric Weeks, Chris Lotts at Ralph Vicinanza, Ltd., Cindy Lee Berryhill, T.V. Reed, and all of you who have expressed your interest and support. The Theodore Sturgeon Literary Trust can be accessed at www.theodoresturgeontrust.com.

BOOKS BY THEODORE STURGEON

Without Sorcery (1948)
The Dreaming Jewels [aka *The Synthetic Man*] (1950)
More Than Human (1953)
E Pluribus Unicorn (1953)
Caviar (1955)
A Way Home (1955)
The King and Four Queens (1956)
I, Libertine (1956)
A Touch of Strange (1958)
The Cosmic Rape [aka *To Marry Medusa*] (1958)
Aliens 4 (1959)
Venus Plus X (1960)
Beyond (1960)
Some of Your Blood (1961)
Voyage to the Bottom of the Sea (1961)
The Player on the Other Side (1963)
Sturgeon in Orbit (1964)
Starshine (1966)
The Rare Breed (1966)
Sturgeon Is Alive and Well ... (1971)
The Worlds of Theodore Sturgeon (1972)
Sturgeon's West (with Don Ward) (1973)
Case and the Dreamer (1974)
Visions and Venturers (1978)
Maturity (1979)
The Stars Are the Styx (1979)
The Golden Helix (1979)
Alien Cargo (1984)
Godbody (1986)
A Touch of Sturgeon (1987)
The [Widget], the [Wadget], and Boff (1989)
Argyll (1993)
The Ultimate Egoist (1994)
Microcosmic God (1995)
Killdozer! (1996)
Star Trek, The Joy Machine (with James Gunn) (1996)
Thunder and Roses (1997)
The Perfect Host (1998)
Baby Is Three (1999)
A Saucer of Loneliness (2000)
Bright Segment (2002)
And Now the News ... (2003)
The Man Who Lost the Sea (2005)

CONTENTS

Theodore Sturgeon and Harlan Ellison, San Francisco Civic Auditorium, 12 February 1977. Photo by Clay Geerdes.

FOREWORD

Abiding with Sturgeon: Mistral in the Bijou

By Harlan Ellison®

It is unlikely that I could have worshipped him more, the day he came to live with me, had his knock on my door been accompanied by thunder and roses. Let us get this clear between us, right from the git-go: I admired Ted Sturgeon more than words can codify. Not just the writing, but much of the man. Not just the art and craft, but the flawed weird duck who schlepped them.

We both smoked pipes, but Ted tamped his bowl full of a *grape*-flavored tobacco so sweetly and sickly redolent, it could stun a police dog. I was a little over thirty-five years old when Sturgeon came to live with me. Ted was just fluttering his wings around age fifty.

Herewith, the (by actual count) eleventh time I have started to write this recondite introduction to Volume XI of the North Atlantic Books collected *oeuvre* of the iconic H. Hunter Theodore Waldo Sturgeon, simply a Great Writer of Our Time. In preparation for this day—one I had foolishly hoped would never come—I have worried this exercise as would a pit bull with an intruder. But now it's here, and now I have dawdled and postponed and evaded to the point where I got put in the hospital for a couple of days. Evaded? As would the helot duck the knout! Ten times before I sat down here, put my two typing fingers on the keyboard of the stout Olympia manual office machine (that Ted sometimes usurped when he was here), and ten times I have said awfuckit and torn out the paper. Ten times. Now eleven. And everyone is screaming at me for my seemingly dilatory behavior.

And here's the flat of it, friends.

And Ted would understand.

Most of what I know about Ted Sturgeon, I cannot tell you.

* * *

In preparation for this endeavor, I have gone back and done my homework: I have reread all the guest forewords in the ten previous volumes: all twelve in ten big fat wonderful congeries of Ted's phantasmagoria—twelve in ten? Yeah, there were three in volume one—and let me assure you: this will not be a learned, long-bearded exegesis such as Chip Delany's, even though both Chip's and Ted's beards have inspired awe. Ah, but that's just splitting hairs. Nor will it be a charming and pop-pastoral reminiscence overflowing with the chirrups of songbirds reeling through Disneyesque delusions courtesy of LSD, à la Dave Crosby's piece that leads off Volume VI (though both of these friends of mine downed more acid than your local neighborhood hiatic hernia) . . .

* * *

a pause, if you'll indulge me. I never did drugs. Probably because I was on the road at an early age and saw what it could do to the creative process. But Ted did stuff, and I have neither the inclination nor the information to comment on what effect it had on him. But what I wanted to tell you was a sweet little moment tangential to the whole substance thing, and it was this:

Ted and I were at a party thrown by a brilliant young poet named Paul Robbins; something like in 1967. Everybody was toke'n and somebody passed me a doob the size of a stegosaurus coprolith, and I passed it on to Ted, sitting next to me. And, naturally, some yotz, whose paranoid orientation conned him into a sense of an ill wind blowing in the room, snarked at me, "Whassamatter, you don't want a hit?" And before I could tell him to mind his own, Ted said (in that lovely tenor), "Harlan won't use till he comes down."

I couda kissed him. And years later, Ted, commenting on how my stories could seem so hallucinatory when I'd never done drugs, told an interviewer, "Harlan is the only person I know who produces psilocybin in his bloodstream." Couda kissed him again.

Uh, for the record, Ted and I never kissed.

Although two men kissing is fine, just fine. Just saying.

* * *

. . . and this foreword will not be a well-intentioned and elegant homage to someone never met by the Introducing Entity, such as Jonathan Lethem's nice piece of Volume X; and it sure as hell isn't going to be a noblesse oblige accommodation such as the one my old chum Kurt Vonnegut proffered in Volume VIII.

It will no doubt upset the faithful, dismay the shy, outrage the punctilious, and get both Publisher and Series Editor to get off the trolley at downtown nose-outta-jointville. Complaints; oh yes, there will be complaints. I get a lot of complaints about my manner.

Yeah, well, if Ted or I had ever given much of a foof about the penalties pursuant to living our lives by our own manner, we sure as hell wouldn't have behaved the way we did, and still do.

But it is the eleventh attempt to climb this Nanga Parbat, in for a penny is in for a pound, either I do it or I don't. Had I my druthers, I wouldn't. But since Ted called me before he died to say he wanted *me* to do his obit . . .

* * *

. . . since we're in it together at this point, let me pause again to reprint some words. This is what I wrote for *Locus* an hour and a half after Ted died. It was on the first page of that "journal of record" of the science fiction world, June 1985, issue #293 if you care to check.

Theodore Sturgeon Dies

> It began raining in Los Angeles tonight at almost precisely the minute Ted Sturgeon died in Eugene, Oregon. Edward Hamilton Waldo would have cackled at the cosmic silliness of it; but I didn't. It got to me; tonight, May 8th, 1985.
>
> It had been raining for an hour, and the phone rang. Jayne Sturgeon said, "Ted left us an hour ago, at 7:59."
>
> I'd been expecting it, of course, because I'd talked to him—as well as he could gasp out a conversation with the fibrosis stealing his breath—early in March, long distance to Haiku, Maui, Hawaii. Ted had written his last story for me, for the

MEDEA project, and we'd sent him the signature plates for the limited edition. He said to me, "I want you to write the eulogy."

I didn't care to think about that. I said, "Don't be a pain in the ass, Ted. You'll outlive us all." Yeah, well, he *will,* on the page; but he knew he was dying, and he said it again, and insisted on my promise. So I promised him I'd do it, and a couple of weeks ago I came home late one night to find a message on my answering machine: it was Ted, and he'd come home, too. Come home to Oregon to die, and he was calling to say goodbye. It was only a few words, huskingly spoken, each syllable taking it out of him, and he gave me his love, and he reminded me of my promise; and then he was gone.

Now I have to say important words, extracted from a rush of colliding emotions. About a writer and a man who loomed large, whose faintest touch remains on everyone he ever met, whose talent was greater than the vessel in which it was carried, whose work influenced at least two generations of the best young writers, and whose brilliance remains as a reminder that this poor genre of dreams and delusions can be literature.

Like a very few writers, his life was as great a work of artistic creation as the stories. He was no myth, he was a legend. Where he walked, the ether was disturbed by his passage.

For some, he was the unicorn in the garden; for others, he was a profligate who'd had ten hot years as the best writer in the country, regardless of categorizations (even the categorization that condemned him to the ghetto); for young writers he was an icon; for the old hands who'd lived through the stages of his unruly life he was an unfulfilled promise. Don't snap at me for saying this: he liked the truth, and he wouldn't care to be remembered sans limps and warts and the hideous smell of that damned grape-scented pipe tobacco he smoked.

But who the hell needs the truth when the loss is still so painful? Maybe you're right; maybe we shouldn't speak of that.

It's only been an hour and a half since Jayne called, as I

write this, and my promise to Ted makes me feel like the mommy who has to clean up her kid's messy room. I called CBS radio, and I called the *Herald-Examiner,* and that will go a ways toward getting him the hail-and-farewell I think he wanted, even though I know some headline writer will say SCI-FI WRITER STURGEON DEAD AT 67.

And the kid on the night desk at the newspaper took the basics—Ted's age, his real name, the seven kids, all that—and then he said, "Well, can you tell me what he was known for? Did he win any awards?" And I got crazy. I said, with an anger I'd never expected to feel, "Listen, sonny, he's only gone about an hour and a half, and he was as good as you get at this writing thing, and no one who ever read *The Dreaming Jewels* or *More Than Human* or *Without Sorcery* got away clean because he could squeeze your heart till your life ached, and he was one of the best writers of the last half a century, and the tragedy of his passing is that *you* don't know who the fuck he was!" And then I hung up on him, because I was angry at his ignorance, but I was *really* angry at Ted's taking off like that, and I'm angry that I'm trying to write this when I don't know what to write, and I'm furious as hell that Ted made me promise to do this unthinkable thing, which is having to write a eulogy for a man who could have written his own, or any other damned thing, better than I or any of the rest of us could do it.

—Harlan Ellison®

* * *

... and since Noël won't spill the beans in *her* tureen, yet expects *me* to do it—"Get in there and suck up them bullets!" she said sweetly—even though she knows most of what I know—though not even between us can we seem to make the dates properly coincide—at least I have a living witness that what I write here is true. Ted's daughter and the Trustee of his Literary Estate; she has read this and vetted this.

Other forewords in this series have brilliantly dissected Ted's style, analyzed his widening circle effect on other writers ...

* * *

When I encounter the encomia of other writers about Sturgeon, and they gush something like, "I learned so much from him," or "his work taught me how to write," I think they are either fools, or they're lying. No, wait, that's unfair: not lying ... deluding themselves; so stunned by what Ted could do seemingly effortlessly, oblivious to what agony accompanied the doing of it, that they've become tropes of what Stephen King noticed about writers, if you leave sour milk open in the refrigerator, pretty soon *everything* in the box takes on the smell.

Yes, he certainly laid down a new architectural elevation every time a story left his nest (onward, madly onward flew the farraginous metaphors); and to be sure, any scribbling idiot can perceive his facility with language, like a pizza chef whirling that expansible crust aloft; and no question that there are glimmers of Ted's auctorial seminar *every*where these days; nonetheless, you *cannot* learn to write from Sturgeon any more conveniently than one could learn how to dance by studying Fred Astaire.

Ted was among the very best there ever were. And the way we're going, he may be among the very best there ever *will* be. He loved the sound of words the way trees love the wind, the way yin loves yang, the way the halves of Velcro love their mate (and Ted often contended that he had "invented" Velcro in one of his stories). Ted played and sang not only with the guitar, but with words like the best chum you ever had, like dopey kids drunk on the summertime, careering through an empty lot. Words were, to Ted, the best chums possible.

Inspirational, but out of reach. What he did, he did like Blackstone or Houdini, with lock-picks and escape engines from flaw-free fetters under his tongue, in his butt, up his nose. Ted was, in the purest sense of the word, a runesmith. (Yeah, that's the title of the story we wrote together—at least the one you know about—and it's in this very book if you want to pause and go read it and come back here ...

* * *

Don't say I'm not considerate of your feelings.)

Anyone who misbelieves that they learned to write by deconstructing a Sturgeon story—try it with "A Way of Thinking" in Volume VII, I double-dog-dare you!—is not only building castles in the air, he or she is trying to move furniture *into* it. Sturgeon was what he called me once: *rara avis*. Weird bird, existent in the universe in the number of one.

* * *

Do I interrupt myself? Very well then, I interrupt myself. I am large, I contain multitudes.

Here's what Ted wrote in 1967 as an introduction to my book of short stories, *I Have No Mouth & I Must Scream*. It goes here, correctly, because it was one of the spurs that moved and shook him to come stay with me. I was in deep anguish in 1967, some of the toughest times of my life, and Ted wrote this, in part:

> ... *You hold in your hands a truly extraordinary book. Taken individually, each of these stories will afford you that easy-to-take, hard-to-find,* very *hard-to-accomplish quality of entertainment. Here are strange and lovely bits of bitterness like "Eyes of Dust" and the unforgettable "Pretty Maggie Moneyeyes," phantasmagoric fables like "I Have No Mouth & I Must Scream" and "Delusion for a Dragon Slayer"* ...
>
> *There are a great many unusual things about Harlan Ellison and his work—the speed, the scope, the variety. Also the ugliness, the cruelty, the compassion, the anger, the hate. All seem larger than life-size—especially the compassion which, his work seems to say, he hates as something which would consume him if he let it. This is the explanation of the odd likelihood (I don't think it's every happened, but I think it could) that the beggar who taps you for a dime, and whom I ignore, will get a punch in the mouth from Harlan.*
>
> *One thing I found fascinating about this particular collection—and it's applicable to the others as well, once you find it out—is that the earlier stories, like "Big Sam," are at first*

glance more tightly knit, more structured, than the later ones. They have beginnings and middles and endings, and they adhere to their scene and their type, while stories like "Maggie Moneyeyes" and "I Have No Mouth" straddle the categories, throw you curves, astonish and amaze. It's an interesting progression, because most beginners start out formless and slowly learn structure. In Harlan's case, I think he quickly learned structure because within a predictable structure he was safe, he was contained. When he got big enough —confident *enough— he began to write it as it came, let it pour out as his inner needs demanded. It is the confidence of freedom, and the freedom of confidence. He breaks few rules he has not learned first.*

(There are exceptions. He is still doing battle with "lie" and "lay," and I am beginning to think that for him "strata" and "phenomena" will forever be singular.)

Anyway . . . he is a man on the move, and he is moving fast. He is, on these pages and everywhere else he goes, colorful, intrusive, abrasive, irritating, hilarious, illogical, inconsistent, unpredictable, and one hell of a writer. Watch him."

Theodore Sturgeon
Woodstock, New York 1967

And as I wrote for Ted's attention in a 1983 reprint of the book, for which I refused any number of Big Name offers to supplant Ted's 1967 essay: "Ted Sturgeon's dear words were very important to me in 1967 when they were shining new and this collection became the instrument that propelled my work and my career forward. To alter those words, or to solicit a new introduction by someone else, would be to diminish the gift that Ted conferred on me. This book has been in print constantly for sixteen years. . . . Only this need be said: I have learned the proper use of 'lie' and 'lay,' Ted."

* * *

"Watch him," he said. That was the lynch-pin of our long and no-bullshit, honest-speaking friendship. We were a lot alike. (Noël's son, age 16, has also read these pages and he declares I'm "a fantastic writer, and arrogant as hell." You just described your grandfather, kiddo.) A *lot* alike, and we watched each other. Avis to avis, two bright-eyed, cagey, weird birds assaying a long and often anguished observation of each other—Ted, I think, seeing in me where and who he had been—me, for certain, seeing in him where I was bound and who I would be in my later years, which are now. We were foreshadow and *déjà vu*. We were chained to each other, in more a creepy than an Iron John way.

I had watched him from afar, before I met him, when I reviewed the just published *More Than Human* in the May-July issue #14 (1954) of my mimeographed fanzine, *Dimensions*. I was an extremely callow nineteen, Ted was only thirty-six and married to Marion, living back East in Woodstock, I think; Noël still had two years to go before she could get borned.

With all the imbecile *sangfroid* of, oh, I'd say, an O-Cel-O sponge mop, I pontificated the following comment on Sturgeon at his most exalted best:

> Book reviewers, like Delphic Oracles, are a breed of individuals self-acknowledged to be authorities on everything—including everything. Thus it is with some feelings of helplessness that a reviewer finds he is totally unprepared or capable in describing a book.
>
> It happens only once in every thousand years or so, and is greater tribute to any book than a word of praise for each of those years. So enjoy the spectacle, dear reader.
>
> Theodore Sturgeon has expanded his Galaxy novella "*Baby Is Three*" into a tender and deeply moving chronicle of *people*, caught in the maelstrom of forces greater than any of them. The book, in case you missed it above, is *More Than Human*, and insures the fact that if Ballantine Books were to cease all publication with this volume, their immortality would be ensured.
>
> We have dragged out more than we thought we could. Sturgeon is impeccable in this novel. Unquestionably the finest piece of work in the last two years, and the closest approach to literature science fiction has yet produced.

* * *

We watched the hell out of each other. After we met, if I remember accurately, in the autumn of 1954, I remember taking offense at a remark the late Damon Knight had made about Ted's story "The Golden Egg" (he opined, the story "starts out gorgeously and develops into sentimental slop"), and Ted just snickered and said, "Damon can show a mean streak sometimes."

Later in life, one day I remembered that and chuckled to myself and thought, "No shit."

Ted called me one time, before he lived here, and sang me the lyrics to "Thunder and Roses." I wrote them down, ran them in *Dimensions,* in issue #15, and when next Ted called me, we sang it together. Ted wrote quite a few songs. They were awful, just awful. What I'm trying to vouchsafe here is that in terms of songwriting, both Pinder and Cole Porter felt no need of stirring in their respective graves at the eminence of Sturgeon's lyricism. He was superlative at what he did superlatively, but occasionally even Ted pulled a booger.

Oh, wait a minute, I have just *got* to tell you this one . . .

* * *

. . . no, hold it, before I tell you *that* one—Ted and the guy reading *The Dreaming Jewels*—I've got to tell you *this* one, which Noël just reminded me of, he said ending a sentence with a preposition.

One early evening, I was rearranging a clothes closet, and I unshipped a lot of crap that had been gathering dust on a top shelf. And Ted was just hanging out watching, for no reason (we used to talk books a lot but I don't think on that particular evening he was again driving me crazy in his perseverance, trying to turn me on to Eugene Sue's *The Wandering Jew* or *The Mysteries of Paris*). And I pulled down this neat tent that I'd used years before, when I was a spelunker; and Ted got interested in it, and he unzipped and unrolled it, and of a sudden this nut-case says to me, "We should go camp out."

Now, two things you should know, one of which Noël remarked when she reminded me of this anecdote. "The two *least* Boy Scouts in the world!" And she laughed so hard her cheek hit the cancel button on her cell-phone, and that was the end of *that* conversation. (Which is a canard, because I was, in fact, an actual Cub and Boy Scout, WEBELOS and all, with merit badges, when I was a kid, so take *that,* Ms. Smartass Sturgeon.) And the second thing you should know is that my home, Ellison Wonderland, aka The Lost Aztec Temple of Mars, sits at the edge of two hundred acres of watershed land and riparian vegetation, high in the Santa Monica Mountains, facing what is known as Fossil Ridge—two million year old aquatic dead stuff in the rocks—now part of what the Santa Monica Mountains Conservancy has designated Edgar Rice Burroughs Park because the land that Carl Sagan and Leonard Nimoy and I saved from developers is *exactly* where the creator of Tarzan and Barsoom used to have picnics, back in the early 1900s.

Okay, so now you know that, and now you know why this resident nut-case Sturgeon is saying to me, "Let's go and camp out."

Which—don't ask me why, it *seemed* like a good idea at the time—is why I found myself the next night in a tent, outdoors, in the middle of a very humid spring night, with semi-nekkid Sturgeon, eating gypsy stew out of a tin can that fuckin' exPLOded, festooning the inside of the tent wherein I slept till the mosquitoes and no-see'ms gorged on my flesh and I crawled moaning back to the house at three a.m....

* * *

Here's the one I was going to tell you before I got feetnoted: Ted had a surfeit of hubris. Every *good* writer has it, especially those who scuff toe in the dirt and do an aw-shucks-ma it weren't nothin'. (John Clute, the critic, just calls it "shucksma.") False humility is bullshit or, as Gustave Flaubert put is much more elegantly, "Modesty is a kind of groveling."

But Ted had that scam down pat. He could act as shy as the unicorn in the garden, but inside he was festooned with bunting and firecrackers for his talent. One would have to be in a coma to be as good as he was, as often as he was, not to revel inwardly at the power. He was selfish and self-involved, even as you and I. He was also generous, great-hearted, and loyal.

Yet in all the analyses I've read in the previous ten volumes, no one else seems to have perceived that Ted—who was touted, by me as well as others, as knowing all there was to know about love—was a man in flames. He had loathings and animosities and an elitism that ran deep. He knew genuine anguish. But he also knew more cleverly than anyone else I've ever met, that it was an instant turn-off; if he wanted to get what he wanted, he had to sprinkle dream dust; and so he filtered his frustration and enmity like Sterno through a loaf of pumpernickel, distilling it into a charm that could Svengali a Mennonite into a McCormick Thresher.

From the starting blocks, Ted had been lumbered with the words "science fiction," and unlike Bierce or Poe or Dunsany, he never got out of the ghetto. Dean Koontz and Steve King know what I'm talking about; and so does Kurt, who created Kilgore Trout, who was Sturgeon. He wanted passionately to get out of the penny-a-word gulag, and he *knew* he was better than most of those who'd miraculously accomplished the trick.

Ted had gotten into writing because he understood all the way to the gristle the truth of that Japanese aphorism: *The nail that stands too high will be hammered down.* And while I'm citing clever sources, Ted also got into the writing in resonance to Heinrich Von Kleist's "I write only because I cannot stop."

But he also knew it was a gig. It was a job. Masonry and pig-iron ingots and pulling the plough. Not a lifetime job for guys like Ted and me, weird ducks who'd rather play than labor. A kind of frenetic, always-working laziness. Tardy, imprecise, careless of the feelings of others, obsessed and selfish. He was, I am, it's a fair cop. So he and I have produced enough work to shame a plethora of others, enough to fill more than a dozen big fat *Complete Sturgeon*s or *Essential Ellison*s. What no one ever realizes is that it's all the product of guilt and laziness, guilt *because* of the laziness.

We know what we *can* be, but we cannot get out of our own way. Ted was the king of that disclosure. He could not cease being Sturgeon for a moment, and he was chained to the genre that was too small for him.

(Ted once told me, and everyone I have dealt with since has told me I'm full of shit and lying, that he *hated* the title, "A Saucer of Loneliness" that Horace Gold attached to the story before he'd even finished writing it—because UFOs were "hot" and "sexy" at that time—and that he'd originally wanted to call it just "Loneliness" and sell it to a mainstream, non-sf market. Apparently he wrote it as a straight character study, couldn't move it—same with "Hurricane Trio" he said—and did it as Gold had suggested.)

(Had a helluva fight with the brilliant Alan Brennert over titling "Saucer" when Alan wrote his teleplay for *The Twilight Zone* on CBS in 1985 when we worked the series together.)

No matter how congenial, how outgoing, how familial, Ted knew way down in the gristle what Hunter Thompson identified as "... the dead end loneliness of a man who makes his own rules." And it made for anguish because he was imprisoned in a literary gulag where there was—and continues to be—such an acceptance of mediocrity that it is as odious as a cultural cringe. And Ted wanted more. Always *more.*

More life, more craft, more acceptance, more love, more of a shot at Posterity. Not to be categorized, seldom to be challenged, just famous enough that even when he wasn't at top-point efficiency everyone was so in awe of him that they were incapable of slapping him around and making him work better. That kind of adulation is death to a writer as incredibly *Only* as was Theodore Sturgeon. He hungered for better, and he deserved better, but he could not get out of his own way, and so ... for years and years ...

He burned, and he coveted, and he continued decanting those fiery ingots, all the while leading a life as disparate and looney as Munchausen's. He knew love, no argument, but it was the saving transmogrification from fevers and railings against the nature of his received world. And this anecdote I want to relate—as funny as it tells now—was idiomatic of Ted's plight.

Here's what happened.

What we were doing in a Greyhound bus station, damned if I can remember. But there we were, about five of us—I think Bill Dignin was one of the group, and I seem to recall Gordy Dickson, as well. But Ted and I and the rest of these guys were going somewhere chimerical, the sort of venue my Susan likes to refer to as Little Wiggly-On-Mire. And there we sat at a table waiting for our bus, chowing down on grilled cheese and tomato sandwiches, or whatever, and one of the guys nudged Ted and did a "Psst," and indicated a guy at the counter, who was (so help me) reading the Pyramid paperback reissue of Ted's terrific novel, *The Dreaming Jewels* (under the re-title *The Synthetic Man*). And it just tickled Ted, and he came all a-twinkle, and whispered to us, "Watch this, you'll love it."

And Ted got up, sidled over to the dude, slid onto the stool next to him and, loud enough for us to hear, cozened the guy with the remark, "Watchu readin'?" and the dude absently flashed the cover, said it was something like a fantasy novel, and Ted said archly, "How can you waste your time reading such crap?"

And we waited for the guy to defend his taste in reading matter to this impertinent buttinski. We held our breaths waiting for the guy to correct this stranger with lofty praise for what a great writer this Theodore Sturgeon was.

The guy looked down at the book for a scant …

Shrugged, and said, "Y'know, you're right," and he flipped it casually across the intervening abyss into the cavernous maw of a huge mound-shaped gray trash container. Then he paid his coffee tab, slid off the stool, and moto-vated out of the Greyhound station.

We knew better than to laugh.

Ted came back; and he had the look of ninth inning strike three. None of us mentioned it again.

It seemed funny at the time. Not so funny when I write about it.

* * *

Here's a funny one. I don't have this authenticated, that is to say, I (thankfully) have no photos, but I sort of always knew that Ted had an inclination toward, well, not wearing clothes. *Your* doctor would call it nudity. Now, as I say, I don't know if Ted was a card-carrying *nudist* at any time in his life, but around here he started walking around *sans raiment*. I could not have that. Not just because we had studio people and other writers and girl friends and the one or two people who made up my "staff" *also in situ*, but mostly because bare, Ted was not any more divine an apparition than are each of you reading this. He had blue shanks, scrawny old guy legs, muscular but ropey; he wasn't inordinately hairy, but what there was . . . well . . . it was *disturbing;* a little pot belly that pooched out, *also* mildly distressing; I will not speak of his naughty bits. But there they were, wagglin' in the breeze. I am, I know, a middle-class disappointment to Ted's ghost, that I am thus so hidebound, but I simply could not have it. Particularly, especially, notably after The Incidents:

Primus: he decided to make *Paella* for me and a select group of dinner party favorites. So we got him this big *olla,* and amassed for him the noxious ingestibles (did I mention, I not only *hate* this olio, would rather have someone hot-glue my tongue to a passing rhino than to partake of *Paella*), and off into the kitchen went the naked Sturgeon. A day he took. A whole day. No one went near the kitchen. I sent *out* for my coffee. And here's what is the Incident aspect of it: as he mish'd that mosh, he used his hands, alternately digging into the heating morass and then occasionally *scratching his ass.* I am not, I swear on the graves of my Mom and Dad, not making this up. I have no idea if others in the house saw it, but I did, and I got to tell you, had I not loathed *Paella* out of the starting-gate, that tableau from The Great Black Plague would have put me off it at least till the return of the Devonian.

(Another footnote within an anecdote inside a reminiscence: Ted was impeccable. Clean. This was a clean old man I'm talkin' here. Not obsessive about it, not some pathological nut washing his hands every seven minutes, but *clean.* So don't get the idea that the horror! the horror! of The *Paella* Incident stemmed from Sturgeon uncleanliness, it was just straightforward here-is-a-dude-slopping-his-claws-in-our-dinner-and-then-maybe-skinning-a-squirrel-who's-to-know.)

Secundus: he liked being helpful; little chores; nice short houseguest strokes that won one's loyalty and affection. Did I mention, Ted used charm the way Joan of Arc used Divine Inspiration. He could sell sandboxes to Arabs. Charm d'boids outta the trees. Devilish weaponry. So: little aids and assists. Such as answering the doorbell every now and then. Which was all good, all fine, except most of the time he forgot he was *bareass nekkid!* Capped as Incident on the afternoon, as god—even though I'm an atheist—is my witness, he answered the door and the Avon cosmetics lady in her Ann Taylor suit and stylish pumps gave a strangled scream, dropped her attaché sample case, her ordering pad, her gloves (I think), and flailed away down the street like a howler monkey.

Tertius: after the cops left, I laid down the law. No more Incidents. Put the fuck some *clothes* on, Ted! I don't care if it's SCUBA gear, mukluks and a fur parka, a suit of body armor, but you *will* henceforth go forth *avec* apparel!

So he started wearing a tiny fire-engine red Speedo.

I cannot begin to convey how disturbing *that* was, mostly because the li'l pot belly overhung that *sexe-cache* the way the demon Chernabog overhung the valley in Disney's *Fantasia.*

Avon has never sent a rep to my house since that day, decades ago. Also, Pizza Hut will not deliver. Go figure.

* * *

And so it went on with us for more than thirty years. Ted growing more ensnared by a received universe that was both too small to contain him while simultaneously telling him he was a titan. It is hideously bifurcating to go among one's readers, many of whom look upon you as the mortal avatar of The Inviolable Chalice of Genius, having had to borrow the bus-fare to get cross-country to the convention. He grew more and more careless of what his actions and life-choices would do to those he left behind, yet to those who met him casually he was more charming than a cobra at a mongoose rally.

And we continued to watch each other; sometimes to watch *over* each other. I have a letter I'd like to insert here. It was written during that very tough time in 1966–67 I mentioned earlier in this jaunt.

Thought it may not seem so, this long in the wind, this exegesis is not about me. It is about the trails Ted and I cut with each other. The other guest introductions are variously great, good, okay and slight; but this one is the only one that minutely tries to codify the odd parameters of an odd friendship, a human liaison. So I'll not go into particulars about the shitstorm under which I went to my knees in '67–'68, save to tell you true that I was neither feckless nor freshly kicked off the turnip truck.

Nonetheless, I got hit hard, and Ted wrote this to me, dated April 18, 1966:

Dear Harlan:

For two days I have not been able to get my mind off your predicament. Perhaps it would be more accurate to say that your predicament is on my mind, a sharp-edged crumb of discomfort which won't whisk away or dissolve or fall off, and when I move or think or swallow, it gigs me.

I suppose the aspect that gigs me the most is "injustice." Injustice is not an isolated homogeneous area any more than justice is. A law is a law and is either breached or not, but justice is reciprocal. That such a thing should have happened to you is a greater injustice than if it happened to most representatives of this exploding population.

I know exactly why, too. It is an injustice because you are on the side of the angels (who, by the way, stand a little silent for you just now). You are in the small company of Good Guys. You are that, not by any process of intellectualization and decision, but reflexively, instantly, from the glands, whether it shows at the checkout in a supermarket where you confront the Birchers, or in a poolroom facing down a famous bully, or in pulling out gut by the hank and reeling it up on the platen of your typewriter.

There is no lack of love in the world, but there is a profound shortage in places to put it. I don't know why it is, but most people who, like yourself, have an inherent ability to claw their way up the sheerest rock faces around, have little of it or have so equipped themselves with spikes and steel hooks that you can't see it. When it shows in such a man—like it does in you—when it lights him up, it should be revered and cared for. This is the very nub of the injustice done you. It should not happen at all, but if it must happen, it should not happen to you.

You have cause for many feelings, Harlan: anger, indignation, regret, grief. Theodore Reik, who has done some brilliant anatomizations of love, declares that its ending is in none of these things: if it is, there is a good possibility that some or one or all of them were there all along. It is ended with indifference— *really ended with a real indifference. This is one of the saddest things I know. And in all my life, I have found one writer, once, who was able to describe the exact moment when it came, and it is therefore the saddest writing I have ever read. I give it to you now in your sadness. The principle behind the gift is called 'counter-irritation.' Read it in good health — eventual.*

. . . and in case you think you misheard me over the phone, I would like you to know that if it helps and sustains you at all, you have my respect and affection.

Yours, T. H. Sturgeon

Accompanying the letter was number 20 of *Twenty Love Poems Based on the Spanish by Pablo Neruda,* by Christopher Logue, from *Songs* (1959). And then, quickly, *Dangerous Visions* was published, Ted's marriage to Marion underwent heartbreak, Ted and I talked cross-country virtually every day, and in the wake of the notoriety of DV and his story, "If All Men Were Brothers, Would You Let One Marry Your Sister?" which I had chivvied him into writing after a protracted writer's block dry spell and financial reverses, Ted came to live with me.

It was 1966, '67, and at various times I think it was for a full year, at other times memory insists it was longer, but separate inputs staunchly declare it was only six, eight, ten months. I can't recall precisely, now more than forty years later, but it seemed to go on forever.

I have all of Ted's books, of course, but the only two he ever signed were my copy of *Dangerous Visions* with *all* the authors logged on—a rare artifact existent in the universe, as I've said, in the number of one—and my personal library copy of his first collection, *Without Sorcery,* Prime Press 1948, for which I paid a buck fifty (marked down from $3.00) in 1952. Here is what he wrote on the front flyleaf in May of 1966 during my birthday gathering:

To Harlan Ellison –
Who has, at an equivalent stage in his career, done so much more — so much better.
Theodore Sturgeon

That's gracious crap, of course, but what I *did* do was get Theodore Sturgeon writing again.

In the wake of my own day and night hammering on one of the half dozen or so Olympia office machines (never mind how many Olympia portables I had stashed), Ted grew chagrined at his facility to *talk* new story-ideas but not to *write* them, and I rode him mercilessly. The phrase "your fifteen minutes of fame has drained out of the hourglass" became taunt and tautology. I showed him no mercy; and with so many other younger writers passing through the way station of my home, all of them on the prod, worshipful but competitive, Ted ground his teeth and set up shop in the blue bedroom, and began writing.

I'd long-since gotten him inside *Star Trek,* but now—for the fastest money in town—I opened the market at *Knight* magazine. Sirkay Publications. Holloway House. The low-end men's magazines: *Adam, Cad, Knight, The Adam Bedside Reader.* Two hundred and fifty, three hundred, sometimes a little more, each pop . . . paid within 24 hours. Sometimes we'd kick the story around at the breakfast table; sometimes he'd come into my then tiny office at the front of the house, dead of night, as I was pounding away under the unrelenting pressure of studio or publication deadlines, and we'd noodle something out. Sometimes it was a snag in one of my stories, sometimes it was a glitch in his.

And we wrote "Runesmith" together. And he wrote or plotted or set aside a snippet of the following, here at Ellison Wonderland: "The Patterns of Dorne," "It Was Nothing—Really!" and "Brownshoes," "Slow Sculpture," and "Suicide," "It's You," and "Jorry's Gap," "Crate," and "The Girl Who Knew What They Meant." Maybe others, I can't remember. But most of the stories that he finished when he was living with Wina about a mile away from me down the hill at 14210 Ventura Boulevard, La Fonda Motel, he plotted and started here before I threw him out.

Here's the flat of it, friends.

And Ted would understand this.

Most of what I know about Theodore Sturgeon I cannot tell you.

* * *

We watched each other. He looked after me. I tried to help him. And then came out *Sturgeon Is Alive and Well . . .*

Many of the stories from that last, final collection of (almost) new fictions, got born here. Right downstairs in the blue bedroom. And I harassed my buddy Digby Diehl, the now-famous editor, who was at that time the editor of the *Los Angeles Times Book Review* section, to let me review *Alive and Well.* And he did, beneath the copy editor's headline "Sturgeon's Law Overtakes Him."

No good deed . . .

Here, reprinted for the first time, is that review, from the April 18th, 1971 *Los Angeles Times.*

You will kindly note the cost of this 221 page hardcover in the early Seventies. This will give you an idea of the kind of money a writer as excellent as Sturgeon had to subsist on, it will also inform your understanding of the love-hate attitude even as lauded an artist as Sturgeon had with his work environment.

Sturgeon Is Alive and Well
A new collection of stories by
Theodore Sturgeon
(G.P. Putnam's Sons—$4.95)

Alive and well, yes definitely. But up to the level of his past brilliance, no I'm afraid not.

Theodore Sturgeon, you see, is without argument one of the finest writers—of any kind—this country has ever produced. His novels *More Than Human, Some of Your Blood,* and *The Dreaming Jewels* stand untarnished by time and endless re-readings as purest silver. His short stories have so completely examined the parameters of love in a genre of imagination woefully shy in that particular, that the words *love* and *Sturgeon* have become synonymous. The word *syzygy* also belongs to him.

He is also much-quoted as the author of Sturgeon's Law, a Deep Thought that suggests 90% of *every*thing is mediocre . . . puddings, plays, politicians; cars, carpenters, coffee; people, books, neurologists . . . *every*thing. A realistic assessment of the impossibility of achieving perfection that, till now, has applied to everyone and everything save Sturgeon. Sadly, and at long last, his own Law has caught up with him. Ninety per cent of this new collection of stories is mediocre.

After a long and painful dry spell in which the creative well seemed emptied, Sturgeon began writing again three years ago, and eleven of the twelve stories herein contained date from this latest period of productivity. Only two of them approach the brilliance of stories like "The Silken-Swift," "A Saucer of Loneliness," "Killdozer," or "Bianca's Hands." It has been said time and again about Sturgeon, that had he not suffered the ghastly stigmatizing ghettoization of being tagged a "science fiction" writer, he might easily surpass John Collier, Donald Barthelme, Ray Bradbury, or even Kurt Vonnegut as a mainstream fantasist of classic stature. Yet here, freed of that restriction, the fictions seem thin and too slick and forgettable; stories that could have been written by men not one thousandth as special as Theodore Sturgeon.

"To Here and the Easel," a 1954 novelette printed here in hardcover for the first time (and the only story to have a previous publication), is the longest, and the dullest. A fantasy of schizophrenia in which a painter who can't paint swings back and forth between his life as Giles, helpless before his empty white canvas, and his life as Rogero, a knight out of *Orlando Furioso,* this overlong and rococo morality play seems embarrassingly reminiscent of the kind of pulp writing typified by L. Ron Hubbard's *Slaves of Sleep,* a novel bearing almost exactly the same plot-device Sturgeon employs.

Of the remaining eleven tales, five are straight mainstream, four are clearly s-f oriented, and two are borderline. However, only two crackle with the emotional load *aficionados* have come to revere in Sturgeon's work. In "Take Care of Joey," a man whose world-view is built on the concept that no one performs a seemingly unselfish act "without there's something in it for him," finds just such a situation operating. A nasty, troublemaking little bastard named Joey is watched over by a guy named Dwight, who obviously hates the little rat. He goes way out of his way to keep Joey from getting the crap kicked out of him, up to and past the point where Dwight himself gets stomped. The narrator of the story has to find out why, and he does, and he finds out something else that makes this eleven-page short a stunning example of Sturgeon's off-kilter insight and humanity.

"The Girl Who Knew What They Meant" is the other winner and it is so carefully-constructed, so meticulously-spun that not until the last twenty-seven words, the final three sentences, does the reader know he has had his soul wrung like the neck of a chicken. It is Sturgeon transcendent. And if Martha Foley's *Best American Short Stories* overlooks it this year, surely there is no justice.

On sum, though the book is weak and for the most part a terrible disappointment, merely having Sturgeon writing again—and being able to prove it with slugs of type—is a blessing. And even with typographical errors rampant (a felony heretofore difficult to charge to Putnam's) it is a book well worth having done. Not just for those two incredible little short stories but by the same rationale that insists we preserve every letter and laundry list written by a Lincoln, a Hemingway or a Melville.

What I'm trying to say, is that Sturgeon is one of our best. He will be read and enjoyed a hundred years from now. So we *must* see it all, even the least successful of it.

This has been a difficult review to write.

* * *

Ted never told me what he thought of that piece. We had no bitterness over it, but we never sat down to bagels and lox about it, either. We were friends, and both of us knew that meant unshakeable trust in the truth that we loved each other, that we respected and admired the best of each other's work in such a way that to blow smoke and/or sunshine up each other's kilt would have been to poison that trust. Unlike many writers who expect their friends to write blurbs and dispense encomia on the basis of camaraderie rather than the absolute quality of the work, Ted and I understood that we could lie to others that way, but never to each other.

So. Enough.

I have more, endless more that I could set down about Ted, about abiding with Ted, about the chill wind blowing through the burlesque houses of both of our lives, but enough is enough.

Noël has suggested that I take the eulogy I wrote for Ted in 1985, that appears near the beginning of this essay, and move it back here, because every time she reads it, she cries.

And she thinks it is a proper end for this love letter to my friend now dead more than two decades.

No, dear Noël, it has to stay where it is; and I'll tell you my thinking here.

Ted wanted me to write his eulogy. He made me promise. And I did it. But I was so wracked by loss at the time, it was brief, far briefer than *this* eulogy. And thus I left out most of what's set down here in print for the first—and last—time. It is the for-real eulogy Ted probably wanted, and which I have perceived is being read over my shoulder as I've written it, by Ted's ghost. Not for you, Noël, not for any of Ted's other kids, not for Marion, not for the publisher who is herewith getting a major piece unexpectedly, and sure as hell not for admirers, fans, readers of Ted's work.

I have written this because Ted needs to read it, and because it is a picture of The Great Artist that cannot exist via *hoi polloi*. It had to be done by me, kiddo; and if you think this is all of it . . .

Most of what I know about Theodore Sturgeon I cannot tell you.

I haven't told you about the two times we fought, the first being the imbroglio over that meanspirited piss-ant, the toweringly talented British novelist Anthony Burgess, who was a nasty little shit; and the second time subsequent to Ted doing one of the most awful things I've ever known of a human being doing to others, resulting in my telling him to get the fuck outta my house, now, tonight, this minute!

I haven't told you about Ted and the Meatgrinder; Ted and the Tongue-Tied Germans; Ted and the Apollo Trip; Ted and Chuck Barris in Movieland; Ted and the Wing-Walker; Ted and the Naked Monkey. Oh, trust me, I could go on for days. But . . .

Enough.

I would have liked to've written more extensively about how Ted and I wrote together, but Paul Williams has covered some of that in the story-notes, and the rest is whispers and memories. So, at last, after more than twenty years, Ted, I've kept my promise. In full.

* * *

To say, at finish, only this. I miss my friend. I miss Ted's charm, his chicanery, his talent, his compassion. I miss them because they will never, not ever, not embodied in anyone or anything, never ever exist on any plane we can perceive. Those of you who never met him, who have only read him, can know what an emptiness there will forever be in your life. Because I know the emptiness in mine.

Harlan Ellison®
30 January 2007
Sherman Oaks, CA

Ride In, Ride Out

Beware the fury of a patient man.
—John Dryden, *Absalom and Achitophel*

Midafternoon and he came to a fork in the road. Just like the rest of us in all our afternoons, whether we know it at the time or not.

Younger Macleish liked the left fork. His horse's sleepy feet preferred the right, a bit downgrade as it was, and Macleish thought what the hell, he was ready to like the right fork too. He liked the country right, left, and whatever, from the white peaks feeding snow water to high timber and good grama range, across and down through the foothills where the low curly bunch-grass grew, and on to the black-earthed bottomland. But then it didn't need to be all that good to please Younger Macleish today. He was of a mind to like salt-flat or sage, crows, cactus or a poison spring, long as the bones lay pretty there.

Around the mountain (right fork, left fork, it's all the same) and three hundred miles beyond lay fifteen thousand well-fenced acres and a good warm welcome. Ninety-nine times Younger Macleish had said no to his cousin's offer, for he had some distances to pace off and some growing up to do on his own. Now he'd said yes and was ambling home to a bubbling spring and an upland house; not too far away lived a pair of the prettiest blue-eyed sisters since crinolines were invented, while down the other way—if a man found he couldn't choose—lived an Eastern school-marm with a bright white smile and freckles on her nose. Right now he had four months pay in his poke, his health, a sound horse, a good saddle, and no worriments. If a man likes where he's been and where he's headed, he's fair bound to like where he is.

As the shadows grew longer, this horse, he thought approvingly, has the right idea, for the trail is good and the passes this side of the mountain might make a little more sense after all. And if things are as they should be, there'll be a settlement down yonder, maybe big enough for a hotel with a sheet on the bed and a bite of something other than trail bacon and boiled beans.

With the thought came the settlement, opening up to him as the trail rounded a bluff. It was just what he had in mind, plus a cut extra—a well-seasoned cowtown with a sprinkling of mining. It had two hotels, he saw as he rode in, the near one with a restaurant and a livery right handy to it. There was a mercantile, more cow than plow, and half the barber shop was an assay office.

Younger Macleish rode up to the livery and slid off. He hooked an elbow around the horn and arched his back hard.

"Ridin' long?"

Macleish turned around and grinned at the tubby little old baldhead who stood in the carriage door. "My back says so . . . Treat hosses po'ly here, do you?"

The old man grinned in return and took the bridle. "Misable," he asserted. "Whup 'em every hour."

"Well, whack this'n with a oat or two an' give him water if he wants it or not."

"He'll rue the day," said the oldster, his eyes twinkling.

Macleish followed him far enough inside for a glance to assure him that water really was there and that the hay was hay. Then he unbuckled his saddlebags and heaved them over his shoulder. "Which one o' them hotels is best?"

"One of 'em ain't rightly a hotel."

"I'll start out at the other."

"The near one, then. Miz Appleton, now, she *feeds*." The old man colored his information by casting his eyes upward most devoutly.

"Now, you know I ain't et since my last meal?" Chuckling, Younger Macleish humped his saddlebags and stepped out into the street. It was only a step to the hotel porch, barely time enough to say howdy twice to passers-by. Macleish mounted the steps and thudded inside. It was small in there, but it had a stairway with a landing up the left and across the back, and under the landing, just like in the city but littler, a regular hotel kind of desk. He knew something was cooking right now, somewhere in the place, with onions and butter both, and he knew that not long ago something had been baked with vanilla in it. Everything was so clean he wanted to go out and shine his boots and come in again. Behind the desk was a doorway covered by nothing at all but red and blue beads. These moved and fell to again behind a little lady fat as the old livery man, but half his age and not the least bit bald. Her face was soft and plump as a sofa pillow and she had a regular homecoming smile.

"You'll be Miz Appleton."

"Come in. Put down those bags. You've come a ways, the looks of you. You hungry?"

Macleish looked around him, at the snowy antimacassars and the doilies under the vases of dried ferns and bright paper flowers, all of it spotless. "I feel dirtier'n I do hongry, but if I git any hongrier I'll be dead of it. My name's Younger Macleish."

"You hurry and wash," she ordered him like kinfolk, "while I set another something on the stove. You'll find water and soap on the stand in your room, first right at the head of the stairs." She gave him a glad smile and was gone through the wall of beads before he could grin back.

He shouldered his saddlebags and climbed the stairs, finding the room just where she had said, and just what the immaculate downstairs had led him to expect. He stood a moment in it shyly, feeling that a quick move would coat the walls with his personal grime, then shrugged off the feeling and turned to the washstand.

He had no plan to get all that fancied up; he just wanted to be clean. But clean or not, just plain shirtsleeves didn't feel right to him in that place, and all he had to put over it was his Santiago vest. It had on it some gold-braid curlicues and a couple extra pockets and real wild satin lapels that a puncher might call Divin' W if it was a brand. He put it on after he'd shaved till it hurt and reamed out his ears; he had half an idea Miz Appleton would send him back upstairs if they weren't clean. He took off his pants and whacked off what dust he could, and put them on again and did his best to prettify the boots. When he was done he cleaned up from his cleaning up, setting the saddlebags in a corner and folding away his dirty shirt. He hung up his gunbelt, never giving it a second thought, or much of the first one either, bent to look in the mirror and paste down a lock of hair which sprang up again like a willow sapling, and went downstairs.

Miz Appleton clasped her hands together and cried out when she saw him: "Glo-ry! Don't he look nice!" and Younger Macleish looked behind him and all around to see who she was talking about, until he saw there was no one there but himself and the lady. "It ain't me, honest, ma'am," he said. "It's only this here gold braid."

"Nonsense! You're a fine-looking, clean-cut youngster. Wherever did you get that curly hair?"

He felt his ears get hot. He never had figured an answer to that. Women were always asking him that. Next thing you know she'd be saying he'd ought to be an actor. But she was asking him if he was ready to eat. He grinned his answer and she led him through a door at the end of the little lobby into the restaurant.

The restaurant had a door also into the street, which Macleish thought was pretty clever. It was a rectangular room, just big enough for three square tables and one long one. On each was a bowl of the dried flowers he had seen in the lobby. The big table had two of them. The whole place smelled like Sunday supper in the promised land. At one of the tables, two punchers and a man in a black coat were shoveling away silently as if the promise was being kept.

Along the back wall was a doorway covered with the same kind of bead curtain. Through it he could just barely make out another table, smaller than the others, covered with blinding white linen. He saw glasses there and a silver vase and a silver candlestick that matched it.

"Just you set," said Miz Appleton, waving at one of the bare square tables, "and I'll be right with you."

Macleish said, "Real nice place here." He pointed at the bead-screened alcove. "Who's that for?"

"You want to see it?" Proudly beaming, she went to the alcove, took a wooden match from a box in her apron pocket, leaned in and lit the candle in the silver candlestick.

"Well, hey," breathed Younger Macleish.

The alcove was just big enough for two people and the table. The seats were built right on to the wall like a window box. They had velour cushions and backs on them. Two places were set. At each place were three forks, two knives, four spoons, three glasses, and a starched napkin folded in a circle like a king's crown, with the eight points sticking straight up. The cutlery looked all mismatched, but the handles were all the same: wide fork, narrow fork, thin knife, wide knife. The same with the glasses, all different shapes but with identical bases. He had never seen anything like it.

He asked again, "Who's this for?"

"Anyone who likes to eat this way."

"Now who would that be?" asked Macleish, honestly perplexed.

"I might say anyone who knows the difference between eating and dining." She laughed at him suddenly. He was walleyed as a new calf seeing his first bull. "Or anybody that might like to learn."

He wet his lips. "Me?"

She laughed at him again. "You're right welcome, Mr. Macleish." Then, in tones of real apology, "It's got to cost a little more, though, and take a while to fix."

"Oh that's all right," he said quickly, his eyes on the gleaming table. He picked up a salad fork between his fingertips and carefully set it down again. "You're goin' to have to break trail for me through all this."

She laughed again and told him to set right down. She seemed to think he was no end funny, and he imagined he was; but there's ways and ways of getting laughed at, and he didn't mind her way. He sat down, careful not to bump anything, and she whisked away the second place setting and left with it.

She was back in a moment with a dish, a long narrow oval of cut glass in which were arranged six celery stalks and a mound of what looked like olives only they were shiny black. She set it down and gently removed the napkin from under his chin and spread it on his lap, while he sat rigidly with his big scrubbed hard-work hands hidden under the edge of the table. "I 'spect some folks think I'm addled in the head," she chattered, "but I always say that good manners are the only real difference between the men and the beasts. I don't reckon there's another table like this this side of San Diego, not till you reach St. Louis. Don't just stare at those olives, boy—eat 'em!... It just does me good to have someone *dine* instead of feed. Or learn it," she added quickly and kindly. "Here." And from under her arm she took a great big card and laid it before him.

MENU, it announced itself in block type at the top. All the rest was in script—flowery curly Spencerian script, so neat and straight and pretty that he just wagged his head in amazement over it. He could make out every single letter—but not one of the words.

"It's in French," she explained. "All real high-toned menus in real high-toned places are written in French. This one's from the Hotel Metropole in San Francisco. I had my honeymoon there with Mister Appleton." She smiled a little more brightly, even, than usual, and Macleish had the vague feeling that something hurt her. "I put that menu away and kep' it for twelve years, and I said to myself that someday I'd serve up that dinner again in a place of my own, and now I do. These," she explained, "are the appetizers, and this is the soup. Down here is fish and then meat. Here and here are vegetables and potatoes and all that, and then dessert and so on."

"Appetizers?"

"They hone up your appetite. Make you hungry."

He wagged his head again at the idea of folks needing to be made hungry at dinnertime. He squinted at the card and said, "Chat. Chat."

"Chateaubriand," she read out. "You cook beef in wine."

"Why?"

She laughed. "Ask yourself that when you've tasted it."

He forlornly handed her back the card. "I better leave all this to you, Miz Appleton. You just bring it on and tell me what to do."

She left him munching on a stalk of celery. Each stick was packed full of a gooey, blue-y stuff that tasted like cheese and, as Miz Appleton explained to him when she came back to pour him a glass of very dry sherry, *was* cheese. He inhaled the whole dishful and drank the wine at a gulp, and sat there with his stomach growling for more.

So Younger Macleish ate a fragrant thin soup with crisp tiny fried cubes of bread afloat in it, some tender flakes of trout meat, four popovers, five salted breadsticks and two rolls; another dish of stuffed celery and olives, three helpings of the Chateaubriand and all the fixings that went with it; and four pieces of lemon meringue pie you could have sneezed off the plate it was so light. He drank white wine and red wine, sharp and thin, and at the end, in a third glass, a heavy red port that his tongue roots couldn't believe. Nuts came with this, and a silver thing to crack them with, and a little bitty doll's house sort of cup of coffee. Somewhere along the line he had lost the conviction that genteel folk didn't know anything about eating, the helpings seemed so small; because they kept coming and coming, until at last he had to sneak a quick pull on his cinches and let his belt out a notch, silently commanding his liver to move over and make more room. Packed with well-being until it showed on his face in a sheen of sweat, he pressed limply at a nut in the nutcracker and wondered if Mr. Appleton was still alive or had died happy of eating.

"Mr. Appleton was killed on the way back," said the little lady when she brought more coffee, smiling that brighter-than-usual smile. "The trace chain broke. He threw me clear but he went over with the horses. The only thing I can't give you," she went on rapidly, "is a brandy. At the Metropole you'll see the gentlemen sitting around after their dinner smoking their fine Havana see-gars, and there'll be brandy. Just a little drop of it in the bottom of a big glass like a flower vase. That's so they can smell it better. Or sometimes they'll call for a shot-glass too and pour in a little brandy and dip the end of their see-gar into it. Or put a drop or two right into their coffee. I do wish I had a bit of fine old brandy for you, so you'd know how it is. They always used to call for the oldest brandy, because that's best."

Killed on the way back, Macleish silently repeated to himself. That would be from the honeymoon. He said, "It's all right about the brandy, Miz Appleton. I doubt I'd git a drop of anything all the way down. Not till tomorrow noon or so anyhow."

"Well, I wish you had it all the same. How do you feel?"

"Miz Appleton," he said with all his heart, "I ain't lived such a life that I deserved all this."

"I think you have," she told him. "I think you will. You're a nice young man, Mr. Macleish."

He felt his ears getting hot again and stood up and batted his way through the red and blue beads and got clear of the alcove. Either he had to escape from all this goodness or he had to take a walk and shake down this dinner so he'd be able to lie down without spilling. He thanked her again and left her beaming after him, with her quick small hands folded together under her apron.

He'd already been past the livery and the mercantile, so he naturally ambled the other way. The town had its quota of bars, and a school right in town, and a church. Then there was a bank and a long row of dwellings and what do you know, a second mercantile, this one with a feed and grain warehouse attached. Then a smithy, and then the other hotel which, as the livery man had told him, wasn't rightly a hotel. He passed the entrance with a glance over the bat-wings, went on three paces and then stopped.

It wasn't the off-voice piano that stopped him, nor the size of the place, which was considerable for such a town, nor the glimpse of pink satin and soft hair somewhere along the bar, nor even the bar itself, the longest and most elaborate he had ever seen. It was the array behind the bar—four tiers all of twenty feet long each, rows and rows of bottles of all sizes and shapes. He had to wonder if there wasn't a fine old brandy there. He didn't want it or need it, and he didn't know if he'd like it or not, but Miz Appleton had said he ought to have it. It was like a service to her. The dinner seemed to mean more to her even than it had to him, and it just seemed right to finish it off the way she said.

So he turned back and went into the place.

The bartender was a squint-eyed oldster wrapped in a long white butcher's apron. You had an idea who he was talking to when you were by yourself at the bar, but it must have been pretty mystifying when the place was crowded.

"You got any brandy?" Macleish asked.

One of the man's eyes scanned Younger Macleish's fancy vest while the other one raked the northwest corner.

"Reckon we have."

"Real old brandy?"

"It's old."

"You got see-gars?"

"Two kinds. Most men wouldn't smoke the one, an' most men wouldn't pay for the other."

"Gimme the best," said Younger Macleish. He remembered something else and said "Uh," as the bartender was about to turn away. He couldn't see himself asking for a flower vase to drink his brandy out of, so he asked for the other instead. "Bring me a extra shot-glass with the brandy."

The bartender walked to the far end and got an old kitchen chair with the back off it, and carried it back and set it down. Grunting, he got up on it and reached for a bottle on the fourth tier. He brought it down and held it so Macleish could see the label, but didn't set it down and didn't bring glasses. "Suit you?"

The question was asked in a way that seemed to mean more than it said. Macleish wondered if it had anything to do with money. He noticed suddenly that the girl, the one with the pink satin dress and all that hair, was watching him. He went into his poke and got a gold ten dollars and laid it on the wood. "It'll do," he said as if he knew what he was talking about.

The bartender put the bottle down then and pulled the cork, and reached underneath for a glass with a small stem and a big bell, and the extra shot-glass. Macleish figured that if you drink brandy out of a big glass like that it must be something like beer; but when the bartender poured in only about a finger and quit, he remembered what Miz Appleton had said about the men smelling it. He took it and smelled it while the bartender went for the cigars. It smelled fine.

The bartender brought the cigar box and handed the whole thing to him, and he took out three. Two he stuck in his vest and got the other one going. The smoke was full-fleshed and kind to him. He took a little taste of the brandy and waited a second, and it was as if a good spirit had sat down in his throat in velvet pants. Turning his back to the bar and hooking up his elbows, he began a wordless worship of Miz Appleton and all her works. He was vaguely aware that the bartender was leaning across the far end, talking to the girl in pink, that the piano player expressed his disbelief in his own abilities by working with his fingers crossed, and that two faro games were operating in the corner. But none of this mattered to him; and as he swung around to dunk his cigar in the shot-glass and caught the pink girl's eye as she climbed the stairs to the gallery, the moment of self-consciousness was lost in pure joy when he took his first drag of the brandied smoke.

He stood in this golden trance for some minutes and nobody bothered him until the girl came back downstairs and walked over to him. He smiled at her because he was ready to smile at anything, but if it was the first word she waited for, she'd have to give it; he couldn't think of a one.

"Hello," she said.

Well, that was a good one. He gave it right back to her.

"Stranger here, aren't you?" She was older than he had first thought, but not much. She had a real different kind of nose, thin as the back of a knife between her close-set eyes, and flaring out at the nostrils, which pointed more forward than down and were constantly aquiver. She was pretty enough, though, with all that hair. He admitted that he was a stranger, and took another smell of the brandy because he then and there ran out of anything else to say.

"Come to stay?" she asked him.

"Nope," said Younger Macleish.

"That's too bad," said the girl, and then laughed briefly and loudly. "My," she said, "you're quite a one for talk, aren't you? . . . You going to buy me a drink?"

"Oh!" said Macleish, feeling stupid. "Uh—sure."

She nodded over his shoulder and the bartender brought her a pale something in a small glass. He also brought back change from Macleish's money. He didn't bring much.

"What are you going to do with yourself all evening?"

"Look around," said Macleish uncomfortably.

It seemed to him that she waited altogether too long to say anything else, watching him the whole time. The bartender was watching him too, or her; he wouldn't know. At last she burrowed into a pink beaded bag and withdrew a heavy gold compact. "Look here," she said, and opened the lid. Macleish became aware of a faint tinkling. He leaned close and discovered that in shrill small bell-like notes, the compact was playing "Peas, peas, goober peas."

"Well, hey," said Younger Macleish.

"I got more of them," said the girl. "I got a powder box that plays a waltz and another one—that one's only a straight music box—that plays the Trish-Trash Polka."

"You *do?*" said Macleish, sounding quite as impressed as he was.

"You want to see 'em? I got them upstairs."

He looked at her numbly. In his mind he had a swift flash of two crinolined sisters and a white-smiled schoolmarm, and—and the whole idea of going home to settle. Then there was this girl and what she said, it . . . it . . . Well, somehow, something was altogether mismatched.

"I guess I better not," he mumbled.

"Oh—come *on!*" she said; and then, going all tight-lipped, "It's just to see the music boxes. What do you think I *am?*"

He knew his ears were getting red again; he could feel the heat. He wished he could get out of this. He wished he hadn't come in. He wished he could curl up in his cigar-ash and go up in smoke. He said, "Well, all right."

He drank up his brandy and it stung him harder than he wanted it to. He dipped his cigar once more in the shot-glass and followed her up the stairs. He was dead certain that both faro games must have stopped dead while he climbed, everyone watching, but when he flashed a glance from the top everything down there seemed as usual. It was about then he remembered to breathe again. He turned to follow the girl along the gallery.

She had opened a door and was waiting for him. "In here."

It was black dark in there. If he thought anything at all, it was that she would follow him and light a lamp.

The instant he was clear of the door, it was kicked shut with the girl still outside, and he found himself in total blackness. Hands came from nowhere, took both arms, wrenched them behind him. "Whut—" he yelled, and got a stinging blow in the mouth before he could make another syllable. He kicked out and back as hard as he could, and his heel struck what felt like a shinbone. He heard a curse, and the red lightning struck him twice more on the cheek and on the ear.

He stood still then, head down, hauling uselessly at the relentless grip on his arms, and breathed hoarsely.

A blaze of light appeared across the room. It was only a match, but it was so unexpected it hurt him more than fists and made him grunt. The flare dwindled as it stroked the wick of a lamp, and then the lamp-flame came up, yellow and steady.

The room was fixed up like an office. There was a bookcase and a cabinet and, on the wall, a claims map. A big desk stood parallel with the far wall with a heavily curtained window behind it. The lamp stood on the desk, and seated behind it was a thin man with pale gray hair and the brightest blue eyes he had seen yet. The man wore a black coat and a tight white collar and an oversized black Ascot, from the top bulge of which gleamed a single pearl. The man was waving the match slowly back and forth to put it out.

He was smiling. His teeth were very long, especially the eyeteeth.

"So, Mr. Bronzeau," he said in a soft, mellow voice. "We meet at last."

Younger Macleish was far too dazzled to respond. He pulled suddenly at the arms which held him, glanced right and left. He got a blurred picture of one man, heavy-set and running to fat, who smelled of beer and sweat, and another, much younger, with the crazed, craven face of one who can be frightened into being snake-dangerous. One thing was certain: the two of them knew how to hold a man so he couldn't move. To them he said, "Turn me loose."

At this there was a movement in the shadows and a fourth man moved out of the corner. He was a wide man with a wide hat on, and small eyes, and he put two big white hands in the pool of light under the lamp and began to fiddle with a big black and gold signet ring with a black-letter B on it. He was smiling. Younger Macleish said again, "Turn me loose."

"Oh," said the gray-headed man pleasantly, "we will—we will, Mr. Bronzeau. But first Mr. Brannegan here will relieve you of anything sharp or explosive or which in any way might disturb the peace and quiet of our little conversation." He smiled, and then waved his hand in a small flourish at the man with the signet ring. He said, like one politician introducing another politician, "Mr. Brannegan."

The big man came over. Macleish tensed. "Hold real still, sonny," said Brannegan, and went over Macleish rapidly and with an expert touch. He checked everything—even his boot-tops, where men have been known to stash a knife. In the process he got Younger Macleish's money, his cigars, his matches, and even a walnut he had borrowed from Miz Appleton's alcove. These things he put neatly on the desk.

"I shall now show you, Mr. Brannegan, that even you can at times be careless; and you, Mr. Bronzeau, that I know a great deal more about you than you thought I did. Our young friend," he informed Brannegan, "has been seen to reach up as if to scratch his ear, and suddenly hang a weighted throwing knife he carries in a four-by-four thirty yards away. If you will be good enough to look, I think you will find the knife in a sheath between his shoulder blades."

Brannegan swore and reached over Macleish's shoulder, to pound him heavily on the back. The two men holding him tightened their grip as Brannegan grasped Macleish's collar and with one painful wrench broke his string tie and tore out his collar buttons. He slid a hand down the back of Macleish's neck and scrabbled around as if he expected to find the weapon under the skin rather than on it.

"It ain't here," said Brannegan.

For a split second the gray-headed man's eyes got round; then they slitted again and he took to wagging his head sadly, side to side. "You have surprised me," he said to Macleish, "Mr. Bronzeau, you have indeed surprised me, and I concede that I never thought you would. I knew you would follow me here, and I knew you could be induced to come into this room; but I will allow that I never expected you to come unarmed. There is a difference, Mr. Bronzeau, between courage and foolhardiness. I think you will agree that you have passed it. Well then," he barked in a business-like way, "we can settle our little matter all the better, then."

He took a paper out of his breast pocket, unfolded it and put it on the desk. "Here, my young friend, is a transfer form, properly executed, lacking only your signature. Here," he said, moving an inkwell and a feather pen next to the paper, "is something to—"

"Now you looky here," said Younger Macleish, who had suddenly had enough and to spare, and was able to pull his startled wits back into shape. "I don't know you or nothing about you or no paper. Now turn me loose!" he yelled at the two men at his sides, and gave a mighty wrench that ought to be enough to pull a horse off its feet—and wasn't enough to break free of these two.

"Mis-ter Bronzeau!" cried the gray-headed man. He sounded aggrieved—astonished and hurt. "You interrupted me!" He turned to Brannegan, complaining: "Mister Brannegan, he interrupted me."

Brannegan tsk-tsked like a deacon, settled his big ring just the way he wanted, and hit Macleish on the left cheek-bone with it. Then he stepped back and smiled. He said, "You hadn't ought to interrupt, sonny."

The craze-frightened youth snickered. The beer-smelling man brayed. The gray-headed man waited until it was quiet again except for Macleish's heavy breathing. The blood began running from the place the ring had hit.

"First I talk," the gray-headed man explained patiently, "and then you talk, and that's the way gentlemen conduct business. Now then—where were we? Here is a paper, and here is the pen you are going to use to sign it with, and here is something"—he put out a short-handled, long-bladed knife, picked up the matchstick he had used to light the lamp, and delicately split it in two—"we can use to keep this conversation going if we have to; and here," he said as he put the knife down exactly parallel with the pen and opened the desk drawer, "is a little something for dessert, you might say," and next to the knife he put down a nickel-plated, four-barrel gambler's gun. "Just a toy, really, and guaranteed not to hit what you aim at unless," he added, picking up the gun and pointing it playfully at Macleish's belt-buckle, "you've got some way of holding the target still." He laughed genteelly; Brannegan haw-hawed; and late, the youth tittered and the beery man brayed. "Now then," said the gray-headed man, "Mr. Bronzeau had something to say. Go ahead, Mr. Bronzeau."

Younger Macleish looked from one to the other of them and concluded that they were waiting for him to speak. He said, "My name ain't Bronzeau or whatever it was you said. I just rode in an' I'm goin' to ride out in the morning and you got yourselves the wrong man."

"Ah," said the gray-headed man tiredly, "come off it, Bronzeau. We know you. Don't make this take any longer than it has to."

"It's the truth all the same," said Younger Macleish.

"All right, all right; I'll hear it out. Where is it you pretend to be coming from, and what lie have you got ready about where you're going?"

"That," said Macleish, "is my business."

"He's rude, Mr. Brannegan," complained the gray-headed man.

Brannegan hit Macleish on the same place with his ring. It seemed to grow dark in there for a time, or perhaps it was only that the lamp and the room and all the men moved far off for a moment. Then he straightened up and shook his head, and it all came back again, and Brannegan was rubbing his ring and saying, "Don't be rude, sonny."

"Are you going to sign it?"

"No, I ain't."

"Not quite so hard this time, Mr. Brannegan." But Macleish guessed Brannegan did not hear the gray-headed man in time.

The next question he was aware of hearing was "Why? Why? Why put yourself through this, Mr. Bronzeau? Why won't you sign it? Just tell me that."

"Because I told you," said Macleish hoarsely. "I ain't who you think, and this has nothin' to do with me. Now you whoa!" he roared suddenly at Brannegan, who was cocking his signet hand for another pass; and, surprisingly, Brannegan whoaed. Macleish said, "Whatever that is, it won't be worth nothing if I sign it. You might's well sign it yourself. I tell you it's got nothin' to do with me."

"Reasonable, reasonable," nodded the gray-headed man. "Only we just don't believe you." But Macleish noticed he didn't call him "Mr. Bronzeau" this time.

Brannegan said to the gray-headed man, "He ought to've had that there throwin' knife."

"A point, a point," allowed the gray-headed man, who apparently always repeated himself when he was thinking. "What impresses me most is that our Mr. Bronzeau is too intelligent to carry this performance of injured innocence on so long. Ergo, this man is as stupid as he acts. Which would indicate that he is after all not our Mr.

Bronzeau." He pulled his low lip carefully away from his lower teeth. They were too long too. "On the other hand, such stupidity might be covering up a very clever man indeed. Indeed." Abruptly he turned from his contemplation of Younger Macleish and said briskly, "Mr. Brannegan, we need to know a little more about our young friend."

Brannegan said to Macleish, "Where at's your horse?"

Macleish said, "In my hip pocket."

"Sonny," said the big man, stroking his ring, "I owe you one for that."

"Take care of it when you come back," said the gray-headed man. "I'm sure all he meant was that his horse is at the livery, and would hardly be anywhere else."

"That's right," said Macleish.

Brannegan went to the door. The gray-headed man said, "If by any chance this is not our Mr. Bronzeau, Brannegan, I should like to know it quickly. I tire soon in the presence of stupid people," and he smiled at Macleish.

"Be right back," said Brannegan, and went out.

The gray-headed man picked up the little gambler's gun and checked the load. "You may as well sit down and be comfortable," he said, waving at a corner chair. "Turn him loose, boys," he said, mimicking Macleish's earlier demand, "and stand by the door, and if he makes a play," he added, smiling his most pleasant smile, "kill him."

The men let go, and Macleish gave each of them a memorizing kind of look, and went and sat in the corner, folding his arms and massaging his biceps.

It grew very quiet in there. Macleish looked at the three, and the three looked back at him. After a while, the gray-headed man rose and came around to the front of the desk, holding the gun loosely. He stood back against the desk and stared at Macleish.

"Didn't you win a silver-digging in a crap game and then put it up in a poker deal with a certain gentleman?"

"Not me," said Younger Macleish.

"And didn't you lose the pot, and renege, and then cut out here to see if the digging was worth-while after all?"

"Not me," said Macleish.

"It was worthwhile," said the gray-headed man.

"Well now," said Macleish.

"Sign this," said the gray-headed man softly, "and nobody reneged, and nobody's mad."

"I ain't mad," said Macleish. He rose suddenly.

The little gun swung to point steadily at him. Late, as usual, the beery man said a wordless *hup!* and his gun was out and, noisily, cocked. The loco-looking youth began to breathe loudly with his mouth open.

"Foot's asleep," said Macleish. He jiggled on it a couple of times and then sat down again.

After that nobody said anything until Brannegan got back.

The gray-headed man went back to his desk chair as Brannegan came in. Brannegan glanced at no one, but went straight to the desk and put down a packet of letters, a piece of polished rock crystal hanging from a fine gold chain, and a pincushion made like a little shepherdess with a full skirt. "Looky yere," said Brannegan. "He plays with dolls."

The gray-headed man was interested only in the letters. He fanned them and dealt them, one by one, picked up one and glanced through it, opened another and closed it right up again. He stacked them neatly and put them away from him next to the doll and the crystal pendant. Then he folded his long pale hands and seemed to close his eyes.

Macleish looked at the things on the desk and wondered if one or the other sister would get the pincushion and the pendant, or if it would be the schoolteacher after all.

The gray-headed man didn't move, but his sharp bright eyes were suddenly on Younger Macleish. "You're really just riding in, riding out."

"I told you," said Macleish.

The gray-headed man cursed. Coming from him, and coming as it did with such violence, the effect was like that match flame a little earlier, which had made Macleish grunt.

"Mr. Brannegan," said the gray-headed man mildly, after he had his breath again, "We've got the wrong man."

Brannegan eyed Macleish with enmity, and said, "All that trouble."

To Macleish, the gray-headed man said, "Say you had a man to see, and you knew he was so good-looking he was practically pretty, and he'd dress so fancy he looked like a clown; and say you knew about him that he'd smoke the best cigars, call for the oldest brandy, and make for the nearest pretty face; and say you set up a trail he had to follow and an ambush he had to walk into. Then suppose just such a clown walked into it."

"I'd say you made a mistake," said Macleish.

"Just so, a mistake." Then he added, showing he was thinking, "A mistake." He sighed. "Mr. Brannegan, we've got to make it up to this young man."

"Sure," said Brannegan heavily.

"Return this man's property to him, Mr. Brannegan."

Brannegan got the things off the desk and gave Macleish his matches, his cigars, his poke, his letters, the crystal pendant. "That's awful pretty," he murmured as he gave Macleish the doll.

Macleish stowed the things in the various pockets of his fancy vest while the gray-headed man went on talking. He said, "I wouldn't want you to resent any of this, you know. An honest mistake. And I wouldn't want you to complain to the sheriff or anything like that. Not that it would make any difference. And I would be especially sad if you should talk about this to anyone you might meet on the trail." He stopped then, and waited.

Younger Macleish said, "I don't never complain."

"Oh fine," said the gray-headed man. Then he said it again, and, "I'd like to be sure of that. I really would."

Macleish shrugged at him. He couldn't think of anything to say.

The gray-headed man placed all the tips of all his fingers together and stared at them mournfully, and said, "A long and eventful life has taught me that there are after all only three kinds of men. One kind gives his word and that's enough. One kind, you pay, and that's enough. And one kind needs a boot in the tail to show that you mean what you say." He paused and said, without looking up, "I do hope you are listening, Mr. Brannegan."

"Oh, every word," said Brannegan happily.

"Now then," said the gray-headed man, "I have his word. Sort of. He said he doesn't complain. Well, I don't know what kind of man he is, and I don't really care very much. So we'll pay him, too. Give him twenty dollars, Mr. Brannegan."

"Give him *what?*" gasped the big man.

The gray-headed man thumbed a coin out of his watch pocket and flipped it ringing across the desk. "Give it to him."

"Well all right," said Brannegan, and took up the coin and handed it to Macleish. Macleish took it and put it away.

"Now," said the gray-headed man, "take him outside and give him a boot in the tail."

"I got just the one," said Brannegan. He came over to Macleish, who stood up. Brannegan eyed him for a moment and said over his shoulder, without looking, "Get your gun out." Macleish heard the beery man's gun cocking and then Brannegan got Macleish's left arm and twisted it behind him, putting the fist tight up between Macleish's shoulder blades. It hurt. He pulled Macleish off balance and ran him out the door and along the gallery to the top of the stairs. Here he gave him a shove outward and followed it with an accurate boot. Macleish spun floundering down the steps and brought up at the bottom, leaning against the newel post like a fence prop. Brannegan, incredibly, was right beside him, got the left fist between his shoulder blades again, and pulled him upright. Macleish looked up. The gray-headed man was leaning over the gallery rail, smiling slightly. Beside him, the youth stood, his mouth wide, tittering. At the head of the stairs stood the beery man, gun in hand. Brannegan ran Macleish the length of the bar and banged him out through the batwings. Macleish cleared the two low steps without touching, clipped the far edge of the duckwalk, and sprawled in the dust outside.

Behind the batwings, somebody yipped a shrill clear dragrider's cattle-drive yip. A number of people helped make a bellow of laughter.

Macleish got to his feet. His face hurt. His hands and elbows hurt, and his left arm clear back to the shoulder bones hurt a whole lot. His fancy vest was a mess and he had a hole in the knee of his pants. He walked back to the hotel.

By the lamplight that streamed from the hotel, Macleish saw a man standing at the foot of the steps. It was the fat little old man from the livery. He had a white handkerchief pressed to his face. He said, "Oh, there you are. Gosh, son, a feller got to your saddle. I tried to stop him."

Macleish gently pulled the handkerchief down away from the old man's face. He had a puffy sort of hole on his cheekbone.

"Feller had a big ring," said the man from the livery. "I tried to stop him," he called apologetically as Macleish climbed the porch.

Some woman Macleish hadn't seen before was in the little lobby. She had a basin of water standing on the hotel desk. Miz Appleton was sitting behind the desk. The woman was dabbing at Miz Appleton's face with a wet clean cloth, and said to Macleish, "Oh, you must be the one. A man got to your things in your room."

Macleish stumped up the stairs, and as he reached the landing he heard Miz Appleton say, "I tried to stop him, Mr. Macleish."

Macleish went on upstairs. The door to his room was open. His saddlebags and spare clothes and blanket, and his Arbuckle coffee and trail bacon and beans were all dumped on the bed. He passed by with a glance and went to the wall peg where his gun-belt hung, and he took it down and strapped it on. He drew the gun, broke and spun it, clicked it straight and holstered it, and went back down the stairs. The women both spoke, but he didn't hear what they said.

He clumped down the duckwalks to the other hotel, looking straight ahead and not exactly hurrying. When he got there he kicked open the batwings and walked in. This time the piano and the faro games, as well as any talking and drinking and moving around that happened to be going on, really did stop, suddenly and altogether. Macleish paid no mind to anyone, but walked straight back to the stairs and went up them two at a time.

Somebody shouted then, but the sound was drowned out by the crash of the door as Macleish shouldered it half off its hinges and stood back.

He could see the desk and the lamp and the gray-headed man, his bright blue eyes all white-rimmed round. The man scooped open a drawer and Macleish drew and shot him through the right forearm and sprang inside.

The gray-headed man shrieked like a woman and curled up like a mealworm bit by a fire ant. Macleish stood in the center of the room, snapped a look to left, to the right. The beery man and the kid stood flat-footed by the end of the desk. Macleish made a motion with his gun and their hands went up as if they had been tied to the same string. Macleish slipped around behind them and got their guns. He threw the guns out through the draped window behind the desk.

He said, "Face the wall," and they were very brisk about doing it. The gray-headed man had fallen and was writhing on the floor behind the desk, crying. Macleish backed around there and booted him out in the open where he could see him. Then he pulled down a drape and put two straight chairs back to back and threw a couple of half-hitches around the uprights at one side. He said, "Come here," and the two gunmen turned uncertainly and came sheepishly across to him. "Sit," he said.

Back to back they sat down. Keeping his gun on them, Macleish circled them twice with the drape, binding them tight to the chairs and to each other. He didn't bother to tie the free end, but just tucked it into itself; it would hold for as long as he wanted it to. He put his gun down on the desk and placed one hand on the kid's face and one on the beery man's face, and whanged the backs of their heads together as hard as he could. When you crack one nut with another nut, practically every time only one of the two will break, and Macleish thought that that gave odds that neither one of these two deserved.

Macleish heard someone running, and he glanced at the door and found it full of frightened faces. He waved his gun at them and they disappeared. He jumped to the door and flattened himself just inside. The running feet ceased and became a deep growl: "Out o' my way!" and Brannegan exploded into the room just the way he himself had. Macleish hit him alongside the head with his gun and he threw out his arms and went forward to his hands and knees, his head hanging. Macleish bent, hooked out his gun, and sent it sailing through the window with one motion. Then he got hold of Brannegan's left wrist, pulled the man kneeling upright, and twisted the arm around and up, meanwhile ramming his gun barrel into Brannegan's kidney. "Up!" he said, and Brannegan stood up. Macleish walked him through the door. There were people out there but they made way.

Macleish brought Brannegan to the top of the stairs and gave him a push and such a fine kick that everyone in the place gasped, including Brannegan, who went out and down like the front end of a rockslide. Macleish bounded down after him and tried to stand him up with the bent-arm thing, but Brannegan couldn't cooperate. Macleish waved his gun and said to throw water on him.

"Yes, *sir!*" said the bartender, shuffling fast around the end of the bar, bringing a big pitcher. Macleish, waiting, moved gun and eyes all around. Everybody watched. Nobody moved.

The water made Brannegan twitch and groan. Macleish snatched up Brannegan's ring hand and caught it between his knees. Looking all around while he did it, he got the ring off Brannegan's finger and put it on his own. The water helped. Then he wrung Brannegan's left hand around behind him and told him "Up!"

Macleish walked him the length of the bar to the batwings, and then swung around to look at the people again. He didn't think any of them looked as if they wanted to stop him. Some followed him and Brannegan up to Miz Appleton's, but he didn't mind that.

He shoved Brannegan up the porch steps with his grip on the arm and also with the end of his gun. He hit the door with Brannegan and heard the latch break; he hadn't meant to do that. Miz Appleton and the other woman screamed.

"Is this the one?" he asked, and they screamed again. He dragged Brannegan to the door and let go of his left arm and pulled his back hair until his face tipped up. Then he hit Brannegan with the ring on the cheekbone, and again on the chin, sending him flying down into the crowd. Down there he saw the little old man from the livery, clasping his hands together over his fat stomach and jumping up and down in glee. He called him.

"Here," he said when the old man had climbed the porch. He handed him the ring. "Give this back to him."

"How?" asked the man, taking the ring and loving it.

"It's your deal," said Macleish, and went inside. He never did find out how the old man dealt it.

He slept well, and departed in the morning before Miz Appleton was up and about. He left her the gold twenty dollars he had been given the night before. In the livery, he liked the looks of his horse. Somebody had bothered to curry him. Macleish saddled up and went to buckling the bags and fixing the blanket roll, and by the time he was finished there was a bug-eyed stable boy yawning down from a little cubby in the mow, who said "Gosh."

"Gosh what?" asked Macleish.

"You're the fellow cleaned out the saloon last night, gosh."

"You tell the old feller," Macleish said, embarrassed, "my horse is happy anyhow. Got it?"

"Your horse is happy anyhow," nodded the boy. Macleish gave him money and mounted, and rode downstreet.

When he passed the other hotel, a woman called. "Mister."

He reined in. The girl with all the hair came running out into the middle of the street. She was all dun-colored in a cape and hood thrown over what was probably night clothes, and no makeup. She said, "I didn't know. I—I had to do what he said."

Macleish asked her, "Did you?" and rode on. He saw her lift her hand slowly and bite it.

A little way on, down where he hadn't been yet, a man called out to him and he stopped again. The man had a star pinned to his shirt. He said, "Look, I got two men bedded up back of the doctor's office, one with a broken arm and one with a cracked head. I got two more locked up in the jail."

Younger Macleish asked him, "Why?"

"Look, I can't hold them 'less you make a complaint."

"I don't complain." He lifted his hand to snap the lines and go, but the man said: "Look, were you thinkin' of maybe settlin' in hereabouts?"

"No," said Younger Macleish.

He rode out.

Assault and Little Sister

Trembling in the bed, Little Sister cried aloud: "They *want* him to!" 'They,' of course, meant the police . . . the newspapers . . . oh, everybody. 'To' meant the—the horror she must go through—again! That's the word, Little Sister: *Again!*—if he came back. *When* he came back. "Oh-h-h . . ." she moaned. But nobody answered. Nobody was there with her.

Nobody was there *yet.*

What was that?

She lay in the dark little room staring at the moon-dappled window, and held her breath. Surely something moved out in the hall? Something was *breathing* out there?

Call out, then. It—could be Peter Poteen, Detective Poteen guarding her after all. He—he could have thought it over, and—

But then, it could be *him.* It could be—the terribly feared one.

Or even, she thought—and her flesh crept cold, crept needly with speckles of cold—a new one. The papers were full of them and word got around, and some men found the victims especially attractive.

Pain banded her chest with the held breath, but still she held it, listening to nothing-at-all out there. But she knew that someone could be out there, holding his breath too, also listening. A roaring began in her ears and listening was useless. She breathed again, gasping open-throated to be silent. When she could, she sat up. She could pant more quietly that way.

And now she could see out and down through the single panel of gauze which covered the lower half of her window. Dim in the moonlight, the not-quite adjoining roof shone in the summer night like an acre of ice. Last summer it had shone too, aching, baking around *him,* hotly holding his flesh, flat as it was, as if it would cup up around him.

She shuddered and rose, and padded on bare feet to the window. The roof outside, a warehouse, was not completely flat, nor altogether unobstructed. The edges rose slightly all around, not by bulwarks, but banked. And not far from Little Sister's window, to the right, jutted a small angular housing or kiosk, to shelter the stairs to the roof.

From inside her room it might seem that the roof was a larger, slightly lower extension of her own floor, but from the window itself she could look down—she seldom did—a dizzy sixty feet to the alley below. Due to the overhang of the warehouse roof, its edge was no more than four and a half feet from her building. Yet the sheer drop between had always been, for her, a magic barrier, an invisible wall between herself and the city and all that near part of the sky which combed itself through the city's stumpy teeth. There was such a lot of it out there, and none of it could see her. Behind her alley-chasm, and her panel of gauze, none of it could see her!

Seen by moonlight, it was as detailed as it had been last summer in the blaze of afternoon. But only to the eye of memory. In actuality, when something moved in the shadows of the kiosk, she couldn't be sure what it was, or even *if* it was. She knew every pebble and crease of the roofing, but pebbles and creases were only what should be there. What should *not* be there, movement or memory, was something she could not be sure of, and memory or movement, it filled her with terror.

Last summer she had stood here speechless, watching the flesh, the tanned flesh, the hard flesh pulsing with life, the unabashedly bare, the sweat-sheened. And there came the moment when her eyes and his had met . . . when in the locking of their gaze she was no longer invisible and he, no longer unseen.

The telephone was next, and the voice of Poteen. That was the first time she heard his voice, the noncommittal, too-understanding Detective Peter Poteen, who said *yes-mam* like the polite cop on a television series, and perhaps was amused at himself for doing it, and, very likely at her, too, for calling. He was immune to the infection of her outrage; he patiently had interrupted her, over and over again, until he had written down her name and her address and had made sure he had them all spelled right—all that, before she could even tell her story.

And then it was yes mam, yes mam, yes mam, to all of it, and his silly question. Was the fellow still out there on the roof? Well of *course* not, she had blurted angrily. He was two hours gone. That was when Poteen's voice got a bit quieter, in that special way he had when he was interested, and also in that special way of his, the amusement showed a bit more. He asked her if she meant she had waited two whole hours to report the man to the police?

She supposed she had, though to this day she could not remember what she had done with the two hours. "I was upset, that's all!" she had shouted into the phone; and "Sure," he had said, "Sure," and he had promised to check on it. Check on it! With the papers full of it, every day, two, three times a day sometimes, the headlines, what happened in parks, alleys, stairways, even in the rooms of women alone. The whole city was aroused, and all the people in it except the police, except Detective Poteen.

Hanging up, she had glared at the bland crooked telephone and "*Oh!*" she had shrieked at it, unable to find a word for what she felt.

A woman alone could be preyed upon, brutalized, murdered. Or worse. *Then* the police would swing into action. Then they would be around with their radios and their fingerprint kits and bloodstain tests and microscopes and things—they were very good at that. Afterwards. After she had been—

Oh! The word was too horrible to say, even to herself.

Check on it. They'd check on it all right. Maybe pass Poteen's cold careful notes around at the precinct station and laugh at her.

It had come night then, that hot summer last year, and she had sat tensely in her wicker chair, glancing in fury at the bland cornerless hulk of the telephone, and then at the textured face of the gauze that shut out the night beyond.

And once—she could still remember it—she had found herself wishing, actually, fervently wishing, that her door would burst open, that one of the fiends, the beasts of prey, would stand there drooling and baring his teeth, and would leap on her ... leaving only enough afterwards to enable her to say through broken lips, *I told you it would happen, Detective Poteen. I told you.* And standing over her bleeding body, Poteen would take off his hat and say *Yes Mam!*

And it had happened, had happened! even as she sat there thinking that, the soft footsteps in the hall, the knock on her door. She had gone rigid, and suddenly the insides of her mouth and throat were dry blotting-paper, while a great cold knot writhed itself into shape in her stomach and drew tight. It wasn't until the knock came again that she was able to answer at all.

"Who is it?"

"You don't know me. The guy on the roof."

She did not answer. She couldn't. In her mind's eye, vividly, she saw through the thin wall. She saw him just as she had seen him by the kiosk in the hot afternoon, standing so shamelessly; she could only imagine him the same way by her door, and again—still—with his gaze locked with hers.

She got up, that hot night a year ago, and, she had never before heard, had never known, the crackles, shrieks, and shouts a wicker chair gives out when a body leaves it. She had crept to the telephone, dialed. Oh! what a noise. What a grinding and clacking a telephone dial makes. Whether or not she could hear him breathing out there, she thought she did, and it was horrible.

He knocked again, louder; it was thunder, it was guns. *Fortieth Precinct; Sergeant Deora,* yelled the phone in her ear.

With her mouth to the telephone's mouth, close like kissing, wet, she said, "I told you this would happen, I told that Mister Poteen, the man, he's breaking in, he—" *This is the police, Sergeant Deora,* rasped the telephone scratchily, tinnily, too loud. *I can't hear you. Who's calling, please?* "Oh, sh! *Shh!!*" Little Sister whispered explosively. "Not so loud, he'll hear you. I called this afternoon—" *May I have your name?*

Angrily, she told him. The knock came again. Out in the hall, a voice, "I got to see you a minute. Come on, I got to talk to you." Little Sister hugged the phone, turned her back to the door. Her eyes were wide and turned so far over to the side that they hurt. "I called this afternoon and told that detective, that Mister Poteen—" *Your address, please.* "Oh!" she cried, but still cried whispering, "Oh! Oh! A man's trying to break in right now, I *told* you he would!" *Yes mam. Now if you will please give me your address.*

Like cursing, she gave her address. "This afternoon—" *We'll check on it.* "But, but, this afternoon—" she said into the phone, the dead phone, he had gone and left her alone, now of all times.

A knock again, only one, but hard; not a knock, a blow. "Come on, I ain't going to hurt you. I got to talk to you a little."

Holding the phone still, she panted, and panted, and suddenly filled her lungs and screamed *No!*

"Cut it out!" said the voice quietly, urgently, close to the crack of the door. "Cut it out, will you? Somebody'll hear. Just open up, let me in a minute, will ya?"

Then she had screamed, and screamed again, and screamed and screamed. Walled in by her own screams, she saw rather than heard the door being pounded on; it trembled; then the knob turned and it shook; then it opened, oh God, it opened. He was there, with his shoulders hunched, his mouth twisted. He hurled himself . . . something struck her across the shoulder-blades; her canned-goods shelf— Then she must have risen, turned, backed away.

"Shut up, wait, be quiet, don't yell like that, don't—" He seemed almost to be pleading. She ducked under the shelf and slid sidewise and turned to flee to—oh, her bed. The sight of her own bed filled her with a new and terrible fear, and she screamed a new scream, a new kind of scream from a new kind of fear.

He touched her.

After that things were misty, swirling. The room was full of people. Somebody turned on the big overhead light and it hurt her eyes. The man from the roof looked some smaller, and a whole lot younger, with three policemen holding him. Younger, well, of course, *these* days.

Then the parade down the stairs and out on the street, the heads popping out of doors, the crowd around the three radio cars with their scything red lights, and a drumming white ambulance, all helter-skelter in the narrow street, and traffic stopped and car doors open with the people out and crowding around, crowding around. All the eyes, the eyes, gloating over her, over *him*.

Coming down the brownstone steps, a woman spat right in his face. In the car, sobbing, and a big policeman saying she was all right now, all right now.

Then questions in a bare bright room, with people coming in and out—and more questions. Once it was *him,* with only two policemen holding him this time; she did not, could not, look at his face, but she knew him all right, and said so; he tried to speak but they told him to shut his mouth. Someone brought her a paper cup of lukewarm tea.

Then the courtroom, and flashbulbs and the smell of dust and old sweat—nothing clean but the flag. *Stand up!* somebody shouted and the judge came in and almost everybody sat down again. It was difficult to follow the proceedings and she did not try. She did not have to.

Her turn came and she was led to the right place to stand and touch the Book, and then to the right place to sit; seated, she was still led; she was asked questions which could only be answered *Yes* and *Yes* and *No* and *Yes;* they thanked her.

He took the stand. She averted her eyes. It was soon over. Home then in a police car, through an avenue of flash-bulbs, on the arm of a policewoman. All a blur, all nothing, really; the real thing was the next thing, the day, the next day.

First there were the papers, the two tabloids with her picture weeping on the front page, and *Story on Page* 3 and *More pictures in Centerfold.* The headline on one was NAB ATTACKER IN ASSAULT ACT and the other one said RAPIST NABBED SENT UP 5 1/2 HRS.

The first one had the story she liked best. It had the reporter's name on it and began "A living nightmare burst upon a lonely lady late last night when . . ." The other one, though it was about her, wasn't so much about *her.* It was mostly about the judge. Her judge and another judge had been having a sort of race.

So many of these terrible attack things coming up had made them revive the old Night Court, and it seems that her Judge had heard and sentenced an attacker in less than twelve hours, so this other judge beat him to it by almost three hours, so this time her judge had packed the convict off to wherever it was he went, just five and a half hours after *he* had knocked on her door. And serve him right, too, said the paper, and all others like him. They had to learn that justice in Our Town was swift and certain.

She wasn't on the front page of the other papers, but she was in them all somewhere. And all that day at the market, people came to see her, to talk to her. People she had worked with for years spoke to her—really spoke to her—for the first time. And some of the men just couldn't get enough of her. Well, they *cared*.

That was the day everyone began to call her Little Sister. And when she walked back from the bus stop in the afternoon; they called out to her—"You okay, Little Sister?" Well, if it took such a terrible thing to show that way down deep people *cared*.... Still, it was a terrible thing, terrible. Everyone said so.

And in about three weeks, that same Detective Poteen came to see her. He had called first, made it convenient, had been very polite and understanding. He was a man who listened a great deal more than he talked. He had that skin that always looks tanned, and glossy black hair and a young face with old pouches under the eyes.

He asked her about the whole thing all over again, right from the beginning. She told it to him, just the way it had been written in the papers. Maybe, she had thought, a police detective is too busy to read the papers. She had asked him why the police were still interested, and he said they weren't, but he was. He was off duty at the time. She thought, at the time, that it was kind of nice.

Then the year went by, and while it was warm, and when it was warm again, she used to sit sometimes in her wicker chair by the window, invisible behind the square of gauze, and gaze out across her unseen barrier—sixty feet, straight down—to the roof. And in her memory's gaze she would see him again, the whole thing ... unseen by him, remote and safe. "You all right, Little Sister?" the people said as she passed. "Watch yourself, now—be careful ..."

The year went by, and this afternoon Poteen called again. She'd been a little slow in responding to him ... that was funny ... it wasn't because she didn't recognize his voice. She did. It was just that for some reason she couldn't believe it. And then with his soft polite voice he had drawn the curtain of terror over her: "I thought I ought to tell you—Clewie Richardson got out yesterday."

"Who's Louie Richardson?"

"Clewie. Clewton W. Richardson. The boy who was sent up on your complaint last year."

She had, of course, seen the name; it just hadn't stayed with her. "I forgot his name. I . . . wanted to forget everything," she said pathetically. Then the full impact of the news struck her. "Got *out?* You mean he's *back?*"

"He lives here," said Poteen's voice gently. Then, very soothing, he said, "Now don't you get excited or worried or anything. There's no danger for you. I just felt I ought to tell you, in case you should see him on the street or something. It's all over, so just don't worry."

"Oh," she said, worried, terribly worried. "Oh dear." While she was saying it he said goodbye quietly and hung up.

That was about three this afternoon; now it was nearly ten, and dark; but for a hazy sliver of moon, peeping and hiding, it was dark, too dark. Yet she would not turn on her light. As night was born, so her worry turned to fright; as the night grew around her and all the world, so her fright turned to terror, until at last it was a haze about her like the one in the sky.

And like the fragile stick of moon out there, all she could do was peep and hide in it, peep and hide, and the blur of her fear filtered common sounds into breathings by her door, and ordinary shifts of moonlight into movement on the roof.

Call the police, she kept telling herself, and *No, what would I say? I thought I saw, I thought I heard . . . ?* Then, *Go!* she would tell herself, and answer, *go where?* . . . and then, since no passion, even the ecstasies of fear, can continue indefinitely, but must ebb and peak, the haze of terror would fitfully clarify and she could get her breath and bearings. Detective Poteen had told her there was nothing to fear. And *he*—Louie or Clewie?—surely he'd have learned his lesson, he wouldn't try to . . .

But then, he would. She knew he would. She knew it so well that she was waiting for him. This is what she kept coming back to as the night grew tight around her, strong and dark, and each time she came back to it, the terror peaked higher. And off again on the climbing spiral: *Call the police.* (No, what would I—) Then, *Go! Go where?* . . . Oh! someone's breathing out there! Something's moving out there . . . Oh!

Something was indeed—someone in the moonlight. Little Sister peered and peered through the gauze, then, because she could not bear to be uncertain, no, not for another second, she took the flimsy panel and held it to one side.

And he, *he* stood there! and when he saw the curtain move, he smiled. She could see the gleam of his teeth in the moonlight.

He began again to take off clothes. He took off a jacket and tossed it behind the kiosk. He took off a shirt. He took off his shoes, balancing like a great bird on one foot, then the other, never taking his eyes off her window. And all the while, smiling.

Whether or not he had learned any lesson, she had, and that was, don't scream. It was only now, this second, that she knew she had learned it, knew what her screams had done last time. She whimpered only, dropped the curtain and fled to the telephone. She lifted it, and, unable to stay away from the window, carried it as close as she could. She took up the receiver—and oh! that blessed hum!—and looking out and back, dialed. And while she was dialing, she saw the dim form outside spring lithely up the side of the kiosk, stand and balance on tiptoe against the flickering sky.

He reached up high over his head, took the faint pencil-line of a wire in his hands, and leapt lightly back to the roof. She heard the twang as the wire parted, and in her hands, like a captured bird, the telephone went dead.

Her breath stopped as the life left the instrument. She thought her heart stopped too. She stood absolutely motionless, gazing at the dead thing, and then she moaned softly, softly replaced the handset, and backed away from the window. And even all the way back, near the bed, she could see him, for he had retired to the middle of the wide roof opposite.

And now he took two springy strides toward her, and now he

skipped once like a diver or an acrobat getting his stride, and now he was sprinting, and up the sloping, ramp-like eave he came, and launched himself into the air!

The square black hole of her open upper sash must have seemed a small target indeed—almost too narrow to admit his shoulders. But through it they went, never touching. His whole long body arrowed through the little opening and came at her like a javelin. And as she tensed herself for the crash of his landing, his body curved downward toward the floor. As his hands touched it he snapped his chin down to his collarbones, curled up in a tight ball, turned all his velocity into a roll. And there was no crash at all, only a great soft complex thud which shook her body and the bed, ending with a bump as he came up standing on his stockinged feet.

For a long moment—forever—they stood silently so, again their gazes locked, he smiling and balanced on his wide-planted feet, she pressed back against the edge of the bed. Then she sighed and fell backwards. She screwed up her eyes and her mouth, and through her twisted lips she gasped, "All right! All right!"

"Little Sister. Little Sister!"

Calling, calling . . . "I told you," she blubbered, "I told you all right."

"All right," the voice echoed her, "You're all right now. You must have fainted."

She let her aching eyes open a crack, and cried out; the big overhead light was on, and it hurt her.

An arm slid cleverly behind her, raised her up. She parted her lips to speak, and cold touched them, a cup, cold water . . . she drank a little and began to tremble. "You're all right now," said the voice over the phone—oh God, not over the phone, right here in the room. She opened her eyes again, now ready for the blaze of light, and looked into the bland quiet face of Detective Sergeant Peter Poteen.

Numbly, she let her gaze fall away, and there across the room, hunched into her wicker chair and much too big for it, was *he, him,* the man on the roof. Louie, Clewie!

Oh!

"I knew he'd try to see you," said Poteen, deftly fixing her pillow behind her. "I was out in the hall. I thought it might save everybody some trouble if I was with him, at the time. I lost him earlier and figured to meet him on the way to the door. Never dreamed he'd fly in like a bird."

Unbelievably, the man, this Louie or Clewie or whatever, he grinned briefly, grinned at Poteen, and it was not at all as if he was a prisoner, or even a criminal. Little Sister began to cry.

Poteen left her alone to cry. He stepped away from her and he and the man talked—chatted was the word—friendly as could be—their faces politely averted while she pulled herself together.

When she was able, she whimpered, "What is it? What happened? What are you doing here?"

Poteen returned to her immediately. He looked at her gravely and then pulled up the straight chair. From the shelf above, he got some tissues from her box. He sat down and gave them to her. She crumpled one and sniffled into it. He said, "Tell me what happened that other time. Last year."

"You know what happened."

"Tell me *all* of what happened."

"That," she remembered, "is what you asked me when you came here that time, three weeks after."

He nodded. "And you told me what you told the papers. I just wanted to know the rest of it."

"There isn't any rest of it."

He breathed deeply once, a patient sound, not exactly a sigh. "That first time you called me, to complain of a Peeping Tom making obscene gestures at you from the roof. Was that the first time you had seen this fellow out on the roof?"

She opened her mouth, drew in air—and then hesitated. There was a certain something about Poteen's bland dark face that was not easy to lie to. "Well," she said at length, "no, it wasn't."

Poteen made no move anyone might describe, but something inside him seemed to relax. "How many times did you see him before?"

"*I* don't know," she said in the beginnings of anger. "How do you expect me to remember, exactly how many times?"

"Ten times? Twenty times? Fifty?"

"Oh, not fifty."

"More than ten?"

"What right have you got to question me like this?" she shouted.

The thing inside him seemed to tighten up again. He reached in his breast pocket and drew out a thick sheaf of mimeo paper. "Know what this is? This is the transcript of his trial. Listen," he said in a tone which gave her no choice but to do as she was told.

He read, "'Q. Did you or did you not indecently expose your person to the view of the plaintiff?

"A. I didn't even—

"'Q. Answer the question. Did you or did not not—

"'A. But I was only—

"'The Court: The witness will answer the question.

"'Q. Did you—

"'A. Yes! Yes! Yes! If that's what I got to say.'"

Poteen held up the transcript so she could see a handwritten line penciled in it. "Here was something off the record but the court stenographer remembered it. His Honor stood up and leaned across the bench and yelled at the witness, 'You did, did you! You got a fat nerve pleading innocent, wasting everybody's time!' Then he said to strike that."

Poteen paused, then struck the papers softly with his free hand. "Let's just say that *this* is my right to question you this way." He folded the transcript and put it away, and went on in exactly the previous voice, "You'd seen him out on the roof before?"

She whispered, "Yes."

"More than ten times?"

". . . Yes."

"More than twenty?"

She glared at him. "No."

"Very well," he shrugged in a way that took all the strength out of her glare; it just didn't matter. "Now, as to what was called in court 'indecent exposure' and 'obscene gestures.' Exactly what was that? Just what did he do? Try to remember."

Little Sister really and truly blushed. "I . . . c-can't say it!"

"All right. Perhaps I can find a way to say it for you. He was relieving himself. Is that about it?"

She put her hands to her cheeks and nodded.

"Very well," he said clinically, not surprised, angry, shocked, anything. "Now—was this the only occasion when you had seen this?"

She would not answer.

"Well?" And the way he produced that one syllable, she had to answer. She shook her head.

"How many times?" He waited, then said, "More than twice? Ten times?"

"Five times," she said at last.

"Five times," he repeated. "All right, let's get back to what he was doing on the roof in the first place."

She made a vague gesture.

"Well . . . tricks."

He waited, and she said, "You know—like, *tricks*. Standing on his hands and all. He had some sort of—well, pipes, like."

"Handstand bars. Like a small parallel bars. Built 'em himself," said Poteen. "One more thing—how was he dressed when he did this?"

"Well, not in much, I can tell you!"

"Would you say it was less, say, than a bathing suit?"

"It *was* a bathing suit."

That inward, indescribable relaxation came to Poteen again, and he said, "Well, we don't need any more of this third degree. Now let me fill in the details for you.

"Clewie Richardson there is what they used to call a circus buff. Ever hear that term? Circus struck when he was barely able to walk. All he ever wanted in his life was to be a flyer—you, know—aerialist. Came to town to get a job and save up enough to get down to Florida; Sarasota, where the circus had winter quarters. Figured he could save up enough to keep him until he could get some sort of a job with them. Got a night loading job in the warehouse, worked hard.

"They let him have a checker's office to sleep in—just a rathole, but they got a kind of watchman out of the deal, and he got to save a few more dollars. Meantime he kept practicing, keeping himself in shape. Last summer he was ready to make the break, go south, try for his break with the circus. Last summer he was seventeen. Three solid years working on his own for that."

"I didn't know!" Little Sister said in defense—in annoyance.

"You didn't want to know," said Poteen mildly. "So he lived in the warehouse, working nights, practicing days. The only washroom is down on the ground floor, by the way, which is why he—" He shrugged. "Technically he was guilty of *something*. That could constitute a nuisance, I suppose. Now then: as to this exposure charge. In all the time he used the roof, he *never* knew he could be seen. Out in the middle, where he had his bars, maybe—there are tall buildings out there, though none nearby.

"But back in this corner, by your window, that stairway-housing thing, that blocks off the view from everywhere except this window. When he stepped behind it, he did it to get out of sight. Yours is the only living quarters on this floor, right? All the rest is loft space. Right?"

Mute, she nodded.

"All right, now I'm going to describe to you exactly what happened that day." He glanced at the boy, and against her will, her gaze was drawn to him too. Clewie Richardson was a big youth, wide, tall, well-muscled, and somehow scrubbed-looking. He sat in her wicker chair dressed in black slacks and a white T-shirt, his stockinged feet crossed at the ankles, his whole large lithe frame leaning raptly toward Poteen.

"He worked out for a couple of hours—oh, it had to be the hours you'd be home, what a break! You and that early-morning job of yours! And then he—well, he committed his nuisance. And it was then for the very first time he saw you looking through your curtain. You can imagine how he felt. Or maybe you can't.

"All right—he cleared out then, and you waited two whole hours—why, I'll never know—and then took it upon yourself to make that phone call. So I said I'd check on it and I did. I talked to the men loading at the warehouse; Clewie was out eating. When he got back and they told him the cops were looking for him, he got all wound up. All he wanted to do was to talk to you, tell you he didn't know you were watching, didn't mean anything by it. He came up and knocked on your door, and next thing you know you started to scream. He wanted to calm you down, explain, but it all blew up in his face.

"Then once the squad-cars got here—" Again, that meaningful shrug. "The way the papers were playing up assault cases this last year, he didn't have a chance. Even the defense attorney told him to save himself trouble and plead guilty. He didn't, and—" Audibly, he tapped the transcript in his breast pocket—"look what that got him."

"I . . . didn't know," said Little Sister, rather differently.

"I didn't either, until next day. I went off duty after I spoke to the guys at the warehouse; then by next morning it was all over and Clewie was upstate. Five and a half hours, my God! Not that I'd've been able to do anything. Or wanted to, at the time. I had the fever, same as everyone else. But later . . . well, it kept bothering me.

"Finally I came to see you and somehow, the way you told the story, it—oh, it was too much the way a sob-sister writes a crime story. So I looked it up. You had that scandal-sheet Page Three story about by heart, didn't you?"

"You—" and for a moment she thought she was going to swear at him, but she changed it. "You could have stayed out of it."

He shook his head and said mildly, "No I couldn't." He looked at her with those understanding dark eyes for too long. She had to turn away, and he said, just like on TV, "I'm a cop, mam. I have to uphold the law. But sometimes I stop and think what the law is. The law in this country is the best we can do to make justice apply to everybody. That's what they get made for and that's how most of 'em work. If they don't work that way then somebody ought to fix the trouble.

"Look here," he said, waving a hand at Clewie Richardson and meaning the whole thing, the, complaint, assault, arrest, imprisonment—all of it. "The law was upheld all down the line, but it took a year out of his life for a misdemeanor. Everything costs,

Little Sister. Somebody pays for everything. Clewie Richardson here paid plenty—for what?

"Partly for newspapers reaching down long handles to stir up some circulation. Partly for rapists who never got caught. Partly for his own ignorance, not knowing his rights, and his own bullheadedness, trying to talk to you. And partly, he paid for something you got out of it. That last is the only part I really don't know about. What did you get out of it, Little Sister?"

"I don't know what you mean, and I don't know why you're . . . *bullying* me like this!"

"I believe you," said Poteen, and there was real wonderment in his voice. "All right, Clewie—you win. You can tell her. Little Sister, this boy lay every night in the reformatory thinking and dreaming of just one thing—to tell you something you ought to know. I didn't think he should because I don't like people to get hurt and because I knew it would get him into more trouble. That's all I wanted to stop him for. But now—go ahead, Clewie."

The boy got up and came across the room on silent feet. He was huge. He was smiling, or perhaps just baring his teeth. She shrank back on the bed. He said softly, "It's the same thing I wanted to tell you that first night, when you screamed so much. You saw me out there that day, and I saw you, just your face, peekin' through that curtain.

"I thought you was a *little funny-lookin' old man.* That's why I took my time, finished what I was doin'. And that's why I had to see you so bad when the cops came around and told the guys they were lookin' for me on a complaint by some *woman.* I had to find you and tell you I never realized it was a woman watchin' me!"

"That was the first time," said Poteen. "Now tell her what you spent every night for a year dreaming about telling her. Go ahead. I think you should."

The boy laughed. "It's the same thing, really. When I saw you through that curtain, I thought you were a funny-lookin' little old man. Well after that I seen you close up, without no curtain, and all I want is to tell you—you still look like a funny little old man!"

Little Sister's face turned grey.

Poteen rose and motioned the boy toward the door. "The circus is in town," he said, "I got him a job with it. That takes care of some of the justice. I think he just took care of the rest."

He let the boy precede him through the door and, with his hand on the knob, turned to face her. "You knew he thought that, didn't you? Is that why? Is that the reason you waited two hours to make your complaint? Is that why you wouldn't let him talk to you? To grab this one chance to tell the world you were a woman, when the world never really knew it before? Is that why you told the reporters 'everybody calls me Little Sister' when nobody ever called you that before?"

"Yes they did!" she shrieked. "Yes they did! My daddy used to call me that!"

Politely, understandingly, Detective Sergeant Peter Poteen closed the door.

When You Care, When You Love

He was beautiful in her bed.

When you care, when you love, when you treasure someone, you can watch the beloved in sleep as you watch everything, anything else—laughter, lips to a cup, a look even away from you; a stride, sun a-struggle lost in a hair-lock, a jest or a gesture—even stillness, even sleep.

She leaned close, all but breathless, and watched his lashes. Now, lashes are thick sometimes, curled, russet; these were all these, and glossy besides. Look closely—there where they curve lives light in tiny serried scimitars.

All so good, *so* very good, she let herself deliciously doubt its reality. She would let herself believe, in a moment, that this was real, was true, was here, had at last happened. All the things her life before had ever given her, all she had ever wanted, each by each had come to her purely for wanting. Delight there might be, pride, pleasure, even glory in the new possession of gift, privilege, object, experience: her ring, hat, toy, trip to Trinidad; yet, with possession there had always been (until now) the platter called *well, of course* on which these things were served her. For had she not wanted it? But this, now—*him*, now ... greatest of all her wants, ever; first thing in all her life to transcend want itself and knowingly become need: this she had at last, at long (how long, now) long last, this she had now for good and all, for always, forever and never a touch of *well, of course*. He was her personal miracle, he in this bed now, warm and loving her. He was the reason and the reward of it all—her family and forebears, known by so few and felt by so many, and indeed, the whole history of mankind leading up to it, and all she herself had *been* and done and felt; and loving him, and losing him, and seeing him dead and bringing him back—it was all for this moment and because the moment had to be, he and this peak, this warmth in these sheets, this *now* of hers. He was all life and all life's beauty, beautiful in her bed; and now she could be sure, could believe it, believe . . .

"I do," she breathed. "I do."

"What do you do?" he asked her. He had not moved, and did not now.

"Devil, I thought you were asleep."

"Well, I was. But I had the feeling someone was looking."

"Not looking," she said softly. "Watching." She was watching the lashes still, and did not see them stir, but between them now lay a shining sliver of the gray, cool aluminum of his surprising eyes. In a moment he would look at her—just that—in a moment their eyes would meet and it would be as if nothing new had happened (for it would be the same metal missile which had first impaled her) and also as if everything, everything were happening again. Within her, passion boiled up like a fusion fireball, so beautiful, so huge—

—and like the most dreaded thing on earth, without pause the radiance changed, shifting from the hues of all the kinds of love to all the tones of terror and the colors of a cataclysm.

She cried his name . . .

And the gray eyes opened wide in fear for her fears and in astonishment, and he bounded up laughing, and the curl of his laughing lips turned without pause to the pale writhing of agony, and they shrank apart, too far apart while the white teeth met and while between them he shouted his hurt. He fell on his side and doubled up, grunting, gasping in pain . . . grunting, gasping, wrapped away from her, unreachable even by her.

She screamed. She screamed. She—

A Wyke biography is hard to come by. This has been true for four generations, and more true with each, for the more the Wyke holdings grew, the less visible have been the Wyke family, for so Cap'n Gamaliel Wyke willed it after his conscience conquered him. This (for he was a prudent man) did not happen until after his retirement from what was euphemistically called the molasses trade. His ship—

later, his fleet—had carried fine New England rum, made from the molasses, to Europe, having brought molasses from the West Indies to New England. Of course a paying cargo was needed for the westward crossing, to close with a third leg this profitable triangle, and what better cargo than Africans for the West Indies, to harvest the cane and work in the mills which made the molasses?

Ultimately affluent and retired, he seemed content for a time to live among his peers, carrying his broadcloth coat and snowy linen as to the manor born, limiting his personal adornment to a massive golden ring and small square gold buckles at his knee. Soberly shop-talking molasses often, rum seldom, slaves never, he dwelt with a frightened wife and a silent son, until she died and something—perhaps loneliness—coupled his brain again to his sharp old eyes, and made him look about him. He began to dislike the hypocrisy of man and was honest enough to dislike himself as well, and this was a new thing for the Cap'n; he could not deny it and he could not contain it, so he left the boy with the household staff and, taking only a manservant, went into the wilderness to search his soul.

The wilderness was Martha's Vineyard, and right through a bitter winter the old man crouched by the fire when the weather closed in, and, muffled in four great gray shawls, paced the beaches when it was bright, his brass telescope under his arm and his grim canny thoughts doing mighty battle with his convictions. In the late spring, he returned to Wiscassett, his blunt certainty regained, his laconic curtness increased almost to the point of speechlessness. He sold out (as a startled contemporary described it) "everything that showed," and took his son, an awed, obedient eleven, back to the Vineyard where, to the accompaniment of tolling breakers and creaking gulls, he gave the boy an education to which all the schooling of all the Wykes for all of four generations would be mere addenda.

For in his retreat to the storms and loneliness of the inner self and the Vineyard, Gamaliel Wyke had come to terms with nothing less than the Decalogue.

He had never questioned the Ten Commandments, nor had he knowingly disobeyed them. Like many another before him, he attributed the sad state of the world and the sin of its inhabitants to their refusal to heed those Rules. But in his ponderings, God Himself, he at last devoutly concluded, had underestimated the stupidity of mankind. So he undertook to amend the Decalogue himself, by adding "... or cause ..." to each Commandment, just to make it easier for a man to work with:

"... or cause the Name of the Lord to be taken in vain."

"... or cause stealing to be done."

"... or cause dishonor to thy father and thy mother."

"... or cause the commission of adultery."

"... or cause a killing to be done."

But his revelation came to him when he came to the last one. It was suddenly clear to him that all mankind's folly—all greed, lust, war, all dishonor—sprang from humanity's almost total disregard for this edict and its amendment: "Thou shall not covet ... *nor cause covetousness!*"

It came to him then that to arouse covetousness in another is just as deadly a sin as to kill him or to cause his murder. Yet all around the world empires rose, great yachts and castles and hanging gardens came into being, tombs and trusts and college grants, all for the purpose of arousing the envy or covetousness of the less endowed—or having that effect no matter what the motive.

Now, one way for a man as rich as Gamaliel Wyke to have resolved the matter for himself would be St. Francis' way; but (though he could not admit this, or even recognize it) he would have discarded the Decalogue and his amendments, all surrounding Scripture and his gnarled right arm rather than run so counter to his inborn, ingrained Yankee acquisitiveness. And another way might have been to take his riches and bury them in the sand of Martha's Vineyard, to keep them from causing covetousness; the very thought clogged his nostrils with the feel of dune-sand and he felt suffocation; to him money was a living thing and should not be interred.

And so he came to his ultimate answer: Make your money, enjoy it, but *never let anyone know.* Desire, he concluded, for a neighbor's wife, or a neighbor's ass, or for anything, presupposed knowing about these possessions. No neighbor could desire anything of his if he couldn't lay a name to it.

So Gamaliel brought weight like granite and force like gravity to bear upon the mind and soul of his son Walter, and Walter begat Jedediah, and Jedediah begat Caiaphas (who died) and Samuel, and Samuel began Zebulon (who died) and Sylva; so perhaps the true beginning of the story of the boy who became his own mother lies with Cap'n Gamaliel Wyke and his sand-scoured, sea-deep, rock-hard revelation.

—fell on his side on the bed and doubled up, grunting, gasping, wrapped away from her, even her, unreachable even by her.

She screamed. She screamed. She pressed herself up and away from him and ran naked into the sitting room, pawed up the ivory telephone: "Keogh," she cried; "For the love of God, *Keogh!*"

—and back into the bedroom where he lay open-mouthing a grating horrible *uh uh!* while she wrung her hands, tried to take one of his, found it agony-tense and unaware of her. She called him, called him, and once, screamed again.

The buzzer sounded with inexcusable discretion.

"Keogh!" she shouted, and the polite buzzer *shhh'*d her again—the lock, oh the damned lock . . . she picked up her negligee and ran with it in her hand through the dressing room and the sitting room and the hall and the living room and the foyer and flung open the door. She pulled Keogh through it before he could turn away from her; she thrust one arm in a sleeve of the garment and shouted at him, "Keogh, please, please, Keogh, what's wrong with him?" and she fled to the bedroom, Keogh sprinting to keep up with her.

Then Keogh, chairman of the board of seven great corporations, board-member of a dozen more, general manager of a quiet family holding company which had, for most of a century, specialized in the ownership of corporate owners, went to the bed and fixed his cool blue gaze on the agonized figure there.

He shook his head slightly.

"You called the wrong man," he snapped, and ran back to the sitting-room, knocking the girl aside as if he had a been a machine on tracks. He picked up the phone and said, "Get Rathburn up here. *Now.* Where's Weber? You don't? Well, find him and get him here

. . . I don't care. Hire an airplane. *Buy* an airplane."

He slammed down the phone and ran back into the bedroom. He came up behind her and gently lifted the negligee onto her other shoulder, and speaking gently to her all the while, reached round her and tied the ribbon belt. "What happened?"

"N-nothing, he just—"

"Come on, girl—clear out of here. Rathburn's practically outside the door, and I've sent for Weber. If there's a better doctor than Rathburn, it could only be Weber, so you've got to leave it to them. Come!"

"I won't leave him."

"Come!" Keogh rapped, then murmured, looking over her shoulder at the bed, "He wants you to, can't you see? He doesn't want you to see him like this. *Right?*" he demanded, and the face, turned away and half-buried in the pillow shone sweatly; cramp mounded the muscles on the side of the mouth they could just see. Stiffly the head nodded; it was like a shudder. "And . . . shut . . . door . . . tight . . ." he said in a clanging half whisper.

"Come," said Keogh. And again, "Come." He propelled her away; she stumbled. Her face turned yearningly until Keogh, both hands on her, kicked at the door and it swung and the sight of the bed was gone. Keogh leaned back against the door as if the latch were not enough to hold it closed.

"What is it? Oh, what is it?"

"I don't know," he said.

"You do, you do . . . you always know everything . . . why won't you let me stay with him?"

"He doesn't want that."

Overcome, inarticulate, she cried out.

"Maybe," he said into her hair, "he wants to scream too."

She struggled—oh, strong, lithe and strong she was. She tried to press past him. He would not budge, so at last, at last she wept.

He held her in his arms again, as he had not done since she used to sit on his lap as a little girl. He held her in his arms and looked blindly toward the unconcerned bright morning, seen soft-focused through the cloud of her hair. And he tried to make it stop, the morning, the sun, and time, but—

—but there is one certain thing only about a human mind, and that is that it acts, moves, works ceaselessly while it lives. The action, motion, labor differ from that of a heart, say, or an epithelial cell, in that the latter have functions, and in any circumstance perform their functions. Instead of a function, mind has a duty, that of making of a hairless ape a human being . . . yet as if to prove how trivial a difference there is between mind and muscle, mind must move, to some degree, always change, to some degree, always while it lives, like a stinking sweat gland . . . holding her, Keogh thought about Keogh.

The biography of Keogh is somewhat harder to come by than that of a Wyke. This is not in spite of having spent merely half a lifetime in this moneyed shadow; it is because of it. Keogh was a Wyke in all but blood and breeding: Wyke owned him and all he owned, which was a great deal.

He must have been a child once, a youth; he could remember if he wished but did not care to. Life began for him with the *summa cum laude,* the degrees in both business and law and (so young) the year and a half with Hinnegan and Bache, and then the incredible opening at the International Bank; the impossible asked of him in the Zurich-Plenum affair, and his performance of it, and the shadows which grew between him and his associates over the years, while for him the light grew and grew as to the architecture of his work, until at last he was admitted to Wyke, and was permitted to realize that Wyke *was* Zurich and Plenum, and the International Bank, and Hinnegan and Bache; was indeed his law school and his college and much, so very much more. And finally sixteen—good heavens, it was eighteen years ago, when he became General Manager, and the shadows dark to totally black between him and any other world, while the light, his own huge personal illumination, exposed almost to him alone an industrial-financial complex unprecedented in his country, and virtually unmatched in the world.

But then, the beginning, the *other* beginning, was when Old Sam Wyke called him in so abruptly that morning, when (though General Manager with many a board chairman, all unbeknownst, under him in rank) he was still the youngest man in that secluded office.

"Keogh," said old Sam, "this is my kid. Take 'er out. Give 'er anything she wants. Be back here at six." He had then kissed the girl on the crown of her dark straw hat, gone to the door, turned and barked, "You see her show off or brag, Keogh, you fetch her a good one, then and there, hear? I don't care what else she does, but don't you let her wave something she's got at someone that hasn't got it. That's Rule One." He had then breezed out, leaving a silent, startled young mover of mountains locking gazes with an unmoving mouse of an eleven-year-old girl. She had luminous pale skin, blue-black silky-shining hair, and thick, level, black brows.

The *summa cum laude,* the acceptance at Hinnegan and Bache—all such things, they were beginnings that he knew were beginnings. This he would not know for some time that it was a beginning, any more than he could realize that he had just heard the contemporary version of Cap'n Gamaliel's "Thou shalt not . . . cause covetousness." At the moment, he could only stand nonplussed for a moment, then excuse himself and go to the treasurer's office, where he scribbled a receipt and relieved the petty cashbox of its by no means petty contents. He got his hat and coat and returned to the President's office. Without a word the child rose and moved with him to the door.

They lunched and spent the afternoon together, and were back at six. He bought her whatever she wanted at one of the most expensive shops in New York. He took her to just the places of amusement she asked him to.

When it was all over, he returned the stack of bills to the petty cash box, less the one dollar and twenty cents he had paid out. For at the shop—the largest toy store in the world—she had carefully selected a sponge rubber ball, which they packed for her in a cubical box. This she carried carefully by its string for the rest of the afternoon.

They lunched from a pushcart—he had one hot dog with kraut, she had two with relish.

They rode uptown on the top of a Fifth Avenue double-decker, open-top bus.

They went to the zoo in Central Park and bought one bag of peanuts for the girl and the pigeons, and one bag of buns for the girl and the bears.

Then they took another double-decker back downtown, and that was it; that was the afternoon.

He remembered clearly what she looked like then: like a straw-hatted wren, for all it was a well-brushed wren. He could not remember what they had talked about, if indeed they had talked much at all. He was prepared to forget the episode, or at least to put it neatly in the *Trivia: Misc.: Closed* file in his compartmented mind, when, a week later, old Sam tossed him a stack of papers and told him to read them through and come and ask questions if he thought he had to. The only question which came to mind when he had read them was, "Are you sure you want to go through with this?" and that was not the kind of question one asked old Sam. So he thought it over very carefully and came up with "Why me?" and old Sam looked him up and down and growled, "She likes you, that's why."

And so it was that Keogh and the girl lived together in a cotton mill town in the South for a year. Keogh worked in the company store. The girl worked in the mill; twelve-year-old girls worked in cotton mills in the South in those days, and had three hours' school in the afternoons. Up until ten o'clock on Saturday nights they watched the dancing from the sidelines. On Sundays they went to the Baptist church. Their name while they were there was Harris. Keogh used to worry frantically when she was out of his sight, but one day when she was crossing the catwalk over the water-circulating sump, a sort of oversized well beside the mill, the catwalk broke and pitched her into the water. Before she could so much as draw a breath a Negro stoker appeared out of nowhere—actually, out of the top of the coal chute—and leapt in and had her and handed her up to the sudden crowd. Keogh came galloping up from the company store as they were pulling the stoker out, and after seeing that girl was all right, knelt beside the man, whose leg was broken.

"I'm Mr. Harris, her father. You'll get a reward for this. What's your name?"

The man beckoned him close, and as he bent down, the stoker, in spite of his pain, grinned and winked. "You don' owe me a thang, Mr. Keogh," he murmured. In later times, Keogh would be filled with rage at such a confidence, would fire the man out of hand: this first time he was filled with wonder and relief. After that, things were easier on him, as he realized that the child was surrounded by Wyke's special employees, working on Wyke land in a Wyke mill and paying rent in a Wyke row-house.

In due time the year was up. Someone else took over, and the girl, now named Kevin and with a complete new background in case anyone should ask, went off for two years to a very exclusive Swiss finishing school, where she dutifully wrote letters to a Mr. and Mrs. Kevin who held large acreage in the Pennsylvania mountains, and who just as dutifully answered her.

Keogh returned to his own work, which he found in apple-pie order, with every one of the year's transactions beautifully abstracted for him, and an extra amount, over and above his astronomical salary, tucked away in one of his accounts—an amount that startled even Keogh. He missed her at first, which he expected. But he missed her every single day for two solid years, a disturbance he could not explain, did not examine, and discussed with no one.

All the Wykes, old Sam once grunted to him, did something of the sort. He, Sam, had been a logger in Oregon and a year and a half as utility man, then ordinary seaman on a coastwise tanker.

Perhaps some deep buried part of Keogh's mind thought that when she returned from Switzerland, they would go for catfish in an old flat-bottomed boat again, or that she would sit on his lap while he suffered on the hard benches of the once-a-month picture show. The instant he saw her on her return from Switzerland, he knew that would never be. He knew he was entering some new phase; it troubled and distressed him and he put it away in the dark inside himself; he could do that; he was strong enough. And she—well, she flung her arms around him and kissed him; but when she talked with this new vocabulary, this deft school finish, she was strange and awesome to him, like an angel. Even a loving angel is strange and awesome . . .

They were together again then for a long while, but there were no more hugs. He became a Mr. Stark in the Cleveland office of a brokerage house and she boarded with an elderly couple, went to the local high school and had a part-time job filing in his office. This was when she learned the ins and outs of the business, the size of it. It would be hers. It became hers while they were in Cleveland: old Sam died very suddenly. They slipped away to the funeral but were back at work on Monday. They stayed there for another eight months; she had a great deal to learn. In the fall she entered a small private college and Keogh saw nothing of her for a year.

"Shhh," he breathed to her, crying, and *sssh!* said the buzzer.

"Go take a bath," he said. He pushed her.

She half-turned under his hand, faced him again blazing. "No!"

"You can't go in there, you know," he said, going for the door. She glared at him, but her lower lip trembled.

Keogh opened the door. "In the bedroom."

"Who—" then the doctor saw the girl, her hands knotted together, her face twisted, and had his answer. He was a tall man, gray, with quick hands, a quick step, swift words. He went straight through foyer, hall and rooms and into the bedroom. He closed the door behind him. There had been no discussion, no request and refusal; Dr. Rathburn had simply, quickly, quietly shut them out.

"Go take a bath."

"No."

"Come on." He took her wrist and led her to the bathroom. He reached into the shower stall and turned on the side jets. There were four at each corner; the second from the top was scented. Apple blossom. "Go on."

He moved toward the door. She stood where he had let go of her wrist, pulling at her hands. "Go on," he said again. "Just a quick one. Do you good." He waited. "Or do you want me to douse you myself? I bet I still can."

She flashed him a look; indignation passed instantly as she understood what he was trying to do. The rare spark of mischief appeared in her eyes and, in perfect imitation of a mill-row redneck, she said, "Y'all try it an Ah'll tall th' shurff Ah ain't rightly yo' chile." But the effort cost her too much, and she cried again. He stepped out and softly closed the door.

He was waiting by the bedroom when Rathburn slid out and quickly shut the door on the grunt, the gasp.

"What is it?" asked Keogh.

"Wait a minute." Rathburn strode to the phone. Keogh said, "I sent for Weber."

Rathburn came almost ludicrously to a halt. "Wow," he said. "Not bad diagnosing, for a layman. Is there anything you can't do?"

"I can't understand what you're talking about," said Keogh testily.

"Oh—I thought you knew. Yes, I'm afraid it's in Weber's field. What made you guess?"

Keogh shuddered. "I saw a mill hand take a low blow once. I know *he* wasn't hit. What exactly is it?"

Rathburn darted a look around. "Where is she?" Keogh indicated the bathroom. "I told her to take a shower."

"Good," said the doctor. He lowered his voice. "Naturally I can't tell without further examination and lab—"

"What is it?" Keogh demanded, not loud, but with such violence that Rathburn stepped back a pace.

"It could be choriocarcinoma."

Tiredly, Keogh wagged his head. "Me diagnose that? I can't even spell it. What is it?" He caught himself up, as if he had retrieved the word from thin air and run it past him again. "I know what the last part of it means."

"One of the—" Rathburn swallowed, and tried again. "One of the more vicious forms of cancer. And it . . ." He lowered his voice again. "It doesn't always hit this hard."

"Just how serious is it?"

Rathburn raised his hands and let them fall.

"Bad, eh? Doc—*how bad?*"

"Maybe some day we can . . ." Rathburn's lowered voice at last disappeared. They hung there, each on the other's pained gaze.

"How much time?"

"Maybe six weeks."

"Six weeks!"

"Shh," said Rathburn nervously.

"Weber—"

"Weber knows more about internal physiology than anybody. But I don't know if that will help. It's a little like . . . your, uh, house is struck by lightning, flattened, burned to the ground. You can examine it and the weather reports and, uh, know exactly what happened. Maybe some day we can . . ." he said again, but he said it so hopelessly that Keogh, through the rolling mists of his own terror, pitied him and half-instinctively put out a hand. He touched the doctor's sleeve and stood awkwardly.

"What are you going to do?"

Rathburn looked at the closed bedroom door. "What I did." He made a gesture with a thumb and two fingers. "Morphine."

"And that's all?"

"Look, I'm a G.P. Ask Weber, will you?"

Keogh realized that he had pushed the man as far as he could in his search for a crumb of hope; if there was none, there was no point in trying to squeeze it out. He asked, "Is there anyone working on it? Anything new? Can you find out?"

"Oh, I will, I will. But Weber can tell you off the top of his head more than I could find out in six mon . . . in a long time."

A door opened. She came out, hollow-eyed, but pink and glowing in a long white terry-cloth robe. "Dr. Rathburn—"

"He's asleep."

"Thank God. Does it—"

"There's no pain."

"What is it? What happened to him?"

"Well, I wouldn't like to say for sure . . . we're waiting for Dr. Weber. He'll know."

"But—but is he—"

"He'll sleep the clock around."

"Can I . . ." The timidity, the caution, Keogh realized was so unlike her. "Can I see him?"

"He's fast asleep!"

"I don't care. I'll be quiet. I won't—touch him or anything."

"Go ahead," said Rathburn. She opened the bedroom door and

eagerly, silently slipped inside.

"You'd think she was trying to make sure he was there."

Keogh, who knew her so very well, said, "She is."

But a biography of Guy Gibbon is *really* hard to come by. For he was no exceptional executive, who for all his guarded anonymity wielded so much power that he must be traceable by those who knew where to look and what to look for, and cared enough to process detail like a mass spectroscope. Neither was Guy Gibbon born heir to countless millions, the direct successor to a procession of giants.

He came from wherever it is most of us come from, the middle or the upper-middle, or the upper-lower middle or the lower-upper middle, or some other indefinable speck in the mid-range of the inter-flowing striations of society (the more they are studied, the less they mean). He belonged to the Wyke entity for only eight and a half weeks, after all. Oh, the bare details might not be too hard to come by (birth date, school record), and certain main facts (father's occupation, mother's maiden name), as well, perhaps as a highlight or two (divorce, perhaps, or a death in the family); but a biography, a real biography, which does more than describe, which *explains* the man—and few do—now, *this* is an undertaking.

Science, it is fair to assume, can do what all the king's horses and all the king's men could not do, and totally restore a smashed egg. Given equipment enough, and time enough ... but isn't this a way of saying, "given money enough?" For money can be not only means, but motive. So if enough money went into the project, perhaps the last unknown, the last vestige of anonymity could be removed from a man's life story, even a young man from (as the snobs say) nowhere, no matter how briefly—though intimately—known.

The most important thing, obviously, that ever happened to Guy Gibbon in his life was his first encounter with the Wyke entity, and like many a person before and since, he had not the faintest idea he had done so. It was when he was in his late teens, and he and Sammy Stein went trespassing.

Sammy was a school sidekick, and this particular day he had a secret; he had been very insistent on the day's outing, but refused to say why. He was a burly-shouldered, good-natured, reasonably chinless boy whose close friendship with Guy was based almost exclusively on the attraction of opposite poles. And since, of the many kinds of fun they had had, the most fun was going trespassing, he wanted it that way on this particular occasion.

"Going trespassing," as an amusement, had more or less invented itself when they were in their early teens. They lived in a large city surrounded (unlike many today) by old suburbs, not new ones. These included large—some, more than large—estates and mansions, and it was their greatest delight to slip through a fence or over a wall and, profoundly impressed by their own bravery, slip through field and forest, lawn and drive, like Indian scouts in settler country. Twice they had been caught, once to have dogs set on them—three boxers and two mastiffs, which certainly would have torn them to very small pieces if the boys had not been more lucky than swift—and once by a dear little old lady who swamped them sickeningly with jelly sandwiches and lonely affection. But over the saga of their adventures, their two captures served to spice the adventure; two failures out of a hundred successes (for many of these places were visited frequently) was a proud record.

So they took a trolley to the end of the line, and walked a mile, and went straight ahead where the road turned at a discreet NO ADMITTANCE sign of expensive manufacture and a high degree of weathering. They proceeded through a small wild wood, and came at last to an apparently unscalable granite wall.

Sammy had discovered this wall the week before, roaming alone; he had waited for Guy to accompany him before challenging it, and Guy was touched. He was also profoundly excited by the wall itself. Anything this size should have been found, conjectured about, campaigned against, battled and conquered long since. But as well as being a high wall, a long wall, and mysterious, it was a distant wall, a discreet wall. No road touched it but its own driveway, which was primitive, meandering, and led to ironbound, solid oak gates without a chink or crack to peek through.

They could not climb it nor breach it—but they crossed it. An ancient maple on this side held hands with a chestnut over the crown of the wall, and they went over like a couple of squirrels.

They had, in their ghost-like way, haunted many an elaborate property, but never had they seen such maintenance, such manicure, such polish of a piece of land and, as Sammy said, awed out of his usual brashness, as they stood in a solid marble pergola overlooking green plush acres of rolling lawn, copses of carven boxwood, park-lake woods and streams with little Japanese bridges and, in their bends, humorful little rock-gardens: "—and there's goddamn *miles* of it."

They had wandered a bit, that first time, and had learned that there were after all some people there. They saw a tractor far away, pulling a slanted gang of mowers across one of the green-plush fields. (The owners doubtless called it a lawn; it was a field.) The machines, rare in that time, cut a swath all of thirty feet wide, "and that," Sammy said, convulsing them, "ain't hay." And then they had seen the house—

Well, a glimpse. Breaking out of the woods. Guy had felt himself snatched back. "House up there," said Sammy. "Someone'll see us." There was a confused impression of a white hill that was itself the house, or part of it; towers, turrets, castellations, crenellations; a fairy-tale palace set in this legendary landscape. They had not been able to see it again; it was so placed that it could be approached nowhere secretly nor even spied upon. They were struck literally speechless by the sight and for most of an hour had nothing to say, and that expressible only by wags of the head. Ultimately they referred to it as "the shack," and it was in this vein that they later called their final discovery "the ol' swimmin' hole."

It was across a creek and over a wooded hill. Two more hills rose to meet the wood, and cupped between the three was a pond, perhaps a lake. It was roughly L-shaped, and all around it were shadowed inlets, grottoes, inconspicuous stone steps leading here to a rustic pavilion set about with flowers, there to a concealed forest glade harboring a tiny formal garden.

But the lake, the ol' swimmin' hole . . .

They went swimming, splashing as little as possible and sticking to the shore. They explored two inlets to the right (a miniature waterfall and a tiny beach of obviously imported golden sand) and three to the left (a square-cut one, lined with tile the color of patina, with a black glass diving tower overhanging water that must have been dredged to twenty feet; a little beach of snow-white sand; and one they dared not enter, for fear of harming the fleet of perfect sailing ships, none more than a foot long, which lay at anchor; but they trod water until they were bone-cold, gawking at the miniature model waterfront with little pushcarts in the street, and lamp-posts, and old-fashioned houses) and then, weary, hungry, and awestruck, they had gone home.

And Sammy cracked the secret he had been keeping—the thing which made this day an occasion: he was to go wild-hairing off the next day in an effort to join Chennault in China.

Guy Gibbon, overwhelmed, made the only gesture he could think of: he devotedly swore he would not go trespassing again until Sammy got back.

"Death from choriocarcinoma," Dr. Weber began, "is the result of—"

"But he won't die," she said. "I won't let him."

"My dear," Dr. Weber was a small man with round shoulders and a hawk's face. "I don't mean to be unkind, but I can use all the euphemisms and kindle all the false hope, or I can do as you have asked me to do—explain the condition and make a prognosis. I can't do both."

Dr. Rathburn said gently, "Why don't you go and lie down? I'll come when we've finished here and tell you all about it."

"I don't want to lie down," she said fiercely. "And I wasn't asking you to spare me anything. Dr. Weber, I simply said I would not let him die. There's nothing in that statement which keeps you from telling me the truth."

Keogh smiled. Weber caught him at it and startled; Keogh saw his surprise. "I know her better than you do," he said, with a touch of pride. "You don't have to pull any punches."

"Thanks, Keogh," she said. She leaned forward. "Go ahead, Dr. Weber."

Weber looked at her. Snatched from his work two thousand miles away, brought to a place he had never known existed, of a magnificence which attacked his confidence in his own eyes, meeting a woman of power—every sort of power—quite beyond his experience ... Weber had thought himself beyond astonishment. Shock, grief, fear, deprivation like hers he had seen before, of course; what doctor has not? but when Keogh had told her baldly that this disease killed in six weeks, *always,* she had flinched, closed her eyes for an interminable moment, and had then said softly, "Tell us everything you can about this—this disease. Doctor." And she had added, for the first time, "He isn't going to die. I won't let him"; and the way she held her head, the way her full voice handled the words, he almost believed her. Heaven knows, he wished he could. And so he found he could be astonished yet again.

He made an effort to detach himself, and became not a man, not this particular patient's doctor, but a sort of source-book. He began again:

"Death from choriocarcinoma is a little unlike other deaths from malignancies. Ordinarily a cancer begins locally, and sends its chains and masses of wild cells growing through the organ on which it began. Death can result from the failure of that organ; liver, kidney, brain, what have you. Or the cancer suddenly breaks up and spreads through the body, starting colonies, throughout the system. This is called metastasis. Death results then from the loss of efficiency of many organs instead of just one. Of course, both these things can happen—the almost complete impairment of the originally cancerous organ, and metastatic effects at the same time.

"Chorio, on the other hand, doesn't originally involve a vital organ. Vital to the species, perhaps, but not to the individual." He permitted himself a dry smile. "This is probably a startling concept, to most people in this day and age, but it's nonetheless true. However, sex cells, at their most basic and primitive, have peculiarities not shared by other body cells.

"Have you ever heard of the condition known as ectopic pregnancy?" He directed this question at Keogh, who nodded. "A fertilized ovum fails to descend to the uterus; instead it attaches itself to the side of the very fine tube between the ovaries and the womb.

And at first everything proceeds well with it—and this is the point I want you to grasp—because in spite of the fact that only the uterus is truly specialized for this work, the tube wall not only supports the growing ovum but feeds it. It actually forms what we call a counterplacenta; it enfolds the early fetus and nurtures it. The fetus, of course, has a high survival value, and is able to get along quite well on the plasma which the counterplacenta supplies it with. And it grows—it grows fantastically. Since the tube is very fine—you'd have difficulty getting the smallest sewing needle up through it—it can no longer contain the growing fetus, and ruptures. Unless it is removed at that time, the tissues outside will quite as readily take on the work of a real placenta and uterus, and in six or seven months, if the mother survives that long, will create havoc in the abdomen.

"All right then: back to chorio. Since the cells involved are sex cells, and cancerous to boot, they divide and redivide wildly, without pattern or special form. They develop in an infinite variety of shapes and sizes and forms. The law of averages dictates that a certain number of these—and the number of distorted cells is astronomical—resemble fertilized ova. Some of them resemble them so closely that I personally would not enjoy the task of distinguishing between them and the real thing. However, the body as a whole is not that particular; anything which even roughly resembles a fertilized egg-cell is capable of commanding that counterplacenta.

"Now consider the source of these cells—physiologically speaking, gland tissue—a mass of capillary tubes and blood vessels. Each and every one of these does its best to accept and nurture these fetal limitations, down to the tiniest of them. The thin walls of the capillaries, however, break down easily under such an effort, and the imitations—selectively, the best of them, too, because the tissues yield most readily to them—they pass into the capillaries and then into the bloodstream.

"There is one place, and only one place, where they can be combed out; and it's a place rich in oxygen, lymph, blood and plasma: the lungs. The lungs enthusiastically take on the job of forming placentae for these cells, and nurturing them. But for every segment of lung given over to gestating an imitation fetus, there is one less segment occupied with the job of oxygenating blood. Ultimately the lungs fail, and death results from oxygen starvation."

Rathburn spoke up. "For years chorio was regarded as a lung disease, and the cancerous gonads as a sort of side effect."

"But lung cancer—" Keogh began to object.

"It isn't lung cancer, don't you see? Given enough time, it might be, through metastasis. But there is never enough time. Chorio doesn't have to wait for that, to kill. That's why it's so swift." He tried not to look at the girl, and failed; he said it anyway: "And certain."

"Just exactly how do you treat it?"

Weber raised his hands and let them fall. It was precisely the gesture Rathburn had made earlier, and Keogh wondered distantly whether they taught it in medical schools. "Something to kill the pain. Orchidectomy might make the patient last a little longer, by removing the supply of wild cells to the bloodstream. But it wouldn't save him. Metastasis has already taken place by the time the first symptom appears. The cancer becomes generalized . . . perhaps the lung condition is only God's mercy."

"What's 'orchidectomy'?" asked Keogh.

"Amputation of the—uh—source," said Rathburn uncomfortably.

"No!" cried the girl.

Keogh sent her a pitying look. There was that about him which was cynical, sophisticated, and perhaps coldly angry, at anyone who lived as he could never live, had what he could never have. It was a stirring of the grave ancient sin which old Cap'n Gamaliel had isolated in his perspicacious thoughts. Sure, amputate, if it'll help, he thought. What do you think you're preserving—his virility? What good's it to you now? . . . but sending her the look, he encountered something different from the romantically based horror and shock he expected. Her thick level brows were drawn together, her whole face intense with taut concentration. "Let me think," she said, oddly.

"You really should—" Rathburn began, but she shushed him with an impatient gesture. The three men exchanged a glance and settled back; it was as if someone, something had told them clearly and specifically to wait. What they were waiting for, they could not imagine.

The girl sat with her eyes closed. A minute crawled by. "Daddy used to say," she said, so quietly that she must surely be talking to herself, "that there's always a way. All you have to do is think of it."

There was another long silence and she opened her eyes. There was a burning down in them somewhere; it made Keogh uneasy. She said, "And once he told me that I could have anything I wanted; all it had to be was . . . possible. And . . . the only way you can find out if a thing is impossible is to try it."

"That wasn't Sam Wyke," said Keogh. "That was Keogh."

She wet her lips and looked at them each in turn. She seemed not to see them at all. "I'm not going to let him die," she said. "You'll see."

Sammy Stein came back two years later, on leave, and full of plans to join the Army Air Force. He'd had, as he himself said, the hell kicked out of him in China and a lot of the hellishness as well. But there was enough of the old Sammy left to make wild wonderful plans about going trespassing; and they knew just where they were going. The new Sammy, however, demanded a binge and a broad first.

Guy, two years out of high school, working for a living, and by nature neither binger nor wencher, went along only too gladly. Sam seemed to have forgotten about the "ol swimmin' hole" at first, and halfway through the evening, in a local bar-and-dance emporium, Guy was about to despair of his ever remembering it, when Sam himself brought it up, recalling to Guy that he had once written Sam a letter asking Sam if it had really happened. Guy had, in his turn, forgotten the letter, and after that they had a good time with "remember-when"—and they made plans to go trespassing the very next day, and bring a lunch. And start early.

Then there was a noisy involvement with some girls, and a lot more drinks, and out of the haze and movement somewhere after midnight, Guy emerged on a sidewalk looking at Sammy shoveling a girl into a taxicab. "Hey!" he called out, "what about the you know, ol' swimmin' hole?"

"Call me Abacus, you can count on me," said Sammy, and laughed immoderately. The girl with him pulled at his arm; he shook her off and weaved over to Guy. "Listen," he said, and gave a distorted wink, "if this makes—and it will—I'm starting no early starts. Tell you what, you go on out there and meet me by that sign says keep out or we'll castigate you. Say eleven o'clock. If I can't make it by then I'm dead or something." He bellowed at the cab, "You gon' kill me, honey?" and the girl called back, "I will if you don't get into this taxi." "See what I mean?" said Sammy in a grand drunken non-sequitur, "I got to go get killed." He zigged away, needing no zag because even walking sidewise he reached the cab in a straight line, and Guy saw no more of him that leave.

That was hard to take, mostly because there was no special moment at which he knew Sammy wasn't coming. He arrived ten minutes late, after making a super-human effort to get there. His stomach was sour from the unaccustomed drinking, and he was sandy-eyed and ache-jointed from lack of sleep. He knew that the greater probability was Sammy had not arrived yet or would not at all; yet the nagging possibility existed that he had come early and gone straight in. Guy waited around for a full hour, and some more minutes until the little road was clear of traffic and sounds of traffic, and then plunged alone into the woods, past the NO ADMITTANCE sign, and in to the wall. He had trouble finding the two trees, and once over the wall, he could not get his bearings for a while; he was pleased, of course, to find the unbelievably perfect lawns still there by the flawless acre, the rigidly controlled museums of carven box, the edge-trimmed, rolled-gravel walks meandering prettily through the woods. The pleasure, however, was no more than confirmation of his memory, and went no further; the day was spoiled.

Guy reached the lake at nearly one o'clock, hot, tired, ravenously hungry and unpleasantly nervous. The combination hit him in the stomach and made it echo; he sat down on the bank and ate. He wolfed down the food he had brought for himself and Sammy's as well—odds and ends carelessly tossed into a paper sack in the bleary early hours. The cake was moldy but he ate it anyway. The orange juice was warm and had begun to ferment. And stubbornly, he determined to swim, because that was what he had come for.

He chose the beach with the golden sand. Under a thick cover of junipers he found a stone bench and table. He undressed here and scuttled across the beach and into the water.

He had meant it to be a mere dip, so he could say he'd done it. But around the little headland to the left was the rectangular cove with the diving platform; and he remembered the harbor of model ships; and then movement diagonally across the foot of the lake's L caught his eye, and he saw models—not the anchored ships this time, but racing sloops, which put out from an inlet and crossed its mouth and sailed in again; they must be mounted on some sort of underwater wheel or endless chain, and moved as the breeze took them. He all but boiled straight across to them, then decided to be wise and go round.

He swam to the left and the rocky shore, and worked his way along it. Clinging close (the water seemed bottomless here) he rounded the point and came face to face (literally; they touched) with a girl.

She was young—near his age—and his first impression was of eyes of too complex an architecture, blue-white teeth with pointed canines quite unlike the piano-key regularity considered beautiful in these times, and a wide cape of rich brown hair afloat around her shoulders. By then his gasp was completed, and in view of the fact that in gasping he had neglected to remove his mouth from the water, he was shut off from outside impressions for a strangling time, until he felt a firm grasp on his left biceps and found himself returned to the side of the rock.

"Th-thanks," he said hoarsely as she swam back a yard and trod water. "I'm not supposed to be here," he added inanely.

"I guess I'm not either. But I thought you lived here. I thought you were a faun."

"Boy am I glad to hear that. I mean about you. All I am is a trespasser. Boy."

"I'm not a boy."

"It was just a finger of speech," he said, using one of the silly expressions which come to a person as he grows, and blessedly pass. She seemed not to react to it at all, for she said gravely, "You have the most beautiful eyes I have ever seen. They are made of aluminum.

And your hair is all wiggly."

He could think of nothing to say to that, but tried; all that emerged was, "Well, it's early yet," and suddenly they were laughing together. She was so strange, so different. She spoke in a grave, unaccented, and utterly incautious idiom as if she thought strange thoughts and spoke them right out. "Also," she said, "you have lovely lips. They're pale blue. You ought to get out of the water."

"I can't!"

She considered that for a moment, treading away from him and then back to the yard's distance. "Where are your things?"

He pointed across the narrow neck of the lake which he had circumnavigated.

"Wait for me over there," she said, and suddenly swam close, so close she could dip her chin and look straight into his eyes. "You got to," she said fiercely.

"Oh I will," he promised, and struck out for the opposite shore. She hung to the rock, watching him.

Swimming, reaching hard, stretching for distance warmed him, and the chill and its accompanying vague ache diminished. Then he had a twinge of stomach-ache, and he drew up his knees to ease it. When he tried to extend himself again, he could, but it hurt too much. He drew up his knees again, and the pain followed inward so that to flex again was out of the question. He drew his knees up still tighter, and tighter still followed the pain. He needed air badly by then, threw up his head, tried to roll over on his back; but with his knees drawn up, everything came out all wrong. He inhaled at last because he had to, but the air was gone away somewhere; he floundered upward for it until the pressure in his ears told him he was swimming downward. Blackness came upon him and receded, and came again; he let it come for a tired instant, and was surrounded by light, and drew one lungful of air and one of water, and got the blackness again; this time it stayed with him . . .

Still beautiful in her bed, but morphine-clouded, fly-papered, and unstruggling in viscous sleep, he lay with monsters swarming in his veins . . .

Quietly, in a corner of the room, she spoke with Keogh:

"You don't understand me. You didn't understand me yesterday when I cried out at the idea of that—that operation. Keogh, I love him, but I'm *me*. Loving him doesn't mean I've stopped thinking. Loving him means I'm more me than ever, not less. It means I can do anything I did before, only more, only better. That's why I fell in love with him. That's why I am in love with him. Weren't you ever in love, Keogh?"

He looked at the way her hair fell, and the earnest placement of her thick soft brows, and he said, "I haven't thought much about it."

"There's always a way. All you have to do is think of it," she quoted. "Keogh, I've accepted what Dr. Rathburn said. After I left you I went to the library and tore the heart out of some books . . . they're right. Rathburn and Weber. And I've thought and I've thought . . . trying the way Daddy would, to turn everything upside down and backwards, to look for a new way of thinking. He won't die, Keogh; I'm not going to let him die."

"You said you accepted—"

"Oh, part of him. Most of him, if you like. We all die, bit by bit, all the time, and it doesn't bother us because most of the dead parts are replaced. He'll . . . he'll lose more parts, sooner, but—after it's over, he'll be himself again." She said it with superb confidence—perhaps it was childlike. If so, it was definitely not childish.

"You have an idea," said Keogh positively. As he had pointed out to the doctors, he knew her.

"All those—those things in his blood," she said quietly. "The struggle they go through . . . they're trying to survive; did you ever think of it that way, Keogh? They want to live. They want most terribly to go on living."

"I hadn't thought about it."

"His body wants them to live too. It welcomes them wherever they lodge. Dr. Weber said so."

"You've got hold of something," said Keogh flatly, "and whatever it is I don't think I like it."

"I don't want you to like it," she said in the same strange quiet voice. He looked swiftly at her and saw again the burning deep in her eyes. He had to look away. She said, "I want you to hate it. I want you to fight it. You have one of the most wonderful minds I have ever known, Keogh, and I want you to think up every argument you can think of against it. For every argument I'll find an answer, and then we'll know what to do."

"You'd better go ahead," he said reluctantly.

"I had a pretty bad quarrel with Dr. Weber this morning," she said suddenly.

"This m—when?" He looked at his watch; it was still early.

"About three, maybe four. In his room. I went there and woke him up."

"Look, you don't do things like that to Weber!"

"I do. Anyway, he's gone."

He rose to his feet, the rare bright patches of anger showing in his cheeks. He took a breath, let it out, and sat down again. "You'd better tell me about it."

"In the library," she said, "there's a book on genetics and it mentions some experiments on Belgian hares. The does were impregnated without sperm, with some sort of saline or alkaline solution."

"I remember something about it." He was well used to her circuitous way of approaching something important. She built conversational points, not like a hired contractor, but like an architect. Sometimes she brought in portions of her lumber and stacked them beside the structure. If she ever did that, it was material she needed and would use. He waited.

"The does gave birth to baby rabbits, all female. The interesting thing was that they were identical to each other and to the mother. Even the blood-vessel patterns in the eyeball were so similar that an expert might be fooled by photographs of them. 'Impossibly similar' is what one of the experimenters called it. They had to be identical because everything they inherited was from the mother. I woke Dr. Weber up to tell him about that.

"And he told you he'd read the book."

"He wrote it," she said gently. "And then I told him that if he could do that with a Belgian hare, he could do it with—" she nodded toward her big bed—"him."

Then she was quiet, while Keogh rejected the idea, found it stuck to his mind's hand, not to be shaken off; brought it to his mind's eye and shuddered away from it, shook again and failed, slowly brought it close and turned it over, and turned it again.

"Take one of those—those things like fertilized ova—make it grow . . ."

"You don't *make* it grow. It wants desperately to grow. And not one of them, Keogh. You have thousands. You have hundreds more every hour."

"Oh my God."

"It came to me when Dr. Rathburn suggested the operation. It came to me all at once, a miracle. If you love someone that much," she said, looking at the sleeper, "miracles happen. But you have to be willing to help them happen." She looked at him directly, with an intensity that made him move back in his chair. "I can have anything I want—all it has to be is possible. We just have to make it possible. That's why I went to Dr. Weber this morning. To ask him."

"He said it wasn't possible."

"He said that at first. After a half hour or so he said the odds against it were in the billions or trillions . . . but you see, as soon as he said that, he was saying it was possible."

"What did you do then?"

"I dared him to try."

"And that's why he left?"

"Yes."

"You're mad," he said before he could stop himself. She seemed not to resent it. She sat calmly, waiting.

"Look," said Keogh at last, "Weber said those distorted—uh—*things* were *like* fertilized ova. He never said they were. He could have said—well, I'll say it for him—they're *not* fertilized ova."

"Bat he did say they were—some of them, anyway, and especially those that reached the lungs—were very much like ova. How close do you have to get before there's no real difference at all?"

"It can't be. It just can't."

"Weber said that. And I asked him if he had ever tried."

"All right, all right! It can't happen, but just to keep this silly argument going, suppose you got something that would grow. You won't, of course. But if you did, how would you keep it growing? It has to be fed, it has to be kept at a certain critical temperature, a certain amount of acid or alkali will kill it . . . you don't just plant something like that in the yard."

"Already they've taken ova from one cow, planted them in another, and gotten calves. There's a man in Australia who plans to raise blooded cattle from scrub cows that way."

"You *have* done your homework."

"Oh, that isn't all. There's a Dr. Carrel in New Jersey who has been able to keep chicken tissue alive for months—he says indefinitely—in a nutrient solution, in a temperature-controlled jar in his lab. It grows, Keogh! It grows so much he has to cut it away every once in a while."

"This is crazy. This is—it's insane," he growled. "And what do you think you'll get if you bring one of these monsters to term?"

"We'll bring thousands of them to term," she said composedly. "And one of them will be—*him.*" She leaned forward abruptly, and her even tone of voice broke; a wildness grew through her face and voice, and though it was quiet, it shattered him: "It will be his flesh, the pattern of him, his own substance grown again. His hair, Keogh. His fingerprints. His—eyes. His—his *self.*"

"I can't—" Keogh shook himself like a wet spaniel, but it changed nothing; he was still here, she, the bed, the sleeper, and this dreadful, this inconceivably horrible, wrong idea.

She smiled then, put out her hand and touched him; incredibly, it was a mother's smile, warm and comforting, a mother's loving, protective touch; her voice was full of affection. "Keogh, if it won't work, it won't work, no matter what we do. Then you'll be right. I think it will work. It's what I want. Don't you want me to have what I want?"

He had to smile, and she smiled back. "You're a young devil," he said ardently. "Got me coming and going, haven't you? Why did you want me to fight it?"

"I didn't," she said, "but if you fight me, you'll come up with problems nobody else could possibly think of, and once we've thought of them, we'll be ready, don't you see? I'll fight with you, Keogh," she said, shifting her strange bright spectrum from tenderness to a quiet, convinced, invincible certainty. "I'll fight with you, I'll lift and carry, I'll buy and sell and kill if I have to, but I am going to bring him back. You know something, Keogh?"

She waved her hand in a gesture that included him, the room, the castle and grounds and all the other castle and grounds; the pseudonyms, the ships and trains, the factories and exchanges, the mountains and acres and mines and banks and the thousands of people which, taken together, were Wyke: "I always knew that all this *was,*" she said, "and I've come to understand that this is mine. But I used to wonder sometimes, what it was all *for.* Now I know. Now I know."

A mouth on his mouth, a weight on his stomach. He felt boneless and nauseated, limp as grease drooling. The light around him was green, and all shapes blurred.

The mouth on his mouth, the weight on his stomach, a breath of air, welcome but too warm, too moist. He needed it desperately but did not like it, and found a power-plant full of energy to gather it up in his lungs and fling it away; but his weakness so filtered all that effort that it emerged in a faint bubbling sigh.

The mouth on his mouth again, and the weight on his stomach and another breath. He tried to turn his head but someone held him by the nose. He blew out the needed, unsatisfactory air and replaced it by a little gust of his own inhalation. On this he coughed; it was too rich, pure, too good. He coughed as one does over a pickle-barrel; good air hurt his lungs.

He felt his head and shoulders lifted, shifted, by which he learned that he had been flat on his back on stone, or something flat and quite that hard, and was now on smooth, firm softness. The good sharp air came and went, his weak coughs fewer, until he fell into a dazed peace. The face that bent over his was too close to focus, or he had lost the power to focus; either way, he didn't care. Drowsily he stared up into the blurred brightness of that face and listened uncritically to the voice—

—the voice crooning wordlessly and comfortingly, and somehow, in its wordlessness, creating new expressions for joy and delight for which words would not do. Then after all there were words, half sung, half whispered; and he couldn't catch them, and he couldn't catch them and then . . . and then he was sure he heard: "How could it be, such a magic as this: all this and the eyes as well . . ." Then, demanding, "You are the shape of the not-you; tell me, are *you* in there?"

He opened his eyes wide and saw her face clearly at last and the dark hair, and the eyes were green—true deep sea-green. Her tangled hair, drying, crowned her like vines, and the leafy roof close above seemed part of her and the green eyes, and threw green light on the unaccountably blond transparency of her cheeks. He genuinely did not know, at the moment, what she was. She had said to him (was it years ago?) "I thought you were a faun . . ." He had not, at the moment, much consciousness, not to say whimsy, at his command; she was simply something unrelated to anything in his experience.

He was aware of gripping, twisting pain rising, filling, about to explode in his upper abdomen. Some thick wire within him had kinked, and knowing well that it should be unbent, he made a furious, rebellious effort and pulled it through. The explosion came, but in nausea, not in agony. Convulsively he turned his head, surged upward, and let it go.

He saw with too much misery to be horrified the bright vomit surging on and around her knee, and running into the crevice between thigh and calf where she had her leg bent and tucked under her, and the clots left there as the fluid ran away. And she—

She sat where she was, held his head, cradled him in her arms, soothed him and crooned to him and said that was good, good; he'd feel better now. The weakness floored him and receded; then shakily he pressed away from her, sat up, bowed his head and gasped for breath. "Whooo," he said.

"Boy," she said; and she said it in exact concert with him. He clung to his shins and wiped the nausea-tears from his left eye, then his right, on his knee-cap. "Boy oh boy," he said, and she said it with him in concert.

So at last he looked at her.

He looked at her, and would never forget what he saw, and exactly the way it was. Late sunlight made into lace by the bower above clothed her; she leaned toward him, one small hand flat on the ground, one slim supporting arm straight and straight down; her weight turned up that shoulder and her head tilted toward it as if drawn down by the heavy darkness of her hair. It gave a sense of yielding, as if she were fragile, which he knew she was not. Her other hand lay open across one knee, the palm up and the fingers not quite relaxed, as if they held something; and indeed they did, for a spot of light, gold turned coral by her flesh, lay in her palm. She held it just so, just right, unconsciously, and her hand held that rare knowledge that closed, a hand may not give nor receive. For his lifetime he had it all, each tiniest part, even to the gleaming big toenail at the underside of her other calf. And she was smiling, and her complex eyes adored.

Guy Gibbon knew his life's biggest moment during the moment itself, a rarity in itself, and of all times of life, it was time to say the unforgettable, for anything he said now would be.

He shuddered, and then smiled back at her. "Oh . . . *boy,*" he breathed.

And again they were laughing together until, puzzled, he stopped and asked, "Where am I?"

She would not answer, so he closed his eyes and puzzled it out. Pine bower . . . undress somewhere . . . swimming. Oh, swimming. And then across the lake, and he had met—He opened his eyes and looked at her and said, "You." Then swimming back, cold, his gut full of too much food and warm juice and moldy cake to boot, and, ". . . you must have saved my life."

"Well somebody had to. You were dead."

"I should've been."

"No!" she cried. "Don't you ever say that again!" And he could see she was absolutely serious.

"I only meant, for stupidity. I ate a lot of junk, and some cake I think was moldy. Too much, when I was hot and tired, and then like a bonehead I went right into the water, so anybody who does that deserves to—"

"I meant it," she said levelly, "never again. Didn't you ever hear of the old tradition of the field of battle, when one man saved another's life, that life became his to do what he wanted with?"

"What do you want to do with mine?"

"That depends," she said thoughtfully. "You have to give it. I can't just take it." She knelt then and sat back on her heels, her hands trailing pine-needles across the bower's paved stone floor. She bowed her head and her hair swung forward. He thought she was watching him through it; he could not be sure.

He said, and the thought grew so large that it quelled his voice and made him whisper. "Do you want it?"

"Oh, yes," she said, whispering too. When he moved to her and put her hair back to see if she was watching him, he found her eyes closed, and tears pressed through. He reached for her gently, but before he could touch her she sprang up and straight at the leafy wall. Her long golden body passed through it without a sound, and seemed to hang suspended outside; then it was gone. He put his head through and saw her flashing along under green water. He hesitated, then got an acrid whiff of his own vomit. The water looked clean and the golden sand just what he ached to scrub himself with. He climbed out of the bower and floundered clumsily down the bank and into the water.

After his first plunge he came up and spun about, looking for her, but she was gone.

Numbly he swam to the tiny beach and, kneeling, scoured himself with the fine sand. He dove and rinsed, and then (hoping) scrubbed himself all over again. And rinsed. But he did not see her.

He stood in the late rays of the sun to dry, and looked off across the lake. His heart leapt when he saw white movement, and sank again as he saw it was just the wheel of boats bobbing and sliding there.

He plodded up to the bower—now at last he saw it was the one behind which he had undressed—and he sank down on the bench.

This was a place where tropical fish swam in ocean water where there was no ocean, and where fleets of tiny perfect boats sailed with no one sailing them and no one watching, and where priceless statues stood hidden in clipped and barbered glades deep in the woods and—and he hadn't seen it all; what other impossibilities were possible in this impossible place?

And besides, he'd been sick. (He wrinkled his nostrils.) Damn near . . . drowned. Out of his head for sure, for a while anyway. She couldn't be real. Hadn't he noticed a greenish cast to her flesh, or was that just the light? . . . anybody who could make a place like this, run a place like this, could jimmy up some kind of machine to hypnotize you like in the science fiction stories.

He stirred uneasily. Maybe someone was watching him, even now.

Hurriedly, he began to dress.

So she wasn't real. Or maybe all of it wasn't real. He'd bumped into that other trespasser across the lake there, and that was real, but then when he'd almost drowned, he'd dreamed up the rest.

Only—he touched his mouth. He'd dreamed up someone blowing the breath back into him. He'd heard about that somewhere, but it sure wasn't what they were teaching this year at the Y.

You are the shape of the not-you. Are you in there?

What did that mean?

He finished dressing dazedly. He muttered, "What'd I hafta go an' eat that goddamn cake for?" He wondered what he would tell Sammy. If she wasn't real, Sammy wouldn't know what he was talking about. If she was real there's only one thing he would talk about, yes, and from then on. You mean you had her in that place and all you did was throw up on her? No—he wouldn't tell Sammy. Or anybody.

And he'd be a bachelor all his life.

Boy oh boy. What an introduction. First she has to save your life and then you don't know what to say and then oh, look what you had to go and do. But anyway—she wasn't real.

He wondered what her name was. Even if she wasn't real. Lots of people don't use their real names.

He climbed out of the bower and crossed the silent pine carpet behind it, and he shouted. It was not a word at all, and had nothing about it that tried to make it one.

She was standing there waiting for him. She wore a quiet brown dress and low heels and carried a brown leather pocketbook, and her hair was braided and tied neatly and sedately in a coronet. She looked, too, as if she had turned down some inward tone control so that her skin did not radiate. She looked ready to disappear, not into thin air, but into a crowd—any crowd, as soon as she could get close to one. In a crowd he would have walked right past her, certainly, but for the shape of her eyes. She stepped up to him quickly and laid her hand on his cheek and laughed up at him. Again he saw the whiteness of those unusual eyeteeth, so sharp . . . "You're blushing!" she said.

No blusher in history was ever stopped by that observation. He asked, "Which way do you go?"

She looked at his eyes, one, the other, both, quickly; then folded her long hands together around the strap of her pocketbook and looked down at them.

"With you," she said softly.

This was only one of the many things she said to him, moment by moment, which gained meaning for him as time went on. He took her back to town and to dinner and then to the West Side address she gave him and they stood outside it all night talking. In six weeks they were married.

"How could I argue?" said Weber to Dr. Rathburn.

They stood together watching a small army of workmen swarming over the gigantic stone barn a quarter-mile from the castle, which, incidentally, was invisible from this point and unknown to the men. Work had begun at three the previous afternoon, continued all night. There was nothing, nothing at all that Dr. Weber had specified which was not only given him, but on the site or already installed.

"I know," said Rathburn, who did.

"Not only, how could I argue," said Weber, "why should I? A man has plans, ambitions. That Keogh, what an approach! That's the first thing he went after—my plans for myself. That's where he starts. And suddenly everything you ever wanted to do or be or have is handed to you or promised to you, and no fooling about the promise either."

"*Oh* no. They don't need to fool anybody . . . You want to pass a prognosis?"

"You mean on the youngster there?" He looked at Rathburn. "Oh no—that's not what you mean. You're asking me if I can bring one of those surrogate fetuses to term. An opinion like that would make a damn fool out of a man, and this is no job for a damn fool. All I can tell you is, I tried it—and that is something I wouldn't've dreamed of doing if it hadn't been for her and her crazy idea. I left here at four a.m. with some throat smears and by nine I had a half dozen of them isolated and in nutrient solution. Beef blood plasma—the quickest thing I could get ready. And I got mitosis. They divided, and in a few hours I could see two of 'em dimpling to form the gastrosphore. That was evidence enough to get going; that's all I think and that's all I told them on the phone. And by the time I got here," he added, waving toward the big barn, "there's a research lab four fifths built, big enough for a city medical center. Argue?" he demanded, returning to Dr. Rathburn's original question. "How could I argue? Why should I? . . . And that *girl.* She's a force, like gravity. She can turn on so much pressure, and I mean by herself and personally, that she could probably get anything in the world she wanted even if she didn't own it, the world I mean. Put that in the northeast entrance!" he bellowed at a foreman. "I'll be down to show you just where it goes." He turned to Rathburn; he was a man on fire. "I got to go."

"Anything I can do," said Dr. Rathburn, "just say it."

"That's the wonderful part of it," said Weber. "That's what everybody around here keeps saying, and they mean it!" He trotted down toward the barn, and Rathburn turned toward the castle.

About a month after his last venture at trespassing, Guy Gibbon was coming home from work when a man at the corner put away a newspaper and, still folding it, said, "Gibbon?"

"That's right," said Guy, a little sharply.

The man looked him up and down, quickly, but giving an impression of such thoroughness, efficiency, and experience that Guy would not have been surprised to learn that the man had not only catalogued his clothes and their source, their state of maintenance and a computation therefrom of his personal habits, but also his state of health and even his blood type. "My name's Keogh," said the man. "Does that mean anything to you?"

"No."

"Sylva never mentioned the name?"

"Sylva! N-no, she didn't."

"Let's go somewhere and have a drink. I'd like to talk to you." Something had pleased this man. Guy wondered what. "Well, okay," he said. "Only I don't drink much, but well, okay."

They found a bar in the neighborhood with booths, in the back. Keogh had a Scotch and soda and Guy, after some hesitation, ordered a beer. Guy said, "You know her?"

"Most of her life. Do you?"

"What? Well, sure. We're going to get married." He looked studiously into his beer and said uncomfortably, "What are you anyway, Mr. Keogh?"

"You might say," said Keogh, "I'm *in loco parentis.*" He waited for a response, then added, "Sort of a guardian."

"She never said anything about a guardian."

"I can understand that. What has she told you about herself?"

Guy's discomfort descended to a level of shyness, diffidence, even a touch of fear—which did not alter the firmness of his words, however they were spoken. "I don't know you, Mr. Keogh. I don't think I ought to answer any questions about Sylva. Or me. Or anything." He looked up at the man. Keogh searched deeply, then smiled. It was an unpracticed and apparently slightly painful process with him, but was genuine for all that. "Good!" he barked, and rose. "Come on." He left the booth and Guy, more than a little startled, followed. They went to the phone booth in the corner. Keogh dropped in a nickel, dialed, and waited, his eyes fixed on Guy. Then Guy had to listen to one side of the conversation:

"I'm here with Guy Gibbon." (Guy had to notice that Keogh identified himself only with his voice.)

". . . Of course I knew about it. That's a silly question, girl."

". . . Because it *is* my business. *You* are my business."

"... Stop it? I'm not trying to stop anything. I just have to know, that's all."

"... All right. All right ... He's here. He won't talk about you or anything, which is good. Yes, very good. Will you please tell him to open up?"

And he handed the receiver to a startled Guy, who said tremulously, "Uh, hello," to it while watching Keogh's impassive face.

Her voice suffused and flooded him, changed this whole unsettling experience to something different and good. "Guy, darling."

"Sylva—"

"It's all right. I should have told you sooner, I guess. It had to come some time. Guy, you can tell Keogh anything you like. Anything he asks."

"Why, honey? Who is he, anyway?"

There was a pause, then a strange little laugh. "He can explain that better than I can. You want us to be married, Guy?"

"Oh yes!"

"Well all right then. Nobody can change that, nobody but you. And listen, Guy. I'll live anywhere, any way you want to live. That's the real truth and all of it, do you believe me?"

"I always believe you."

"All right then. So that's what we'll do. Now you go and talk to Keogh. Tell him anything he wants to know. He has to do the same. I love you, Guy."

"Me too," said Guy, watching Keogh's face. "Well, okay then," he added when she said nothing further. "Bye." He hung up and he and Keogh had a long talk.

"It hurts him," she whispered to Dr. Rathburn.

"I know." He shook his head sympathetically. "There's just so much morphine you can rain into a man, though."

"Just a little more?"

"Maybe a little," he said sadly. He went to his bag and got the needle. Sylva kissed the sleeping man tenderly and left the room. Keogh was waiting for her.

He said, "This has got to stop, girl."

"Why?" she responded ominously.

"Let's get out of here."

She had known Keogh so long, and so well, that she was sure he had no surprises for her. But this voice, this look, these were something new in Keogh. He held the door for her, so she preceded him through it and then went where he silently led.

They left the castle and took the path through a heavy copse and over the brow of the hill which overlooked the barn. The parking lot, which had once been a barnyard, was full of automobiles. A white ambulance approached; another was unloading at the northeast platform. A muffled generator purred somewhere behind the building, and smoke rose from the stack of the new stone boiler room at the side. They both looked avidly at the building but did not comment. The path took them along the crest of the hill and down toward the lake. They went to a small forest clearing in which stood an eight-foot Diana, the huntress Diana, chaste and fleet-footed, so beautifully finished she seemed not like marble at all, not like anything cold or static. "I always had the idea," said Keogh, "that nobody can lie anywhere near her."

She looked up at the Diana.

"Not even to themselves," said Keogh, and plumped down on a marble bench.

"Let's have it," she said.

"You want to make Guy Gibbon happen all over again. It's a crazy idea and it's a big one too. But lots of things were crazier, and some bigger, and now they're commonplace. I won't argue on how crazy it is, or how big."

"What then?"

"I've been trying, the last day or so, to back way out, far off, get a look at this thing with some perspective. Sylva, you've forgotten something."

"Good," she said. "Oh, good. I knew you'd think of things like this before it was too late."

"So you can find a way out?" Slowly he shook his head. "Not this time. Tighten up the Wyke guts, girl, and make up your mind to quit."

"Go ahead."

"It's just this. I don't believe you're going to get your carbon copy, mind you, but you just might. I've been talking to Weber, and by God you just about might. But if you do, all you've got is a container, and nothing to fill it with. Look, girl, a man isn't blood and bone and body cells, and that's all."

He paused, until she said, "Go on, Keogh."

He demanded, "You love this guy?"

"Keogh!" She was amused.

"Whaddaya love?" he barked. "That skrinkly hair? The muscles, skin? His nat'ral equipment? The eyes, voice?"

"All that," she said composedly.

"All that, and that's all?" he demanded relentlessly. "Because if your answer is yes, you can have what you want, and more power to you, and good riddance. I don't know anything about love, but I will say this: that if that's all there is to it, the hell with it."

"Well of *course* there's more."

"Ah. And where are you going to get that, girl? Listen, a man is the skin and bone he stands in, plus what's in his head, plus what's in his heart. You mean to reproduce Guy Gibbon, but you're not going to do it by duplicating his carcass. You want to duplicate the whole man, you're going to have to make him live the same life again. And that you can't do."

She looked up at the Diana for a long time. Then, "Why not?" she breathed.

"I'll tell you why not," he said angrily. "Because first of all you have to find out *who he is.*"

"I know who he is!"

He spat explosively on the green moss by the bench. It was totally uncharacteristic and truly shocking. "You don't know a particle, and I know even less. I had his back against a wall one time for better than two hours, trying to find out who he is. He's just another kid, is all. Nothing much in school, nothing much at sports, same general tastes and feelings as six zillion other ones like him. Why him, Sylva? Why him? What did you ever see in a guy like that to be worth the marrying?"

"I . . . didn't know you disliked him."

"Oh hell, girl, I don't! I never said that. I can't—can't even find anything to dislike."

"You don't know him the way I do."

"There, I agree. I don't and I couldn't. Because you don't know anything either—you *feel,* but you don't *know.* If you want to see Guy Gibbon again, or a reasonable facsimile, he's going to have to live by a script from the day he's born. He'll have to duplicate every experience that this kid here ever had."

"All right," she said quietly.

He looked at her, stunned. He said, "And before he can do that, we have to write the script. And before we can write it, we have to get the material somehow. What do you expect to do—set up a foundation or something dedicated to the discovery of each and every moment this—this unnoticeable young man ever lived through? And do it secretly, because while he's growing up he can't ever know? Do you know how much that would cost, how many people it would involve?"

"That would be all right," she said.

"And suppose you had it, a biography written like a script, twenty years of a lifetime, every day, every hour you could account for; now you're going to have to arrange for a child, from birth, to be surrounded by people who are going to play this script out—and who will never let anything else happen to him but what's in the script and who will never let him know."

"That's it! That's it!" she cried.

He leapt to his feet and swore at her. He said, "I'm not planning this, you lovestruck lunatic, I'm objecting to it!"

"Is there anymore?" she cried eagerly. "Keogh, Keogh, try—try hard. How do we start? What do we do first? Quick, Keogh."

He looked at her, thunderstruck, and at last sank down on the bench and began to laugh weakly. She sat by him, held his hand, her eyes shining. After a time he sobered, and turned to her. He drank the shine of those eyes for awhile; and after, his brain began to function again . . . on Wyke business . . .

"The main source of who he is and what he's done," he said at last, "won't be with us much longer . . . We better go tell Rathburn to get him off the morphine. He has to be able to think."

"All right," she said. "All right."

When the pain got too much to permit him to remember any more, they tried a little morphine again. For a while they found a balance between recollection and agony, but the agony gained. Then they severed his spinal cord so he couldn't feel it. They brought in people—psychiatrist, stenographers, even a professional historian.

In the rebuilt barn, Weber tried animal hosts, cows even, and primates—everything he could think of. He got some results, though no good ones. He tried humans too. He couldn't cross the bridge of body tolerance; the uterus will not support an alien fetus any more than the hand will accept the graft of another's finger.

So he tried nutrient solutions. He tried a great many. Ultimately he found one that worked. It was the blood plasma of pregnant women.

He placed the best of the quasi-ova between sheets of sterilized chamois. He designed automatic machinery to drip the plasma in at arterial tempo, drain it at venous rate, keep it at body temperature.

One day fifty of them died, because of the chloroform used in one of the adhesives. When light seemed to affect them adversely, Weber designed containers of bakelite. When ordinary photography proved impractical, he designed a new kind of film sensitive to heat, the first infrared film.

The viable fetuses he had at sixty days showed the eye-spot, the spine, the buds of arms, a beating heart. Each and every one of them consumed, or was bathed in, over a gallon of plasma a day, and at one point there were one hundred and seventy-four thousand of them. Then they began to die off—some malformed, some chemically unbalanced, many for reasons too subtle even for Weber and his staff.

When he had done all he could, when he could only wait and see, he had fetuses seven months along and growing well. There were twenty-three of them. Guy Gibbon was dead quite a while by then, and his widow came to see Weber and tiredly put down a stack of papers and reports, urged him to read, begged him to call her as soon as he had.

He read them, he called her. He refused what she asked.

She got hold of Keogh. He refused to have anything to do with such an idea. She made him change his mind. Keogh made Weber change his mind.

The stone barn hummed with construction again, and new machinery. The cold tank was four by six feet inside, surrounded by coils and sensing devices. They put her in it.

By that time the fetuses were eight and a half months along. There were four left. One made it.

Author's note: To the reader, but especially to the reader in his early twenties, let me ask: did you ever have the feeling that you were getting pushed around? Did you ever want to do something, and have all sorts of obstacles thrown in your way until you had to give up, while on the other hand some other thing you wanted, was made easy for you? Did you ever feel that certain strangers know who you are? Did you ever meet a girl who made you explode inside, who seemed to like you—and who was mysteriously plucked out of your life, as if she shouldn't be in the script?

Well, we've all had these feelings. Yet if you've read the above, you'll allow it's a little more startling than just a story. It reads like an analogy, doesn't it? I mean, it doesn't have to be a castle, or the ol' swimmin' hole, and the names have been changed to protect the innocent . . . author.

Because it could be about time for her to wake up, aged only two or three years for her twenty-year cold sleep. And when she meets you, it's going to be the biggest thing that ever happened to you since the last time.

Holdup à la Carte

Gladys McGonigle, who was known as Happy, was not.

She stood behind the counter of Hart Calway's restaurant, and cried. In her hand was the bakelite grip of a glass coffee-maker. At her feet were the glittering shards of what had been, until a moment ago, a twelve-cup lower bowl.

"It's his fault and I *hate* him," she said untruthfully. Of course, it was only remotely Hart's fault that she had broken the coffee-maker, and burned sixteen slices of toast that morning, and told the milkman not to bring buttermilk when she *knew* buttermilk biscuits were on the menu. It was Hart's fault because when he was not there her mind was full of Hart's wide shoulders and Hart's crisp blond hair and Hart's smile.... Sometimes the smile made a small, sweet chucking noise, when it was sudden enough.

She began to smile at the thought, and the cry-puckers over her winged nostrils smoothed out and let the bright tears run. She set the bakelite handle down in the center of a bowl of mayonnaise and dabbed at her cheeks with a paper napkin. "I do try," she sniffed.

It wasn't the job. A girl as pretty as Happy could get plenty of jobs. A girl who was as good a waitress as Happy usually was, could get jobs easily too. "I'm just no good *here,*" she sobbed.

"I hate him," she repeated, and then uttered a woeful moan as she saw the mayonnaise bowl. "He hates me too. He *makes* me do things like this." She picked out the bakelite handle, shook the surplus mayonnaise from it, and dropped it into the garbage bin. "Leaving me alone with robbers and murderers," she muttered.

She was thinking of the reason for Hart's absence—a meeting of the Clay Street Merchants' Association to discuss emergency measures for dealing with a particularly slick crook who was apparently determined to hold up every member of the Association, in turn. "It won't be a long meeting," he had said. "Hold the fort, will you, Hap? You don't have to serve anything but short orders, and there'll be enough customers in to make it safe."

Well, he was wrong there. There hadn't been a soul in the place except herself and one fly since he left. "But Hap—keep your eyes peeled all the same. The whole week's receipts are in the cash drawer. I'd take 'em to the night depository before the meeting only I'm late already. I'll do it as soon as I get back—got to run; the boys are waiting."

The boys, Hap thought bitterly as she mopped the counter. He'll entertain, the boys with tales of the big one that got away, and how hard the tarpon struck his line that day. Fishing and working—that's all he ever thinks about! She could take fishing or she could leave it alone; but to be fair about it, she had to admit that the way he worked was one of the things she loved about him—that, and his eyes, of course. And the way he—

She smiled again as she thought of his intense face the day after he had hired her. "You're going to think I'm crazy, Miss McGonigle. And tough too, maybe. But this place is all I have in the world. Every penny I could save by working for other people is in those fixtures and that equipment. It's only a little short-order place, but a lot of big things have started small. And this is going to be as big as I can make it. Work and economize, work and economize—that's all I can have around here."

And she had looked up at him and said, "You call me Hap, then. It's more economical"—and he had given her the smile, the wide sudden one, and had touched her shoulder.

"You'll do."

She touched the shoulder now. She hadn't "done." She had tried so hard to help, and had fallen all over herself, and everything had gone wrong.

She went to the end of the counter and slid open the old-fashioned cash drawer. There was no register—just a sturdy wooden drawer with partitions in front for change and a deep recess in the back for the heavy canvas sack the bank issued for night deposits. She felt the strong fabric and the chunky packet of notes inside it, and they gave her a sudden chill.

He'd been so patient with her. She had done some of the stupidest, *stupidest* things, and never once had he bawled her out. Well, not really. With his eyes, and twice with a sort of resigned sigh that made her want to run away and hide her head. Suppose she was held up tonight? Suppose he came back and found the entire week's receipts gone, and the rent due, and the meat wholesaler not yet paid? What would he think of her then? What would he do?

He'd say quietly, "Hap, I'm sorry, but this is the last straw. This is too much. I'm afraid you'll have to go." That's what he'd say, and she'd just die, right there in front of him.

Imagine going to work somewhere else, and never seeing him again! Imagine maybe meeting him on the street and see his politest, coldest smile flick at her as he walked past, not wanting even to talk to her.

"Oh, *dear!*"

She stood for a moment with her hand on the canvas bag, quite overcome by her own imagination. And then she began to think—hard.

And then she did an extraordinary thing. She got a hammer and nails from the tool chest. She got a needle and thread from the dish-towel closet. And with the claw of the hammer she grimly pried off the hasp of Hart Calway's personal, private locker . . .

A half hour later Happy was standing by the door looking out, hoping that she might get a glimpse of Hart striding toward her down the dark street. The man she saw reminded her of him. Tall men reminded her of him because he was tall, and short men reminded her of him because he was tall.

She shook her head sadly and looked at the man who was now approaching.

He was short, balding, and pudgy. He wore a jacket almost the color of the pumpkin pies she had spoiled last week, and not-quite-shabby brown trousers. He glanced up at her as he shambled past. A few feet farther on he stopped and peered through the restaurant window, right at the end where he could see down behind the counter. He seemed to be thinking something over. Then he turned and came back.

"Got anything to eat?"

"Why, yes!" A customer, this late! Hart would be pleased. "Come in."

He followed her in and sat down at one of the tables. She put a menu in front of him—the one Hart had laughed at so, because she had typed "Hart and Eggs" on it.

"Lamb chops," said the pudgy man. "Peas and mashed. Apple pie and coffee."

"Lamb chops," she repeated, then "Lamb chops! But I—but the boss—" There are only two lamb chops left, you silly man, she thought, and Hart didn't have his dinner yet, and he'll want those lamb chops. He *likes* lamb chops! Aloud she said, "Maybe a nice small steak . . ."

"It says here—" the man pointed "—it says lamb chops. You got lamb chops?"

"I—" The customer, Hart kept saying, is always right. "Yes, sir." She went dolefully back to the stove, and turned it on. Maybe, she thought as she greased the grill, maybe she could fix Hart something special. A potpie, perhaps. Then he would tell her that kind of food was for cash customers; he, Hart, was hired help the same as she was, even if he did own the place. But he did *so* like lamb chops . . .

She tonged a hot potato out of the steam table and pressed it through the ricer, mashed it deftly, and pulled it up to a cone with the tines of a fork. A pat of butter on top, the way Hart had shown her and a sprinkling of paprika to make it look luscious. Bright green peas around it in a ring, flanked by the sizzling chops. Pretty. Bread on a plate, a glass of water, and everything on a tray. Hart would have been proud of her. If, of course, she didn't tangle up her feet on the way and drop the tray in his lap.

She set the plate before the customer, saw to his salt and pepper and catsup, and then went behind the counter again. The man ate steadily and hungrily. She kept an eye on him, and when he had only a single forkful left on his plate, she was there with the pie and coffee. That's the way to do it. That's how to run a restaurant. Let the boss go to his old cops-and-robbers merchant meetings. She'd run things like a clock.

She cleared off the dishes he had used, washed them immediately, and put them away. Then she made out the check, adding it three times to be sure it was right. She laid it properly, face down, at his left, and went away again.

He ate the pie as slowly and deliberately as he had the rest of the meal, then reached for the check and patted his right hip pocket.

Then he patted his left hip pocket. Then his coat pockets.

"Miss," he called.

"Yes, sir?"

He coughed apologetically. "I—ah—seem to have left my wallet in my other clothes."

"You—why you—"

The oldest gag in the restaurant business, and it had to happen to her! Fury mounted in her. Burned toast and broken coffee-makers—and now this! A free meal—and Hart's lamb chops!

She searched futilely for a word, found an "Oh!", tried again, and said, "Why, I ought to have you arrested!"

"I beg your pardon," said the pudgy man. "Really, miss. It could happen to anyone. I don't know what to say. I could—I could leave you my name and address."

"I'm not interested in the address of an empty lot," she said coldly. "Haven't you any money at all?"

He shook his head, patting forlornly at his pockets.

Her eyes filled with tears—angry ones. "I don't know *what* my boss will say. I wish a policeman would walk *in* here right now, that's what I wish!"

And at that moment a policeman did walk in. The pudgy man half rose, opened his mouth, closed his mouth, and sat down again.

Happy whirled and stared. He was a big policeman, with hard eyes and a big face, and he had a big gun and a big nightstick. He said, "What's going on here?"

The pudgy man seemed to wilt. He sagged down in his chair, but he said nothing. Happy suddenly felt a twinge of pity. "This man didn't pay for his dinner," she said, in a considerably softer voice. "But it's all right. I can handle it, I—I think."

"A deadbeat, eh?" said the policeman. He looked around the

restaurant, out into the deserted street, and licked his lips. "I got just the treatment for deadbeats." He swung his nightstick by its leather thong, caught the handle deftly and advanced on the pudgy man.

"No!" cried Happy. "Don't hit him, officer! It's—it's all right. I'll take care of the bill myself." The look of fear on the pudgy man's face as he started out of his chair had simply torn her apart. Why, he was little, and hungry, that was all!

"You keep out of this now, kiddo," said the policeman. He brought his stick point downward on the checked tablecloth with a crash. "Out of my way—I'll fix him!"

Happy pushed between him and the table. "No! No!"

The policeman swept her aside with one easy motion, leaned over, and tapped the pudgy man behind the ear with the stick. The deadbeat sighed and slid under the table.

"See how easy?" said the policeman.

"You *pushed* me!" gasped Happy.

"And you hit that poor little man, why you great big—" and she ran out of words. Then her temper burst through, and she rushed at him, forgetting his gun, his stick, his size, his uniform, everything. He was nothing but a cruel bully, and she felt just as she had when she was a child and saw a man beating a dog.

Her attack was so sudden that even though her figure was small and her pert face soft, Happy could pack a surprising wallop. She hit the policeman's blue-clad chest as if she had been fired from a cannon, like the girl in the circus. The policeman staggered back, tripped over the pudgy man's leg, which stuck out from under the table, and went down like tall timber.

For a blind moment the smoke of fury curled around Hap's brain and she saw nothing—only a blur. Then her vision cleared.

Two broken chairs. A table and some dishes in a rubble on the floor. The still figure of the pudgy man. And the policeman, groaning, feebly feeling the side of his head where it had struck the counter. He rolled over and began to drag one knee under him.

Happy uttered a mouse-like squeak and fled.

This was the end. This was the complete, utter, final finish of everything.

She ran, sobbing, down the street, not caring where she was going. She had attacked a policeman, wrecked the restaurant, maybe cost Hart Calway everything he had worked so hard to accumulate. And now Hart would never want to see her again.

She ran right into his arms.

"Oh, oh dear!" she gasped. "Policeman. Oh, Hart! The little man couldn't pay lamb chops hit him on the head!"

"What?"

There were two men with Hart. One of them said, "Sounds like someone got hit on the head with some lamb chops."

"Shut up, Frank. There's something wrong here. Bill, blow your whistle."

A shrill blast ripped out. For some reason it loosed a flood of tears in Happy.

Hart put an arm around her shoulders. "Come on, Happy darling," he said gently. "Let's go back and straighten it all out."

Happy looked up into his face. She had caught one word, and fixed on it. She said it. "Darling."

"Why—Happy!"

"Come on!" said the man called Bill.

Somehow Happy got her feet under her and found another breath or two. They ran back down the street. At the corner near the restaurant they were joined by two policemen.

"Who blew that whistle?"

"Come on!" Hart said urgently. They skidded to a stop in front of the restaurant. One of the policemen barked, "Down! Get *down!*"

The next thing Happy knew she was sitting on the pavement in front of the restaurant, dragged down by Hart. "Sorry, darling, but that man inside's got a gun."

Slowly she raised her head. She could just see into the restaurant.

The big policeman who had hit the deadbeat was behind the counter with his hand in the cash drawer. He was staring at the pudgy man, who was walking toward him on the balls of his feet. Suddenly the little man ran two delicate steps and leaped over the counter.

The policeman tried to reach his gun, but before he could grasp it, the little man was on him like a dervish. There was a flurry of action and the little man backed off, the gun in his hand.

The two policemen, the three merchants, and Happy crowded into the restaurant. One of the policemen said, "Why—it's the Chief!"

The pudgy man straightened up. "Hello, boys," he panted; "Get the handcuffs on him. We'll book him for everything from armed robbery to impersonating an officer. Know him?"

Hart looked at the limp blue figure behind the counter. "I know him," he said.

"Me too," said the man called Frank. "That's Eddie Lowell. He was bootlegging from the back room of a drug store, and the Merchants' Association ran him out. No wonder he's been working us over, one by one."

Happy's head was whirling. "Please," she said faintly. "Will s-somebody tell me what—I mean—are *you* the Chief of Police?"

The pudgy man smiled and nodded. "You, young lady, are worth your weight in gold. I mean it. This fellow has a record as long as my arm, and rewards to go with it.

"Chief," said Hart in a bewildered voice, "will you please start from the beginning and tell me just what's been going on here?"

"Why, sure, son." The Chief leaned back against an undamaged table. "The way I got into it—well, I must confess that you Association men shamed me into it. If merchants have to get together for protection against a holdup man, instead of relying on the police, why, it's a sad business. I put on these old clothes and mooched around trying to think like a criminal. I spotted this place as a natural for a holdup. Only a girl to watch it—but what a girl! Know what she did? She booby-trapped the cash drawer, and on top of that, she knocked Lowell down and ran for the police."

"Knocked—" Hart looked at her with amazement. "And what do you mean, booby-trapped the cash drawer?"

Happy gulped. "I was scared about the cash. So I b-broke into your locker, Hart, and got all your fishhooks and sewed them into the cash bag with their points downward. And I nailed the bag to the bottom of the drawer, so if anyone tried to get it out, they couldn't, and they'd have to reach into it for the money and—*oh!*"

"What's the matter?" asked the Chief.

Happy said, "You really did leave your wallet in your other clothes, didn't you?"

The Chief's eyes twinkled. "I really did. I never want you for an enemy, young lady. You had sparks flying out of you! Anyway, this crook Lowell didn't recognize me. He was probably going to pretend to guard me while he sent the girl for the police. Then he'd take the money and run, and the poor old deadbeat—me!—would be in for it. Of course, I knew he wasn't one of my boys the minute I laid eyes on him, so I decided to sit tight and try to catch him in the act. You beat me to it, young lady," he finished, wagging his head admiringly.

After they had all gone, after Hart had laughingly waved off the Chief's insistence that he owed him for a meal, Happy turned to right the overturned table. Hart caught her arm. "Hap—"

She waited.

"Hap, I—" She had never heard him stumble over his words before. "Hap, what do you suppose a fellow works for—works hard and saves and tries to build something up?"

"To get ahead."

"Yes, but not only in business. Hap, I've worked twice as hard since I—you came here. Some day maybe I'll have enough—*be* enough to—to—" He stopped, turned her to face him. "Would you wait until then?"

She lowered her voice. "If I had a part interest in this place I don't think I'd break things, Hart."

"You mean you—"

"—and with the reward money I get, you could buy a cash register and—and—because husbands and wives can jointly own—oh, *Hart!*"

How to Forget Baseball

Once upon a possible (for though there is only one past, there are many futures), after twelve hours of war and forty-some years of reconstruction, and at a time when nothing had stopped technology (for technological progress not only accelerates, so does the *rate* at which it accelerates), the country was composed of strip-cities, six blocks wide and up to eighty miles long, which rimmed the great superhighways, and wildernesses. And at certain remote spots in the wilderness lived primitives, called Primitives, a hearty breed that liked to stay close to nature and the old ways. And it came about that a certain flack, whose job it was to publicize the national pastime, a game called Quoit, was assigned to find a person who had never seen the game; to invite him in for one game, to get his impressions of said game and to use them as flacks use such things. He closed the deal with a Primitive who agreed to come in exchange for the privilege of shopping for certain trade goods. So . . .

The dust cloud had a chromium nose and a horrible hiss. It labored down the lane, swinging from side to side, climbed the final rise, slowed beside the rustic gate with the ancient enameled legend OURSER over it, slewed around and stopped, whereupon it was enveloped in its own streaming tail. The hissing subsided, and the dust cloud seemed to slump at its swirling heart. In the silence the dust settled on and around the ground-effect vehicle, its impregnable, scratchproof, everlasting finish ignominiously surrendering its gleam and glitter to the pall of bone-dry marl. There was a moment of silence, accented by the *râles* of cooling metal and the barbarous comments of faraway frightened crickets and a nearby unabashed frog. Then the vehicle emitted a faint rising whine as a circular section in a side window began to spin; in a second the sound was up out of the audible range and the dust vanished from the rotating part of the window, presenting a dark porthole in which a jovial head appeared, browless, hairless, and squinting nervously at all the unconditioned air. It stared through the bars of the gate at what would have been a footpath except that there were two of them, parallel and winding up through the meadow to a stand of maples. From these, in due course, issued an impossibility outside the pages of some historical treatise—not annealed plastic, but formed metal; not hovering, but wheeled; streamlined outlandishly only where it showed and, most surprising of all, producing constant sound from the power plant.

The man in the hovercraft watched with incredulity the stately progress of this wheeled fossil as it bumped across the meadow and came to a stop on the other side of the gate. From it stepped a tall man dressed embarrassingly, bearing a burden of some kind. He closed the door of his antique and locked it with a key, and walked to the other side to try the door there. At last he turned to face the hovercar. He did so with an expression of distaste, which he wore the whole time he approached.

The hairless man touched a stud on the dash and listened intently to the murmur that came from surrounding speakers. Then he palmed a pale spot on the dash and the side panel snicked out of sight, gone up, down, sidewise—who could tell?—and repeated what the recorder had told him: "Hello. Hello. Bil Ferry speaking. Is Mr. Ourser there?"

The tall man put out a searching hand, found that there was indeed an opening and got in. The driver brushed the pale spot and the opening went *snick!* and was no longer an opening. The newcomer winced, then said, "I'm Ourser."

"Did I get it right?" asked Bil Ferry.

"You mean the 'hello, hello' bit? That's for the telephone," said Mr. Ourser mercilessly.

"Damn dim research department," grumbled the flack, and started the hovercraft. "Anyway, I tried."

"Nobody but a Primitive *tries,*" said Mr. Ourser starchily. "There's no reason to."

"Passpoint unreason there, classmate," said Bil Ferry rapidly. "Y'll know it, comes Ol' Florio flippin."

"I," said Mr. Ourser, "am a scholar, and among other things I am devoted to the purity of the tongue. I do not dig you one bit, man."

"Sorr, so sorr. All I mean, you'll see Florio put out lots effort, plenty, today. You find me?"

"I follow the general trend. This Florio, I take it, is your favorite and champion. *Slow down, you idiot!*" The hovercraft, as always when not automatically guided, had begun to indulge in its proclivity for heading at forty-five degrees to the direction it was traveling. Bil Ferry wrestled the tiny figure-eight–shaped wheel, corrected the heading and said, unabashed, "Positive, poz-poz-poz," and slowed to a comparative crawl. "Every rockhead in the world thinks he's an expert driver," grumbled the Primitive. "Not me, classmate," said the other cheerfully. "Who needs it? I am expert flack."

The hovercar hissed over the undulating marl road with its high wide white mantle of dust airborne in its wake. In time it turned onto the remains of a blacktop feeder road, the potholes and weed patches of which the craft ignored, and came at last to the superway approach. Bil Ferry placed the vehicle carefully on the center stripe of the approach ramp and accelerated to match the flowing patches of violet on its buff background. There was the soft syllable of a gong, and a saucer-sized purple light appeared at the center of the dash. Bil Ferry sighed, folded up the steering wheel with a snap and pushed it forward, where it was swallowed without a trace by a gateway in the dash. The flack sighed again and swung his seat around on its pivot with his back to the windshield. Mr. Ourser was sitting rigid, perspiration starting visibly from his temples and his eyes tight closed, as the hovercraft swept around the curve of the ramp accelerating (100, 130, 150, 165) to the straightaway.

"What's the matter, classmate?"

"I hate these things," said Mr. Ourser. "Hate this."

Bil Ferry settled himself comfortably. "Now I got a chance to brief you about the Q this after."

"Please don't," said the Primitive. "It never made any sense to me before and I don't think it or anything else would make any sense to me just now." He opened his eyes, took in the blur of continuous village at the sides, the hurtling hovercraft that preceded them a precise one hundred yards ahead and the other, which followed one hundred yards behind, all three vehicles strung on the broad yellow stripe of the center line. He glanced at, and winced from, the luminous yellow figures that seemed to hang unsupported three inches away from the dash, with the information (175) he so little desired at the moment. "Talk if you want. Just don't ask me to think."

"Kay," said the unpuncturable Bil Ferry agreeably. "You don't got a Q stadium your place, poz?"

"We haven't, we can't, we wouldn't and, as you say, we don't."

"What you do instead?"

"Instead of what?"

"Sitement. Root. You trace me? The big game."

"Oh. Well, football. Then in the winter there's basketball and hockey. And some of us like tennis. But the main thing is baseball."

The flack shook his head. "Not baseball. Nobody can und'stan' baseball."

"Not understand baseball?" cried Mr. Ourser.

"I researched baseball," said Bil Ferry. "Chit and chat with you, home ground, friendly, you find me? I don't und'stan' it. RBI. MVP. Earned runs. Hittin zungos."

"Fungos. Anyone can understand baseball! Why—"

And so it was that the Primitive began to lecture the flack, the one still tensely gripping the sides of his seat and averting his eyes from the outscape, the other relaxed and puzzled, listening with birdlike cockings of the head and bright, unreceptive eyes. It would have been clear to Mr. Ourser, had he been observing the evolution of the flack's expression from interest through perplexity, that the flack had eventually tuned him out and was just listening to the noise.

"What I *don't* und'stan'," said Bil Ferry at length, "is, everything stay still, yes? First base here, third base here, foul line here, home run here, poz?"

"Home plate. Yes."

"Thass dead, classmate. You want everything movin. Well, alive is movin, you find me? Now, what you should do, you should get those bases movin around a circle. You get your pitcher to turn and turn to follow. He got a special throw to lead the target, hey?"

"That wouldn't be baseball!" cried Mr. Ourser.

"And hey," said the flack eagerly, "why you want one team up, th'other team up? It take all day. What you want, you got two diamonds, one on top the other, you find me? You put your pitchers out there back to back an the whole thing goin round and round. Now it *moves,* classmate, hey? Alive?"

"You keep your obscenities to yourself!"

"Kay," said Bil Ferry, uninsulted. "So I don't und'stan' baseball, and I don't und'stan' you Primmies either. P'centage points, magic numbers to win or lose, battin' averages, and they tell me you live computerless."

"Our cornerstone," acknowledged Mr. Ourser. "Then y'r all unsane," said Bill Ferry amiably. "Y'r all like this baseball thing. Fella stand on a place, uses knowledge skill and ergs to get himself where? Right back where he started only he's tired. Gimme a Q any day. We're here."

What "here" turned out to be was an exit ramp, one like a dozen others they had passed. The flack turned into it by touching the right-hand one of two wartlike lumps on the dash. It began to flash lime-green, and the hovercraft edged off the center line onto the buff roadway and then the blue margin and began to decelerate. Mr. Ourser fixed his companion with an apprehensive gaze, opened his mouth to speak, thought better of it, and started to tremble. The hovercraft, still decelerating, followed the ramp across a bewildering web of crossroads and cloverleafs and rushed by a lake and two thousand-foot cylindrical housing units encrusted with balconies and standing on stilts. Ahead was the chiaroscuro of one of the nation's few remaining cities—and it was less a city than the monstrous clutter caused by the crossing of five major highways and their strip-villages. The skyline showed a heavy preponderance of "inverted structure"—the architectural gimmickry of the period which, by using superstrength materials below and ultralight ones above, created buildings like upside-down pyramids and impossibly leaning and curving towers.

Mr. Ourser, past the point of tact and even reason, suddenly screamed, "The wheel! For the love of God, you forgot your wheel!" At that moment the lime-green light gonged softly and went out. The flack reached behind him (he still sat with his back to the windshield) and touched the wart again; it resumed its flashing and the machine whirled off again to the right, this time on a much narrower ramp which was now a ramp, now a tunnel, now an arrow-straight path through swampland and meadow. "The wheel, who needs it?" laughed the flack, as the car banked sharply around a turn like that of a bobsled run, braked silently almost to a halt and settled, with the descending whine of its throttled-out turbines, to rest on a moving belt.

Above and ahead, great shining letters hung in the sky, surrounded by a nutating ring of blue light. The letters read QUOIT TODAY and then FLORIO and then ADAM THE GREAT, and then again QUOIT TODAY. The hovercraft was borne down perhaps a hundred feet, then turned broadside and decanted into a niche between two other cars, part of a row, a rank, a serried myriad of distance-dwindled shining cars. The flack touched the doorplate, and the side of the car snicked out of existence. "Out, classmate. We're here."

Mr. Ourser, still trembling, dismounted and reached back in for his burden, at which the flack raised the ridges from which his eyebrows had been shaved, but made no comment. The flack led the way and assisted his unwilling guest onto the first and second bands of a slideway on which they were whisked, standing, to the gateway. Mr. Ourser flicked self-conscious glances at the people around him and their impossible clothes. There was a preponderance of a substance that was colored like skin and clung like skin to areas of skin and showed no margin where the substance stopped and skin began. This made possible such effects as braided earlobes and skintight torso coverings, which to all intents and purposes did not cover. There were also bald girls and men with shoes that looked like bare feet with no toes. Mr. Ourser and the flack were grateful, each in his way, for the tradition that made clothing style the privilege of each individual, and derogatory comments inexpressible. "Modesty is not so simple a virtue as honesty," a wise man once said, and he said it before entire populations lived in an air-conditioned environment.

Bil Ferry flashed a medallion, swung from a chain around his neck, at the gate-keeping machine, and they were admitted and swept by another slideway under the stadium and through to daylight on their aisle. Their box was perhaps seven rows back from the edge of the playing field but, once in it, Mr. Ourser had the feeling it was suspended in space over the action. Before he could determine how this was done he was diverted by the flack's demonstration of the box's conveniences: heat control, cold control, refreshments, the scoreboard (a blank bulkhead at the moment) and the Options.

"What are Options?"

Bil Ferry pointed to the two nubs on the scoreboard section of the bulkhead. "Each quarter, the quoiters run up provisional score, shows here. Now we decide if it adds zero-sum or nonzero-sum."

"I do not," said the Primitive, "know what you are talking about."

"Oh," said the flack, and thought for a moment. "Look. You got something out wildernessville called 'games theory'?"

"I've heard of it. A kind of high-grade math, or logic."

"Right-eo. Games theory derived from games, hey? Well, Quoit is first game derived from games theory." He looked at Mr. Ourser's expression and shrugged. "Skip, classmate. Y'll und'stan' better at the quarter when the scores come up."

"I doubt it," said the Primitive, and sat down (with all but an astonished yelp at the seat's superb softness) and directed his attention to the field.

The field was oval, about two hundred feet long and a hundred wide, and covered with what seemed to be perfect greensward. Centered in the oval was a circle fifty feet in diameter. "Thass the Track," said Bil Ferry, pointing to the circle. "There's three things you got to know: the Track, the Quoit, the Spot. Track's fifty feet across. Quoit rolls on it. Spot is where edge of Quoit touches Track."

"I don't see this Spot. Or the Quoit either."

"You will. This is North," said the flack, waving left, "and this is South. Object is for South to get his body, or part of it, into the Spot while Spot's traveling in North's side of the track. You trace me?"

"And to keep the North player out of the Spot when it's in his own territory."

"You listen real good, classmate," the flack said approvingly.

"How fast does this Spot travel around the track?"

"Four times a minute. Once in fifteen seconds. Bout seven miles 'n hour."

"And a player scores by getting into the Spot?"

"Any part of his body, for five seconds. He gets points 'pending on where Spot is at end of five seconds."

"You mean he gets more or fewer points depending on where the Spot is."

"Positiv-eo. From centerfield, into North, goes from zero to ninety and back to zero."

"In degrees."

"In points. Degrees is points, points is degrees."

"I guess I understand it."

"Simpler'n a Texas leaguer an' a fielder's choice. Here come the girls."

As if by magic, from unmarked areas in the end zones, girls appeared briskly, perhaps two per second, springing and dancing off in all directions. In a matter of moments the field was a kaleidoscope of leaping, running, bending forms, each wearing—Mr. Ourser would have said "bearing"—the most exquisite arrays of trailing plumes and ribbons, cobwebby streamers of all the colors there are, all at once and ever-changing, some trailing real smoke from slim anklets and bracelets, green, purple, yellow, orange. Mr. Ourser could smell the smoke now—pine, heliotrope, sea breeze, vanilla, fresh bread. Music appeared from nowhere, everywhere, perhaps from the girls, who seemed a part of it. It heightened its tempo, and the girls began to form into patterns and lines, intermingle, cluster and whirl, then break into disorganized riots of color that instantly turned into avenues and orchards of beauty and motion.

Bil Ferry rose and crossed in front of Mr. Ourser. "Look down there," he said. Mr. Ourser moved to the side rail and looked down into a square pit between their box and the next. He saw three uniformed men there, each bearing the insignia of the slanted, glowing blue Quoit with a scarlet thread through it. On the front, or field-side, wall were thirty or more monitor screens. In the center were four immense trideo tanks bearing closeup three-dimensional images of the pageantry on the field. "Broadcast monitors," explained the flack. "The 2-D screens are for the ref'ree—him over there on the high chair. The other citizens 're techs, one for stadium management—sound, lights, force screens and all—an' the other's a Quoit tech. See that big red handle? Thass it, classmate. Thass the big one. Thass the Quoit."

Mr. Ourser, intrigued by a movement in the trideo tanks, turned his attention back to the field. At a twinkling run the girls had formed themselves into two large Xs, one in each end zone, and raced into the mysterious spot from which they had come, the Xs swallowing themselves up in their own apexes.

"Where do they go to?"

"Down under. They got like a four-sided pyramid with gateways, on'y you can't see it. Force field."

"What are these force fields? How do they work?"

"How sh'd I know? Look, y'r belly can take y'r lunch an turn it into that big happy smile an bright eyes, poz? You know how that works? Does y'r belly know? If it works, who cares? If y'want technol'gy, classmate, ask one of those techs down there after the game, don't ask a flack. Now watch the clown."

The clown was tall and gangling and many-jointed, bobbing and staggering and falling over his feet. Bil Ferry pointed into the control tank, and Mr. Ourser saw the Quoit tech draw down the big red handle.

The stadium, even the most habituated fans in it, gasped; Mr. Ourser was thunderstruck. A mighty toroid, or doughnut shape, of transparent blue light, with a threadlike core of aching red, the Quoit was tilted at thirty degrees, with one edge contacting the ground just on the circular path of the Track. Where it touched, a circular patch of brilliant light appeared, the Spot. About twelve feet across and exactly bisected by the Track, it was green on the infield side and orange on the outfield side, and it traveled the Track at a steady pace as the huge Quoit moved. The motion of the Quoit was that of a saucer spinning on its edge and slowing down, so that it rolls on its perimeter. The Quoit, however, did not slow down, but nutated at its steady four revolutions per minute, the bicolored Spot moving with it. "Watch clown."

The gangling clown, jelly-legged, spaghetti-armed, did a boneless dance on the Track. The crowd shrieked at him as the Quoit approached. He stopped dancing and looked at the stands, cupping one ear. With the Quoit upon him, he turned and leaped in mock panic, and tried to lurch out of its way. The red thread at the heart of the Quoit sliced down through his bobbing bustle, severing it neatly. The crowd howled. The clown, hands clapped to his backside, scampered across the infield, making the stadium rock with bursts of shrill amplified laughter.

"Ol' core cut anything—steel, bones, bottoms or rice puddin," chuckled the flack. "Para-matter field."

"How does it work?"

"I tol' you, ask the techs. All I know is that red core cuts off hand, foot, anything. Line only a few molecules thick. Seals it, heals it and makes you laugh."

"Who laughs?"

"I jingle you not, classmate—it's some sort of shock. Cut off your behind, you laugh like hell."

"Doesn't it hurt?"

"They say not. Not for a while anyhoo. Then the medicos stick it back on good as new."

"Good as new?"

Bil Ferry shrugged. "Most times. Sometimes numb. Sometimes rots off." He laughed suddenly and pointed at the clown, who had tripped over his feet and sprawled across the Track just as the Quoit arrived. To the horror of the Primitive, the deadly red thread cut through both the clown's legs at the knees. The clown howled with merriment, flopped like a fish into the danger zone again, where the line crossed his neck. The head rolled away and then exploded with a loud bang, for it had been some kind of balloon. Out of the headless torso stepped a diminutive and enchanting female, who rushed to the retreating Spot, caught up with it and did a roundoff, a handspring and a perfect layout back somersault over the scarlet core. She bowed charmingly and skipped to the North centerfield, where she disappeared.

"Now the quoiters," said the flack, leaning forward expectantly. Mr. Ourser found himself doing the same; perhaps it was the music, which thundered and diminished and, with the unresolved chord, waited. "Here comes Florio."

The local hero was greeted enthusiastically as he appeared in the South centerfield. His name floated above him in huge block letters as he bowed to the right, to the left and ahead. He was dark, compact, and extraordinarily muscled. "Mother-naked!" gasped the Primitive. Bil Ferry shook his head and thumbed down into the control pit. Mr. Ourser could see, in the immense magnification of the trideo tanks, the quoiter advancing down the field with little mincing steps, his arms out like a tightrope walker's. And if one could see no garments, one could also see no details: he was, if naked, as smoothly streamlined as a teenage-boy doll. "He got his minibiki," said Bil Ferry.

"Minibiki," muttered Mr. Ourser, by some alchemy of inflection making the word sound like giggling from behind the barn, "Minibiki."

From centerfield North, out of thin air, pranced a tall golden figure wearing long yellow hair and a minibiki which, like his opponent's, exactly matched the color of his skin. He was all of six feet six and broad and flat. He sprinted forward, bending as he ran, until he was hurtling along stooped almost double, his long arms wide and curved forward a few inches above the ground; he rushed Florio as if to scoop him up like a mail sack. Florio half knelt, one foot far forward, braced his rear foot, expanded his enormous chest, bunched his shoulder and arm muscles and waited there like some artist's conception of The Immovable Object. At the last possible moment Adam the Great stopped, poised in an amazing and perfect arabesque, and then left the ground. His elevation was phenomenal, and he soared over the stocky Florio's head like a big golden bird. The crowds loved it, and said so.

"This is Quoit? It looks more like a dance recital," scoffed Mr. Ourser.

"Positiv-eo!" cried the flack, not offended. He took his own fingers one by one and rattled off, "Quoit is dance and prizefight, wrestling, bullfight, bearbait, gym meet, track, everything."

"Except baseball."

Bil Ferry laughed and turned back to the field, just as the Quoit flickered on and off twice, still moving. There was a long silver note from the sourceless band, and the whole place fell silent, a breathing velvet silence in which nothing moved but the great wheeling blue Quoit. The two quoiters stood, each in his own infield, legs apart, hands clasped behind them, heads bowed.

"What's happening?" Mr. Ourser demanded, and was answered by a chorus of growls and shushes from the people around. "Minute silence memory dead quoiters," murmured Bil Ferry.

The silence, commanded by the noiseless hypnotic undulations of the mighty Quoit, seemed much longer than the sixty seconds it actually was. Then the music came up with organ tones and a crescendo clear from the marrow and all the way up to the wailing wall, and broke into a nippy little trot, and everyone relaxed. "Two cut in th' last three months," explained Bil Ferry. "Fans take it serious."

"I thought you said the doctors could fix them up."

"Most times. Not through the head."

A Gabriel trumped, and instantly the infield, the wonderful smooth greensward, developed spokes ten degrees apart. From the center line around to the North, nine segments glowed with spectral colors, red to indigo. From the North around again to the center line, indigo to red. And the same at the South side of the circular playing field. At the same time a hitherto unsuspected (by Mr. Ourser) force field over the entire stadium went opaque. Daylight was inked out, and the intensity of everything—the Quoit, the spoked circular centerfield, and the traveling Spot, green inside the Track, orange outside—it all was stepped up, so that the eye had to narrow and blink to accommodate it. And the two men, still standing at ease with their hands behind them, had acquired a glow of their own: Florio the local champion, silver, Adam the Great, a glowing gold.

"Are they painted?"

"Taint paint," said the flack. "They got to spray 'em so the sensors know who's in the Spot or over the line so they c'n send to the computers so they c'n score 'em. Hey, Quoit!" he bellowed, and it seemed as if half the world was bellowing with him. Mr. Ourser recognized the equivalent of "Play ball!" and was also aware of the wildly partisan nature of the crowd. At the South end the boxes seemed almost to rock with a rhythmic chant of "Florio! Flo-ri-o!" mostly from an idolizing younger group, while at the North end a large block of upper seats flared with the letters A-D-A-M spelled out in glowing cards. The two quoiters trotted to the center line and extended their hands. They touched fingertips and then turned and went completely across to touch ground at the ninety degree point in their own territory.

"You want to watch that Adam," said Bil Ferry tensely. "He got a trouble. He be champ by now sept for that."

"What trouble?"

Bil Ferry tapped his own head. "He gets mad."

Mr. Ourser tsked. Even to the wilderness it had penetrated that there is something vulgar about anger; it was the new obscenity. Children learned to control their anger before they could toddle. It was thought that this might, in the long run, prevent war. The entire civilized world was studded with methods and devices, rituals and reflexes designed to drain off anger, or to transmute it into something else. One did not—simply did not—make public displays of anger. "You mean he's a sore loser, something like that?" asked Mr. Ourser.

"Neg-a neg-a no," the flack said. "He take that all right-eo. But don't make him look like a damn fool, you find me? There they go."

The Spot was just leaving North—Adam's territory—and as it entered the South segment Adam began to move. Florio, watching him intently, faded slowly back. As he crossed the center line, Adam shortened his steps, every fourth or fifth one being a small feint to right or left, to which Florio responded as if he were wired to the other's central nervous system, going up on his toes to balance there, arms out, tensed, ready to go anywhere including straight up.

"Now," said Mr. Ourser, explaining it aloud to himself, "he has to get past Florio and keep himself in the Spot for five seconds to score anything."

"Poz. Or maybe keep Florio in it for five. Florio lose points. In his own ter'tory." He laughed excitedly. "But I bet Florio say no."

The teenagers in the next box were shrieking at Florio to stop Adam, to rush him, to look out for him. But it was Adam who rushed. His great size making the speed completely deceptive, he took two long strides and left the ground in one of his exquisite leaps. It was planned to carry him over Florio's head and down just in advance of the Spot as it entered the eighty degree segment. He could then stay in its green area, inside the Track, for the necessary five seconds or more, while fighting Florio off.

But Florio was not deceived and had plans of his own.

As the magnificently arched and balanced figure soared overhead he reached up almost casually and tipped up the trailing ankle. Florio then made an immense bound, landing a dozen feet away even before his flailing, tumbling adversary hit the ground. Catlike the big man might be, but a cat he was not; he landed on his shoulder and the side of his face, the speed of his passage then carrying his long body up and over. His head was twisted almost under his armpit, and his legs just missed the rising red threat of the Quoit's core as it passed through the ninety degree segment. The crowd gasped.

"Now Florio usin' his think-tank!" crowed the flack. "You see him jump?"

"Yes. What did he do that for?"

"Rule say no direct contusions. No punchin', kickin', stompin', or bitin'. If you dump a quoiter an he gets contused, that's all right, you find me? But you don't pick him up and whang him on the ground or it costs you. So if you get away before he hits, he can't claim. Hey, look that Florio."

By now the Spot had swung into North territory. The golden giant still lay where he had fallen. Mr. Ourser rose anxiously. Half the stadium was on its feet. Florio was strutting with a cocky little heel-and-toe into enemy country, blandly ignoring the Spot, though pacing it, until it should get into a high-scoring area. He waved to someone high up in the stands. He blew a kiss. And then as if the joy in him simply could not be contained, he cut across the infield of North's territory with a roundoff, two crisp back handsprings and a high back somersault which took him over the Spot, over the core and out of bounds. He was back in again with a dive and roll as if he had bounced off something solid, having used up only the narrowest slice of the second that would have cost him points. The crowd roared approval.

"But what about him?" cried Mr. Ourser, pointing at the still figure of Adam the Great. "He could be hurt. He could be dead!"

"Patience, classmate. We find that out end of quarter. Look that Florio now!"

Florio was staring at the ninety degree segment, play-acting an immense concentration, holding his chin and wagging his head. Suddenly he turned his back and walked away. "Score! Score!" shrieked his partisans, but Florio shook his head, and someone suddenly shouted, "He don't need it! He don't need it!" and everyone took up the cry, laughing and cheering and pounding one another on the back. And in the midst of the bedlam Mr. Ourser took Bil Ferry by the shoulders and shook him, trying to be heard: "Somebody should go out there and see. Somebody—Ferry! Ferry!" he bellowed, and found himself inarticulate. "The thing, the thing there, the what-you-call it, red thing, that core, it'll take off his legs! Make 'em stop the Quoit, Ferry, damn it, you hear? You've got to make 'em stop the Quoit!" he cried, shocked and horrified to his Primitive bones.

This got through to the flack, and no mistake about it. Ferry's eyes went wide, his jaw dropped, he gasped. Then, "Stop the Quoit? They never stop the Quoit!" he intoned, more shocked, even, than his guest.

Florio disdainfully trotted along in the undefended Spot as it passed through the low-scoring segment. On the bulkhead before him Mr. Ourser saw luminous letters and numbers appear: SOUTH 5, but he could not think about that at the moment. The scarlet thread at the core of the great ghostly Quoit pursued its stately way, with the brilliant bicolored disc of light centered on and traveling with the Quoit's point of contact with the ground. The stadium was in total uproar. Incredibly to Mr. Ourser, it seemed like laughter. Inexcusably, it was, for Florio had flopped down on his stomach and was pretending to pull up blades of grass and pick his teeth with them. And now, along with the roars and shrieks of laughter, there was an undercurrent of something else—a low-pitched buzz of terror and intoxication and something unforgivably akin to delight—the mob sound which, once heard, can never be forgotten or mistaken for anything else. And here and there, widely separated, ineffective, was a scream of horror, a cry of protest as the Quoit's core, like the slow-motion picture of a whiplash, red already for its deadly work, moved down toward the motionless Adam.

Adam lay with his legs across the Track in South's eighty degree segment. As the green-and-orange Spot approached the sixty-five degree mark, something like a silver torpedo hurtled across the arena from the North infield. How Florio had converted himself from a lolling, grass-chewing sloth into this projectile—how any human being could move this fast—was beyond Mr. Ourser's comprehension. One second he was belly down on the sward and taking his ease, the next he was flashing across the playing field, the third he had Adam by the wrists and had jerked him clear of the Quoit. It seemed as if everybody in the place was on his feet but one. Mr. Ourser fell back into his seat, covered his face and trembled.

Bil Ferry plumped down beside him and pounded his shoulder. "Now, *thass* Quoit. Thass really Quoit. Now you know. Is great, neg-a neg-a no, hey?" he crowed. Then before the dazed Primitive could react he gave a wordless shout and pointed. Florio was standing over the prone giant bowing to the crowd, when with one of those bewildering transitions from stasis to full movement, from fear to hilarity, from combat to playfulness that seemed to characterize this game, Adam the Great rose fluidly from what had seemed to be total unconsciousness, caught the smaller man by the thighs, and came up standing with him in a fetal position in his arms. The closeup in the trideo tanks showed the heavy strain it took for Adam to hold Florio this way—and that he was capable of it. It showed, too, what seemed to be unalloyed fury on the big man's face, and the effortful but still amused expression of the little one in his arms.

Adam stalked across the infield with his burden. He could not hope to overtake the Spot as it left the high-scoring area, so he cut across and intercepted it. To score, he must be in it for five seconds, and all he got out of it was a 7 as it approached midfield and his own territory. But it was enough to top Florio's score and to send Adam's adherents into transports of joy. At the midfield point he unceremoniously dropped Florio on his rump and stalked off after the Spot.

Florio sat where he was for a moment, shook himself like a wet spaniel, bounced to his feet and crossed to midfield at the Track, just where the Spot would enter his territory. Here he braced himself, and when the Spot crossed over into South, he shoulder-shunted Adam aside and placed himself between Adam and the Spot. They followed it around this way, the golden giant trying to step into the pool of light, which would mean a score, or trying to box his opponent into it, which would mean his loss of points, but each failing, all around the South traverse. Once it crossed midfield, they reversed positions like dancers, with Adam now defending against Florio's feints and attacks. It was, in its way, beautiful to watch: the golden and the silver bodies tense and speeding, waiting and leaping, the brilliant glowing spokes of the playing field, the majestic loop and fall of the nutating Quoit with its blue body and the lethal red thread at its heart. The contestants were in constant motion as they led and followed the traveling Spot, now defending, now attacking, now bounding away to take up an ambush point somewhere along the Track. The effect on the crowd seemed to be one of satisfaction, as if the explosive opening had set the game on a high plane and it was all right to turn it to this wondrous display of feint and fence. And at last, with a shocking effect on Mr. Ourser's eyeballs, the Quoit disappeared, the luminous spectral cartwheel of the playing field became the green oval bearing its innocent circle; the light shield over the stadium flicked out of existence, and it was again a warm outdoor afternoon, with a pleased and applauding crowd colorful in the sunlight. The first quarter was over.

"Well, you like? You like?" asked the flack gleefully.

"I don't really know," said Mr. Ourser as honestly as he could. "I was scared there for a minute, I don't mind telling you. Was Adam really unconscious?"

The flack shrugged. "Pozzo, neggo, who's to say-a? Long as it's good Quoit. Watch, here's the scoring."

The public address system began to thrum: "Zerosum, nonzero-sum. Zero-sum, nonzero-sum . . ."

"What's that mean? Zero what?"

"Zero-sum, you trace? Like-uh-poker. You have poker out there in the wilderness?"

"Well, sure."

"Kay. You and I play poker, everything won plus everything lost equals zero. Hey?"

"Uh—well, yes."

"Fine. Now, nonzero-sum is like, well, baseball. The scores add up to more than zero."

"I see."

"Good-eo." The flack pointed to the bulkhead, where the score floated: North 7 South 5. "Thass provisional, you und'stan'. Now, if we score it zero-sum, we give each one 50 points—you got to have something to play with, same like poker, you find me? Now, Adam got 7, Florio got 5, provisional. Two points apart. If scoring's zero-sum, we take two points f'm Florio and give 'em to Adam. Score North 52, South 48."

"Uh, I think I've got it."

"Now, nonzero-sum. They get jus' what they earned, sept for one thing—underdog gets 50–point bonus."

"You mean if it's scored that way Adam would get his seven points, but Florio would get 55?"

"You oiled up and squeakless, Mr. O.," said the flack. Mr. Ourser recognized this as some sort of compliment and all but smiled. "But why should the underdog get 50 points?"

"Crowd likes his style."

"So by pushing one of those buttons"—he pointed to the bulkhead—"the crowd votes on whether to score it zero-sum or nonzero-sum."

The public-address system gave its muezzinlike cry once more, followed by a long chime. "Ten seconds. You want to push?"

"You do it."

The flack pushed the nonzero-sum button and leaned back. In two or three seconds the final first-quarter score appeared: SOUTH 55 NORTH 7. Florio's rescue of Adam had pleased the crowd. "Adam, he not goin to love that no way nohow negativ-eo," Bil Ferry said.

The infield abruptly took on its spokes of color, the sky went out, the Quoit appeared, and the players were magically in place again. The crowd sighed and settled itself.

This time there was no meeting and salutation. Florio shot across and into the Spot the second it was in North's territory. Adam sprang at him and, grasping him by the shoulders, flung him out before he had been in the green more than two seconds. Florio, surprisingly, raced away from him to the other side of the Track, by the center line, and lay down laughing on the Track.

Bil Ferry, and the whole stadium, shouted. Mr. Ourser was perplexed. "What's he doing?"

"He just laying there," chortled the flack. "Once was a champ name of Cream used to do that. War o'nerves, trace me? He snatched Adam away f'm the core, right? Now he give Adam the chance to do same thing. Adam got to. Look how mad he is, and he got to!"

"But suppose Adam just doesn't?"

"Oh, he got to. You think the crowd stand f' that?'"

"Florio made a damn fool of him. You said—"

"Oh—Watch the game, classmate."

The mighty Quoit nutated on. Its brilliant scarlet core knifed along the Track. The stadium grew hushed, as if at the bidding of a slowly turned volume control. Florio lay back on the Track, put his hands behind his head, and laughed up at the darkened sky. Adam the Great stalked over and stood looking down on him, glowering and (as seen in the trideo) chewing hard on his own teeth. The green-and-orange Spot arrived. The blue glow of the Quoit arrived. Adam still looked down, motionless.

And then, unbelievably, the red core cut Florio right in two, from groin to crown and through both the wrists which were behind his head. In the trideo tank Mr. Ourser saw the two halves of his body fall open like a book, the complex of colors which flooded out flashing on its glazed cut surfaces.

There seemed then to be a silence that went on forever, though it could not have been long. The Quoit disappeared and the sky came into being when the core had advanced only another two or three yards. The only thing that would come to Mr. Ourser's lips was a whispered, "I thought they never stopped the Quoit." And came Bil Ferry's whispered answer, "But the game's over now," and as whispers they could be clearly heard.

Then there was a wild, inconsolable screaming that seemed to set off an explosion in every human being in the place. Teenagers began vaulting over the rail into the control pit; Mr. Ourser saw some confused fighting going on down there and uniformed men being trampled. The crowd, in ones, in twos, then by dozens and hundreds, began to jump over the barriers and pour onto the arena.

Adam the Great stood for perhaps a minute after the bisection of his opponent, his hands on his hips and his jaws working. He slowly raised his head and watched the people leaping, falling, vaulting onto the greensward. Then his eyes widened and he turned and sprinted for the invisible gateway in the North outfield. He reached it yards ahead of the nearest spectators and seemed to be scrabbling at thin air. He ran around in a half circle and tried again, with the same result.

Mr. Ourser now understood why the teenagers had dropped into the control pit—it was to lock those exits. Adam, fleeing across toward the South exit, apparently understood this, because he suddenly stopped trying. Right in the center of the arena he stopped and crouched at bay. More people came. They closed in, slowly. He whirled, and those behind him jumped back, but others jumped forward. He got his hands on a man and whirled with him and threw him. He knocked down two more. He ran then, and was tripped and went down.

There was a huge hooting sound. Bil Ferry paled. "Less cut out, classmate. Ther'll be police helis over here like flies in four seconds flat," he said. They stumbled out, the Primitive clinging to his burden to the last, up the aisle, out to the slideway stage.

Mr. Ourser looked back.

Someone in the wild flailing melee in the control pit had pulled the big red handle. The Quoit was in motion through the crowd. Nothing of that was ever to stay with Mr. Ourser but one sharp picture: a young, slender, bald girl sitting on the sward with the crowd milling around her, holding a severed and bloodless leg in both hands and laughing and laughing and laughing . . .

The slideway, the parking lot, the hovercraft. When at last they were clear of the stadium and out on a feeder road, Bil Ferry said to the Primitive, in tones of outrage that echoed back through the years to the once-familiar syllables: "I say, that's not cricket." "Mr. O.," he said, "that wasn't Quoit. That wasn't Quoit."

"I know. I know," said Mr. Ourser, comforting him.

And it was at that moment that Mr. Ourser destroyed the Primitives forever. He did not do it all at once, but he did it completely. "Do you suppose," he said, "that a Quoit installation—just a simple one—might be put in a wilderness location?"

"I c'n have Survey an' Estimate out there in the morning, y'ronner," said Bil Ferry. (He never called Mr. Ourser "classmate" again, that being a concession to the ideal of equality and used only on members of classes lower than one's own. A prospect, now, a real prospect, was "y'ronner" no matter what his station.) "I c'n also up your priorities one notch for the trade goods."

So Mr. Ourser opened his burden—an attaché case—and got out his shopping list, and with the improved priorities they were able to fill it, even to the timer for a 1962 RCA Whirlpool washing machine, even to the set of points for a 1964 Mercury.

The Nail and the Oracle

Despite the improvements, the Pentagon in 1970 was still the Pentagon, with more places to walk than places to sit. Not that Jones had a legitimate gripe. The cubical cave they had assigned to him as an office would have been more than adequate for the two-three days he himself had estimated. But by the end of the third week it fit him like a size-6 hat and choked him like a size-12 collar. Annie's phone calls expressed eagerness to have him back, but there was an edge to the eagerness now which made him anxious. His hotel manager had wanted to shift his room after the first week and he had been stubborn about it; now he was marooned like a rock in a mushroom patch, surrounded by a back-to-rhythm convention of the Anti-Anti-Population Explosion League. He'd had to buy shirts, he'd had to buy shoes, he'd needed a type-four common-cold shot, and most of all, he couldn't find what was wrong with ORACLE.

Jones and his crew had stripped ORACLE down to its mounting bolts, checked a thousand miles of wiring and a million solid-state elements, everything but its priceless and untouchable memory banks. Then they'd rebuilt the monster, meticulously cross-checking all the way. For the past four days they had been running the recompleted computer, performance-matching with crash-priority time on other machines, while half the science boys and a third of the military wailed in anguish. He had reported to three men that the machine had nothing wrong with it, that it never had had anything wrong with it, and that there was no reason to believe there ever would be anything wrong with it. One by one these three had gone (again) into ORACLE's chamber, and bolted the door, and energized the privacy field, and then one by one they had emerged stern and disappointed, to tell Jones that it would not give them an answer: an old admiral, an ageless colonel, and a piece of walking legend whom Jones called to himself the civilian.

Having sent his crew home—for thus he burned his bridges—having deprived himself of Jacquard the design genius and the twenty-three others, the wiring team, all the mathematicians, everyone, Jones sighed in his little office, picked up the phone again and called the three for a conference. When he put the instrument down again he felt a little pleased. Consistencies pleased Jones, even unpleasant ones, and the instant response of all three was right in line with everything they had done from the time they had first complained about ORACLE's inability to answer their questions, all through their fiddling and diddling during every second of the long diagnostic operation. The admiral had had an open line installed to Jones' office, the colonel had devised a special code word for his switchboard, the civilian had hung around personally, ignoring all firm, polite hints until he had turned his ankle on a cable, giving Jones a reason to get him out of there. In other words, these three didn't just want an answer, they *needed* it.

They came, the admiral with his old brows and brand-new steel-blue eyes, the colonel with starch in his spine and skin like a post-maneuver proving-grounds, the civilian limping a bit, with his head tilted a bit, turned a bit, a captivating mannerism which always gave his audiences the feeling that history cared to listen to them. Jones let them get settled, this admiral whose whole career had consisted of greater and greater commands until his strong old hand was a twitch away from the spokes of the helm of the ship of state; this colonel who had retained his lowly rank as a mark of scorn for the academy men who scurried to obey him, whose luxurious quarters were equipped with an iron barracks bed; and this civilian with the scholarly air, with both Houses and a Cabinet rank behind him, whose political skills were as strong, and as deft, and as spiked as a logroller's feet.

"Gentlemen," said Jones, "this may well be our last meeting. There will, of course, be a written report, but I understand the—uh—practicalities of such a situation quite well, and I do not feel it necessary to go into the kind of detail in the report that is possible to us in an informal discussion." He looked at each face in turn and congratulated himself. That was just right. This is just between us boys. Nobody's going to squeal on you.

"You've dismissed your crew," said the civilian, causing a slight start in the admiral and a narrowing of the colonel's eyes and, in Jones, a flash of admiration. This one had snoopers the services hadn't even dreamed up yet. "I hope this is good news."

"Depends," said Jones. "What it means primarily is that they have done all they can. In other words, there is nothing wrong with ORACLE in any of their specialties. Their specialties include everything the computer is and does. In still other words, there's nothing wrong with the machine."

"So you told us yesterday," gritted the colonel, "but I got no results. And—I want results." The last was added as an old ritual which, apparently, had always gotten results just by being recited.

"I followed the procedures," said the admiral, intoning this as a cardinal virtue, "and also got no results." He held up a finger and suspended operations in the room while he performed some sort of internal countdown. "Had I not done so, ORACLE would have responded with an 'insufficient data' signal. Correct?"

"Quite correct," said Jones.

"And it didn't."

"That was my experience," said the civilian, and the colonel nodded.

"Gentlemen," said Jones, "neither I nor my crew—and there just is not a better one—have been able to devise a question that produced that result."

"It was not a result," snapped the colonel.

Jones ignored him. "Given the truth of my conclusion—that there is nothing wrong with the machine—and your reports, which I can have no reason to doubt, there is no area left to investigate but one, and that is in your hands, not mine. It's the one thing you have withheld from me." He paused. Two of them shifted their feet. The colonel tightened his jaw.

The admiral said softly, but with utter finality, "I can*not* divulge my question."

The colonel and the civilian spoke together: "Security—" and

"This is a matter—" and then both fell silent.

"Security." Jones spread his hands. To keep from an enemy, real or potential, matters vital to the safety of the nation, that was security. And how easy it was to wrap the same blanket about the use of a helicopter to a certain haven, the presence of a surprising little package in a Congressional desk, the exact relations between a certain officer and his—*argh!* This, thought Jones, has all the earmarks of, not *our* security, but three cases of *my* security . . . I'll try just once more.

"Thirty years ago, a writer named William Tenn wrote a brilliant story in which an Air Force moon landing was made, and the expedition found an inhabited pressure dome nearby. They sent out a scout, who was prepared to die at the hands of Russians or even Martians. He returned to the ship in a paroxysm, gentlemen, of laughter. The other dome belonged to the U.S. Navy."

The admiral projected two loud syllables of a guffaw and said, "Of course." The colonel looked pained. The civilian, bright-eyed, made a small nod which clearly said, One up for you, boy.

Jones put on his used-car-salesman face. "Honestly, gentlemen, it embarrasses me to draw a parallel like that. I believe with all my heart that each of you has the best interests of our nation foremost in his thoughts. As for myself—security? Why, I wouldn't be here if I hadn't been cleared all the way back to *Pithecanthropus erectus*.

"So much for you, so much for me. Now, as for ORACLE, you know as well as I do that it is no ordinary computer. It is designed for computations, not of math, specifically, nor of strictly physical problems, though it can perform them, but for the distillation of human thought. For over a decade the contents of the Library of Congress and other sources have poured into that machine—everything: novels, philosophy, magazines, poetry, textbooks, religious tracts, comic books, even millions of personnel records. There's every shade of opinion, every quality of writing—anything and everything that an army of over a thousand microfilming technicians have been able to cram into it. As long as it's printed and in English, German, Russian, French, or Japanese, ORACLE can absorb it. Esperanto is the funnel for a hundred Oriental and African languages. It's the greatest repository of human thought and thought-directed action the world has ever known, and its one most powerful barrier against error in human affairs is the sheer mass of its memory and the wide spectrum of opinion that has poured into it.

"Add to this its ability to extrapolate—to project the results of hypothetical acts—and the purposely designed privacy structure—for it's incapable of recording or reporting who asked it what question—and you have ORACLE, the one place in the world where you can get a straight answer based, not in terms of the problem itself, but on every ideological computation and cross-comparison that can be packed into it."

"The one place I couldn't get a straight answer," said the civilian gently.

"To your particular question. Sir, if you want that answer, you have got to give me that question." He checked a hopeful stir in the other two by adding quickly, "and yours. And yours. You see, gentlemen, though I am concerned for your needs in this matter, my prime concern is ORACLE. To find a way to get one of the answers isn't enough. If I had all three, I might be able to deduce a common denominator. I already have, of course, though it isn't enough: you are all high up in national affairs, and very close to the center of things. You are all of the same generation" (translation: near the end of the road) "and, I'm sure, equally determined to do the best you can for your country" (to get to the top of the heap before you cash in). "Consider *me*," he said, and smiled disarmingly. "To let me get this close to the answer *I* want; namely, what's wrong with ORACLE, and then to withhold it—isn't that sort of cruel and unusual punishment?"

"I feel for you," said the civilian, not without a twinkle. Then, sober with a coldness that would freeze helium into a block, he said, "But you ask too much."

Jones looked at him, and then at the others, sensing their unshakable agreement. "OK," he said, with all the explosive harshness he could muster, "I'm done here, I'm sick of this place and my girl's sick of being by herself, and I'm going home. You can't call in anyone else cause there isn't anyone else: my company built ORACLE and my men were trained for it."

This kind of thing was obviously in the colonel's idiom. From far back in his throat, he issued a grinding sound that came out in words: "You'll finish the job you were ordered to do, mister, or you'll take the consequences."

Jones shouted at him, "Consequences? What consequences? You couldn't even have me fired, because I can make a damn good case that you prevented me from finishing the job. I'm not under your orders either. This seems a good time to remind you of the forgotten tradition that with this"—he took hold of the narrow lapel of his own sports jacket—"I outrank any uniform in this whole entire Pentagon." He caught the swift smile of the civilian, and therefore trained his next blast on him. "Consequences? The only consequence you can get now is to deny yourself and your country the answer to your question. The only conclusion I can come to is that something else is more important to you than that. What else?" He stood up. So did the officers.

From his chair, the civilian said sonorously, "Now, now . . . gentlemen. Surely we can resolve this problem without raising our voices. Mr. Jones, would the possession of two of these questions help you in your diagnosis? Or even one?"

Breathing hard, Jones said, "It might."

The civilian opened his long white hands. "Then there's no problem after all. If one of you gentlemen—"

"Absolutely not," said the admiral instantly.

"Not me," growled the colonel. "You want compromise, don't you? Well, go ahead—you compromise."

"In this area," said the civilian smoothly, "I possess all the facts, and it is my considered judgment that the disclosure of my question would not further Mr. Jones' endeavors." (Jones thought, the admiral said the same thing in two words.) "Admiral, would you submit to my judgment the question of whether or not security would be endangered by your showing Mr. Jones your question?"

"I would not."

The civilian turned to the colonel. One look at that rock-bound countenance was sufficient to make him turn away again, which, thought Jones, puts the colonel two points ahead of the admiral in the word-economy business.

Jones said to the civilian, "No use, sir, and by my lights, that's the end of it. The simplest possible way to say it is that you gentlemen have the only tools in existence that would make it possible for me to repair this gadget, and you won't let me have them. So fix it yourself, or leave it the way it is. I'd see you out," he added, scanning the walls of the tiny room, "but I have to go to the john." He stalked out, his mind having vividly and permanently photographed the astonishment on the admiral's usually composed features, the colonel's face fury-twisted into something like the knot that binds the lashes of a whip, and the civilian grinning broadly.

Grinning broadly?

Ah well, he thought, slamming the men's-room door behind him—and infuriatingly, it wouldn't slam—Ah well, we all have our way of showing frustration. Maybe I could've been just as mad more gently.

The door moved, and someone ranged alongside at the next vertical bathtub. Jones glanced, and then said aloud, "Maybe I could've been just as mad more gently."

"Perhaps we all could have," said the civilian, and then with his free hand he did four surprising things in extremely rapid succession. He put his finger to his lips, then his hand to the wall and then to his ear. Finally he whisked a small folded paper out of his breast pocket and handed it to Jones. He then finished what he was doing and went to wash up.

Shh. The walls have ears. Take this.

"All through history," said the civilian from the sink, his big old voice booming in the tiled room, "we read about the impasse, and practically every time it's mentioned, it's a sort of preface to an explanation of how it was solved. Yet I'll bet history's full of impasses that just couldn't be solved. They don't get mentioned because when it happens, everything stops. There just isn't anything to write down in the book anymore. I think we've just seen such an occasion, and I'm sorry for each of us."

The old son of a gun! "Thanks for that much, anyway, sir," Jones said, tucking the paper carefully away out of sight. The old man, wiping his hands, winked once and went out.

Back in his office, which seemed three times larger than it had been before the conference, Jones slumped behind his desk and teased himself with the small folded paper, not reading it, turning it over and over. It had to be the old man's question. Granted that it was, why had he been so willing to hand it over now, when three minutes earlier his refusal had been just about as adamant as—adamant? So, Jones, quit looking at the detail and get on the big picture. What was different in those three minutes?

Well, they were out of one room and into another. Out of one room that was damn well not bugged and into one which, the old man's pantomime had informed him, may well be. Nope—that didn't make sense. Then—how about this? In the one room there had been witnesses. In the second, none—not after the finger on the lips. So if a man concluded that the civilian probably never had had an objection to Jones' seeing and using the question, but wanted it concealed from anyone else—maybe specifically from those other two . . . why, the man had the big picture.

What else? That the civilian had not said this, therefore would not bring himself to say it in so many words, and would not appreciate any conversation that might force him to talk it over. Finally, no matter how reluctant he might be to let Jones see the paper, the slim chance Jones offered him of getting an answer outweighed every other consideration—except the chance of the other two finding out. So another part of the message was: I'm sitting on dynamite, Mr. Jones, and I'm handing you the detonator. Or: I trust you, Mr. Jones.

So be it, old man. I've got the message.

He closed his eyes and squeezed the whole situation to see if anything else would drip out of it. Nothing . . . except the faint conjecture that what worked on one might work on the other two. And as if on cue, the door opened and a bland-faced major came in a pace, stopped, said "Beg pardon, sir. I'm in the wrong room," and before Jones could finish saying "That's all right," he was gone. Jones gazed thoughtfully at the door. That major was one of the colonel's boys. That "wrong room" bit had a most unlikely flavor to it. So if the man hadn't come in for nothing, he'd come in for something. He hadn't taken anything and he hadn't left anything, so he'd come in to find something out. The only thing he could find out was whether Jones was or was not here. Oh: and whether he was or was not alone.

All Jones had to do to check that out was to sit tight. You can find out if a man is alone in a room for now, but not for ten minutes from now, or five.

In two minutes the colonel came in.

He wore his "I don't like you, mister" expression. He placed his scarred brown hands flat on Jones' desk and rocked forward over him like a tidal wave about to break.

"It's your word against mine, and I'm prepared to call you a liar," grated the colonel. "I want you to report to me and no one else."

"All right," said Jones, and put out his hand. The colonel locked gazes with him for a fair slice of forever, which made Jones believe that the Medusa legend wasn't necessarily a legend after all. Then the officer put a small folded paper into Jones' outstretched palm. "You get the idea pretty quick, I'll say that, mister"; he straightened, about-faced and marched out.

Jones looked at the two scraps of folded paper on the desk and thought, I will be damned.

And one to go.

He picked up the papers and dropped them again, feeling like a kid who forces himself to eat all the cake before he attacks the icing. He thought, maybe the old boy wants to but just doesn't know how.

He reached for the phone and dialed for the open line, wondering if the admiral had had it canceled yet.

He had not, and he wasn't waiting for the first ring to finish itself. He knew who was calling and he knew Jones knew, so he said nothing, just picked up the phone.

Jones said, "It was kind of crowded in here."

"Precisely the point," said the admiral, with the same grudging approval the colonel had shown. There was a short pause, and then the admiral said, "Have you called anyone else?"

Into four syllables Jones put all the outraged innocence of a male soprano accused of rape. "Certainly not."

"Good man."

The Britishism amused Jones, and he almost said Gung ho, what?; but instead he concentrated on what to say next. It was easy to converse with the admiral if you supplied both sides of the conversation. Suddenly it came to him that the admiral wouldn't want to come here—he had somewhat farther to travel than the colonel had—nor would he like the looks of Jones' visiting him at this particular moment. He said, "I wouldn't mention this, but as you know, I'm leaving soon and may not see you. And I think you picked up my cigarette lighter."

"Oh," said the admiral.

"And me out of matches," said Jones ruefully. "Well—I'm going down to ORACLE now. Nice to have known you, sir." He hung up, stuck an unlit cigarette in his mouth, put the two folded papers in his left pants pocket, and began an easy stroll down the catacombs called corridors in the Pentagon.

Just this side of ORACLE's dead-end corridor, and not quite in visual range of its security post, a smiling young ensign, who otherwise gave every evidence of being about his own business, said, "Light, sir?"

"Why, thanks."

The ensign handed him a lighter. He didn't light it and proffer the flame; he handed the thing over. Jones lit his cigarette and dropped the lighter into his pocket. "Thanks."

"That's all right," smiled the ensign, and walked on.

At the security post, Jones said to the guard, "Whoppen?"

"Nothing and nobody, Mr. Jones."

"Best news I've had all day." He signed the book and accompanied the guard down the dead end. They each produced a key and together opened the door. "I shouldn't be too long."

"All the same to me," said the guard, and Jones realized he'd been wishfully thinking out loud. He shut the door, hit the inner lock switch, and walked through the little foyer and the swinging door which unveiled what the crew called ORACLE's "temple."

He looked at the computer, and it looked back at him. "Like I told you before," he said conversationally, "for something that causes so much trouble, you're awful little and awful homely."

ORACLE did not answer, because it was not aware of him. ORACLE could read and do a number of more complex and subtle things, but it had no ears. It was indeed homely as a wall, which is what the front end mostly resembled, and the immense size of its translators, receptors, and the memory banks was not evident here. The temple—other people called it Suburbia Delphi—contained nothing but that animated wall, with its one everblooming amber "on" light (for the machine never ceased gulping its oceans of thought), a small desk and chair, and the mechanical typewriter with the modified Bodoni typeface which was used for the reader. The reader itself was nothing more than a clipboard (though with machined guides to hold the paper exactly in place) with a large push button above it, placed on a strut which extended from the front of the computer, and lined up with a lens set flush into it. It was an eerie experience to push that button after placing your query, for ORACLE scanned so quickly and "thought" so fast that it was rapping away on its writer before you could get your thumb on the button.

Usually.

Jones sat at the desk, switched on the light and took out the admiral's lighter. It was a square one, with two parts which telescoped apart to get to the tank. The tight little roll of paper was there, sure enough, with the typescript not seriously blurred by lighter fluid. He smoothed it out, retrieved the other two, unfolded them, stacked them all neatly; and then, feeling very like Christmas morning, said gaily to the unresponsive ORACLE:

"Now!"

Seconds later, he was breathing hard. A flood of profanity welled upward within him—and dissipated itself as totally inadequate.

Wagging his head helplessly, he brought the three papers to the typewriter and wrote them out on fresh paper, staying within the guidelines printed there, and adding the correct code symbols for the admiral, the colonel and the civilian. These symbols had been assigned by ORACLE itself, and were cross-checked against the personnel records it carried in its memory banks. It was the only way in which it was possible to ask a question including that towering monosyllable "I."

Jones clipped the first paper in place, held his breath and pushed the button.

There was a small flare of light from the hood surrounding the lens as the computer automatically brought the available light to optimum. A relay clicked softly as the writer was activated. A white tongue of paper protruded. Jones tore it off. It was blank.

He grunted, then replaced the paper with the second, then the third. It seemed that on one of them there was a half-second delay in the writer relay, but it was insignificant: the paper remained blank.

"Stick your tongue out at me, will you?" he muttered at the computer, which silently gazed back at him with its blank single eye. He went back to the typewriter and copied one of the questions, but with his own code identification symbols. It read:

THE ELIMINATION OF WHAT SINGLE MAN COULD RESULT IN MY PRESIDENCY?

He clipped the paper in place and pushed the button. The relay clicked, the writer rattled and the paper protruded. He tore it off. It read (complete with quotes):

"JOHN DOE"

"A wise guy," Jones growled. He returned to the typewriter and again copied one of the queries with his own code:

IF I ELIMINATE THE PRESIDENT, HOW CAN I ASSURE PERSONAL CONTROL?

Wryly, ORACLE answered:

DON'T EAT A BITE UNTIL YOUR EXECUTION.

It actually took Jones a couple of seconds to absorb that one, and then he uttered an almost hysterical bray of laughter.

The third question he asked, under his own identification, was:

CAN MY SUPPORT OF HENNY BRING PEACE?

The answer was a flat NO, and Jones did not laugh one bit. "And you don't find anything funny about it either," he congratulated the computer, and actually physically shuddered.

For Henny—the Honorable Oswaldus Deeming Henny—was an automatic nightmare to the likes of Jones. His weatherbeaten saint's face, his shoulder-length white hair (oh, what genius of a public-relations man put him onto that?), his diapason voice, but most of all, his "Plan for Peace"' had more than once brought Jones up out of a sound sleep into a cold sweat. Now, there was once a man who entranced a certain segment of the population with a slogan about the royalty in every man, but he could not have taken over the country, because a slogan is not a political philosophy. And there was another who was capable of turning vast numbers of his countrymen—for a while—against one another and toward him for protection: and he could not have taken over the country, because the manipulation of fear is not an economic philosophy. This Henny, however, was the man who had both, and more besides. His appearance alone gave him more non-thinking, vote-bearing adherents than Rudolph Valentino plus Albert Schweitzer. His advocacy of absolute isolation brought in the right wing, his demand for unilateral disarmament brought in the left wing, his credo that science could, with a third of munitions-size budgets, replace foreign trade through research, invention and ersatz, brought in the tech segment, and his dead certainty of lowering taxes had a thick hook in everyone else. Even the most battle-struck of the war-wanters found themselves shoulder to shoulder with the peace-at-any-price extremists, because of the high moral tone of his disarmament plan, which was to turn our weapons on ourselves and present any aggressor with nothing but slag and cinders—the ultimate deterrent. It was the most marvelous blend of big bang and beneficence, able to cut chance and challenge together with openhanded Gandhiism, with an answer for everyone and a better life for all.

"All of which," complained Jones to the featureless face of the computer, "doesn't help me find out why you wouldn't answer those three guys, though I must say, I'm glad you didn't." He went and got the desk chair and put it down front and center before the computer. He sat down and folded his arms and they stared silently at each other.

At length he said, "If you were a people instead of a thing, how would I handle you? A miserable, stubborn, intelligent snob of a people?"

Just how do I handle people? he wondered. I do—I know I do. I always seem to think of the right thing to say, or to ask. I've already asked ORACLE what's wrong, and ORACLE says nothing is wrong. The way any miserable, stubborn, intelligent snob would.

What I do, he told himself, is to empathize. Crawl into their skins, feel with their fingertips, look out through their eyes.

Look out through their eyes.

He rose and got the admiral's query—the one with the admiral's own identification on it—clipped it to the board, then hunkered down on the floor with his back to the computer and his head blocking the lens.

He was seeing exactly what the computer saw.

Clipboard. Query. The small bare chamber, the far wall. The . . .

He stopped breathing. After a long astonished moment he said, when he could say anything, and because it was all he could think of to say: "Well, I . . . be . . . damned . . ."

The admiral was the first in. Jones had had a busy time of it for the ninety minutes following his great discovery, and he was feeling a little out of breath, but at the same time a little louder and quicker than the other guy, as if he had walked into the reading room after a rub-down and a needle-shower.

"Sit down, Admiral."

"Jones, did you—"

"Please, sir—sit down."

"But surely—"

"I've got your answer, Admiral. But there's something we have to do first." He made waving gestures. "Bear with me."

He wouldn't have made it, thought Jones, except for the colonel's well-timed entrance. Boy oh boy, thought Jones, look at 'm, stiff as tongs. You come on the battlefield looking just like a target. On the other hand, that's how you made your combat reputation, isn't it? The colonel was two strides into the room before he saw the admiral. He stopped, began an about-face and said over his left epaulet, "I didn't think—"

"Sit down, Colonel," said Jones in a pretty fair imitation of the man's own brass gullet. It reached the officer's muscles before it reached his brain and he sat. He turned angrily on the admiral, who said instantly, "This wasn't my idea," in a completely insulting way.

Again the door opened and old living history walked in, his head a little to one side, his eyes ready to see and understand and his famous mouth to smile, but when he saw the tableau, the eyes frosted over and the mouth also said: "I didn't think—"

"Sit down, sir," said Jones, and began spieling as the civilian was about to refuse, and kept on spieling while he changed his mind, lowered himself guardedly onto the edge of a chair and perched his old bones on its front edge as if he intended not to stay.

"Gentlemen," Jones began, "I'm happy to tell you that I have succeeded in finding out why ORACLE was unable to perform for you—thanks to certain unexpected cooperation I received." Nice touch, Jones. Each one of 'em will think he turned the trick, single-handedly. But not for long. "Now I have a plane to catch, and you all have things to do, and I would appreciate it if you would hear me out with as little interruption as possible." Looking at these bright, eager, angry, sullen faces, Jones let himself realize for the first time why detectives in whodunits assemble all the suspects and make speeches. Why they *personally* do it—why the author has them do it. It's because it's fun.

"In this package"—he lifted from beside his desk a brown paper parcel a yard long and fifteen inches wide—"is the cause of all the trouble. My company was founded over a half century ago, and one of these has been an appurtenance of everyone of the company's operations, each of its major devices and installations, all of its larger utility equipment—cranes, trucks, bulldozers, everything. You'll find them in every company office and in most company cafeterias." He put the package down flat on his desk and fondled it while he talked. "Now, gentlemen. I'm not going to go into any part of the long argument about whether or not a computer can be conscious of what it's doing, because we haven't time and we're not here to discuss metaphysics. I will, however, remind you of a childhood chant. Remember the one that runs: 'For want of a nail the shoe was lost; for want of a shoe the horse was lost; for want of a horse the message was lost; for want of the message the battle was lost; for want of the battle the kingdom was lost—and all for the want of a horseshoe nail.'"

"Mr. Jones," said the admiral, "I—we—didn't come here to—"

"I just said that," Jones said smoothly, and went right on talking until the admiral just stopped trying. "This"—he rapped the package—"is ORACLE's horseshoe nail. If it's no ordinary nail, that's because ORACLE's no ordinary computer. It isn't designed to solve problems in their own context; there are other machines that do that. ORACLE solves problems the way an educated man solves them—by bringing everything he is and has to bear on them. Lacking this one part"—he thumped the package again—"it can then answer your questions, and it accordingly did." He smiled suddenly. "I don't think ORACLE was designed this way," he added musingly. "I think it . . . became . . . this way . . ." He shook himself. "Anyway, I have your answers."

Now he could afford to pause, because he had them. At that moment, the only way any of them could have been removed was by dissection and haulage.

Jones lined up his sights on the colonel and said, "In a way, your question was the most interesting, Colonel. To me professionally, I mean. It shows to what detail ORACLE can go in answering a wide theoretical question. One might even make a case for original creative thinking, though that's always arguable. Could a totally obedient robot think if you flatly ordered it to think? When does a perfect imitation of a thing become the thing itself?"

"You're not going to discuss my question here," said the colonel as a matter of absolute, incontrovertible fact.

"Yes I am," said Jones, and raised his voice. "You listen to me, before you stick that trigger finger of yours inside that tunic. Colonel. I'm in a corny mood right now and so I've done a corny thing. Two copies of a detailed report of this whole affair are now in the mail, and, I might add, in a mailbox outside this building. One goes to my boss, who is a very big wheel and a loyal friend, with as many contacts in business and government as there are company machines operating, and that puts him on the damn moon as well as all over the world. The other goes to someone else, and when you find out who that is it'll be too late, because in two hours he can reach every paper, every wire service, every newscasting organization on earth. Naturally, consistent with the corn, I've sent these out sealed with orders to open them if I don't phone by a certain time—and I assure you it won't be from here. In other words, you can't do anything to me and you'd better not delay me. *Sit down, Admiral,*" he roared.

"I'm certainly not going to sit here and—"

"I'm going to finish what I started out to do whether you're here or not." Jones waved at the other two. "They'll be here. You want that?"

The admiral sat down. The civilian said, in a tolling of mighty sorrow, "Mr. Jones, I had what seemed to be your faithful promise—"

"There were overriding considerations," said Jones. "You know what an overriding consideration is, don't you, sir?" and he held up the unmistakable ORACLE query form. The civilian subsided.

"Let him finish," gritted the colonel. "We can—well, let him finish."

Jones instantly, like ORACLE, translated: *We can take care of him later.* He said to the colonel, "Cheer up. You can always deny everything, like you said." He fanned through the papers before him and dealt out the colonel's query. He read it aloud:

"'IF I ELIMINATE THE PRESIDENT, HOW CAN I ASSURE PERSONAL CONTROL?'"

The colonel's face could have been shipped out, untreated, and installed on Mount Rushmore. The civilian gasped and put his knuckles in his mouth. The admiral's slitted eyes went round.

"The answer," said Jones, "makes that case for creative thinking I was talking about. ORACLE said: 'DETONATE ONE BOMB WITHIN UNDERGROUND H.Q. SPEND YOUR SUBSEQUENT TENURE LOOKING FOR OTHERS.'"

Jones put down the paper and spoke past the colonel to the other two. "Get the big picture, gentlemen? 'UNDERGROUND H.Q.' could only mean the centralized control for government in the mountains. Whether or not the President—or anyone else—was there at the time is beside the point. If not, he'd find another way easily enough. After that happened, our hero here would take the posture of the national savior, the only man competent to track down a second bomb, which could be anywhere. Imagine the fear, the witch-hunts, the cordons, the suspicion, the 'Emergency' and 'For the Duration' orders and regulations." Suddenly savage, Jones snarled, "I've got just one more thing to say about this warrior and his plans. All his own strength, and the entire muscle behind everything he plans for himself, derives from the finest *esprit de corps* the world has ever known. I told you I'm in a corny mood, so I'm going to say it just the way it strikes me. That kind of *esprit* is a bigger thing than obedience or devotion or even faith, it's a species of love. And there's not a hell of a lot of that to go around in this world. Butchering the President to make himself a little tin god is a minor crime compared to his willingness to take a quality like that and turn it into a perversion."

The civilian, as if unconsciously, hitched his chair a half inch away from the colonel. The admiral trained a firing-squad kind of look at him.

"Admiral," said Jones, and the man twitched, "I'd like to call your attention to the colonel's use of the word 'eliminate' in his query. You don't, you know, you just *don't* eliminate a live President." He let that sink in, and then said, "I mention it because you, too, used it, and it's a fair conjecture that it means the same thing. Listen: 'WHAT SINGLE MAN CAN I ELIMINATE TO BECOME PRESIDENT?'"

"There could hardly be any *one* man," said the civilian thoughtfully, gaining Jones' great respect for his composure. Jones said, "ORACLE thinks so. It wrote your name, sir."

Slowly the civilian turned to the admiral. "Why, you sleek old son of a bitch," he enunciated carefully, "I do believe you could have made it."

"Purely a hypothetical question," explained the admiral, but no one paid the least attention.

"As for you," said Jones, rather surprised that his voice expressed so much of the regret he felt, "I do believe that you asked your question with a genuine desire to see a world at peace before you passed on. But, sir—it's like you said when you walked in here just now—and the colonel said it, too: 'I didn't think . . .' You are sitting next to two certifiable first-degree murderers; no matter what their overriding considerations, that's what they are. But what you planned is infinitely worse."

He read, "'CAN MY SUPPORT OF HENNY BRING PEACE?' You'll be pleased to know—oh, you already know; you were just checking, right?—that the answer is Yes. Henny's position is such right now that your support would bring him in. But—you didn't *think*. That demagogue can't do what he wants to do without a species of thought-policing the like of which the ant-heap experts in China never even dreamed of. Unilateral disarmament and high morality scorched-earth! Why, as a nation we couldn't do that unless we meant it, and we couldn't mean it unless every man, woman and child thought alike—and with Henny running things, they would. Peace? Sure we'd have peace! I'd rather take on a Kodiak bear with boxing gloves than take my chances in that kind of a world. These guys," he said carelessly, "are prepared to murder one or two or a few thousand. You," said Jones, his voice suddenly shaking with scorn, "are prepared to murder every decent free thing this country ever stood for."

Jones rose. "I'm going now. All your answers are in the package there. Up to now it's been an integral part of ORACLE—it was placed exactly in line with the reader, and has therefore been a part of everything the machine has ever done. My recommendation is that you replace it, or ORACLE will be just another computer, answering questions in terms of themselves. I suggest that you make similar installations in your own environment . . . and quit asking questions that must be answered in terms of *your*selves. Questions which in the larger sense would be unthinkable."

The civilian rose, and did something that Jones would always remember as a decent thing. He put out his hand and said, "You are right. I needed this, and you've stopped me. What will stop *them?*"

Jones took the hand. "They're stopped. I know, because I asked ORACLE and ORACLE said this was the way to do it." He smiled briefly and went out. His last glimpse of the office was the rigid backs of the two officers, and the civilian behind his desk, slowly unwrapping the package. He walked down the endless Pentagon corridors, the skin between his shoulder blades tight all the way: ORACLE or no, there might be overriding considerations. But he made it, and got to the first outside phone booth still alive. Marvelously, wonderfully alive.

He heard Ann's voice and said, "It's a real wonderful world, you know that?"

"Jones, darling! . . . you certainly have changed your tune. Last time I talked to you it was a horrible place full of evil intentions and smelling like feet."

"I just found out for sure three lousy kinds of world it's not going to be," Jones said. Ann would not have been what she was to him if she had not been able to divine which questions not to ask. She said, "Well, good," and he said he was coming home.

"Oh, darling! You fix that gadget?"

"Nothing to it," Jones said. "I just took down the

THINK

sign."

She said, "I never know when you're kidding."

If All Men Were Brothers, Would You Let One Marry Your Sister?

The Sun went Nova in the Year 33 A.E. "A.E." means "After the Exodus." You might say the Exodus was a century and a half or so A.D. if "A.D." means "After the Drive." The Drive, to avoid technicalities, was a device somewhat simpler than Woman and considerably more complicated than sex, which caused its vessel to cease to exist *here* while simultaneously appearing *there,* bypassing the limitations imposed by the speed of light. One might compose a quite impressive account of astrogation involving the Drive, with all the details of orientation *here* and *there* and the somewhat philosophical difficulties of establishing the relationships between them, but this is not that kind of a science fiction story.

It suits our purposes rather to state that the Sun went Nova with plenty of warning, that the first fifty years A.D. were spent in improving the Drive and exploring with unmanned vehicles which located many planets suitable for human settlement, and that the next hundred years were spent in getting humanity ready to leave. Naturally there developed a number of ideological groups with a most interesting assortment of plans for one Perfect Culture or another, most of which were at bitter odds with all the rest. The Drive, however, had presented Earth with so copious a supply of new worlds, with insignificant subjective distances between them and the parent, that dissidents need not make much of their dissent, but need merely file for another world and they would get it. The comparisons between the various cultural theories are pretty fascinating, but this is not that kind of a science fiction story either. Not quite.

Anyway, what happened was that, with a margin of a little more than three decades, Terra depopulated itself by its many thousands of ships to its hundreds of worlds (leaving behind, of course, certain die-hards who died, of course, certainly) and the new worlds were established with varying degrees of bravery and a pretty wide representation across the success scale.

It happened, however (in ways much too recondite to be described in this kind of a science fiction story), that Drive Central on Earth, a computer central, was not only the sole means of keeping track of all the worlds; it was their only means of keeping track with one another; and when this installation added its bright brief speck to the ocean of Nova-glare, there simply was no way for all the worlds to find one another without the arduous process of unmanned Drive-ships and search. It took a long while for any of the new worlds to develop the necessary technology, and an even longer while for it to be productively operational, but at length, on a planet which called itself Terratu (the suffix meaning both "too" and "2") because it happened to be the third planet of a GO-type sun, there appeared something called the Archives, a sort of index and clearinghouse for all known inhabited worlds, which made this planet the communications central and general dispatcher for trade with them all and their trade with one another—a great convenience for everyone. A side result, of course, was the conviction on Terratu that, being a communications central, it was also central to the universe and therefore should control it, but then, that is the occupational hazard of all conscious entities.

We are now in a position to determine just what sort of a science fiction story this really is.

"Charli Bux," snapped Charli Bux, "to see the Archive Master."

"Certainly," said the pretty girl at the desk, in the cool tones reserved by pretty girls for use on hurried and indignant visitors who are clearly unaware, or uncaring, that the girl is pretty. "Have you an appointment?"

He seemed like such a nice young man in spite of his hurry and his indignation. The way, however, in which he concealed all his niceness by bringing his narrowed eyes finally to rest on her upturned face, and still showed no signs of appreciating her pretty-girlhood, made her quite as not-pretty as he was not-nice.

"Have you," he asked coldly, "an appointment book?"

She had no response to that, because she had such a book; it lay open in front of her. She put a golden and escaloped fingernail on his name therein inscribed, compared it and his face with negative enthusiasm, and ran the fingernail across the time noted. She glanced at the clockface set into her desk, passed her hand over a stud, and said, "A Mr. Charli, uh, Bux to see you, Archive Master."

"Send him in," said the stud.

"You may go in now."

"I know," he said shortly.

"I don't like you."

"What?" he said, but he was thinking about something else, and before she could repeat the remark he had disappeared through the inner door.

The Archive Master had been around long enough to expect courtesy, respect, and submission, to get these things, and to like them. Charli Bux slammed into the room, banged a folio down on the desk, sat down uninvited, leaned forward, and roared redly, "Goddamnit—"

The Archive Master was not surprised because he had been warned. He had planned exactly what he would do to handle this brash young man, but faced with the size of the Bux temper, he found his plans somewhat less useful than worthless. Now he was surprised, because a single glance at his gaping mouth and feebly fluttering hands—a gesture he thought he had lost and forgotten long ago—accomplished what no amount of planning could have done.

"Oh-h-h . . . bitchballs," growled Bux, his anger visibly deflating. "Buggerly bangin' bumpkin' *bitch*balls." He looked across at the old man's horrified eyebrows and grinned blindingly. "I guess it's not your fault." The grin disappeared. "But of all the hydrocephalous, drool-toothed, cretinoid runarounds I have ever seen, this was the stupidest. Do you know how many offices I've been into and out of with this"—he banged the heavy folio—"since I got back?"

The Archive Master did, but, "How many?" he asked.

"Too many, but only half as many as I went to before I went to

Vexvelt." With which he shut his lips with a snap and leaned forward again, beginning his bright penetrating gaze at the old man like twin lasers. The Archive Master found himself striving not to be the first to turn away, but the effort made him lean slowly back and back, until he brought up against his chair cushions with his chin up a little high. He began to feel a little ridiculous, as if he had been bamboozled into Indian wrestling with some stranger's valet.

It was Charli Bux who turned away first, but it was not the old man's victory, for the gaze came off his eyes as tangibly as a pressing palm might have come off his chest, and he literally slumped forward as the pressure came off. Yet if it was Charli Bux's victory, he seemed utterly unaware of it. "I think," he said after his long, concentrated pause, "that I'm going to tell you about that—about how I happened to get to Vexvelt. I wasn't going to—or at least, I was ready to tell you only as much as I thought you needed to know. But I remember what I had to go through to get there, and I know what I've been going through since I got back, and it looks like the same thing. Well, it's not going to be the same thing. Here and now, the runaround stops. What takes its place I don't know, but by all the horns of all the owls in Hell's northeast, I have been pushed around my last push. All right?"

If this was a plea for agreement, the Archive Master did not know what he would be agreeing to. He said diplomatically, "I think you'd better begin *somewhere.*" Then he added, not raising his voice, but with immense authority, "And quietly."

Charli Bux gave him a boom of laughter. "I never yet spent upwards of three minutes with anybody that they didn't shush me. Welcome to the Shush Charli Club, membership half the universe, potential membership, everybody else. And I'm sorry. I was born and brought up on Biluly where there's nothing but trade wind and split-rock ravines and surf, and the only way to whisper is to shout." He went on more quietly, "But what I'm talking about isn't that sort of shushing. I'm talking about a little thing here and a little thing there and adding them up and getting the idea that there's a planet nobody knows anything about."

"There are thousands—"

"I mean a planet nobody *wants* you to know anything about."

"I suppose you've heard of Magdilla."

"Yes, with fourteen kinds of hallucinogenic microspores spread through the atmosphere, and carcinogens in the water. Nobody wants to go there, nobody wants anybody to go—but nobody stops you from getting information about it. No, I mean a planet not ninety-nine percent Terran Optimum, or ninety-nine point ninety-nine, but so many nines that you might just as well shift your base reference and call Terra about ninety-seven percent in comparison."

"That would be a little like saying 'one hundred and two percent normal,'" said the Master smugly.

"If you like statistical scales better than the truth," Bux growled. "Air, water, climate, indigenous flora and fauna, and natural resources six nines or better, just as easy to get to as any place else—and nobody knows anything about it. Or if they do, they pretend they don't. And if you pin them down, they send you to another department."

The Archive Master spread his hands. "I would say the circumstances prove themselves. If there is no trade with this, uh, remarkable place, it indicates that whatever it has is just as easily secured through established routes."

Bux shouted, "In a pig's bloody and protruding—" and then checked himself and wagged his head ruefully. "Sorry again, Archive Master, but I just been too mad about this for too long. What you just said is like a couple troglodytes sitting around saying there's no use building a house because everybody's living in caves." Seeing the closed eyes, the long white fingers tender on the white temples, Bux said, "I said I was sorry I yelled like that."

"In every city," said the Archive Master patiently, "on every settled human planet in all the known universe, there is a free public clinic where stress reactions of any sort may be diagnosed, treated or prescribed for, speedily, effectively, and with dignity. I trust you will not regard it as an intrusion on your privacy if I make the admittedly unprofessional observation (you see, I do not pretend to be a therapist) that there are times when a citizen is not himself aware that he is under stress, even though it may be clearly, perhaps painfully obvious to others. It would not be a discourtesy, would it, or an unkindness, for some understanding stranger to suggest to such a citizen that—"

"What you're saying, all wrapped up in words, is I ought to have my head candled."

"By no means. I am not qualified. I did, however, think that a visit to a clinic—there's one just a step away from here—might make—ah—communications between us more possible. I would be glad to arrange another appointment for you, when you're feeling better. That is to say, when you are ... ah ..." He finished with a bleak smile and reached toward the calling stud.

Moving almost like a Drive-ship, Bux seemed to cease to exist on the visitor's chair and reappeared instantaneously at the side of the desk, a long thick arm extended and a meaty hand blocking the way to the stud. "Hear me out first," he said, softly. Really softly. It was a much more astonishing thing than if the Archive Master had trumpeted like an elephant. "Hear me out. Please."

The old man withdrew his hand, but folded it with the other and set the neat stack of fingers on the edge of the desk. It looked like stubbornness. "I have a limited amount of time, and your folio is very large."

"It's large because I'm a bird dog for detail—that's not a brag, it's a defect: sometimes I just don't know when to quit. I can make the point quick enough—all that material just supports it. Maybe a tenth as much would do, but you see, I—well, I give a damn. I really give a high, wide, heavy damn about this. Anyway—you just pushed the right button in Charli Bux. 'Make communication between us more possible.' Well, all right. I won't cuss, I won't holler, and I won't take long."

"Can you do all these things?"

"You're goddamn—whoa, Charli." He flashed the thirty-thousand-candlepower smile and then hung his head and took a deep breath. He looked up again and said quietly, "I certainly can, sir."

"Well, then." The Archive Master waved him back to the visitor's chair: Charli Bux, even a contrite Charli Bux, stood just too tall and too wide. But once seated, he sat silent for so long that the old man shifted impatiently. Charli Bux looked up alertly, and said, "Just getting it sorted out, sir. A good deal of it's going to sound as if you could diagnose me for a stun-shot and a good long stay at the funny farm, yeah, and that without being modest about your professional knowledge. I read a story once about a little girl was afraid of the dark because there was a little hairy purple man with poison fangs in the closet, and everybody kept telling her no, no, there's no such thing, be sensible, be brave. So they found her dead with like snakebite and her dog killed a little hairy purple man and so on. Now if I told you there was sort of a conspiracy to keep me from getting information about a planet, and I finally got mad enough to go there and see for myself, and 'They' did their best to stop me; 'They' won me a sweepstake prize trip to somewhere else that would use up my vacation time; when I turned that down, 'They' told me there was no Drive Guide orbiting the place, and it was too far to reach in real space (and that's a God, uh, doggone *lie,* sir!) and when I found a way to get there by hops, 'They' tangled up my credit records so I couldn't buy passage; why, then I can't say I'd blame you for peggin' me paranoid and doing me the kindness of getting me cured. Only thing was, these things did happen and they were not delusions, no matter what everybody plus two thirds of Charli Bux (by the time 'They' were done with me) believed. I had an ounce of evidence and I believed it. I had a ton of opinion saying otherwise. I tell you, sir, I *had* to go. I had to stand knee-deep in Vexvelt sweet grass with the cedar smell of a campfire and a warm wind in my face," *and my hands in the hands of a girl called Tyng, along with my heart and my hope and a dazzling wonder colored like sunrise and tasting like tears,* "before I finally let myself believe I'd been right all along, and there is a planet called Vexvelt and it does have all the things I knew it had," *and more, more, oh, more than I'll ever tell you about, old man.* He fell silent, his gaze averted and luminous.

"What started you on this—this quest?"

Charli Bux threw up his big head and looked far away and back at some all-but-forgotten detail. "Huh! I'd almost lost that in the clutter. Workin' for Interworld Bank & Trust, feeding a computer in the clearin'house. Not as dull as you might think. Happens I was a mineralogist for a spell, and the cargoes meant something to me besides a name, a quantity and a price. Huh!" came the surprised I've-found-it! little explosion. "I can tell you the very item. Feldspar. It's used in porcelain and glass, antique style. I got a sticky mind, I guess. Long as I'd been there, feldspar ground and bagged went for about twenty-five credits a ton at the docks. But here was one of our customers bringing it in for eight and a half F.O.B. I called the firm just to check; mind, I didn't care much, but a figure like that could color a statistical summary of imports and exports for years. The bookkeeper there ran a check and found it was so: eight and a half a ton, high-grade feldspar, ground and bagged. Some broker on Lethe: they hadn't been able to contact him again.

"It wasn't worth remembering until I bumped into another one. Niobium this time. Some call it columbium. Helps make steel stainless, among other things. I'd never seen a quotation for rod stock at less than a hundred and thirty-seven, but here was some—not much, mind you—at ninety credits *delivered.* And some sheets too, about thirty percent less than I'd ever seen it before, freight paid. I checked that one out too. It was correct. Well-smelted and pure, the man said. I forgot that one too, or I thought I had. Then there was that space-hand." *Moxie Magiddle—honest! That was his name. Squint-eyed little fellow with a great big laugh bulging the walls of the honky-tonk out at the spaceport. Drank only alcohol and never touched a needle. Told me the one about the fellow had a big golden screwhead in his belly button. Told me about times and places all over—full of yarns, a wonderful gift for yarning.* "Just mentioned in passing that Lethe was one place where the law was 'Have Fun' and nobody ever broke it. The whole place just one big transfer point and rest-and-rehab. A water world with only one speck of land in the tropics. Always warm, always easy. No industry, no agriculture, just—well, services. Thousands of men spent hundreds of thousands of credits, a few dozen pocketed millions. Everybody happy. I mentioned the feldspar, I guess just so I would sound as if I knew something about Lethe too." *And laid a big fat egg, too. Moxie looked at me as if he hadn't seen me before and didn't like what he saw. If it was a lie I was telling it was a stupid one. "Y'don't dig feldspar out of a swamp, fella. You puttin' me on, or you kiddin' y'rself?" And a perfectly good evening dried up and blew away.* "He said it couldn't possibly have come from Lethe—it's a water world. I guess I could have forgotten that too but for the coffee beans. Blue Mountain Coffee, it was called; the label claimed it descended in an unbroken line from Old Earth, on an island called Jamaica. It went on to say that it could be grown only in high cool land in the tropics—a real mountain plant. I liked it better than any coffee I ever tasted, but when I went back for more they were sold out. I got the manager to look in the records and traced it back to through the Terratu wholesaler to the broker and then to the importer—I mean, I *liked* that coffee!

"And according to him, it came from Lethe. High cool mountain land and all. The port at Lethe was tropical all right, but to be cool it would have to have mountains that were really mountains.

"The feldspar that did, but couldn't have, come from Lethe—and at those prices!—reminded me of the niobium, so I checked on that one too. Sure enough—Lethe again. You don't—you just do *not* get pure niobium rod and sheet without mines and smelters and mills.

"Next off-day I spent here at Archives and got the history of Lethe halfway back, I'll swear, to Yiem and the Big Bang. It was a swamp, it practically always has been a swamp, and something was wrong.

"Mind you, it was only a little something, and probably there was a good simple explanation. But little or not, it bothered me." *And besides, it had made me look like a horse's ass in front of a damn good man. Old man, if I told you how much time I hung around the spaceport looking for that bandy-legged little spacegnome, you'd stop me now and send for the stun-guns. Because I was obsessed—not a driving addiction kind of thing, but a very small deep splinter-in-the-toe kind of thing, that didn't hurt much but never failed to gig me every single step I took. And then one day—oh, months later—there was old Moxie Magiddle, and he took the splinter out. Hyuh! Ol' Moxie ... he didn't know me at first, he really didn't. Funny little guy, he has his brains rigged to forget anything he doesn't like—honestly forget it. That feldspar thing, when a fella he liked to drink with and yarn to showed up to be a know-it-all kind of liar, and to boot, too dumb to know he couldn't get away with it—well, that qualified Charli for zero minus the price of five man-hours of drinking. Then when I got him cornered—I all but wrestled him—and told about the feldspar and the niobium and now the mountain-grown coffee, all of it checked and cross-checked, billed, laded, shipped, insured—all of it absolutely Lethe and here's the goddamn proof, why, he began to laugh till he cried, a little at himself, a little at the situation, and a whole lot at me. Then we had a long night of it and I drank alcohol and you know what? I'll never in life find out how Moxie Magiddle can hold so much liquor. But he told me where those shipments came from, and gave me a vague idea why nobody wanted much to admit it. And the name they call all male Vexveltians.* "I mentioned it one day to a cargo handler," Bux told the Archive Master, "and he solved the mystery—the feldspar and niobium and coffee came from Vexvelt and had been transshipped at Lethe by local brokers, who, more often than not, get hold of some goods and turn them over to make a credit or so and dive back into the local forgetteries.

"But any planet which could make a profit on goods of this quality at such prices—transshipped, yet!—certainly could do much better direct. Also, niobium is Element 41, and Elkhart's Hypothesis has it that, on any planet where you find elements in Periods Three to Five, chances are you'll find 'em all. And that coffee! I used to lie awake at night wondering what they had on Vexvelt that they liked too much to ship, if they thought so little of their coffee that they'd let it out.

"Well, it was only natural that I came here to look up Vexvelt. Oh, it was listed at the bank, all right, but if there ever had been trade, it had been cleared out of the records long ago—we wipe the memory cells every fifty years on inactive items. I know at least that it's been wiped four times, but it could have been blank the last three.

"What do you think Archives has on Vexvelt?"

The Archive Master did not answer. He *knew* what Archives had on the subject of Vexvelt. He knew where it was, and where it was not. He knew how many times this stubborn young man had been back worrying at the mystery, how many ingenious approaches he had made to the problem, how little he had gotten, how much less he or anyone would get if they tried it today. He said nothing.

Charli Bux held up fingers to count. "Astronomical: no observations past two light-years. Nothing but sister planets (all dead) and satellites within two light-years. Cosmological: camera scan, if ever performed (but it must have been performed, or the damn thing wouldn't even be listed at all!), missing and never replaced. So there's no way of finding out where in real space it is, even. Geological: unreported. Anthropological: unreported. Then there's some stuff about local hydrogen tension and emission of the parent star, but they're not much help. And the summation in Trade Extrapolation: untraded. Reported undesirable. Not a word as to who reported it or why he said it.

"I tried to sidle into it by looking up manned exploration, but I could find only three astronauts' names in connection with Vexvelt. Troshan. He got into some sort of trouble when he came back and was executed—we used to kill certain criminals six, seven hundred years ago, did you know that?—but I don't know what for. Anyway, they apparently did it before he filed his report. Then Balrou. Oh—Balrou—he did report. I can tell you his whole report word for word: 'In view of conditions on Vexvelt contact is not recommended,' period. By the word, that must be the most expensive report ever filed."

It was, thought the Archive Master, but he did not say it aloud.

"And then somebody called Allman explored Vexvelt but—how did the report put it—'it was found on his return that Allman was suffering from confinement fatigue and his judgment was so severely impaired that his report is discounted.' Does that mean it was destroyed, Archive Master?"

Yes, thought the old man, but he said, "I can't say."

"So there you are," said Charli Bux. "If I wanted to present a classic case of what the old books called persecution mania, I'd just have to report things exactly as they happened. Did I have a right to suspect, even, that 'They' had picked me as the perfect target and set up those hints—low-cost feldspar, high-quality coffee—bait I couldn't miss and couldn't resist. Did I have the right to wonder if a living caricature with a comedy name—Moxie for-god's-sake Magiddle—was working for 'Them'? Then, what happened next, when I honestly and openly filed for Vexvelt as my next vacation destination? I was told there was no Drive Guide orbiting Vexvelt—it could only be reached through normal space. That happens to be a lie, but there's no way of checking on it here, or even on Lethe—Moxie never knew. Then I filed for Vexvelt via Lethe and a real-space transport, and was told that Lethe was not recommended as a tourist stop and there was no real-space service from there anyhow. So I filed for Botil, which I *know* is a tourist stop, and which I know has real-space shuttles and charter boats, and which the star charts call Kricker III while Lethe is Kricker V, and that's when I won the God—uh, the sweepstakes and a free trip to beautiful, beautiful Zeenip, paradise of paradises with two indoor 36-hole golf courses and free milk baths. I gave it to some charity or other, I said to save on taxes, and went for my tickets to Botil, the way I'd planned. I had it all to do over because they'd wiped the whole transaction when they learned about the sweepstakes. It seemed reasonable but it took so long to set it all up again that I missed the scheduled transport and lost a week of my vacation. Then when I went to pay for the trip my credit showed up zero, and it took another week to straighten out that regrettable error. By that time the tour service had only one full passage open, and in view of the fact that the entire tour would outlast my vacation by two weeks, they wiped the whole deal again—they were quite sure I wouldn't want it."

Charli Bux looked down at his hands and squeezed them. The Archives Office was filled with a crunching sound. Bux did not seem to notice it. "I guess anybody in his right mind would have got the message by then, but 'They' had underestimated me. Let me tell you exactly what I mean by that. I *don't* mean that I am a man of steel and by the Lord when my mind is made up it stays made. And I'm not making brags about the courage of my convictions. I had very little to be convinced about, except that there was a whole chain of coincidences which nobody wanted to explain even though the explanation was probably foolishly simple. And I never thought I was 'specially courageous.

"I was just—scared. Oh, I was frustrated and I was mad, but mostly I was scared. If somebody had come along with a reasonable explanation I'd've forgotten the whole thing. If someone had come back from Vexvelt and it was a poison planet (with a pocket of good feldspar and one clean mountainside) I'd have laughed it off. But the whole sequence—especially the last part, trying to book passage—really scared me. I reached the point where the only thing that would satisfy me as to my own sanity was to stand and walk on Vexvelt and *know* what it was. And that was the one thing I wasn't being allowed to do. So I couldn't get my solid proof and who's to say I wouldn't spend the next couple hundred years wondering when I'd get the next little splinter down deep in my toe? A man can suffer from a thing, Master, but then he can also suffer for fear of suffering from a thing. No, I was scared and I was going to stay scared until I cleared it up."

"My." The old man had been silent, listening, for so long that his voice was new and arresting. "It seems to me that there was a much simpler way out. Every city on every human world has free clinics where—"

"That's twice you've said that," crackled Charli Bux. "I have something to say about that, but not now. As to my going to a patch-up parlor, you know as well as I do that they don't change a thing. They just make you feel good about being the way you are."

"I fail to see the distinction, or what is wrong if there is one."

"I had a friend come up to me and tell me he was going to die of cancer in the next eight weeks, 'just in time,' he says, and whacks me so hard I see red spots, 'just in time for my funeral,' and off he goes down the street whooping like a loon."

"Would it be better if he huddled in his bed terrified and in pain?"

"I can't answer that kind of a question, but I do know what I saw is just as wrong. Anyway—there was something out there called Vexvelt, and it wouldn't make me feel any better to get rolled through a machine and come out thinking there isn't something called Vexvelt, and don't tell me that's not what those friendly helpful spot removers would do to me."

"But don't you see, you'd no longer be—"

"Call me throwback. Call me radical if you want to, or ignorant." Charli Bux's big voice was up again and he seemed angry enough not to care. "Ever hear that old line about 'in every fat man there's a thin man screaming to get out'? I just can't shake the idea that if something is *so,* you can prick, poke, and process me till I laugh and scratch and giggle and admit it ain't so after all, and even go out and make speeches and persuade other people, but away down deep there'll be a me with its mouth taped shut and its hands tied, bashing up against my guts trying to get out and say it is so after all. But what are we talking about me for? I came here to talk about Vexvelt."

"First tell me something—do you really think there was a 'They' who wanted to stop you?"

"*Hell* no. I think I'm up against some old-time stupidity that got itself established and habitual, and that's how come there's no information in the files. I don't think anybody today is all that stupid. I like to think people on this planet can look at the truth and not let it scare them. Even if it scares them they can think it through. As to that rat race with the vacation bookings, there seemed to be a good reason for each single thing that happened. Science and math have done a pretty good job of explaining the mechanics of 'the bad break' and 'a lucky run', but neither of them ever got repealed."

"So." The Master tented his fingers and looked down at the ridgepole. "And just how did you manage to get to Vexvelt after all?"

Bux flicked on his big bright grin. "I hear a lot about this free society, and how there's always someone out to trim an edge off here and a corner there. Maybe there's something in it, but so far they haven't got around to taking away a man's freedom to be a damn fool. Like, for example, his freedom to quit his job. I've said it was just a gruesome series of bad breaks, but bad breaks can be outwitted just as easily as a superpowerful masterminding 'They.' Seems to me most bad breaks happen inside a man's pattern. He gets out of phase with it and every step he takes is between the steppin' stones.

If he can't phase in, and if he tries to maintain his pace, why there's a whole row of stones ahead of him laid just exactly where each and every one of them will crack his shins. What he should do is head upstream. It might be unknown territory, and there might be dangers, but one thing for sure, there's a whole row of absolutely certain, absolutely planned agonies he is just not going to have to suffer."

"How did you get to Vexvelt?"

"I told you." He waited, then smiled. "I'll tell you again. I quit my job. 'They,' or the 'losing streak,' or the stinking lousy Fates, or whatever had a bead on me—they could do it to me because they always knew where I was, when I'd be the next place, and what I wanted. So they were always waiting for me. So I headed upstream. I waited till my vacation was over and left the house without any luggage and went to my local bank and had all my credits before I could have any tough breaks. Then I took a Drive jumper to Lunatu, booked passage on a semi-freight to Lethe."

"You booked passage, but you never boarded the ship."

"You know?"

"I was asking."

"Oh," said Charli Bux. "Yeah, I never set foot in that cozy little cabin. What I did, I slid down the cargo chute and got buried in Hold No. 2 with a ton of oats. I was in an interesting position, Archive Master. In a way I'm sorry nobody dug me out to ask questions. You're not supposed to stow away but the law says—and I know exactly what it says—that a stowaway is someone who rides a vessel without booking passage. But I did book passage, and paid in full, and all my papers were in order for where I was going. What made things a lot easier, too, was that where I was going nobody gives much of a damn about papers."

"And you felt you could get to Vexvelt through Lethe."

"I felt I had a chance, and I knew of no others. Cargoes from Vexvelt *had* been put down on Lethe, or I wouldn't have been sucked into this thing in the first place. I didn't know if the carrier was Vexveltian or a tramp (if it was a liner I'd have known it) or when one might come or if it would be headed for Vexvelt when it departed. All I knew was that Vexvelt had shipped here for sure, and this was the only place where maybe they might be back. Do you know what goes on at Lethe?"

"It has a reputation."

"Do you *know?*"

The old man showed a twinge of irritation. Along with respect and obedience, he had become accustomed to catechizing and not to being catechized. "Everyone knows about Lethe."

Bux shook his head. "They don't, Master."

The old man lifted his hands and put them down. "That kind of thing has its function. Humanity will always—"

"You approve of Lethe and what goes on there."

"One neither approves nor disapproves," said the Archive Master stiffly. "One knows about it, recognizes that for some segments of the species such an outlet is necessary, realizes that Lethe makes no pretensions to being anything but what it is, and then—one accepts, one goes on to other things. How did you get to Vexvelt?"

"On Lethe," said Charli Bux implacably, "you can do anything you want to or with any kind of human being, or any number of combination of them, as long as you can pay for it."

"I wouldn't doubt it. Now, the next leg of your trip—"

"There are men," said Charli Bux, suddenly and shockingly quiet, "who can be attracted by disease—by sores, Archive Master, by the stumps of amputated limbs. There are people on Lethe who cultivate diseases to attract such men. Crones, Master, with dirty leather skin, and boys and little—"

"You will cease this nauseating—"

"In just a minute. One of the unwritten and unbreakable traditions of Lethe is that, what anyone pays to do, anyone else may pay to watch."

"Are you finished?" It was not Bux who shouted now.

"You accept Lethe. You condone Lethe."

"I have not said I approve."

"You trade with Lethe."

"Well, of course we do. That doesn't mean we—"

"The third day—night, rather, that I was there," said Bux, overriding what was surely about to turn into a helpless sputter, "I turned off one of the main streets and into an alley. I knew this might be less than wise, but at the moment there was an ugly fight going on between me and the corner, and some wild gunning. I was going to turn right and go to the other avenue anyway, and I could see it clearly through the alley.

"I couldn't describe to you how fast this happened, or explain where they came from—eight of them, I think, in an alley, not quite dark and very narrow, when only a minute before I had been able to see it from end to end.

"I was grabbed from all sides all over my body, lifted, slammed down flat on my back and a bright light jammed in my face.

"A woman said, 'Aw shoot, 'tain't him.' A man's voice said to let me up. They picked me up. Somebody even started dusting me off. The woman who had held the light began to apologize. She did it quite nicely. She said they had heard that there was a—Master, I wonder if I should use the word."

"How necessary do you feel—"

"Oh, I guess I don't have to; you know it. On any ship, any construction gang, in any farm community—anywhere where men work or gather, it's the one verbal bullet which will and must start a fight. If it doesn't, the victim will never regain face. The woman used it as casually as she would have said Terran or Lethean. She said there was one right here in town and they meant to get him. I said, 'Well, how about that.' It's the one phrase I know that can be said any time about anything. Another woman said I was a good big one and how would I like to tromp him. One of the men said all right, but he called for the head. Another began to fight him about it, and a third woman took off her shoe and slapped both their faces with one swing of the muddy sole. She said for them to button it up or next time she'd use the heel. The other woman, with the light, giggled and said Helen was Veddy Good Indeed that way. She spoke in a beautifully cultivated accent. She said Helen could hook out an eye neat as a croupier. The third woman suddenly cried out, 'Dog turds!' She asked for some light. The dog turds were very dry. One of the men offered to wet them down. The women said no—they were her dog turds and she would do it herself. Then and there she squatted. She called for a light, said she couldn't see to aim. They turned the light on her. She was one of the most beautiful women I have ever seen. Is there something wrong, Master?"

"I would like you to tell me how you made contact with Vexvelt," said the old man a little breathlessly.

"But I am!" said Charli Bux. "One of the men pressed through, all grunting with eagerness, and began to mix the filth with his hands. And then, by a sort of sixth sense, the light was out and they were simply—*gone!* Disappeared. A hand came out of nowhere and pulled me back against a house wall. There wasn't a sound—not even breathing. And only then did the Vexveltian turn into the alley. How they knew he was coming is beyond me.

"The hand that had pulled me back belonged to the woman with the light, as I found out in a matter of seconds. I really didn't believe her hand meant to be where I found it. I took hold of it and held it, but she snatched it away and put it back. Then I felt the light bump my leg. And the man came along toward us. He was a big man, held himself straight, wore light-colored clothes, which I thought was more foolhardy than brave. He walked lightly and seemed to be looking everywhere—and still could not see us.

"If this all happened right this minute, after what I've learned about Vexvelt—about Lethe too—I wouldn't hesitate, I'd know exactly what to do. What you have to understand is that I didn't know anything at all at the time. Maybe it was the eight against one that annoyed me." He paused thoughtfully. "Maybe that coffee. What I'm trying to say is that I did the same thing then, in my ignorance, that I'd do now, knowing what I do.

"I snapped the flashlight out of the woman's hand and got about twenty feet away in two big bounds. I turned the light on and played it back where I'd come from. Two of the men had crawled up the sheer building face like insects and were ready to drop on the victim. The beautiful one was crouched on her toes and one hand; the other, full of filth, was ready to throw. She made an absolutely animal sound and slung her handful, quite uselessly. The others were flattened back against wall and fence, and in the light, for a long second, they flattened all the more, blinking. I said over my shoulder,

'Watch yourself, friend. You're the guest of honor, I think.'

"You know what he did? He laughed. I said. 'They won't get by me for a while. Take off.' 'What for?' says he, squeezing past me. 'There're only eight of them.' And he marches straight down on them.

"Something rolled under my foot and I picked it up—half a brick. What must have been the other half of it hit me right on the breastbone. It made me yelp, I couldn't help it. The tall man said to douse the light, I was a target. I did, and saw one of them in silhouette against the street at the far end, standing up from behind a big garbage can. He was holding a knife half as long as his forearm, and he rose up as the big man passed him. I let fly with the brick and got him right back of the head. The tall man never so much as turned when he heard him fall and the knife go skittering. He passed one of the human flies as if he had forgotten he was there, but he hadn't forgotten. He reached up and got both the ankles and swung the whole man screaming off the wall like a flail, wiping the second one off and tumbling the both of them on top of the rest of the gang.

"He stood there with the back of his hands on his hips for a bit, not even breathing hard, watching the crying, cursing mix-up all over the alley pavement. I came up beside him. One, two got to their feet and ran limping. One of the women began to scream—curses, I suppose, but you couldn't hear the words. I turned the light on her face and she shut right up.

"'You all right?' says the tall man.

"I told him, 'Caved in my chest is all, but that's all right, I can use it for a fruit bowl lying in bed.' He laughed and turned his back on the enemy and led me the way he had come. He said he was Vorhidin from Vexvelt. I told him who I was. I said I'd been looking for a Vexveltian, but before we could go on with that a black hole opened up to the left and somebody whispered, 'Quick, quick.' Vorhidin clapped a hand on my back and gave me a little shove. 'In you go, Charli Bux of Terratu.' And in we went, me stumbling all over my feet down some steps I didn't know were there, and then again because they weren't there. A big door boomed closed behind us. Dim yellow light came on. There was a little man with olive skin and a shiny, oily mustache. 'Vorhidin, for the love of God, I told you not to come into town, they'll kill you.' Vorhidin only said, 'This is Charli Bux, a friend.' The little man came forward anxiously and began to pat Vorhidin on the arms and ribs to see if he was all right.

"Vorhidin laughed and brushed him off. 'Poor Tretti! He's always afraid something is going to happen! Never mind me, you fusspot. See to Charli here. He took a shot in the bows that was meant for me.' The little one, Tretti, sort of squeaked and before I could stop him he had my shirt open and the light out of my hand switched on and trained on the bruise. 'Your next woman can admire a sunset,' says Vorhidin. Tretti's away and back before you can blink and sprays on something cool and good and most of the pain vanished.

"'What do you have for us?' and Tretti carries the light into another room. There's stacks of stuff, mostly manufactured goods, tools, and instruments. There was a big pile of trideo cartridges, mostly music and new plays, but a novel or so too. Most of the other stuff was one of a kind. Vorhidin picked up a forty-pound crate and spun it twice by diagonal corners till it stopped where he could read the label. 'Molar spectroscope. Most of this stuff we don't really need but we like to see what's being done, how it's designed. Sometimes ours are better, sometimes not. We like to see, that's all.' He set it down gently and reached into his pocket and palmed out a dozen or more stones that flashed till it hurt. One of them, a blue one, made its own light. He took Tretti's hand and pulled it to him and poured it full of stones. 'That enough for this load?' I couldn't help it—I glanced around the place and totted it up and made a stab estimate—a hundred each of everything in the place wouldn't be worth that one blue stone. Tretti was goggle-eyed. He couldn't speak. Vorhidin wagged his head and laughed and said, 'All right, then,' and reached into his pants pocket again and ladled out four or five more. I thought Tretti was going to cry. I was right. He cried.

"We had something to eat and I told Vorhidin how I happened to be here. He said he'd better take me along. I said where to? and he said Vexvelt. I began to laugh. I told him I was busting my brains trying to figure some way to make him say that, and he laughed too and said I'd found it, all right, twice over. 'Owe you a favor for that,' he says, dipping his head at the alley side of the room. 'Reason two, you wouldn't live out the night on Lethe if you stayed here.' I wanted to know why not, because from what I'd seen there were fights all the time, then you'd see the fighters an hour later drinking out of the same bowl. He says it's not the same thing. Nobody helps a Vexveltian but a Vexveltian. Help one, you are one, far as Lethe was concerned. So I wanted to know what Lethe had against Vexvelt, and he stopped chewing and looked at me a long time as if he didn't understand me. Then he said, 'You really don't know anything about us, do you?' I said, not much. 'Well,' he says, 'now there's three good reasons to bring you.'

"Tretti opened the double doors at the far end of the storeroom. There was a ground van in there, with another set of doors into the street. We loaded the crates into it and got in, Vorhidin at the tiller. Tretti climbed a ladder and put his eyes to something and spun a wheel. 'Periscope,' Vorhidin told me. 'Looks like a flagpole from outside.' Tretti waved his hand at us. He had tears running down his cheeks again. He hit a switch and the doors banged out of the way. The van screeched out of there as the doors bounced and started back. After that Vorhidin drove like a little old lady. One-way glass. Sometimes I wondered what those crowds of drunks and queers would do if they could see in. I asked him, 'What are they afraid of?' He didn't seem to understand the question. I said, 'Mostly when people gang up on somebody, it's because one way or another they're afraid. What do they think you're going to take away from them?'

"He laughed and said, 'Their decency.' And that's all the talk I got out of him all the way out to the spaceport.

"The Vexveltian ship was parked miles away from the terminal, way the hell and gone at the far end of the pavement near some trees. There was a fire going near it. As we got closer I saw it wasn't near it, it was spang under it. There was a big crowd, maybe half a hundred, mostly women, mostly drunk. They were dancing and staggering around and dragging wood up under the ship. The ship stood up on its tail like the old chemical rockets in the fairy stories. Vorhidin grunted. 'Idiots,' and moved something on his wrist. The rocket began to rumble and everybody ran screaming. Then there was a big explosion of steam and the wood went every which way, and for a while the pavement was full of people running and falling and screaming, and cycles and ground cars milling around and bumping each other. After a while it was quiet and we pulled up close. The high hatch opened on the ship and a boom and frame came out and lowered. Vorhidin hooked on, threw the latches on the van bed, beckoned me back there with him, reached forward and set the controls of the van, and touched the thing on his wrist. The whole van cargo section started up complete with us, and the van started up and began to roll home by itself.

"The only crew he carried," said Charli Bux carefully, "was a young radio officer." *With long shining black wings for hair and bits of sky in her tilted eyes, and a full and asking kind of mouth. She held Vorhidin very close, very long, laughing the message that there could be no words for this: he was safe. "Tamba, this is Charli. He's from Terratu and he fought for me." Then she came and held him too, and she kissed him; that incredible mouth, that warm strong soft mouth, why, he and she shared it for an hour; for an hour he felt her lips on his, even though she had kissed him for only a second. For an hour her lips could hardly be closer to her than they were to his own astonished flesh.* "The ship blasted off and headed sunward and to the celestial north. It held this course for two days. Lethe has two moons, the smaller one just a rock, an asteroid. Vorhidin matched velocities with it and hung half a kilo away, drifting in."

And the first night he had swung his bunk to the after bulkhead and had lain there heavily against the thrust of the jets, and against the thrust of his heart and his loins. Never had he seen such a woman—only just become woman, at that. So joyful, so utterly and so rightly herself. Half an hour after blastoff: "Clothes are in the way on ship, don't you think? But Vorhidin says I should ask you, because customs are different from one world to another, isn't that so?"

"Here we live by your customs, not mine," Charli had been able to say, and she had thanked him, thanked him! and touched the bit of glitter at her throat, and her garment fell away. "There's much more privacy this way," she said, leaving him. "A closed door means

more to the naked; it's closed for a real reason and not because one might be seen in one's petticoat." She took her garment into one of the state-rooms. Vorhidin's. Charli leaned weakly against the bulkhead and shut his eyes. Her nipples were like her mouth, full and asking. Vorhidin was casually naked, but Charli kept his clothes on, and the Vexveltians made no comment. The night was very long. For a while part of the weight on Charli turned to anger, which helped. Old bastard, silver-temples. Old enough to be her father. But that could not last, and he smiled at himself. He remembered the first time he had gone to a ski resort. There were all kinds of people there, young, old, wealthy, working, professionals; but there was a difference. The resort, because it was what it was, screened out the pasty-faced, the round-shouldered lungless sedentaries, the plumping sybarites. All about him had been clear eyes, straight backs, and skin with the cosmetics of frost and fun. Who walked idled not, but went somewhere. Who sat lay back joyfully in well-earned weariness. And this was the aura of Vorhidin—not a matter of carriage and clean color and clear eyes, though he certainly had all these, but the same qualities down to the bone and radiating from the mind. A difficult thing to express and a pleasure to be with. Early on the second day Vorhidin had leaned close when they were alone in the control room and asked him if he would like to sleep with Tamba tonight. Charli gasped as if he had been clapped on the navel with a handful of crushed ice. He also blushed, saying, "If she, if she—" wildly wondering how to ask her. He need not have wondered, for "He'd love to, honey," Vorhidin bellowed. Tamba popped her face into the corridor and smiled at Charli. "Thank you so much," she said. And then (after the long night) it was going to be the longest day he had ever lived through, but she let it happen within the hour instead, sweetly, strongly, unhurried. Afterward he lay looking at her with such total and long-lasting astonishment that she laughed at him. She flooded his face with her black hair and then with her kisses and then all of him with her supple strength; this time she was fierce and most demanding until with a shout he toppled from the very peak of joy straight and instantly down into the most total slumber he had ever known. In perhaps twenty minutes he opened his eyes and found his gaze plunged deep in a blue glory, her eyes so close their lashes meshed. Later, talking to her in the wardroom, holding both her hands, he turned to find Vorhidin standing in the doorway. He was on them in one long stride, and flung an arm around each. Nothing was said. What could be said?

"I talked a lot with Vorhidin," Charli Bux said to the Archive Master. "I never met a man more sure of himself, what he wanted, what he liked, what he believed. The very first thing he said when I brought up the matter of trade was 'Why?' In all my waking life I never thought to ask that about trade. All I ever did, all anyone does, is to trade where he can and try to make it more. 'Why?' he wanted to know. I thought of the gemstones going for that production-line junk in the hold, and pure niobium at manganese prices. One trader would call that ignorance, another would call it good business and get all he could—glass beads for ivory. But cultures have been known to trade like that for religious or ethical reasons—always give more than you get in the other fellow's coin. Or maybe they were just—*rich*. Maybe there was so much Vexvelt that the only thing they could use was—well, like he said: manufactures, so they could look at the design 'sometimes better than ours, sometimes not.' So I asked him.

"He gave me a long look that was, at four feet, exactly like" *drowning in the impossibly blue lakes of Tamba's eyes, but watch yourself, don't think about that when you talk to this old man* "holding still for an X-ray continuity. Finally he said, 'Yes, I suppose we're rich. There's not much we need.'

"I told him, all the same, he could get a lot higher prices for the little he did trade. He just laughed a little and shook his head. 'You have to pay for what you get or it's no good. If you "Trade well," as you call it, you finish with more than you started with; you didn't pay. That's as unnatural as energy levels going from lesser to greater, it's contrary to ecology and entropy.' Then he said, 'You don't understand that.' I didn't and I don't."

"Go on."

"They have their own Drive cradle back of Lethe's moon, and their own Guide orbiting Vexvelt. I told you—all the while I thought the planet was near Lethe; well, it isn't."

"Now, that I do *not* understand. Cradles and guides are public utilities. Two days, you say it took. Why didn't he use the one at the Lethe port?"

"I can't say, sir. Uh—"

"Well?"

"I was just thinking about that drunken mob building a fire under the ship."

"Ah yes. Perhaps the moon cradle is a wise precaution after all. I have always known, and you make it eminently clear, that these people are not popular. All right—you made a Drive jump."

"We made a Drive jump." Charli fell silent for a moment, reliving that breathless second of revelation as black, talcdusted space and a lump moonlet winked away to be replaced by the great arch of a purple-haloed horizon, marbled green and gold and silver and polished blue, with a chromium glare coming from the sea on the planet's shoulder. "A tug was standing by and we got down without trouble." The spaceport was tiny compared even with Lethe—eight or ten docks, with the warehouse area under them and passenger and staff areas surrounding them under a deck. "There were no formalities—I suppose there's not enough space travel to merit them."

"Certainly no strangers, at any rate," said the old man smugly.

"We disembarked right on the deck and walked away." *Tamba had gone out first. It was sunny, with a warm wind, and if there was any significant difference between this gravity and that of Terratu, Charli's legs could not detect it. In the air, however, the difference was profound. Never before had he known air so clear, so winy, so clean—not unless it was bitter cold, and this was warm. Tamba stood by the silent, swiftly moving "up" ramp, looking out across the foothills to the most magnificent mountain range he had ever seen, for they had everything a picture-book mountain should have—smooth vivid high-range, shaggy forest, dramatic gray, brown, and ocher rock cliff, and a starched white cloth of snowcap tumbled on the peaks to dry in the sun. Behind them was a wide plain with a river for one margin and foothills for the other, and then the sea, with a wide golden beach curving a loving arm around the ocean's green shoulder. As he approached the pensive girl the warm wind curled and laughed down on them, and her short robe streamed from her shoulders like smoke, and fell about her again. It stopped his pace and his breath and his heart for a beat, it was so lovely a sight. And coming up beside her, watching the people below, the people rising on one ramp and sliding down the other, he realized that in this place clothing had but two conventions—ease and beauty. Man, woman and child, they wore what they chose, ribbon or robe, clogs, coronets, cummerbunds or kilts, or a ring, or a snood, or nothing at all. He remembered a wonderful line he had read by a pre-Nova sage called Rudofsky, and murmured it:* Modesty is not so simple a virtue as honesty. *She turned and smiled at him; she thought it was his line. He smiled back and let her think so. "You don't mind waiting a bit? My father will be along in a moment and then we'll go. You're to stay with us. Is that all right?"*

Did he mind. Would he wait, bracketed by the thundering colors of that mountain, the adagio of the sea. Is that all right.

There was nothing, no way, no word to express his response but to raise his tense fists as high as he could and shout as loud as he could and then turn it into laughter and to tears.

Vorhidin, having checked out his manifests, joined them before Charli was finished. He had locked gazes with the girl, who smiled up at him and held his forearm in both her hands, stroking and he laughed and laughed. "He drank too much Vexvelt all at once," she said to Vorhidin. Vorhidin put a big warm hand on Charli's shoulder and laughed with him until he was done. When he had his breath again, and the water-lenses out of his eyes, Tamba said, "That's where we're going."

"Where?"

She pointed, very carefully. Three slender dark trees like poplars came beseeching out of a glad tumble of luminous light willow-green. "Those three trees."

"I can't see a house ..."

Vorhidin and Tamba laughed together: this pleased them. "Come."

"We were going to wait for—"

"No need to wait any longer. Come."

Charli said, "The house was only a short walk from the port, but you couldn't see the one from the other. A big house, too, trees all around it and even growing up through it. I stayed with the family and worked." He slapped the heavy folio. "All this. I got all the help I needed."

"*Did* you indeed." The Archive Master seemed more interested in this than in anything else he had heard so far. Or perhaps it was a different kind of interest. "Helped you, did they? Would you say they're anxious to trade?"

The answer to this was clearly an important one. "All I can say," Charli Bux responded carefully, "is that I asked for this information—a catalogue of the trade resources of Vexvelt, and estimates of F.O.B. prices. None of them are very far off a practical, workable arrangement, and every single one undercuts the competition. There are a number of reasons. First of all, of course, is the resources themselves—almost right across the board, unbelievably rich. Then they have mining methods like nothing you've ever dreamed of, and harvesting, and preserving—there's no end to it. At first blush it looks like a pastoral planet—well, it's not. It's a natural treasure house that has been organized and worked and planned and understood like no other planet in the known universe. Those people have never had a war, they've never had to change their original cultural plan; it works, Master, it *works*. And it has produced a sane healthy people which, when it goes about a job, goes about it single-mindedly and with . . . well, it might sound like an odd term to use, but it's the only one that fits: with joy . . . I can see you don't want to hear this."

The old man opened his eyes and looked directly at the visitor. At Bux's cascade of language he had averted his face, closed his eyes, curled his lip, let his hands stray over his temples and near his ears, as if it was taking a supreme effort to keep from clapping the palms over them.

"All I can hear is that a world which has been set aside by the whole species, and which has kept itself aloof, is using you to promote a contact which nobody wants. Do they want it? They won't get it, of course, but have they any idea of what their world would be like if this"—he waved at the folio—"is all true? How do they think they could control the exploiters? Have they got something special in defenses as well as all this other?"

"I really don't know."

"I know!" The old man was angrier than Bux had yet seen him. "What they are is their defense! No one will *ever* go near them, not *ever*. Not if they strip their whole planet of everything it has, and refine and process the lot, and haul it to their spaceport at their own expense, and give it away free."

"Not even if they can cure cancer?"

"Almost all cancer is curable."

"They can cure *all* cancer."

"New methods are discovered every—"

"They've had the methods for I don't know how many years. Centuries. *They have no cancer.*"

"Do you know what this cure is?"

"No, I don't. But it wouldn't take a clinical team a week to find out."

"The incurable cancers are not subject to clinical analysis. They are all deemed psychosomatic."

"I know. That is exactly what the clinical team would find out."

There was a long, pulsing silence. "You have not been completely frank with me, young man."

"That's right, sir."

Another silence. "The implication is that they are sane and cancer-free because of the kind of culture they have set up."

This time Bux did not respond, but let the old man's words hang there to be reheard, reread. At last the Archive Master spoke again in a near whisper, shaking and furious. "Abomination! Abomination!" Spittle appeared on his chin: he seemed not to know. "I would—rather—die—eaten alive—with cancer—and raving *mad* than live with such sanity as that."

"Perhaps others would disagree."

"No one would disagree! Try it? Try it! They'll tear you to pieces! That's what they did to Allman. That's what they did to Balrou! We killed Troshan ourselves—he was the first and we didn't know then that the mob would do it for us. That was a thousand years ago, you understand that? And a thousand years from now the mob will still do it for us! And that—that *filth* will go to the locked files with the others, and someday another fool with too much curiosity and not enough decency and his mind rotten with perversion will sit here with another Archive Master, who will send him out as I'm sending you out, to shut his mouth and save his life or open it and be torn to pieces. Get *out!* Get *out!* Get *out!*" His voice had risen to a shriek and then a sort of keening, and had rasped itself against itself until it was a painful forced whisper and then nothing at all: the old eyes glared and the chin was wet.

Charli Bux rose slowly. He was white with shock. He said quietly, "Vorhidin tried to tell me, and I wouldn't believe it. I couldn't believe it. I said to him, 'I know more about greed that you do; they will not be able to resist those prices.' I said, I know more about fear than you do; they will not be able to stand against the final cancer cure.' Vorhidin laughed at me and gave me all the help I needed.

"I started to tell him once that I knew more about the sanity that lives in all of us, and very much in some of us, and that it could prevail. But I knew while I was talking that I was wrong about that. Now I know that I was wrong in everything, even the greed, even the fear, and he was right. And he said Vexvelt has the most powerful and the least expensive defense ever devised—sanity. He was right."

Charli Bux realized then that the old man, madly locking gazes with him as he spoke, had in some way, inside his head, turned off his ears. He sat there with his old head cocked to one side, panting like a foundered dog in a dust bowl, until at last he thought he could shout again. He could not. He could only rasp, he could only whisper-squeak, "Get out! Get out!"

Charli Bux got out. He left the folio where it was; it, like Vexvelt, defended itself by being immiscible—in the language of chemistry, by being noble.

It was not Tamba after all, but Tyng who captured Charli's heart.

When they got to the beautiful house, so close to everything and yet so private, so secluded, he met the family. Breerho's radiant—almost heat-radiant—shining red hair, and Tyng's, showed them to be mother and daughter. Vorhid and Stren were the sons, one a child, the other in his mid-teens, were straight-backed, wide-shouldered like their father, and by the wonderful cut and tilt of their architectured eyes, were brothers to Tyng, and to Tamba.

There were two other youngsters, a lovely twelve-year-old girl called Fleet, who was singing when they came in, and for whose song they stopped and postponed the introductions, and a sturdy tumblebug of a boy they called Handr, possibly the happiest human being any of them would ever see. In time Charli met the parents of these two, and black-haired Tamba seemed much more kin to the mother than to flame-haired Breerho.

It was at first a cascade of names and faces, captured only partially, kaleidoscoping about in his head as they all did in the room, and making a shyness in him. But there was more love in the room than ever the peaks of his mind and heart had known before, and more care and caring.

Before the afternoon and evening were over, he was familiar and accepted and enchanted. And because Tamba had touched his heart and astonished his body, all his feelings rose within him and narrowed and aimed themselves on her, hot and breathless, and indeed she seemed to delight in him and kept close to him the whole of the time. But when the little ones went off yawning, and then others, and they were almost alone, he asked her, he begged her to come to his bed. She was kind as could be, and loving, but also completely firm in her refusal. "But, darling, I just can't now. I can't. I've been away to Lethe and now I'm back and I *promised.*"

"Promised who?"

"Stren."

"But I thought . . ." He thought far too many things to sort out or even to isolate one from another. Well, maybe he hadn't understood the relationships here—after all, there were four adults and six children and he'd get it straight by tomorrow who was who, because otherwise she—oh. "You mean you promised Stren you wouldn't sleep with me."

"No, my silly old dear. I'll sleep with Stren tonight. Please, darling, don't be upset. There'll be other times. Tomorrow. Tomorrow morning?" She laughed and took his cheeks in her two hands and shook his whole head as if she could make the frown drop off. "Tomorrow morning *very* early?"

"I don't mean to be like this my very first night here. I'm sorry, I guess there's a lot I don't understand," he mumbled in his misery. And then anguish skyrocketed within him and he no longer cared about host and guest and new customs and all the rest of it. "I love you," he cried, "don't you know that?"

"Of course, of course I do. And I love you, and we will love one another for a long, long time. Didn't you think I knew that?" Her puzzlement was so genuine that even through pain-haze he could see it. He said, as close to tears as he felt a grown man should ever get, that he just guessed he didn't understand.

"You will, beloved, you will. We'll talk about it until you do, no matter how long it takes." Then she added, with absolutely guileless cruelty, "Starting tomorrow. But now I have to go, Stren's waiting. Good night, true love," and she kissed the top of his averted head and sprinted away lightly on bare tiptoe.

She had reached something in him that made it impossible for him to be angry at her. He could only hurt. He had not known until these past two days that he could feel so much or bear so much pain. He buried his face in the cushions of the long couch in the—living room?—anyway, the place where indoors and outdoors were as tangled as his heart, but more harmoniously—and gave himself up to sodden hurt.

In time, someone knelt beside him and touched him lightly on the neck. He twisted his head enough to be able to see. It was Tyng, her hair all but luminous in the dimness, and her face, what he could see of it, nothing but compassion. She said, "Would you like me to stay with you instead?" and with the absolute honesty of the stricken, he cried, "There couldn't be anyone else instead!"

Her sorrow, its genuineness, was unmistakable. She told him of it, touched him once more, and slipped away. Sometime during the night he twisted himself awake enough to find the room they had given him, and found surcease in utter black exhaustion.

Awake in daylight, he sought his other surcease, which was work, and began his catalogue of resources. Everyone tried at one time or another to communicate with him, but unless it was work he shut it off (except, of course, for the irresistible Handr, who became his fast and lifelong friend). He found Tyng near him more and more frequently, and usefully so; he had not become so surly that he would refuse a stylus or reference book (opened at the right place) when it was placed in his hand exactly at the moment he needed it. Tyng was with him for many hours, alert but absolutely silent, before he unbent enough to ask her for this or that bit of information, or wondered about weights and measures and man-hour calculations done in the Vexveltian way. If she did not know, she found out with a minimum of delay and absolute clarity. She knew, however, a very great deal more than he had suspected. So the time came when he was chattering like a macaw, eagerly planning the next day's work with her.

He never spoke to Tamba. He did not mean to hurt her, but he could sense her eagerness to respond to him and he could not bear it. She, out of consideration, just stopped trying.

One particularly knotty statistical sequence kept him going for two days and two nights without stopping. Tyng kept up with him all the way without complaint until, in the wee small hours of the third morning, she rolled up her eyes and collapsed. He staggered up on legs gone asleep with too much sitting, and shook the statistics out of his eyes to settle her on the thick fur rug, straighten the twisted knee. In what little light spilled from his abandoned hooded lamp, she was exquisite, especially because of his previous knowledge that she was exquisite in the most brilliant of glares. The shadows added something to the alabaster, and her unconscious pale lips were no longer darker than her face, and she seemed strangely statuesque and non-living. She was wearing a Cretan sort of dress, a tight stomacher holding the bare breasts cupped and supporting a diaphanous skirt. Troubled that the stomacher might impede her breathing, he unhooked it and put it back. The flesh of her midriff where it had been was, to the finger if not to the eye, pinched and ridged. He kneaded it gently and pursued indefinable thoughts through the haze of fatigue: pyrophyllite, Lethe, brother, recoverable vanadium salts, Vorhidin, precipitate, Tyng's watching me. Tyng in the almost dark was watching him. He took his eyes from her and looked down her body to his hand. It had stopped moving some vague time ago, slipped into slumber of its own accord. Were her eyes open now or closed? He leaned forward to see and over-balanced. They fell asleep with their lips touching, not yet having kissed at all.

The pre-Nova ancient Plato tells of the earliest human, a quadruped with two sexes. And one terrible night in a storm engendered by the forces of evil, all the humans were torn in two; and ever since, each has sought the other half of itself. Any two of opposite sexes can make something, but it is usually incomplete in some way. But when one part finds its true other half, no power on earth can keep them apart, nor drive them apart once they join. This happened that night, beginning at some moment so deep in sleep that neither could ever remember it. What happened to each was all the way into new places where nothing had ever been before, and it was forever. The essence of such a thing is acceptance, and lest he be judged, Charli Bux ceased to judge quite so much and began to learn something of the ways of life around him. Life around him certainly concealed very little. The children slept where they chose. Their sexual play was certainly no more enthusiastic or more frequent than any other kind of play—and no more concealed. There was very much less talk about sex than he had ever encountered in any group of any age. He kept on working hard, but no longer to conceal facts from himself. He saw a good many things he had not permitted himself to see before, and found to his surprise that they were not, after all, the end of the world.

He had one more very, very bad time coming to him. He sometimes slept in Tyng's room, she sometimes in his. Early one morning he awoke alone, recalling some elusive part of the work, and got up and padded down to her room. He realized when it was too late to ignore it what the soft singing sound meant; it was very much later that he was able to realize his fury at the discovery that this special song was not his alone to evoke. He was in her room before he could stop himself, and out again, shaking and blind.

He was sitting on the wet earth in the green hollow under a willow when Vorhidin found him. (He never knew how Vorhidin had accomplished this, nor for that matter how he had come there himself.) He was staring straight ahead and had been doing so for so long that his eyeballs were dry and the agony was enjoyable. He had forced his fingers so hard down into the ground that they were buried to the wrists. Three nails were bent and broken over backwards and he was still pushing.

Vorhidin did not speak at all at first, but merely sat down beside him. He waited what he felt was long enough and then softly called the young man's name. Charli did not move. Vorhidin then put a hand on his shoulder and the result was extraordinary. Charli Bux moved nothing visibly but the cords of his throat and his jaw, but at the first touch of the Vexveltian's hand he threw up. It was what is called clinically "projectile" vomiting. Soaked and spattered from hips to feet, dry-eyed and staring, Charli sat still. Vorhidin, who understood what had happened and may even have expected it, also remained just as he was, a hand on the young man's shoulder. "Say the words!" he snapped.

Charli Bux swiveled his head to look at the big man. He screwed up his eyes and blinked them, and blinked again. He spat sour out of his mouth, and his lips twisted and trembled. "Say the words," said Vorhidin quietly but forcefully, because he knew Charli could not contain them but had vomited rather than enunciate them. "Say the words."

"Y-y—" Charli had to spit again. "You," he croaked. "You—her *father!*" he screamed, and in a split second he became a dervish, a windmill, a double flail, a howling wolverine. The loamy hands, blood-muddy, so lacked control from the excess of fury that they never became fists. Vorhidin crouched where he was and took it all. He did not attempt to defend himself beyond an occasional small accurate movement of the head, to protect his eyes. He could heal from almost anything the blows might do, but unless the blows were spent, Charli Bux might never heal at all. It went on for a long time because something in Charli would not show, probably would not even feel, fatigue. When the last of the resources was gone, the collapse was sudden and total. Vorhidin knelt grunting, got painfully to his feet, bent dripping blood over the unconscious Terran, lifted him in his arms, and carried him gently into the house.

Vorhidin explained it all, in time. It took a great deal of time, because Charli could accept nothing at all from anyone at first, and then nothing from Vorhidin, and after that, only small doses. Summarized from half a hundred conversations, this is the gist:

"Some unknown ancient once wrote," said Vorhidin, "'Tain't what you don't know that hurts you; it's what you do know that ain't so.' Answer me some questions. Don't stop to think. (Now that's silly. Nobody off Vexvelt ever stops to think about incest. They'll say a lot, mind you, and fast, but they don't think.) I'll ask, you answer. How many bisexual species—birds, beasts, fish, and insects included—how many show any sign of the incest taboo?"

"I really couldn't say. I don't recall reading about it, but then, who'd write such a thing? I'd say—quite a few. It would be only natural."

"Wrong. Wrong twice, as a matter of fact. *Homo sapiens* has the patent, Charli—all over the wall-to-wall universe, only mankind. Wrong the second: it would *not* be natural. It never was, it isn't, and it never will be natural."

"Matter of terms, isn't it? I'd call it natural. I mean, it comes naturally. It doesn't have to be learned."

"Wrong. It does have to be learned. I can document that, but that'll wait—you can go through the library later. Accept the point for the argument."

"For the argument, then."

"Thanks. What percentage of people do you think have sexual feelings about their siblings—brothers and sisters?"

"What age are you talking about?"

"Doesn't matter."

"Sexual feelings don't begin until a certain age, do they?"

"Don't they? What would you say the age is, on the average?"

"Oh—depends on the indi—but you did say 'average,' didn't you? Let's put it around eight. Nine maybe."

"Wrong. Wait till you have some of your own, you'll find out. I'd put it at two or three minutes. I'd be willing to bet it existed a whole lot before that, too. By some weeks."

"I don't believe it!"

"I know you don't," said Vorhidin. "'Strue all the same. What about the parent of the opposite sex?"

"Now, that would have to wait for a stage of consciousness capable of knowing the difference."

"Wel-l-l—you're not as wrong as usual," he said, but he said it kindly. "But you'd be amazed at how early that can be. They can smell the difference long before they can see it. A few days, a week."

"I never knew."

"I don't doubt that a bit. Now, let's forget everything you've seen here. Let's pretend you're back on Lethe and I ask you, what would be the effects on a culture if each individual had immediate and welcome access to all the others?"

"*Sexual* access?" Charlie made a laugh, a nervous sort of sound. "Sexual excess, I'd call it."

"There's no such thing," said the big man flatly. "Depending on who you are and what sex, you can do it only until you can't do it any more, or you can keep on until finally nothing happens. One man might get along beautifully with some mild kind of sexual relief twice a month or less. Another might normally look for it eight, nine times a day."

"I'd hardly call that normal."

"I would. Unusual it might be, but it's one hundred percent normal for the guy who has it, long as it isn't pathological. By which I mean, capacity is capacity, by the cupful, by the horsepower, by the flight ceiling. Man or machine, you do no harm by operating within the parameters of design. What does do harm—lots of it, and some of the worst kind—is guilt and a sense of sin, where the sin turns out to be some sort of natural appetite. I've read case histories of boys who have suicided because of a nocturnal emission, or because they yielded to the temptation to masturbate after five, six weeks of self-denial—a denial, of course, that all by itself makes them preoccupied, absolutely obsessed by something that should have no more importance than clearing the throat. (I wish I could say that this kind of horror story lives only in the ancient scripts, but on many a world right this minute, it still goes on.)

"This guilt and sin thing is easier for some people to understand if you take it outside the area of sex. There are some religious orthodoxies which require a very specific diet, and the absolute exclusion of certain items. Given enough indoctrination for long enough, you can keep a man eating only (we'll say) 'flim' while 'flam' is forbidden. He'll get along on thin moldy flim and live half starved in a whole warehouse full of nice fresh flam. You can make him ill—even kill him, if you have the knack—just by convincing him that the flim he just ate was really flam in disguise. Or you can drive him psychotic by slipping him suggestions until he acquires a real taste for flam and gets a supply and hides it and nibbles at it secretly every time he fights temptation and loses.

"So imagine the power of guilt when it isn't a flim-and-flam kind of manufactured orthodoxy you're violating, but a deep pressure down in the cells somewhere. It's as mad, and as dangerous, as grafting in an ethical-guilt structure which forbids or inhibits yielding to the need for the B-vitamin complex or potassium."

"Oh, but," Charli interrupted, "now you're talking about vital necessities—survival factors."

"I sure as hell am," said Vorhidin in Charli's own idiom, and grinned a swift and hilarious—and very accurate—imitation of Charli's flash-beacon smile. "Now it's time to trot out some of the things I mentioned before, things that can hurt you much more than ignorance—the things you know that ain't so." He laughed suddenly. "This is kind of fun, you know? I've been to a lot of worlds, and some are miles and years different from others in a thousand ways: but this thing I'm about to demonstrate, this particular shut-the-eyes, shut-the-brains conversation you can get anywhere you go. Are you ready? Tell me, then: what's wrong with incest? I take it back—you know me. Don't tell me. Tell some stranger, some fume-sniffer or alcohol addict in a spaceport bar." He put out both hands, the fingers so shaped that one could all but see light glisten from the imaginary glass he held. He said in a slurred voice, "Shay, shtranger, whut's a-wrong wit' in-shest, hm?" He closed one eye and rolled the other toward Charli.

Charli stopped to think. "You mean, morally, or what?"

"Let's skip that whole segment. Right and wrong depend on too many things from one place to another, although I have some theories of my own. No—let's be sitting in this bar and agree that incest is just awful, and go on from there. What's really wrong with it?"

"You breed too close, you get faulty offspring. Idiots and dead babies without heads and all that."

"I knew it! I knew it!" crowed the big Vexveltian. "Isn't it wonderful? From the rocky depths of a Stone Age culture through the brocades and knee-breeches sort of grand opera civilizations all the way out to the computer technocracies, where they graft electrodes into their heads and shunt their thinking into a box—you ask that question and you get that answer. It's something everybody just *knows*. You don't have to look at the evidence."

"Where do you go for evidence?"

"To dinner, for one place, where you'll eat idiot pig or feeble-minded cow. Any livestock breeder will tell you that, once you have a strain you want to keep and develop, you breed father to daughter and to granddaughter, and then brother to sister. You keep that up indefinitely until the desirable trait shows up recessive, and you stop it there. But it might never show up recessive. In any case, it's rare indeed when anything goes wrong in the very first generation; but you in the bar, there, you're totally convinced that it will. And are you prepared to say that every mental retard is the product of an incestuous union? You'd better not, or you'll hurt the feelings of some pretty nice people. That's a tragedy that can happen to anybody, and I doubt there's any more chance of it between related parents than there is with anyone else.

"But you still don't see the funniest . . . or maybe it's just the oddest part of that thing you know that just ain't so. Sex is a pretty popular topic on most worlds. Almost every aspect of it that is ever mentioned has nothing to do with procreation. For every mention of pregnancy or childbirth, I'd say there are hundreds which deal only with the sex act itself. But mention incest, and the response always deals with offspring. Always! To consider and discuss a pleasure or love relationship between blood relatives, you've apparently got to make some sort of special mental effort that nobody, anywhere, seems able to do easily—some not at all."

"I have to admit I never made it. But then—what *is* wrong with incest, with or without pregnancy?"

"Aside from moral considerations, you mean. The moral consideration is that it's a horrifying thought, and it's a horrifying thought because it always has been. Biologically speaking, I'd say there's nothing wrong with it. Nothing. I'd go even further, with Dr. Phelvelt—ever hear of him?"

"I don't think so."

"He was a biological theorist who could get one of his books banned on worlds that had never censored anything before—even on worlds which had science and freedom of research and freedom of speech as the absolute keystones of their whole structure. Anyway, Phelvelt had a very special kind of mind, always ready to take the next step no matter where it is, without insisting that it's somewhere where it isn't. He thought well, he wrote well, and he had a vast amount of knowledge outside his specialty and a real knack for unearthing what he happened not to know. And he called that sexual tension between blood relatives a survival factor."

"How did he come to that?"

"By a lot of separate paths which came together in the same place. Everybody knows (this one *is* so!) that there are evolutionary pressures which make for changes in a species. Not much (before Phelvelt) had been written about stabilizing forces. But don't you see, inbreeding is one of them?"

"Not offhand, I don't."

"Well, look at it, man! Take a herd animal as a good example. The bull covers his cows, and when they deliver heifers and the heifers grow up, he covers them too. Sometimes there's a third and even fourth generation of them before he gets displaced by a younger bull. And all that while, the herd characteristics are purified and reinforced. You don't easily get animals with slightly different metabolisms which might tend to wander away from the feeding ground the others were using. You won't get high-bottom cows which would necessitate Himself bringing something to stand on when he came courting." Through Charli's shout of laughter he continued, "So there you have it—stabilization, purification, greater survival value—all resulting from the pressure to breed in."

"I see, I see. And the same thing would be true of lions or fish or tree toads, or—"

"Or any animal. A lot of things have been said about Nature, that she's implacable, cruel, wasteful, and so on. I like to think she's—reasonable. I concede that she reaches that state cruelly, at times, and wastefully and all the rest. But she has a way of coming up with the pragmatic solution, the one that works. To build in a pressure which tends to standardize and purify a successful stage, and to call in the exogene, the infusion of fresh blood, only once in several generations—that seems to me most reasonable."

"More so," Charli said, "than what we've always done, when you look at it that way. Every generation a new exogene, the blood kept churned up, each new organism full of pressures which haven't had a chance with the environment."

"I suppose," said Vorhidin, "you could argue that the incest taboo is responsible for the restlessness that pulled mankind out of the caves, but that's a little too simplistic for me. I'd have preferred a mankind that moved a little more slowly, a little more certainly, and never fell back. I think the ritual exogamy that made inbreeding a crime and 'deceased wife's sister' a law against incest is responsible for another kind of restlessness."

He grew very serious. "There's a theory that certain normal habit patterns should be allowed to run their course. Take the sucking reflex, for example. It has been said that infants who have been weaned too early plague themselves all their lives with oral activity—chewing on straws, smoking intoxicants in pipes, drinking out of bottle by preference, nervously manipulating the lips, and so on. With that as an analogy, you may look again at the restlessness of mankind all through his history. Who but a gaggle of frustrates, never in their lives permitted all the ways of love within the family, could coin such a concept as 'motherland' and give their lives to it and for it? There's a great urge to love Father, and another to topple him. Hasn't humanity set up its beloved Fathers, its Big Brothers, loved and worshiped and given and died for them, rebelled and killed and replaced them? A lot of them richly deserved it, I concede, but it would have been better to have done it on its own merits and not because they were nudged by a deep-down, absolutely sexual tide of which they could not speak because they had learned that it was unspeakable.

"The same sort of currents flow within the family unit. So-called 'sibling rivalry' is too well known to be described, and the frequency of bitter quarreling between siblings is, in most cultures and their literature, a sort of cliché. Only a very few psychologists have dared to put forward the obvious explanation that, more often than not, these frictions are inverted love feelings, well salted with horror and guilt. It's a pattern that makes conflict between siblings all but a certainty, and it's a problem which, once stated, describes its own solution . . . Have you ever read Vexworth? No? You should—I think you'd find him fascinating. Ecologist; in his way quite as much of a giant as Phelvelt."

"Ecologist—that has something to do with life and environment, right?"

"Ecology has *everything to* do with life and environment; it studies them as reciprocals, as interacting and mutually controlling forces. It goes without saying that the main aim and purpose of any life form is optimum survival; but 'optimum survival' is a meaningless term without considering the environment in which it has to happen. As the environment changes, the organism has to change its ways and means, even its basic design. Human beings are notorious for changing their environment, and in most of our history in most places, we have made these changes without ecological considerations. This is disaster, every time. This is over-population, past the capabilities of producing food and shelter enough. This is the rape of irreplaceable natural resources. This is the contamination of water supplies. And it is also the twisting and thwarting of psychosexual needs in the emotional environment.

"Vexvelt was founded by those two, Charli—Phelvelt and Vexworth—and is named for them. As far as I know it is the only culture ever devised on ecological lines. Our sexual patterns derive from the ecological base and are really only a very small part of our structure. Yet for that one aspect of our lives, we are avoided and shunned and pretty much unmentionable."

It took a long time for Charli to be able to let these ideas in, and longer for him to winnow and absorb them. But all the while he lived surrounded by beauty and fulfillment, by people, young and old, who were capable of total concentration on art and learning and building and processing, people who gave to each other and to their land and air and water just a little more than they took. He finished his survey largely because he had started it; for a while he was uncertain of what he would do with it.

When at length he came to Vorhidin and said he wanted to stay on Vexvelt, the big man smiled, but he shook his head. "I know you want to, Charli—but do you?"

"I don't know what you mean." He looked out at the dark bole of one of the Vexveltian poplars; Tyng was there, like a flower, an orchid. "It's more than that," said Charli, "more than my wanting to be a Vexveltian. You need me."

"We love you," Vorhidin said simply. "But—need?"

"If I went back," said Charli Bux, "and Terratu got its hands on my survey, what do you think would become of Vexvelt?"

"You tell me."

"First Terratu would come to trade, and then others, and then others; and then they would fight each other, and fight you . . . you need someone here who knows this, really knows it, and who can deal with it when it starts. It will start, you know, even without my survey; sooner or later someone will be able to do what I did—a shipment of feldspar, a sheet of pure metal. They will destroy you."

"They will never come near us."

"You think not. Listen: no matter how the other worlds disapprove, there is one force greater: greed."

"Not in this case, Charli. And this is what I want you to be able to understand, all the way down to your cells. Unless you do, you can never live here. We are shunned, Charli. If you had been born here, that would not matter so much to you. If you throw in your lot with us, it would have to be a total commitment. But you should not make such a decision without understanding how completely you will be excluded from everything else you have ever known."

"What makes you think I don't know it now?"

"You say we need defending. You say other-world traders will exploit us. That only means you don't understand. Charli: listen to me. Go back to Terratu. Make the strongest presentation you can for trade with Vexvelt. See how they react. Then you'll know—then you can decide."

"And aren't you afraid I might be right, and because of me, Vexvelt will be robbed and murdered?"

And Vorhidin shook his big head, smiling, and said, "Not one bit, Charli Bux. Not one little bit."

So Charli went back, and saw (after a due delay) the Archive Master, and learned what he learned, and came out and looked about him at his home world and, through that, at all the worlds like it; and then he went to the secret place where the Vexveltian ship was moored, and it opened to him.

Tyng was there, Tamba, and Vorhidin. Charli said, "Take me home."

In the last seconds before they took the Drive jump, and he could look through the port at the shining face of Terratu for the last time in his life, Charli said, "Why? Why? How did human beings come to hate this one thing so much that they would rather die insane and in agony than accept it? How did it happen, Vorhidin?"

"I don't know," said the Vexveltian.

Afterword:

And now you know what sort of a science fiction story this is, and perhaps something about science fiction stories that you didn't know before.

I have always been fascinated by the human mind's ability to think itself to a truth, and then to take that one step more (truly the basic secret of all human progress) and the inability of so many people to learn the trick. Case in point: "We mean to get that filth off the newsstands and out of the bookstores." Ask why, and most such crusaders will simply point at the "filth" and wonder that you asked.

But a few will take one step more: "Because youngsters might get their hands on it." That satisfies most, but ask: "And suppose they do?" a still smaller minority will think it through to: "Because it's bad for them." Ask again: "In what way is it bad for them?" and a handful can reach this: "It will arouse them." By now you've probably run out of crusaders, but if there are a couple left, ask them, "How does being aroused harm a child?" and if you can get them to take that one more step, they will have to take it out of the area of emotional conviction and into the area of scientific research. Such studies are available, and invariably they show that such arousement is quite harmless—indeed, there is something abnormal about anyone who is not or cannot be so roused. The only possible harm that can result comes not from the sexual response itself but from the guilt-making and punitive attitude of the social environment—most of all that part of it which is doing the crusading.

Casting about for some more or less untouched area in which to exercise this one-step-more technique, I hit on this one. That was at least twenty years ago, and I have had to wait until now to find a welcome for anything so unsettling. I am, of course, very grateful. I hope the yarn starts some fruitful argument.

Runesmith

by Harlan Ellison® and Theodore Sturgeon

Dedicated to the memory of Cordwainer Smith

Crouching there in the darkness on the 102nd floor, Smith fumbled for the skin-bag of knucklebones. Somewhere down below in the stairwell—probably the ninety-fifth or -sixth floor by now, judging from the firefly ricochets of their flashlight beams on the walls, coming up—the posse was sniffing him out. Soundlessly he put his good shoulder against the fire door, but it was solid. Probably bulged and wedged for months, since Smith had made the big mistake.

He was effectively trapped in a chimney. The dead stairwell of the carcass that was the Empire State Building, in the corpse that was New York City, in the mammoth graveyard he had made of the world. And finding the only escape hatch closed off, he reluctantly fumbled at his belt for the skin-bag of knucklebones.

Smith. First and last of the magic men. About to cast the runes again.

The posse had reached the ninety-ninth floor. If he were going to do it—terrible!—he had to do it now . . .

He hesitated a second. There were fifteen or sixteen men and women in that pack. He didn't want to hurt them. Despite their slavering hatred, despite their obvious intention, he was reluctant to call into effect that power again.

He had done it before, and destroyed the world.

"He's gotta be up there," one of them called down to the rest of the pack. "Now we got 'im."

The silence they had maintained since morning, climbing like insects up the inside of the Empire State, was suddenly broken. "Let's take 'im!" yelled another one. The slap-slap of their rag-and-hide-wrapped feet on the metal stairs rose to Smith. He swallowed and it tasted sour, and he upended the skin-bag.

The knucklebones spilled chatteringly on the landing. The pattern was random; he murmured. Hunkered down on his haunches, he called up the power, and there was the faintest hiss of a breeze in the stairwell. A breeze that was peculiarly bittersweet, the way Holland chocolates used to be. A chill breeze that broke sweat out on Smith's spine, in the hollows between his shoulder blades. Then the screams began. Below him, on the one hundredth floor.

Terrible screams. Small creatures with things growing inside them, pushing their vital organs out of alignment, then out through the skin. Watery screams. As solids turned liquid and boiled and ran leaving their containers empty husks. Short, sharp screams. As dull cutting edges appeared where none had been before and severed the flesh that had contained them when they were merely bones. Then the screams stopped. The silence that had climbed with the posse since morning, *that* silence deepened, returned.

Smith crawled away from the knucklebones, far into the corner of the landing, drew his boney knees up to his bearded chin, and whimpered. The breeze—casting about like an animal that was still hungry—reluctantly died away, fled back to the place from which it had come.

Smith, alone. Caster of runes. Reader from a strange grimoire only he could interpret. The only survivor of the catastrophe he had caused. The only survivor because anyone else out there was merely one step away from animal. Smith, whimpering.

Smith, alone.

Alone. The terrible word broke away out of him like projectile vomit: "Alone!" and fled to the walls, rebounded to sting him, turned echo-edged and rebounded again.

"But for me." Then a girl laughed girl-laughter, and down amidst the silence was the sound of quick soft footsteps, and again girl-laughter, not spread about the floor below, but right in the stairwell. And it was laughter again, footstepping up and nearer.

Terror and joy, terror and joy, shock and disbelief. Terror and joy and a terrible fear: oh, guard, oh fight, oh run, *look out!* Grunting *akh!,* grunting *hah!* Smith scrabbled to his knucklebones, so hurried that he would not take standing-time, but hurried hunkering, hams and knuckles to his knucklebones. He swept them into a clack-chattering heap, and "Mind now," he cautioned her (whoever she was), "I'll cast again. I will!" he plucked up a bone, fumbled in the blackness for the magic bag, put in the bone, plucked up another, his shiny-dry dirty hands doing his seeing, for his eyes were elbow-useless for seeing in such a black.

"But oh! I love you," she said, so near now she could say it in a strumming whisper and be heard: oh! What a voice, oh, a clean, warm woman's voice, full of care and meaning: but oh! She loved him.

Terror and joy. He plucked up the last of the bones, his eyes in the black-on-black, driving at the doorway to the stairs, where now a hand-torch flashlightninged an agony into him; and he cried out. The flash was gone a-borning, too brief, almost, to have a name at all, gone before its pointed tip had slashed its way from lens to optic nerve, gone long before its agony was done with him. And something alive, *life alive even after what he had done;* life alive was breathing in the dark.

A threat, a warning—yes and a kind of begging: *be real! and in God's name don't make me do it again!*—he rattled his bag of bones.

The torch lit, arced, wheeling and swording a great blade of light, scraping and spinning across the floor to him. The flashlight struck the one knee he had down and he screamed, not for the knee but for the light sandblasting his unready open eyes. She made wide-smiling, welcome-words: "Here's light, my darling. Look at me."

He hand-heeled the scorching water out of his eyes and picked up the light. He pointed it at the doorway, and the man who stood there was seven feet, one and a half inches tall and wrapped in rags, he had a bloody beard down to his clavicles and a split stomach, and when the light hit him he bowed down and down and crashed dead on his face. He was a man whose liver was homogenized and had sweated out through the pores of his back—all of it, and a liver is a very very large thing, he knew that now.

"Oh please," she begged him, "find me beautiful . . ." and since he had not thought to move the light and the big dead bloody-bearded man stood no longer in the wall, he saw a naked woman standing well back from the doorway, at the head of the stairs.

For a long time he crouched there with the light in one hand and his bag of bones in the other.

He rose to his feet and the bones tumbled a whisper down the path of light to the woman. He was ever so careful, because perhaps if the light left her she might be gone. He took a careful step, because perhaps she would escape. But no, but no, she waited there sculpture-still and he went to her.

She looked straight and unblinking at the light as the light grew and grew near, until at last he could reach her. He transferred the bag to dangle from the fingers which held the light, studying her face as he had studied the darkness. He knew the instant before he touched her what his hand told him when it touched: that she was dead. She toppled away from him backwards and down, and disappeared in the darkness of the stairwell. The final sound of the fall was soft, vaguely moist, but ended.

Smith backed to the wall of the landing. The first finger of his right hand went idly to his lips, and he sucked on it. It had to have been a cruel joke of his own magic. These perambulating corpses. Something inherent in the incantations as they were filtered down through his consciousness, his conscience, his libido, his id. They were sympathetic magic, and that meant he, himself, Smith, was an integral part, not merely the voice-box. Not merely a way station through which the charms worked. He was part *of* them, helped form them, was as necessary as the wood into which the nails were driven to form the shell of the house. And if this were so, then the filtering process was necessarily influenced by what he was, who he was, what he thought. So:

Side-effects.

Like the destruction of the civilization he had known. Like the hideous torments that came to those he was compelled to destroy. Like the walking dead. Like the visible, tangible, terrifying creatures of his mind; that came and went with his magic.

He was alone, this Smith. But unfortunately he was alone inside a skull densely populated with Furies.

In the rabbit warren he called a home, that barricaded cistern to which entrance was only possible through the ripped and sundered walls of the IRT-7th Avenue subway tunnel just north of 36th Street, Smith collapsed with weariness. He had failed to get the canned goods. His mouth had watered for days, for Cling peaches, for that exquisite sweetness. He had left the eyrie late the night before, heading uptown toward a tiny Puerto Rican *bodega* he had known was still intact. A grocery he had seen soon after the mistake, and around which he had danced widdershins, placing a powerful incantation in the air, where it would serve as shield and obstruction.

But crossing Times Square—with the checkerboard pattern of bottomless pits and glass spires—the posse had seen him. They had recognized his blue serge suit immediately, and one of them had unleashed a bolt from a crossbow. It had struck just above Smith's head, on the frame of the giant metal waste basket that asked the now-vanished citizenry of Manhattan to KEEP OUR CITY CLEAN. Then a second bolt, that had grazed his shoulder. He had run, and they had followed, and what had happened, had happened, and now he was back. Peachless. He lay down on the chaise-lounge, and fell asleep at once.

The incubus spoke to the nixie.

Have we opened him up enough yet? No, not nearly enough. We counted too much on the first blast. *But what's left?* Enough is left that I still have difficulty emerging. We'll have to wait. They'll do it to him, and for us. There's all the time in eternity. Stop rushing. *I'm concerned. I have my principals as well as you, and they have equally as unpleasant a way of making their wishes and sorrows known as yours.* They'll have to wait, like mine. *They won't wait.* Well, they'll have to. This is a careful operation. *They've waited two million eternities already.* You turn poetry, but that isn't the figure. *A long time, at any rate.* Then a few more cycles won't twit them that much. *I'll tell them what you said.* You do that. *I can't guarantee anything.* When did you ever? *I do my best.* That's an explanation, not an excuse. *I'm leaving now.* You're fading; it's obvious you're leaving. *You'll stay with Smith?* No, I'll leave him, and go take a rest at the black pool spa . . . of course I'll stay with him! Get out of here. *Arrogance!* Imbecile!

Smith slept, and did not dream. But there were voices. When he awoke, he was more weary than when he had lay down. The grimoire still stood open, propped against the skull on the kitchen table he had set against the wall. The charts were still there, the candle was still half-down.

Something ferocious was gnawing at the back of his mind. He tried to focus on it, but it went chittering away into the darkness. He looked around the cistern. It was chill and empty. The fire had gone out. He swung his legs off the cot and stood up. Bones cracked. There was pain in his shoulder where a crossbow bolt had grazed him. He went to the rack and took out a corked decanter, pulled the cork with his teeth and let the dark gray smoke-fluid within dribble onto the raw, angry wound.

He was trying to remember. Something. What?

Oh . . . yes. Now he remembered. The girl. The one who was spreading the word about him. *Blue serge suit,* she was telling them, crowds of them, rat-packs in the streets, *blue serge suit, a little weasel man, with a limp. He's the one who did it. He's the one who killed the world.*

If he'd been able to get out of the city, he might have been able to survive without having to kill anyone else. But they'd closed off the bridges and tunnels . . . they were now actively looking for him, scouring the city. And beyond the city . . . now . . . it wasn't safe.

Not even for him, for Smith who had done it.

So he had to find the girl. If he could stop her mouth, end her crusade to find him, he might be able to escape them, go to the Bronx, or even Staten Island (no, not Staten Island: it wasn't there).

He knew he must find her quickly. He had had dreams, there in the cistern. He had gone to Nicephorus to glean their meaning, and even though he read Greek imperfectly he found that his dream of burning coals meant a threat of some harm at the hands of his enemies, his dream of walking on broken shells meant he would escape from his enemies' snares, his dream of burning incense foretold danger, and his dream of holding keys meant there was an obstacle in the path of his plans. The girl.

He prepared to go out to find her. He took a piece of virgin parchment from the sealed container on which had been inscribed the perfect square in Latin:

S A T O R

A R E T O

T E N E T

O T E R A

R O T A S

and with the dried beak of a black chicken he wrote in purple ink he had made from grapes and shoe polish, the names of the three Kings, Gaspar, Melchior, and Balthazar. He put the parchment in his left shoe, and as he left the cistern he made the first step with his left foot, pronouncing the names softly.

Thus he knew he would travel without encountering any difficulties. And he wore a black agate, veined with white. To protect him from all danger and to give him victory over his enemies.

Why had they somehow failed him at other times?

It was night. The city glowed with an eerie off-orange color, as though it had lain beneath great waters for ages, then the water had been drained away and the city left to rust.

He conjured up a bat and tied to its clawed foot a kind of kite-tail made from the carefully twined and knotted hair of men he had found lying dead in the streets. Then he swung the bat around and around his head, speaking words that had no vowels in them, and loosed the bat into the rusty night. It flew up and circled and squealed like an infant being skewered, and when it came back down to light on his shoulder, it told him where she was.

He turned the bat free. It swooped twice to bless him, then went off into the sky.

It was a long walk uptown. He took Broadway, after a while avoiding the checkerwork of pits without even seeing them. The buildings had been turned to glass. Many of them had shattered from sounds in the street caverns.

There was a colony of things without hands living in rubble-strewn shops on Broadway and 72nd Street. He got through them using the black agate. It blinded them with darkness and they fell back crying for mercy.

Finally he came to the place the bat told him to find if he wanted to locate the girl. It was, of course, where he had lived when he had made the mistake. He went inside the old building and found the room that had been his.

Here it had all begun, or had it begun when he went to work at the Black Arts Bookstore? or when in college he had sunk himself so deeply in the arcane back in the library stacks that he had flunked out? Or perhaps when as a youth he had first thrilled to the ads in yellowed copies of *Weird Tales: UNLOCK YOUR SECRET POWER, ANCIENT MYSTERIES OF THE PYRAMIDS REVEALED,* or even earlier, when on All Hallows' Eve he and some others had drawn a pentagram in yellow chalk? How old had he been then? Eight? Nine?

There had been the candles and the geometric shape drawn on the floor, and he had begun to chant *Eu-hu, Elihu, Asmodeus, deus deus stygios*—nonsense syllables of course—how could they be anything else? But they had come to him and something in his monotonous soprano had shaped them—no, fleshed them. A glove looks like a hand; thrust a hand into it and it looks the same but is not, it is a far more potent thing. Words are words—nothings—but there seemed to be that in his young chanting that filled, that fleshed them, each of them. And as for the words themselves, they came to him each dictated by the last, like the cadence of pacing feet: being here, there is only one place to go next; from *Ahriman* to *Satani* is somehow simply obvious, and then like hopscotch the young voice bounced on *Thanatos, Thanatos, Thanatos.* It was then that the bulge happened in the middle of the pentagram. The floor couldn't have swelled like that (it showed no signs later), but it did all the same, and the thin pennants of many-colored smoke and the charnel smell did happen, and the crowding feeling of—of—of Something coming up, coming in. Then goggle-eyed kids deliciously ready to be terrified were terrified, ready to scream, screamed, ready to escape, fled in a galloping synergy of wild fears—all but young Smith, who stayed to watch the plumes of smoke subside, the bulge recede . . . for his chant had stopped, a panic-driven sneaker had cut the careful yellow frame of the pentagram, so that soon nothing was left but the echoes of that abandoned abattoir smell and in Smith's heart a terrified yet fascinated dedication; he cried, he whispered: "It really worked . . ."

An old wives' tale once had heart-attack victims munch on the leaves of the foxglove and recover. Along came science and extracted digitalis. In just this way Smith learned what it really is about bat's blood, and the special potency of the body-fat of a baby murdered and bled at the dark of the moon, and how these and many other things may be synthesized and their potency multiplied without recourse to bats or babies, stars or stumpwater, Eucharists, eunuchs, or unicorn horn.

Basics are simple. The theory of solid-state electronic is complicated but the thing itself is not; the tiny block of semi-conductive germanium called transistor, nuvistor, thermistor, tunnel diode is, as any fool can see, a simple thing indeed. So it was that Smith, working his way through matters incomprehensible, indescribable, and unspeakable, came all the way through the complexities of the earnest alchemists and Satanists and the strangely effective religious psychology which steeps the worship of the Nameless One sometimes called the Horned God, and many others, until he reached basics.

Simple as a transistor, as difficult to understand.

And who, using a transistor, needs to understand it?

But a transistor (however precise) without a power supply (however tiny) is useless. The runes and the bones without the runesmith . . . nothing. With one, with the smith called Smith, fear more terrifying than any ever known by humankind; disaster unexpected, inexplicable, seeming random, operating on unknown logic and unleashing unknown forces.

In the hall of the Seven Faceless ones.

Stood the incubus and the nixie.

Before their masters.

Who told them.

Things they needed to know.

The time has come. After time within time that has eaten time till it be gorged on its own substance, the time has come. You have been chosen emissaries. You will go and you will find us an instrument and you will train it and teach it and hone it and mold it to our needs. And when the instrument is ready you will use it to open a portal, and we will pour through and regain what was once and always ours, what was taken from us when we were exiled.

Here.

Where it is cold.

Where it is dark.

Where we receive no nourishment.

You will do this.

I am ready to serve. So am I. But what sort of weapon do you want us to get? *I think I know what they mean.* You always know what they mean; listen, masters, I don't want to be a nuisance, but I can't work with this incubus. He's a complainer and a befuddler and he's got delusions of authority. *Masters, don't listen to him. He's jealous of the faith and trust you've put in me. He rails under the lash of envy. My success with the coven against the Norns infuriates him.* Rails? What the Thoth are you gibbering about? Look, Masters, I serve gladly; there isn't much else for me to do. But I can't work under this lunatic. One of us has to be in charge of things on this. If it's him, then put me on some other duty. If it's me, then put him in his place.

Silence!

You will work together as needs be.

The incubus.

The nixie will be in charge of this matter.

And you will assist.

I serve gladly, Masters. Then why are you foaming? *Shut up!* Darling, you're lovely when you're angry.

We will hear.

No more.

You will begin now.

Find.

The weapon and teach it.

Open the portal.

We long to return.

How you do it is your concern but.

Do not fail us.

The nixie and the incubus had worked together as well as might be expected. The nixie said: We'll give him magic and let him use it. We can't go through, not yet at least, but we can send dreams and thoughts and desires: they'll pass through the veil. *And what good will that do?*

He'll tear a rift in the veil for us. *Oh, I can't believe the stupidity of your ideas.* Stupid or not, it's the way I'm doing it; carefully and smoothly, and you keep your trachimoniae out of it. *Just don't order me about. I'm the highest-ranking incubus—*

Just shut up will you.

Shut up? How dare you speak to me like that? You'd better succeed quickly, nixie. My principals are anxious, and if you go wrong or slow down I'll make certain they have their way with you.

The nixie had found his weapon. Smith. He had given him first a series of dreams. Then a hunger to know the convolutions of black magic. The bulge in the floor. The hunger of curiosity. Leading him, step by step through his life: the Black Arts Book Store, the proper volumes, the revealed secrets, the dusty little room, and at last . . . the power. But given not quite whole. Given in a twisted manner. The runes had been cast, and the mistake made—and Smith had destroyed the world, tearing the veil in the process. But not quite enough for the return of the Faceless Ones.

And the incubus grew impatient for his revenge.

The girl.

Smith was sorry. Standing in the room to which his bat had led him, he was sorry. He hadn't meant to do it. Smith had not, in the deepest sense, known it was loaded (nor had he been meant to know); and when it went off (in this room with half a candle and dust and books bound in human flesh, and the great grimoire) it was aimed at the whole world.

Peking, Paris, Rome, Moscow, Detroit, New York, New Orleans, Los Angeles: Miles of cinders burying cold roast corpses. Checkerboard arrangements of bottomless pits and glass spires. Acres of boiling swamp. Whole cities that were now only curling, rising green mist. Cities and countries that had been, were totally gone.

And in the few cities that remained . . . Water no longer flowed through their veins nor electricity through their nerves, and there they sat, scraping the sky, useless, meaningless, awaiting erosion. And at their dead feet, scurrying loners and human rat-packs, survivors hunting and sometimes eating one another, a species in its glorious infancy with the umbilical cord a thousand ways pinhole-perforated before it had had a chance really to be born; and Smith knew this and had to see it all around him, had to see it and say, "My fault. My fault."

Guilty Smith the runesmith.

Back then, here, to the room where the runes had begun, to trap a girl he sensed would come. He set a noise-trap at the outer door (it opened outward so he propped a 4x4 against it and an old tin washtub under it; open the door and *whamcrash!*) and next to it a rune-trap (which cannot be described here) and he settled down to wait.

The nixie to the incubus:

What have you been doing? *I've lured him back to the focus location.* You fool! He may suspect now. *He suspects nothing. I've implanted a delusion, a girl. When he sleeps we take him and rip the veil completely.* What girl!? What have you done? You can ruin it all, you egomaniac! *There is no girl. A succubus. I tried earlier, but it went wrong. This time he's weaker, he'll sleep, we'll take him.*

What makes you think he'll succumb this time, any more than he did the last time? *Because he's a human and he's weak and stu-*

pid and lonely and filled with guilt and he has never known love. I will give him love. Love that will drain him, empty him. Then he's mine.

Not yours . . . ours!

Not yours at all, Nixie. The Masters will see to you.

He stood in a dark corner, waiting. And sleep suddenly seemed the most important thing in the world to him. He wanted to sleep.

Sleep! Should a man live three-score years, one of them must go to this inert stupidity, a biochemical habit deriving from the accident of diurnal rotation. The caveman must huddle away behind rocks and flame during the hours of darkness because of the nocturnal predators who can see better in the dark than he can. They, in turn, must hide from him. Hence the habit, long outmoded but still inescapable. A third of a life spent sprawled out paralyzed, mostly unconscious, and oh vulnerable. Twenty years wasted out of each life, when life itself is so brief a sparkle in a surrounding immensity of nothingness. Brief as it is, still we must give away a third of it to sleep, for no real reason. Twenty years. Smith had hated and despised sleep, the cruel commanding necessity for sleep, the intrusion, the interruption, the sheer waste of sleep; but never had he hated it so much as now, when everyone in the world was his enemy and all alone he must stand them off. Who would stand sentry over Smith? Only Smith, lying mostly unconscious with his own lids blinding him and his ears turned off and his soft belly upward to whatever soft-footed enemy might penetrate his simple defenses.

But he could not help himself; he *wanted* to sleep.

He lay down fully dressed and pulled a blanket over him. He murmured his goodnight words, which for a long time had been (as he slid toward the edge of slumber's precipice and scanned the day past and the weeks and months since that first terrible rune-work) "I didn't mean it. I didn't mean it. I'm sorry. I'm sorry . . ." and as he tumbled off the edge of waking, he would catch one awful glimpse of tomorrow—more of the same, but worse.

But not tonight. Perhaps it was his exhaustion, the long thirty-six-hour flight up the Empire State Building, trying, out of guilt and compassion, not to use his terrible weapon (how many times had he made that firm resolution ... how many times, falling sickly asleep, had he determined to walk out unarmed, to build an attention aura around himself, to get from the new barbarians that which his guilt deserved?), or perhaps he had reached a new peak of terror and shame, and feared especially the vulnerability of sleep.

As he approached the dark tumble into oblivion, something made him claw at the edge, hold fast, neither asleep nor awake, just at that point through which he usually hurtled, unable to stay awake, on guard no more.

And he heard voices.

Now I send her to him. Now when he's weakest. Wait! Are you sure? This man ... he's ... different. There's been a change in him. *Since we last manipulated him? Don't be ridiculous.* No, wait! There is ... something. Sleep. Yes, that's it. It had to do with sleep. *I'm not waiting; my Principals want through now, in this tick of time, now! I want success more than you, that is why the triumph and the rewards will be mine. The twelve generations it took to breed this Smith as a gateway and the lifetime it took to train him. It's all come down to me, to me to fail or succeed, and I'll succeed! I'm sending the succubus, now! He's never been loved ...* now *he'll be loved.*

No! You fool! Your ego! Sleep is his strength. You have it all wrong. Nothing can harm him when he sleeps!

Success!

Smith had a brief retinal impression of *something* ... it was being a gateway, and what it was like. Mouth open till the flesh tore at the corners. Darkness pouring from within him, then flames that expanded and rolled over the land, filling the sky; and himself burning burning burning.

Then it was gone. Smith clung for one more amazed moment to this place, this delicately-limned turnover point between waking and sleep. This line was a crack in—in something incomprehensible, but it was a crack through which his mind could peep as between boards in a fence.

Something began to beat in him, daring him to move, hope. He quelled it quickly lest it wake him altogether and those—those *others* —know of it. Slipping, slipping, losing his clutch on this half-wakefulness, about to drop and over end into total sleep, he snatched at phrases and concepts, forcing himself to keep and remember them: twelve generations it took to breed this Smith as a gateway . . . lifetime it took to train.

And: nothing can reach him, nothing can harm him while he's asleep.

Sleep.

Sleep the robber, sleep the intruder, sleep the enemy—all his life he had tried to avoid it, had succumbed as little as possible, had fought to live without it. *Who had taught him that?* Why did he want to unlearn it so desperately now? And what did the doctors and poets say about sleep: surcease, strengthener, healer, knitter-up of the raveled sleeve of care. And he had sneered at them. Had he been *taught* to sneer?

He had. For *their* purposes, he had been taught. More; he had been bred for this—twelve generations, was it? And why? To be given the power to decimate humanity so that something unspeakable, something long-exiled could return to possess this world? Would it be the Earth alone, or all the planets, the galaxies, the universe? Could it be time itself? Or other sets of dimensions?

The one thing he must do is sleep. *Nothing can harm him when he sleeps.*

Then she came to him. The girl from the stairwell, alive again, a second time, or how many times back to the inky beginnings he could not even imagine? She came to him through the door, and there was no sound of crashing washtub; she came through the room and there was no stench and death from the rune-trap.

She came toward him, lying there, without clothes, without sound, without pain or anger, and she extended her flawless arms to him in love. The pleasure of her love swept across the room. She wanted to give herself, to give him everything, all she was and all she could be, for no other return than his love. She wanted his love, all of his love, all of him, everything, all the substance and strength of him.

He half-rose to meet her, and then he knew what she was, and he trembled with the force of losing her, of destroying her, and he murmured words without vowels and a slimy darkness began to eat at her feet, her legs, her naked thighs, her torso, and she let one ghastly shriek as something took her, and her face dissolved in slime and darkness, and she was gone . . . and he fell back, weak.

Smith the runesmith let go his shred of wakefulness and plunged joyfully into the healing depths. It was not until he awakened, rested and strong and healthily starving, that he realized fully what else he had let go.

Guilt.

The sin was not his. He had been shaped to do what he had done. A terrible enemy had made him its instrument, its weapon. You do not accuse, condemn, imprison the murder-weapon.

The runesmith, smiling (how long since?) fumbled for the skin-bag of knucklebones. He closed his eyes, his strong, clear rested eyes, and turned his rested mind to the talent (inborn) and skills (instilled) in him alone of all men ever. No jaded blind buckshot in the faces of his kin, done in anguish to stay alive, but the careful, knowing, precise drawing of a bead. The location, direction, range known to Smith the weapon in ways impossible to Smith the man.

The knucklebones spilled chatteringly on the floor.

The pattern was random; his talent and his skills understood it.

He murmured a new murmur.

Hunkered down on his haunches, he called up the power.

There was the faintest hiss of a breeze in the tumbled warren of this focus-room, a breeze that was peculiarly bittersweet, the way Holland chocolates used to be. A chill breeze that broke sweat out on Smith's spine, in the hollows between his shoulder blades.

Then the screams began.

They were screams beyond sound, and surely only and immeasurable fraction of them reached Smith, so different were they in quality and kind from anything remotely human. Yet their echoes and their backlash seemed to blur the world for a moment of horror beyond imagining. A soundless, motionless quake, the terror of countless billions of frightful beings facing death and (unlike the millions who had perished here) knowing it, knowing why.

Smith's skills knew as Smith himself could not, that the universe itself was relieved of a plague.

Was it a long time later? Probably it was—Smith was never able to remember that—when he stood up and filled his lungs with the dusty, sweet air and looked out on tomorrow and forever with clear and guiltless eyes.

He tested his power. It was intact.

He walked to the inner and outer barriers, kicking them down. He looked out at the sunlit ruins of the city.

If I live, he thought (and barring accident I can live forever), I can build it up again. I have magic; they gave it to me and no one can take it away. Magic and science, humanity and the Powers. It's supposed to have worked that way long ago. It will again. Build it up again . . .

And if I don't, if I fail, then at least I've fixed it so they have no enemies but themselves. Terrible as that might be, there are worse things.

He saw a flicker of movement in the distance, something feeble, hungry, misshapen, ragged.

The runesmith stepped out of the shadows, and walked toward the movement in the distance. There was sun now. For the first time. Because he wanted sun. And he wanted cool breezes. And the scent of good things in the air.

He could have it all now. They might never forgive him, but they could not harm him, and he would help them, as they had never been able to help themselves.

They were still alone, but perhaps it would be better now.

Jorry's Gap

"Jorry!"

Dam*damn!* Jorry never said dam*damn* out loud; it was something that happened inside his head when he realized he couldn't get away with whatever, or when it wasn't going the way he wanted it to. "Yeh Mom." How come she could hear him even when Pop had his head in the boob-tube with horses galloping and gunshots and all, every time?

Mom got up and stood in the door of the living room and looked at him as he stood at the bottom of the stairs where he had just stepped over the third step which squeaked and timed it with the big noise on the TV and all. She said, "You're going out."

"Well yeh."

"You're not going out."

"It's early."

"Out till all hours, and where, and who with, I want to know."

"It's Friday."

"Speak to your son."

Without moving his eyes from the tube, Pop said, "What."

Not a question, not an answer, just a flat statement "What."

Mom said to Jorry, "You're not going out."

Up to now it was like wired-in with relays, the way a traffic light does no matter what, red to yellow, yellow to green, green to red again. If he wanted to he could make the whole thing go again: It's early, out till all hours and where and who with, it's Friday, speak to your son, what. So he tried the don't-worry.

"Don't worry, Mom. I'll be back early."

"Early in the morning early, five o'clock in the morning," Mom said. "With that addict Chatz."

"Chazz," he corrected. Chazz had a whole new thing with special words: lid, joint, roach, weed, grass. "You smoke?" meant something brand new. Chazz lied a lot and Jorry had never seen him with anything, and if he acted funny once or twice well, hell, you didn't need to blow a joint to learn that, you could learn it in the movies. Then yesterday Chazz said "I got a stash. You want?" and maybe it was a lie, but it scared Jorry like hell; he was real cool though: "Later, man." Now he said to his mother, "Nothing the matter with Chazz."

"With those eyes close together, round-shouldered," Mom said. "I can tell. Whatever he's taking now, even if he isn't he will and it will lead to something worse. Or it's that Jane."

"Joan." Dam*damn.* The instant he corrected her he knew she knew he had been thinking about pale parted hair and bright knowing laughter with some other guy, but with him a kind of *Finish your sentence, I got to go* even when all he said was hello. "That one," said Mom, "will give you a disease. Speak to your son."

"Wha-at. Wha-at." Pop still didn't take his eyes off the cowboys, but each "what" now had two syllables, and that meant he'd go into action if she gigged him once more.

"You'll hang around that Stube."

"Strobe," he corrected her before he could stop himself. "They don't have anything there, not even beer, only sodas and fruit juice."

"You're going to get killed riding around in that cheap flashy junkheap"—which was a hightailed Mustang with Shelby spoilers, oh wow—"which no man in his right mind would give to a retarded draft dodger like that Highball"—

"Highboy," Jorry said faintly.

—"no matter how much money he has. Speak to your son." Dam*damn.* Now everything depended on how it was with the cowboys. If Pop was locked in to this show, it would be short. If not, this could go on for hours and nobody was going no place.

"What." Back to one syllable, but he yelled it, and he bounced out of the fat chair with a two-handed bang and came out of the living room, wattle-jawed, clamp-lipped, squinch-eyed. "Well what."

Mom said, "He's going out." Pop said, "He's going out?" Mom said, "He's not going out."

Pop said, "So go out, go out, a man has a right to work all day and come home and see one show all the way through."

Good, good, the show was good, this would be short.

"Go, go," Mom yelled, "Go to your creepy friends, never mind here where you get taken care of, eat the best food for your health, I work my fingers to the bone. Go."

Jorry went, feeling funny like he always did when it went this way, getting his way, winning, but all the same like thrown out in the street, nobody cared enough. There is no word for a feeling like that. He went quickly but did not bump the door closed because sometimes that would bring Pop out on the porch, to make him come back. Behind him he could hear Mom starting in on Pop: how can I be his mother and his father all at the same time, he hasn't got a father who cares enough to keep him in the house running around at all hours with those creepy kids, and Pop yelling "After! After!" meaning shut up while he sees his show.

Jorry got as far as Third without seeing anybody, and then from out of nowhere there was Specs, waiting for the light to change. Specs had real bad skin and shorter hair than anyone else but he was always around the action and knew everything. "Highboy got Libby," was his greeting. Libby was a very unreachable chick; you see them carrying the flag at high-school assemblies and president of the Student Council and the honor roll and like that, and clean and kind and pretty and square, man, forget it. But with four hundred horsepower and a tach on the dash, Highboy gets Libby, vooming along dark roads anyplace for anything he wants, and back on time. "What else?" he said, and knew Specs understood him perfectly. The light changed and they walked across. Jorry stopped.

"Strobe," said Specs, announcing and asking.

"Not now." Jorry wasn't sure why not now. Maybe it was not wanting to arrive at the place with Specs; you didn't go anywhere with Specs, you found him there. And maybe it was wanting to be alone on a dark street for a while, to think about Libby on real leather next to you and the tach pushing up towards six, towards seven, towards someplace way out of town where nobody would know, and lots of time there and back early. Spec said, "Later, man," and walked. Jorry stood next to a high hedge and did his thing about the Mustang.

Maybe it took a while and maybe not; there's no time in there, but what brought him back was *bang* on the sidewalk with a little plastic handbag that skittered lipstick and Tampax and a cracked compact and some change all out and around.

It was Joanie with the long pale hair falling away from the clean pink part. She didn't see him and she said, "I don't *care.*" Then she stood quite still for the longest time with her eyes closed. Jorry didn't want to say anything while her eyes were closed, but then under the streetlamp he saw they were not closed tight enough to keep tears in, and the streaks on her face were like cracks in a doll if you put a light inside. So he picked up the handbag and touched her with it and said her name. She gasped and banged at the bridge of her nose with the back of her hand and looked at him. After a while she said, "Jorry," and took the bag.

"I was just standing here," was all he could say, and bent to pick up the compact and the Tampax. He found a quarter and a dime and straightened up. She held out the handbag, open, and he dumped the stuff into it and dropped the compact again. "Are you all right?"

She started to laugh in a way he didn't like at all, but by the time he had dipped down and up for the compact he realized that she wasn't laughing at him. It wasn't even laughing. Whatever it was stopped abruptly and she did something no girl he had ever heard of had ever done; she took his hand and put it against her breast. Never in all his life had he felt anything so soft and alive and wonderful. She asked him in a soft, breathy voice, "Is there anything wrong with that?"

"Well, no," was all he could say.

She lifted her hand away from his; it was up to him whether or not he left it on her. He dropped it away. His hand could still feel her; he had the crazy thought that it always would. She said, very slowly, "I have been so damn lonesome."

He just shook his head a little. He hadn't seen her around for a while but he couldn't ever remember her looking lonesome. Not ever.

"Jorry—"

"What?"

She wet her lips. "You know where I live."

"Well, yes."

"Look, I've got something to do right now, but I'll be home about eleven. There's nobody there tonight. You come."

"Well, I don't—" His mouth was suddenly too dry to release another word.

"I mean," she said, "I just don't *care.*" He was hung on her eyes like a coat on a nail. "Please, Jorry. *Please.*"

"Well, all right," he said, and she held him for a moment and then turned away; he thought his knees were going to buckle. He watched her walking away, long legs, long back, long hair all flogged by the shadows of tree trunks as she walked. "Oh wow," he whispered.

After a while he walked slowly down Third, somehow aware as never before of the impact of heels on pavement, the press of toes, the smell of a lawn mowed that afternoon and a hint of cat pee and how sharp blue starspecks could pierce a small town's Friday skyglow. Then and there he didn't feel any more like I'll-have-to-ask-Mom Jorry, or they-won't-let-me Jorry, or Jorry who was always on the outside looking in, or the inside looking on. "Man," he said quietly to the nighttime, "you got to do your thing." He was quoting somebody or other but he meant it. Then he was in the light, and who should be coming out of the candy store but Chazz.

Chazz had long green eyes and an eagle's beak and no chin, and a funny way of coming up to you as if he was walking a little sidewise. Jorry called him. It seemed to make Chazz glad. "Hey man."

Jorry made a c'mon motion with his head and walked away from lights and people and let Chazz catch up with him. They moved along for a moment and Joanie's, "I don't *care!*" popped into Jorry's head. It made him grin a little and it made a pleasant cold vacuum appear in his solar plexus: fun-fear. He said, in a Chazz-sidewise kind of way, "About that stash."

Pleased astonishment. Chazz banged his hands together once and smiled all around as if at an invisible audience in the dark, to whom he said, "He's with it, he's with it." He hit Jorry. "I about had you wrote off as a brownshoes."

"Me." Jorry knew how to use a question word as a flat statement. He liked how it came out. "Where's this grass?"

Chazz released a sudden roar of laughter and shut it off. Full of glee, he looked all around and sidewised up close, and said in a half whisper, "Man, I been *looking* for you. I just didn't know till now it was you." He began walking purposefully, and Jorry strode along beside him, willing enough but a little puzzled. They got to the next streetlight and Chazz looked all around again. "Roll up your sleeve."

"What?"

"Roll it up. I want to see something."

Jorry started to think something and then didn't want to think it. He rolled up his sleeve. Chazz grasped the biceps with both hands and squeezed and held on. Jorry tugged a bit, but Chazz held on, a great eagerness showing on his face. "What the hell you doing?"

"Shut up a minute," said Chazz, and hung on. He was peering at the crook of Jorry's elbow. Suddenly he released the arm. "Beautiful. Oh man, but beautiful."

"Beautiful what."

"Like that vein, it's a piece of hose, man."

"Chazz, what the hell you talking about?"

"Like you're like me, man. Some cats, you can't find it with an X-ray, but you and me, we got the gates wide open."

Jorry tried out the words. "Chazz, if you're holding we'll smoke. If not we'll Injun rassle or just forget it."

Chazz again produced that cut-off blast of laughter that went on in silent glee. When he could he said, "Smoke! That shit can wait, man. I got us a trip, not a buzz. Like four, six hours at twenty thousand feet with the wind behind us." He came close and whispered, "I got . . . speed."

"Speed."

There was a long pause. Jorry had the painful realization that I'll-have-to-ask-Mom, They-won't-let-me Jorry was maybe standing on a higher step, but he was still around. On the other hand, to have missed being a brownshoes by so close a margin, only to fall right out of this fellowship and back into Squaresville—it was unthinkable. And besides—he was scared. Veins-Speed-God. His mouth was suddenly completely dry, which had the odd effect of reminding him of something. He worked up spit and swallowed hard before he could say, very carefully, "Oh hell, man, six hours. I got a date at eleven. I'm going to need everything I got."

"You don't need the date."

"Oh, huh."

"Who is it?"

"A chick."

"You're putting me on."

"Honest to God. Any other time, Chazz, but not tonight." Apparently he said this just right too, because Chazz sounded real sad when he said "Oh wow," and hopeless when he said "She got a friend?" and Jorry knew for a second (he forgot it later) why round shoulders and a big nose and no chin was looking to shoot speed. Chazz bit on his lip a while and then said nakedly, "Look, I'm going to wait for you. Like I got it and I checked it out and I know how, but man, I don't figure to fly solo, not the first time."

Jorry said, "I dig." What Jorry dug most was how scared Chazz was. He didn't have to look at whether or not he was scared or how much; this could come first and it made him grateful. He hit Chazz and said, "So later," and could see Chazz was grateful too. Then the Mustang flew in *wawoom* to the curb, nosed down and squatted there.

Highboy: crisp hair the color of French vanilla, white shirt, white sweater, white strong teeth, and next to him oh Libby. Oh. Highboy said, "Hey, who wants to make it with us to Little Gate?" Little Gate was forty miles away.

Chazz said so it showed, "Jorry's hung up, he's making out." Jorry thought from what he could see that Highboy liked this and Libby didn't, but what could that matter, ever? Chazz was saying, "But you could drop me by the Strobe, right?"

Highboy waved at his door latch: permission, but Chazz could open it for himself, and said to Jorry, "Keep the beat, baby," which was so-long and also something to do with making out, and made him feel pretty good, but all the same dam*damn* there go the taillights. And the funny thing was, he had to go by the Strobe to get to Joanie's house anyway. You never know why you play it the way you do.

At night (it isn't even there in the daytime) the Strobe is a wide bright storefront on a row of dark ones; light is a lake in front, with lightning; cars whale through it, people shark and minnow through it, and away a bit, once in a while, the Highway Patrol hawks by seeing everything, looking for something. Specs was there, knowing it all, and as soon as he saw Jorry's face he said to it, "Making out." Two words: congratulations, you didn't think you could keep it from me, who is it, if you don't tell me I'll find out anyway, you are maybe becoming something to notice around here, I'm watching you. All of which Jorry acknowledged: "You know how it is." He saw the Mustang in the middle of the light-lake, tail-up in a sprinter's crouch in the shallows two feet away from the curb; Highboy needn't park straight. Chazz wasn't there.

Specs said, "Three guys got burned by the same chick. Their folks got together and went to the school."

Burned. Jorry couldn't grab that, unless—"Who?"

Specs said who, three guys he knew, two of them were in History with him. But that wasn't what he wanted to know. He wanted to know who the girl was. He didn't want to ask and he didn't have to; Specs said it was Joanie. Dam*damn*. At which point Highboy and Libby came out of the Strobe and crossed to the Mustang. Highboy opened her door for her and that shining car fielded her like a good catcher's mitt. Highboy legged around front and slid in, and the chrome pipes growl-howled. From the Strobe came a chick with sit-on-it shining black hair and hip huggers tight as a blister, white, cut so low in front that "They give away shaving cream when you buy those," Specs said in his ear, and Highboy made a gesture that Jorry would remember all his life it was so great, that would last longer in his head even than what else happened right after. Highboy blew her a kiss. Highboy blew her a kiss right in front of and all around Libby and made Libby smile at it. Highboy blew that chick a kiss while he snapped his clutch and the wide ovals screamed him away in a burning launch; he blew her a kiss turning evenly in his luscious-leather bucket; he blew and threw his kiss in a wide steady backhand that ended with him smiling and releasing the last of it through the big wide rear window, all the while scorching rubber and squashed tight, him and Libby, against the welcoming seatbacks. So great.

Also he misfigured his angles. At the end of the row of dark stores and across a small street was no curb or sidewalk but a bare bank, low at first and tipping up steep, and the engineer doesn't live who could design it more perfectly to lift up the right side of a car and flip it, not to spin and flip, but to take off and corkscrew. It wasn't more than seventy, seventy-five yards from the Strobe that the Mustang flew and flipped and hit upside down and against an elm tree and burned. The Highway Patrol always knows what to do and they were there, but knowing how isn't enough sometimes.

Jorry walked home through the dark streets, trying hard to wipe out what was behind him without opening up what was in front, trying to get by himself, not with Jorry-maybe-you're-worth-watching or with Mom-can-I-Jorry, but with himself; and who the hell might that be?

About Chazz and mainlining, about Joanie and the burn, about getting killed in the Mustang, he could have known without leaving the house. Mom said it all, Mom batted one thousand. He could've known it all even if she hadn't said it—but she did say it.

Also she said she worked hard and saw to it he ate and got good clothes and had a place for himself. She said it funny and she said it so often you didn't hear it any more, but she did say it.

Pop also said he worked hard all day and when he came home he had a right. He said it to Mom and he said it to Jorry. Then Jorry would say whatever it was he always said, and nobody heard him either.

Jorry began to walk faster.

Because if there was a way to say something to Mom, and if she could say it to him and to Pop, so that they heard each other, they wouldn't need to stay mad or feel useless, not any of them. Like if somehow you can make people just *listen* to each other, not just listen to you. And you listen too. Everybody.

Jorry began to run because he really believed you could make someone else listen. He knew because he'd done it. He'd listened to every word Mom said about tonight, the only thing was he couldn't hear it until later when those things happened. And now he really believed you could make somebody listen *now.* And would you believe it, after all that had happened it was still only a quarter of twelve.

He went in the back way because no matter what else, Mom always had for him a way in. He locked the door from inside because when he was in Mom liked the rest of everything shut out. This seemed to mean something as he climbed the stairs. He heard their voices up there, hammer-and-tongs. He smiled to himself because he knew something they didn't.

It was the same thing he had heard going away: why can't you speak to your son. And: Coming home I got a right. But it was the same thing drawn out ragged and harsh: Jorry realized that they had been going around and around since he left. Believing that people could listen, listen and hear, he knocked on the door.

Pop, undershirt, galluses down, the last straw was under the angry eaves of his eyes and burning; Mom, gray pigtails (only at night, pigtails) and so worn, so worn altogether out by not being heard.

"Pop, listen."

"I wash my hands," Mom cried. "Do what you want, the waste. Go in the ashcan, live there with your Chatz and the other garbage. I wash my hands."

"Mom, listen."

Pop probably didn't hit him all that hard but it was so unexpected and he wasn't at all ready. Lying down on the floor of the upstairs hall looking up, with Mom screaming, he saw his father big. Huge. Like he hadn't since he was three years old.

"I had this for the last time and never again, you going out and her on my back, so out of my sight," Pop bellowed and spit flew.

Jorry sat up and then knelt up. He said "Pop, listen," or maybe he thought he said it. As he knelt there Pop went for him again, this time not with a man's punch like the other one, but with a push in the face to throw him back and skidding, the kind of push where being hurt isn't any part of it, but insult is. "Out of my sight!" Pop bawled, crack-voiced, and Mom was in the doorway and he pushed her too, back on the bed, and slammed the door. Somewhere in there Jorry stopped believing in anything.

He went back in town and did his thing here, and did it again there, and at a quarter to five he and Chazz were busted for use and holding, and a couple of weeks later the first chancre showed; that was in the House of Correction.

And that's how Jorry got started.

Brownshoes

His name was Mensch; it once was a small joke between them, and then it became a bitterness. "I wish to God I could have you now the way you were," she said, "moaning at night and jumping up and walking around in the dark and never saying why, and letting us go hungry and not caring how we lived or how we looked. I used to bitch at you for it, but I never minded, not really. I held still for it. I would've, just for always, because with it all you did your own thing, you were a free soul."

"I've always done my own thing," said Mensch, "and I did so tell you why."

She made a disgusted sound. "Who could understand all that?" It was dismissal, an old one; something she had recalled and worked over and failed to understand for years, a thing that made tiredness. "And you used to love people—really love them. Like the time that kid wiped out the fire hydrant and the streetlight in front of the house and you fought off the fuzz and the schlock lawyer and the ambulance and everybody, and got him to the hospital and wouldn't let him sign the papers because he was dazed. And turning that cheap hotel upside down to find Victor's false teeth and bring them to him after they put him in jail. And sitting all day in the waiting room the time Mrs. What's-her name went for her first throat cancer treatment, so you could take her home, you didn't even know her. There wasn't anything you wouldn't do for people."

"I've always done what I could. I didn't stop."

Scorn. "So did Henry Ford. Andrew Carnegie. The Krupp family. Thousands of jobs, billions in taxes for everybody. I know the stories."

"My story's not quite the same," he said mildly.

Then she said it all, without hate or passion or even much emphasis; she said in a burnt-out voice, "We loved each other and you walked out."

They loved each other. Her name was Fauna; it once was a small joke between them. Fauna the Animal and Mensch the Man, and the thing they had between them. "Sodom is a-cumen in," he misquoted Chaucer, "Lewd sing cuckold" (because she had a husband back there somewhere amongst the harpsichord lessons and the mildewed unfinished hooked rugs and the skeleton of a play and all the other abandoned projects in the attic of her life). Mensch was the first one she could have carried through, all the way. She was one of those people who waits for the right thing to come along and drops all others as soon as she finds out they aren't the main one. When someone like that gets the right thing, it's forever, and everyone says, my how you've changed. She hasn't changed.

But then when the right thing comes along, and it doesn't work out, she'll never finish anything again. Never.

They were both very young when they met and she had a little house back in the woods near one of those resort towns that has a reputation for being touristy-artsy-craftsy and actually does have a sprinkling of real artists in and around it. Kooky people are more than tolerated in places like that providing only that (a) they attract, or at least do not repel, the tourists and (b) they never make any important money. Nothing disturbs the people who really run a town like that more than an oddball who strikes it rich; people begin to listen to him, and that could change things. Fauna wasn't about to change things. She was a slender pretty girl who liked to be naked under loose floor-length gowns and take care of sick things as long as they couldn't talk—broken-wing birds and philodendrons and the like—and lots of music—lots of *kinds* of music; and cleverly doing things she wouldn't finish until the real thing came along. She had a solid title to the little house and a part-time job in the local frame shop; she was picturesque and undemanding and never got involved in marches and petitions and the like. She just believed in being kind to everyone around her and thought ... well, that's not quite right. She hadn't ever thought it out all the way, but she *felt* that if you're kind to everyone the kindness will somehow spread over the world like a healing stain, and that's what you do about wars and greed and injustice. So she was an acceptable, almost approved fixture in the town even when they paved her dirt road and put the lamppost and fire hydrant in front of it.

Mensch came into this with long hair and a guitar strapped to his back, a head full of good books and a lot of very serious restlessness. He moved in with Fauna the day after she discovered his guitar was tuned like a lute. He had busy hands too, and a way of finishing what he started, yes, and making a dozen more like them—beautifully designed kitchen pads for shopping lists made out of hand-rubbed local woods, which used adding-machine rolls and had a hunk of hacksaw blade down at the bottom so you could neatly tear off a little or a lot, and authentic reproductions of fireplace bellows and apple-peelers and stuff like that which could be displayed in the shoppes (not stores, they were shoppes) on the village green, and bring in his share. Also he knew about transistors and double-helical gears and eccentric linkages and things like Wankels and fuel cells. He fiddled around a lot in the back room with magnets and axles and colored fluids of various kinds, and one day he had an idea and began fooling with scissors and cardboard and some metal parts. It was mostly frame and a rotor, but it was made of certain things in a certain way. When he put it together the rotor began to spin, and he suddenly understood it. He made a very slight adjustment and the rotor, which was mostly cardboard, uttered a shrill rising sound and spun so fast that the axle, a tenpenny nail, chewed right through the cardboard bearings and the rotor took off and flew across the room, showering little unglued metal bits. He made no effort to collect the parts, but stood up blindly and walked into the other room. Fauna took one look at him and ran to him and held him: what is it? what's the matter? but he just stood there looking stricken until the tears began rolling down his cheeks. He didn't seem to know it.

That was when he began moaning suddenly in the middle of the night, jumping up and walking around in the dark. Then she said years later that he would never tell her why, it was true, and it wasn't, because what he told her was that he had something in his head so important that certain people would kill him to get it, and certain other people would kill him to suppress it, and that he wouldn't tell her what it was because he loved her and didn't want her in danger. She cried a lot and said he didn't trust her, and he said he did, but he wanted to take care of her, not throw her to the wolves. He also said—and this is what the moaning and nightwalking was all about—that the thing in his head could make the deserts bloom and could feed hungry people all over the world, but that if he let it loose it could be like a plague too, not because of what it was but because of what people would do with it; and the very first person who died because of it would die because of him, and he couldn't bear the idea of that. He really had a choice to make, but before he could make it he had to decide whether the death of one person was too great a price to pay for the happiness and security of millions, and then if the deaths of a thousand would be justified if it meant the end of poverty for all. He knew history and psychology and he had a mathematician's head as well as those cobbler's hands, and he knew damned well what would happen if he took this way or that. For example, he knew where he could unload the idea and all responsibility for it for enough money to keep him and Fauna—and a couple hundred close friends, if it came to that—in total luxury for the rest of their lives; all he would have to do would be to sign it away and see it buried forever in a corporate vault, for there were at least three industrial giants which would urgently bid against one another for the privilege.

Or kill him.

He also thought of making blueprints and scattering millions of copies over cities all over the world, and of finding good ethical scientists and engineers and banding them together into a firm which would manufacture and license the device and use it only for good things. Well you can do that with a new kind of rat-killer or sewing machine, but not with something so potent that it will change the face of the earth, eliminate hunger, smog, and the rape of raw materials—not when it will also eliminate the petro-chemical industry (except for dyes and plastics), the electric-power companies, the internal-combustion engine and everything involved in making it and fueling it, and even atomic energy for most of its purposes.

Mensch tried his very best to decide not to do anything at all about it, which was the moaning and nightwalking interval, and that just wouldn't work—the thing would not let him go. Then he decided what to do, and what he must do in order to do it. His first stop was at the town barbershop.

Fauna held still for this and for his getting a job at Flextronics, the town's light industry, which had government contracts for small computer parts and which was scorned by the town's art, literature and library segment. The regular hours appalled her, and although he acted the same (he certainly didn't look the same) around the house, she became deeply troubled. She had never seen so much money as he brought in every payday, and didn't want to, and for the first time in her life had to get stubborn about patching and improvising and doing without instead of being able to blame poverty for it. The reasons she found now for living that way seemed specious even to her, which only made her stubborn about it, and more of a kook than ever. Then he bought a car, which seemed to her an immorality of sorts.

What tore it was when somebody told her he had gone to the town-board meeting, which she had never done, and had proposed that the town pass ordinances against sitting on the grass on the village green, playing musical instruments on town thoroughfares, swimming at the town swimming hole after sundown, and finally, for hiring more police. When she demanded an explanation he looked at her sadly for a long time, then would not deny it, would not discuss it, and moved out.

He got a clean room in a very square boarding house near the factory, worked like hell until he got his college credits straightened out, went to night school until he had another degree. He took to hanging around the Legion post on Saturday nights and drank a little beer and bought a lot of whiskey for other people. He learned a whole portfolio of dirty jokes and dispensed them carefully, two-thirds sex, one-third bathroom. Finally he took a leave of absence from his job, which was, by this time, section manager, and moved down the river to a college town where he worked full time on a postgraduate engineering degree while going to night school to study law. The going was very tough around then because he had to pinch every nickel to be able to make it and still keep his pants creased and his brown shoes shiny, which he did. He still found time to join the local church and become a member of the vestry board and a lay preacher, taking as his text the homilies from *Poor Richard's Almanac* and delivering them (as did their author) as if he believed every word.

When it was time he redesigned his device, not with cardboard and glue, but with machined parts that were seventy percent monkey-puzzle-mechanical motions that canceled each other out, and wiring which energized coils which shorted themselves out. He patented parts and certain groupings of parts, and finally the whole contraption. He then took his degrees and graduate degrees, his published scholarly papers, his patents and his short haircut, together with a letter of introduction from his pastor, to a bank, and borrowed enough to buy into a failing company which made portable conveyor belts. His device was built into the drive segment, and he went on the road to sell the thing. It sold very well. It should. A six-volt automobile battery would load coal with that thing for a year without needing replacement or recharging, and no wonder, because the loading was being powered by that little black lump in the drive segment, which, though no bigger than a breadbox, and requiring no fuel, would silently and powerfully spin a shaft until the bearings wore out.

It wasn't too long before the competition was buying Mensch's loaders and tearing them down to see where all that obscene efficiency was coming from. The monkey-puzzle was enough to defeat most of them, but one or two bright young men and a grizzled oldster or so were able to realize that they were looking at something no bigger than a breadbox which would turn a shaft indefinitely without fuel, and wonder what things would be like with this gadget under the hood of a car or in the nacelles of aircraft, or pumping water in the desert, or generating light and power 'way back in the hills and jungles without having to build roads or railways or to string power lines. Some of these men found their way to Mensch.

Either he hired them and tied them up tight with ropes of gold and fringe benefits, or had them watched and dissuaded, or discredited, or, if need be, ruined.

Inevitably someone was able to duplicate the Mensch effect, but by that time Mensch had a whole office building full of lawyers with their pencils sharpened and their instructions ready. The shrewd operator who had duplicated the effect, and who had sunk everything he had and could borrow into retooling an engine factory for it, found himself in such a snarl of infringement, torts, ceases-and-desists, and prepaid royalty demands that he sold his plant at cost to Mensch and gratefully accepted a job managing it. And he was only the first.

The military moved in at about this point, but Mensch was ready for them and their plans to take over his patents and holdings as a national resource. He let himself be bunted higher and higher in the chain of command, while his refusals grew stronger and stronger and the threats greater and greater, until he emerged at the top in the company of the civilian who commanded them all. This meeting was brought about by a bishop, for never in all these busy years did Mensch overlook his weekly duty at the church of his choice, nor his tithes, nor his donations of time for an occasional Vacation Bible School or picnic or bazaar. And Mensch, on this pinnacle of wealth, power and respectability, was able to show the president the duplicate set of documents he had placed in a Swiss bank, which, on the day his patents were preempted by the military, would donate them to research institutes in Albania and points north and east. That was the end of that.

The following year a Mensch-powered car won the Indy. It wasn't as fast as the Granatelli entry; it just voomed around and around the brickyard without making any stops at all. There was, of course, a certain amount of static for a while, but the inevitable end was that the automobile industry capitulated, and with it the fossil-fuel people. Electric light and power had to follow and, as the gas and steam and diesel power sources obsolesce and are replaced by Mensch prime movers, the atomic plants await their turn.

It was right after the Indianapolis victory that Mensch donated his blueprints to Albania anyway—after all, he had never said he wouldn't—and they showed up about the same time in Hong Kong and quickly reached the mainland. There was a shrill claim from the Soviet Union that the Mensch Effect had been discovered in the nineteenth century by Siolkovsky, who had set it aside because he was more interested in rockets, but even the Russians couldn't keep that up for long without laughing along with the audience, and they fell to outstripping all other nations in development work. No monkey-puzzle on earth can survive this kind of effort—monkey-puzzles need jungles of patent law to live and thrive—and it was not long before the Soviets (actually, it was a Czech scientist, which is the same thing, isn't it? Well, the Soviets said it was) were able to proclaim that they had improved and refined the device to a simple frame supporting one moving part, the rotor: each made, of course, of certain simple substances which, when assembled, began to work. It was, of course, the same frame and rotor with which Mensch, in terror and tears, had begun his long career, and the Czech, that is, Soviet "refinement" was, like all else, what he had predicted and aimed himself toward.

For now there wasn't a mechanics magazine in the world, nor hardly a tinkerer's workshop anywhere, that didn't begin turning out Mensch rotors. Infringements occurred so widely that even Mensch's skyscraperful of legal-eagles couldn't have begun to stem the flood. And indeed they did not try, because—

For the second time in modern history (the first was an extraordinary man named Kemal Ataturk) a man of true national-dictator stature set his goal, achieved it, and abdicated. It didn't matter one bit to Mensch that the wiser editorialists, with their knowledgeable index fingers placed alongside their noses, were pointing out that he had defeated himself, shattered his own empire by extending its borders, and that by releasing his patents into the public domain he was making an empty gesture to the inevitable. Mensch knew what he had done, and why, and what other people thought of it just did not matter.

"What does matter," he said to Fauna in her little house by the old fire hydrant and the quaint streetlamp, "is that there isn't a kraal in Africa or a hamlet in Asia that can't pump water and plow land and heat and light its houses by using a power plant simple enough to be built by any competent mechanic anywhere. There are little ones to rock cradles and power toys and big ones to light whole cities. They pull trains and sharpen pencils, and they need no fuel. Already desalted Mediterranean water is pouring into the northern Sahara; there'll be whole new cities there, just as there were five thousand years ago. In ten years the air all over the earth will be measurably cleaner, and already the demand for oil is down so much that offshore drilling is almost completely stopped. 'Have' and 'have-not' no longer mean what they once meant, because everyone has access to cheap power. And that's why I did it, don't you see?" He really wanted very much to make her understand.

"You cut your hair," she said bitterly. "You wore those awful shoes and went to church and got college degrees and turned into a—a typhoon."

"Tycoon," he corrected absently. "Ah, but Fauna, listen: remember when we were kids, how there were protests and riots in the universities? Think of just one small aspect of that. Suppose a crowd of students wanted to take the administration building—how did they do it? They swarmed up the roads and sidewalks, didn't they? Now—oh hear me out!" for she was beginning to shake her head, open her mouth to interrupt. "Up the roads and sidewalks. Now when those roads and walks were built, the planners and architects didn't put them there to be used that way, did they? But that doesn't matter—when the mob wants to get to the administration building, they take the road that's there. And that's all I did. The way to get what I wanted was short hair, was brown shoes, was published postgraduate papers, was the banks and businesses and government and all of those things that were already there for me to use."

"You didn't need all that. I think you just wanted to move things and shake things and be in the newspapers and history books. You could've made your old motor right here in this house and showed it to people and sold it and stayed here and played the lute, and it would have been the same thing."

"No, there you're wrong," said Mensch. "Do you know what kind of a world we live in? We live in a world where, if a man came up with a sure cure for cancer, and if that man were found to be married to his sister, his neighbors would righteously burn down his house and all his notes. If a man built the most beautiful tower in the country, and that man later begins to believe that Satan should be worshipped, they'll blow up his tower. I know a great and moving book written by a woman who later went quite crazy and wrote crazy books, and nobody will read her great one any more. I can name three kinds of mental therapy that could have changed the face of the earth, and in each case the men who found it went on to insane Institutes and so-called religions and made fools of themselves—dangerous fools at that—and now no one will look at their really great early discoveries. Great politicians have been prevented from being great statesmen because they were divorced. And I wasn't going to have the Mensch machine stolen or buried or laughed at and forgotten just because I had long hair and played the lute. You know, it's easy to have long hair and play the lute and be kind to people when everyone else around you is doing it. It's a much harder thing to be the one who does it first, because then you have to pay a price, you get jeered at and they throw stones and shut you out."

"So you joined them," she accused.

"I used them," he said flatly. "I used every road and path that led to where I was going, no matter who built it or what it was built for."

"And you paid your price," she all but snarled. "Millions in the bank, thousands of people ready to fall on their knees if you snap your fingers. Some price. You could have had love."

He stood up then and looked at her. Her hair was much thinner now, but still long and fine. He reached for it, lifted some. It was white. He let it go.

He thought of fat Biafran babies and clean air and unpolluted beaches, cheaper food, cheaper transportation, cheaper manufacturing and maintenance, more land to lessen the pressures and hysteria during the long slow process of population control. What had moved him to deny himself so much, to rebel, to move and shake and shatter the status quo the way he had, rather than conforming—conforming to long hair and a lute? *You could have had love.*

"But I did," he said; and then, knowing she would never, could never understand, he got in his silent fuelless car and left.

It Was Nothing—Really!

Having reached that stage in his career when he could have a personal private washroom in his office, Henry Mellow came out of it and said into the little black box on his desk "Bring your book, please." Miss Prince acknowledged and entered and said "Eeek."

"'Ever since the dawn of history,'" Henry Mellow dictated, "'mankind has found himself face to face with basic truths that—'"

"I am face to face," said Miss Mellow, "with your pants are down, Mr. Mellow, and you are waving a long piece of toilet paper."

"Ah yes, I'm coming to that . . . with basic truths that he cannot see, or does not recognize, or does not understand.' Are you getting this, Miss Prince?"

"I am getting very upset, Mr. Mellow. Please pull up your pants."

Mr. Mellow looked at her for a long moment while he put his thoughts on "hold" and tuned them out, and tuned her in, and at last looked down. "Archimedes," he said, and put his piece of toilet paper down on the desk. Pulling up his pants, he said, "At least I think it was Archimedes. He was taking a bath and when he lay back in it, displacing the water and watching it slop over the sides of the tub, the solution to a problem came to him, about how to determine how much base metal was mixed in with the king's gold ornaments. He jumped out of the bath and ran naked through the streets shouting Eureka, which means in Greek, 'I have found it.' You, Miss Prince, are witnessing such a moment. Or was it Aristotle?"

"It was disgraceful is what it was," said Miss Prince, "and no matter how long I work here you make me wonder. Toilet paper."

"Some of the most profound thinking in human history has come about in toilets," said Henry Mellow. "The Protestant reformation was begun in a toilet, when Luther was sitting there working on his—am I offending you, Miss Prince?"

"I don't know. I guess it depends on what comes next," said Miss Prince, lowering her hands from her ears, but not much. Warily she watched as he arranged his pennant of toilet paper on the desk and began tearing it, placing his hands palm down on the desk and drawing them apart. "You will observe—Miss Prince, are you getting this?"

She picked up her notebook from where she had flung it to cover her ears. "No, sir, not really."

"Then I shall begin again," said Henry Mellow, and began to dictate the memo which was to strike terror into the hearts and souls of the military-industrial complex. Oh yes, they have hearts and souls. It's just that they never used them until Henry Mellow. Notice the structure there. Henry Mellow was more than a man, he was a historical event. You don't have to say "Wilbur and Orville Wright and their first successful experiment at," you just have to say "Kitty Hawk." You can say "Since Hiroshima" or "Dallas" or "Pasteur" or "Darwin" and people know what you are talking about. So it is that things haven't been the same with the military-industrial complex since Henry Mellow.

The Mellow memo reached the Pentagon by the usual channels, which is to say that a Bureau man, routinely going through the segregated trash from the Mellow offices, found three pages done by a new typist and discarded because of forty-three typographical errors, and was assigned, after they had gone through all the layers of the Bureau to the desk of the Chief himself, to burglarize the Mellow offices and secure photographs of a file copy. He was arrested twice and injured once in the accomplishment of this mission, which was not reported in for some time due to an unavoidable accident: he left the papers in a taxicab after stealing them and it took him three weeks to locate the taxi driver and burglarize *him*. Meanwhile the memo had been submitted to the *Times* in the form of a letter, which in turn formed the basis for an editorial; but as usual, appearance of such material in the public media escaped the notice of public and Pentagon alike.

The impact of the memo on the Pentagon, and most especially

on its target point, the offices of Major General Fortney Superpate, was that of an earthquake seasoned with a Dear John letter. His reactions were immediate and in the best military tradition, putting his whole section on Condition Red and invoking Top Secret, so that the emergency would be heard by no one outside his department. What then followed was total stasis for two hours and forty minutes, because of his instant decision to check out Mellow's results. This required toilet paper, and though General Superpate, like Henry Mellow, had a washroom at the corner of his office, he had enough respect for tradition to stifle his impulse to get up and get some, but instead summoned his adjutant, who snapped a smart salute and received the order. From the outer office the adjutant required the immediate attendance in person of the supply sergeant (remember, this was now a classified matter) who was on leave; the qualifications of his corporal had then to be gone into before he could substitute. Requisition papers were made out, with an error in the fourth copy (of six) which had to be adjusted before the roll of toilet paper, double-locked in a black locked equipment case, was delivered to the general. At this point he was interrupted by a Jamestown gentleman named (he said) Mr. Brown: black suit, black tie, black shoes, and a black leather thing in his breast pocket which, when unfolded, displayed a heavy bright badge with eagles and things on it. "Oh damn," said the general, "how did you people find out about this?" which got him a smile—it was the only thing these Mr. Brown types ever really smiled at—while Mr. Brown scooped up the photocopy of the Mellow memo and the locked equipment case containing the roll of toilet paper. He left, whereupon the general, realizing with a soldier's practicality that the matter was now out of his hands, restored Condition Green and lifted Secrecy, and then felt free to step into his own washroom and do his own toilet-paper procurement. He returned with a yard or so of it, spread it out on his immaculate desk, placed his hands palms down on it and began to pull it apart. He turned pale.

The injection of the Mellow Memo into the industrial area is more of a mystery. Certainly it was the cause of Inland Corp's across-the-board six-percent reduction of raw material orders, and when a corporation as big, and as diversified as Inland cuts back six percent, the whole market shakes like a load of jello in a truck with square wheels. This is the real reason for Outland Industries starting merger talks with Inland, because one of their spies had gotten the word to Outland, but not the memo, and the big wheels at Outland figured if they bought Inland, the memo would come along with the deal. Imagine their surprise, then, when the Chairman of the Board at Inland not only agreed enthusiastically to the merger, but sent along a copy of the memo for free. There is no record of the midnight meetings of the top brass of the two industrial giants, but when they broke up they were, it is reported, a badly frightened bunch. The dawn came up on many a wealthy suburb, estate, club, and hotel suite to the soft worried sound of tearing toilet paper.

And paper towels.

And checks from checkbooks.

As for the merger, it was left in its current state of negotiation, neither withdrawn nor pursued, but waiting; meanwhile, Inland's order to reduce raw materials purchases was lowered to a compromised three percent while the world—the little, real world, not the mass, sleeping world—waited to see what would happen.

The Mellow Memo's most frightening impact, however, was on the secret headquarters in Jamestown. (It's probably the most secret headquarters in the world or anywhere else. No signs out front, unmarked cars, and everybody's named Brown. Sometimes twelve, fourteen lunches are delivered to the front office for "Mr. Brown." Nobody knows how they get sorted out. Everybody in town keeps the secret.)

They had done everything they could; Henry Mellow's home, office, person and immediate associates were staked out, tailed, and bugged, his probable movements computed and suitable responses by the Agency programmed, and there was nothing to do but sit around and wait for something to happen. On total assignment to the Mellow affair were three top agents, Red Brown and Joe Brown and a black-power infiltrator called Brown X. Due to the extremely sensitive nature of the Memo, Red Brown had sent Brown X off on an extremely wild goose chase, tracking down and interviewing Henry Mellow's ex-schoolteachers, kindergarten through fourth grade, in places like Enumclaw, Washington and Turtle Creek, Pennsylvania.

Red Brown rose from his pushbuttoned, signal-light-studded desk and crossed the room and closed the door against the permeating susurrus of computers and tapes and rubber footfalls and hand-shrouded phone calls: "Brown here. . . . Ready. Scramble Two. Brown out." Joe Brown watched him alertly, knowing that this meant they were going to discuss their assignment. He knew too that they would refer to Henry Mellow only as "Suspect." Not The suspect or Mr. Suspect: just Suspect.

Red Brown regained his saddle, or control tower—nobody would call it a chair—and said: "Review. Brainstorm."

Joe Brown started the tape recorder concealed in his black jacket and repeated "Review. Brainstorm," and the date and time.

"Just who is Suspect?" Red Brown demanded. Comprehending perfectly that this would be a fast retake of everything pertinent that they knew about Henry Mellow, with an aim of getting new perspectives and insights, no matter how far out; and that he, Joe Brown, was on trial and on the record in a "have you done your homework" kind of way, Joe Brown responded swiftly, clearly, and in official staccato: "WMA, five ten, unmarried, thirty-six years old, eyes hazel, weight one seventy—"

"All right, all right. Occupation."

"Writer, technical, also science fact articles and book reviews. Self-employed. Also inventor, holding patents number—"

"Never mind those or you'll be reeling off numbers all day, and besides you're bragging, Brown: I know that thing you have with numbers."

Joe Brown was crushed but knew better than to show it.

Memorizing numbers was the one thing he did really well and patent numbers were where he could really shine. "Holds patents on kitchen appliances, chemical processes, hand tools, optical systems . . ."

"Genius type, very dangerous. The Bureau's been segregating his garbage for eighteen months."

"What put them onto him?"

"Internal Revenue. Gets royalties from all over the world. Never fails to report any of it."

Joe Brown pursued his lips. "Has to be hiding something."

"Yes, not usual, not normal. Politics?"

"No politics. Registers and votes, but expresses no opinions."

Joe Brown pursued his lips again, the same purse as before, because it was part of the same words: "Has to be hiding something. And what happens if he turns this thing loose on the world?"

"Worse than the bomb, nerve gas, Dederick Plague, you name it."

"And what if he gets sole control?"

"King of the world."

"For maybe ten minutes." Joe Brown squinted through an imaginary telescopic sight and squeezed an invisible trigger.

"Not if he had the Agency."

Joe Brown looked at Red Brown for a long, comprehending moment. Before he had become an Agent, and even for a while when he was in training, he had been very clear in his mind who the Agency worked for. But as time went on that didn't seem to matter any more; agents worked for the Agency, and nobody in or out of the Agency or the Government or anywhere else would dream of asking who the Agency worked for. So if the Agency decided to work for the king of the world, well, why not? Only one man. It's very easy to take care of one man. The agency had long known how things should be, and with sole control of a thing like this the Agency could make them be that way. For everybody, everywhere.

Red Brown made a swift complex gesture which Joe Brown understood. They both took out their concealed recorders and wiped that last sentence from the tape. They put their recorders away again and looked at each other with new and shining eyes. If the two of them should come by sole possession of the Mellow Effect, then their superior, a Mr. Brown, and his superior, who was head of the whole Agency, had a surprise coming.

Red Brown removed a bunch of keys from his belt and selected one, with which he unlocked a compartment, or drawer, in his desk, or console, and withdrew a heavy steel box, like a safety deposit. Flicking a glance at his colleague to be sure he was out of visual range, he turned a combination knob with great care and attention, this way, that, around again and back, and then depressed a handle. The lid of the box rose, and from it he took two photocopies of the Mellow Memo. "We shall now," he said for the record, "read the Mellow Memo."

And so shall you.

THE MELLOW MEMO

Ever since the dawn of history, mankind has found himself face to face with basic truths that, through inattention, preconception, or sheer stupidity, he cannot see, or does not recognize, or does not understand. There have been times when he has done very well indeed with complex things—for example, the Mayan calendar stones and the navigation of the Polynesians—while blindly overlooking the fact that complex things are built of simple things, and that the simple things are, by their nature, all around us, waiting to be observed.

Mankind has been terribly tardy in his discovery of the obvious. Two clear illustrations should suffice:

You can, for a few pennies, at any toy store or fairgrounds, pick up a pinwheel. Now, I have not been able to discover just when this device was invented, where, or by whom, but as far as I know there are no really early examples of it. An even simpler device can be whittled by an eight-year-old from a piece of pine: a two-bladed propeller. Mounted on a shaft, or pin, it will spin freely in the wind. This would seem to be the kind of discovery which could have been made five hundred years ago, a thousand—even five thousand, when Egyptian artisans were turning out far more complex designs and devices. To put the propeller on a fixed shaft, to spin the shaft and create a wind, to immerse the thing in water and envision pumps and propulsion—these seem to be obvious, self-describing steps to take, and yet for thousands of years, nobody took them. Now imagine if you can—and you can't—what the history of civilization would be, where we would now be technologically, had there been propellers and pumps a thousand years ago—or three, or five! All for the lack of one whittling child, one curious primitive whose eye was caught by a twisted leaf spinning on a spiderweb.

One more example; and this time we will start with modern materials and look back. If you drill a one-sixteenth-inch hole in a sheet of tin, and place a drop of water on the hole, it will suspend itself there. Gravity will pull it downward, while surface tension will draw it upward into a dome shape. Viewed from the edge of the piece of tin, the drop of water is in the shape of a lens—and it is a lens. If you look down through it, with the eye close to the drop, at something held under it and well illuminated, you will find that the liquid lens has a focal length of about half an inch and a power of about fifty diameters. (And if by any chance you want a microscope for nothing, drill your hole in the center of the bottom of a soup can, then cut three sides of a square—right, left, top—in the side of the can and bend the tab thus formed inward to forty-five degrees, to let the light in and reflect it upwards. Cut a slip of glass and fix it so it rests inside the can and under the hole. Mount your subject—a fly's foot, a horsehair, whatever you like—on the glass, put a drop of water in the hole, and you will see your subject magnified fifty times. A drop of glycerin, by the way, is not quite as clear but works almost as well and does not evaporate.)

Microscopes and their self-evident siblings, telescopes, did not appear until the eighteenth century. Why not? Were there not countless thousands of shepherds who on countless dewy mornings were in the presence of early sunlight and drops of water captured on cobwebs or in punctured leaves; why did not just one of them look, just once, through a dewdrop at the whorls of his own thumb? And why, seemingly, did the marvelous artisans of glass in Tyre and Florence and ancient Babylon never think to look through their blown and molded bowls and vases instead of at them? Can you imagine what this world would be if the burning glass, the microscope, the eyeglasses, the telescope had been invented three thousand years earlier?

Perhaps by now you share with me a kind of awe at human blindness, human stupidity. Let me then add to that another species of blindness: the conviction that all such simple things have now been observed and used, and all their principles understood. This is far from so. There are in nature numberless observations yet to be made, and many of them might still be found by an illiterate shepherd; but in addition to these, our own technology has produced a whole new spectrum of phenomena, just waiting for that one observant eye, that one undeluded mind which sees things placed right in front of its nose—not once, not rarely, but over and over and over again, shouting to be discovered and developed.

There is one such phenomenon screaming at you today and every day from at least three places in your house—your bathroom, your kitchen, and, if you have a bank account, your pocket.

Two out of five times, on the average, when you tear off a sheet of toilet tissue, a paper towel, or a check from your checkbook, it will tear across the sheet and not along the perforated line. The same is true of note pads, postage stamps, carbon-and-second-sheet tablets, and virtually every other substance or device made to be torn along perforations.

To the writer's present knowledge, no exhaustive study has ever been made of this phenomenon. I here propose one.

We begin with the experimentally demonstrable fact that in a large percentage of cases, the paper will tear elsewhere than on the perforation line. In all such cases the conclusion is obvious: that the perforation line is stronger than the nonperforated parts.

Let us next consider what perforation is—that is to say, what is done when a substance is perforated. Purely and simply: material is removed.

Now if, in these special cases, the substance becomes stronger when a small part of it is removed, it would seem logical to assume that if still more were removed, the substance would be stronger still. And carried to its logical conclusion, it would seem reasonable to hypothesize that by removing more and more material, the resulting substance would become stronger and stronger until at last we would produce a substance composed of nothing at all—which would be indestructible!

If conventional thinking makes it difficult for you to grasp this simple sequence, or if, on grasping it, you find you cannot accept it, please permit me to remind you of the remark once uttered by a Corsican gentleman by the name of Napoleon Bonaparte*: "To find out if something is impossible—try it." I have done just that, and results so far are most promising. Until I have completed more development work, I prefer not to go into my methods nor describe the materials tested—except to say that I am no longer working with paper. I am convinced, however, that the theory is sound and the end result will be achieved.*

A final word—which surely is not needed, for like everything else about this process, each step dictates and describes the next—will briefly suggest the advantages of this new substance, which I shall conveniently call, with a capital letter, Nothing*:*

The original material, to be perforated, is not expensive and will always be in plentiful supply. Processing, although requiring a rather high degree of precision in the placement of the holes, is easily adaptable to automatic machinery which, once established, will require very little maintenance. And the most significant—one might almost say, pleasant—thing about this processing is that by its very nature (the removal of material) it allows for the retrieval of very nearly 100 percent of the original substance. This salvage may be refabricated into sheets which can then be processed, by repeated perforations, into more Nothing*, so that the initial material may be used over and over again to produce unlimited quantities of* Nothing*.*

Simple portable devices can be designed which will fabricate Nothing *into sheets, rods, tubing, beams or machine parts of any degree of flexibility, elasticity, malleability, or rigidity. Once in its final form,* Nothing *is indestructible. Its permeability, conductivity, and chemical reactivity to acids and bases all are zero. It can be made in thin sheets as a wrapping, so that perishables can be packed in* Nothing*, displayed most attractively on shelves made of* Nothing*. Whole buildings, homes, factories, schools can be built of it. Since, even in tight rolls, it weighs nothing, unlimited quantities of it can be shipped for virtually nothing, and it stows so efficiently that as yet I have not been able to devise a method of calculating how much of it could be put into a given volume—say a single truck or air-*

plane, which could certainly carry enough Nothing to build, pave, and equip an entire city.

Since Nothing (if desired) is impermeable and indestructible, it would seem quite feasible to throw up temporary or permanent domes over houses, cities, or entire geographical areas. To shield aircraft, however, is another matter: getting an airflow through the invisible barrier of Nothing and over the wings of an airplane presents certain problems. On the other hand, orbiting devices would not be subject to these.

To sum up: the logical steps leading to the production of Nothing seem quite within the "state of the art," and the benefits accruing to humanity from it would seem to justify proceeding with it.

There was a certain amount of awe in Miss Prince's voice as it emerged from the little black box saying, "A Mr. Brown is here and would like to see you."

Henry Mellow frowned a sort of "Oh, dear" kind of frown and then said, "Send him in."

He came in, black suit, black shoes, black tie, and in his eyes, nothing. Henry Mellow did not rise, but he was pleasant enough as he gestured, "Sit down, Mr. Brown." There was only one chair to sit in, and it was well placed, so Mr. Brown sat. He identified himself with something leathery that opened and shut like a snapping turtle with a mouthful of medals. "What can I do for you?"

"You're Henry Mellow." Mr. Brown didn't ask, he *told.*

"Yes."

"You wrote a memo about Noth—about some new substance to build things with."

"Oh that, yes. You mean Nothing."

"That depends," said Mr. Brown humorlessly. "You've gone ahead with research and development."

"I have?"

"That's what we'd like to know."

"We?"

Mr. Brown's hand dipped in and out of his black jacket and made the snapping turtle thing again.

"Oh," said Henry Mellow. "Well, suppose we just call it an intellectual exercise—an entertainment. We'll send it out to a magazine, say, as fiction."

"We can't allow that."

"Really not?"

"We live in a real world, Mr. Mellow, where things happen that maybe people like you don't understand. Now I don't know whether or not there's any merit in your idea or how far you've gone with it, but I'm here to advise you to stop it here and now."

"Oh? Why, Mr. Brown?"

"Do you know how many large corporations would be affected by such a thing—if there was such a thing? Construction, mining, hauling, prefabrication—everything. Not that we take it seriously, you understand, but we know something about you and we have to take it seriously anyway."

"Well, I appreciate the advice, but I think I'll send it out anyway."

"Then," continued Mr. Brown as if he had not spoken, and acquiring, suddenly, a pulpit resonance, "Then . . . there's the military."

"The military."

"Defense, Mr. Mellow. We can't allow just anybody to get their hands on plans to put impenetrable domes over cities—suppose somebody overseas got them built first?"

"Do you think if a lot of people read it in a magazine, someone overseas would do it first?"

"That's the way we have to think." He leaned closer. "Look, Mr. Mellow—have you thought maybe you've got a gold mine for yourself here? You don't want to turn it over to the whole world."

"Mr. Brown, I don't want a gold mine for myself. I don't much want any kind of mines for anybody. I don't want people cutting down more forests or digging more holes in the ground to take out what they can't put back, not when there are better ways. And I don't want to get paid for not using a better way if I find one. I just want people to be able to have what they want without raping a planet for it, and I want them to be able to protect themselves if they have to, and to get comfortable real quick and real cheap even if it means some fat cats have to get comfortable along with them.

Not thin, Mr. Brown—just comfortable."

"I thought it was going to be something like this," said Mr. Brown. His hand dipped in and out of the black jacket again, but this time it was holding a very small object like a stretched-out toy pistol. "You can come along with me willingly or I'll have to use this."

"I guess you'd better use it, then," said Henry Mellow regretfully.

"It's nice," said Mr. Brown. "It won't even leave a mark."

"I'm sure it won't," said Henry Mellow as the little weapon went off with a short, explosive hiss. The little needle it threw disintegrated in midair.

Mr. Brown turned gray. He raised the weapon again. "Don't bother, Mr. Brown," said Henry Mellow. "There's a sheet of just plain Nothing between us, and it's impenetrable."

Still holding his weapon, Mr. Brown rose and backed away—and brought up sharply against some Nothing behind him. He turned and patted it wildly and then ran to the side, where he struck an invisible barrier that sat him down on the rug. He looked as if he was going to cry.

"Sit in the chair," said Henry Mellow, not unkindly. "Please. There. That's better. Now then: listen to me." And something, at that moment, seemed to happen to Henry Mellow: to Mr. Brown he looked bigger, wider, and, somehow realer than he had been before. It was as if the business he was in had for a long time kept him from seeing people as real, and now, suddenly, he could again.

Henry Mellow said, "I've had a lot longer to think this out than you have, and besides, I don't think the way you do. I guess I don't think the way anybody does. So I've been told. But for what it's worth, here it is: If I tried to keep this thing and control it myself, I wouldn't live ten minutes. (What's the matter, Mr. Brown? Somebody else say that? I wouldn't doubt it.) Or I could just file it away and forget it; matter of fact, I tried that and I just couldn't forget it, because there's a lot of people dying now, and more could die in the future, for lack of it. I even thought of printing it up, in detail, and scattering it from a plane. But then, you know what I wrote about how many shepherds didn't look into how many dewdrops; that could happen again—probably would, and it's not a thing I could do thousands of times. So I've decided to do what I said—publish it in a magazine. But not in detail. I don't want anyone to think they stole it, and I don't want anyone to make a lot out of it and then come looking for me, either to eliminate me (that could happen) or to share it, because I don't want to share it with one person or two or a company—I want to share it with everybody, all the good that comes of it, all the bad. You don't understand that, do you, Mr. Brown?

"You're going to meet a doctor friend of mine in a minute who will give you something that will help you forget. It's quite harmless, but you won't remember any of this. So before you go, I just want to tell you one thing: there's another Mr. Brown downstairs. Mr. Brown X, he said you called him, and all he wanted was the process—not for himself, not for the Agency, but for his people; he said they really know how to get along with Nothing." He smiled. "And I don't want you to feel too badly about this, but your Agency's not as fast on its feet as you think it is. Last week I had a man with some sort of Middle European accent and a man who spoke Ukrainian and two Orientals and a fellow with a beard from Cuba. Just thought I'd tell you. . . .

"So good-bye, Mr. Brown. You'll forget all about this talk, but maybe when you write a check and tear it in two getting it out of the book, or when you rip off a paper towel or a stamp and the perforations hold, something will tell you to stop a minute and think it through." He smiled and touched a second button on his intercom.

"Stand by, Doc."

"Ready," said the intercom.

Henry Mellow moved something under the edge of his desk and the visitor's chair dropped through the floor. In a moment it reappeared, empty. Henry Mellow touched another control, and the sheets of Nothing slid up and away, to await the next one.

So when it happens, don't just say Damn and forget it. Stop a minute and think it through. Somebody's going to change the face of the earth and it could be you.

Take Care of Joey

Talking to this bartender, I forget what about, he said wait and reached for the backbar phone. I hadn't much noticed the little guy in the green sweater but he had. He was eyeing him while he dialed so I did too. The little guy was ambling down the whole length of the place and slowing down, not quite stopping, at each bar stool. Every customer got the eye, a cold, up-down and back kind of hit-me-why-doncha look. Spooky. Some little guys got this banty-cock thing going: you know, I'm little but I'm tough, try me out, and they really are tough. This one wasn't. Somehow his legs didn't work right, I can't say how, it wasn't even a limp, and he was real skinny.

"Hello, Dwight. This is Danny at the Ramble Inn. Joey just come in and it looks like he—Yeah. Yeah. Yeah." He hung up and the both of us watched this little guy, this Joey. Some of the customers turned their back, swing to the left as he come near, swing to the right as he passed, and when that happened he would edge in next to them and hang there until they had to face him. He'd give them that eye and like twitch his upper lip at one side and if they didn't say nothing he would walk on, and they didn't say nothing.

Then some others would look at him what-the-hell, and he would look right back at them until they turned away, and then move on. One customer, he was a big guy and kind of sleepy-looking, but look out for guys like that, he said "You want something?" and this little Joey waits a good long time to answer him, "Maybe later." Then there's me, because I'm down at the bottom end with the bartender. I'm watching him in the mirror by then and he can't know that, so he stands by my elbow doing nothing so long I got to turn around and look at him. I said Hi.

He didn't say nothing. He waited what got to be an awful long time, hanging those boiled-looking eyes on me, and then he spit on the floor. I didn't have to move my feet, but almost. He kept on looking and then rounded me and said to the bartender, "I want to make a boiler."

Danny the bartender got him his shot and chaser and the little guy took the glasses and moved over to a table where he could see everybody. I said, "Guy like that, could be trouble."

"Will be trouble," Danny the bartender says.

Before I can talk any more there comes in a tall man, worried, looked all around but I don't think he could see this Joey because he come straight down to where I am and says to the bartender, "Danny, where. . . ."

"Hi, Dwight. There he is." He points with his eyes.

Dwight, that's the tall one, he flashes a look and then uses the backbar mirror to study out this Joey, seems like he wants to know everything he can by looking without talking to him. I seen him squinch up his face when Joey knocks back the rye and chugalugs his chaser. I hear him say O God when Joey gets up.

Joey puts a cigarette in his chops and kind of sets his chin down and moves halfway up the bar where sits this big sleepy-looking guy who told him before, "You want something?" and he reaches for the guy's cigar which is in an ashtray on the bar. Dwight says in my ear again O God and Danny the bartender says, "Dwight, you better get him out of here," and Sleepy says, "Hey get your goddamn hands off my *seegar.*"

Joey goes right on getting a light off the cigar for his cigarette and paying no mind and Dwight starts moving up toward the two of them and maybe it would of been all right even then but Joey taken the cigar and dropped it in the big guy's highball. Well, of course, that was it and Sleepy takes a swing, but by that time Dwight is there in between them and more than that—he gives little Joey a shoulder that sends him cakewalking back out of the way. For that Dwight has to take the punch on the side of his neck and he puts up his hands like peacemaking and says Cool it or some such.

But Sleepy is not about to cool it now and gets on his feet, and he is a much bigger man than I thought. He winds up a ham-handed right at the end of an arm like a tree-trunk, and I have seen guys who do that and I want to yell at Dwight don't pay no attention to that big looping windup, he wants you to, and sure enough Sleepy's left comes out from under his armpit traveling short and straight and lays Dwight out flat on the floor and sliding.

Disgusted and scared I hear Danny the bartender say "God now I got to call the pleece, I hate to call the pleece," so I told him not to and went up there where the trouble was, Dwight wiggling a little on the floor and Sleepy with his eye on Joey and Joey backing away. I guess I was going to try to talk it through but Sleepy tromps Dwight. He does it still looking at Joey like he don't care where he tromps him and he don't, either. I don't like guys who tromp guys unless they need to, so I told Sleepy to quit and he tromped Dwight again looking at me now and cocking that big phony right-hander my way, and when you see them do that twice in a row you know you got a one-trick fighter, which makes it easy for anyone who knows two, and I know half a hundred.

I showed him some and he never laid a hand on me but the one I grabbed the wrist of and rolled him over my back and airplaned him, and by that time I had got to him four times already and he wasn't about to get up again for a while. I got Dwight up on his feet and over to where my drink was and he hung onto the bar shaking his head. Danny the bartender give him a shot and that seemed to help a little while the customers went back to their stools except a couple over to see about Sleepy. I called over to them not to worry. And meanwhile that little Joey that started it all is standing right where he was where Sleepy had pushed him to.

Danny said for me to drink my drink. "It's on the house, grateful, but get that Joey out of here, he's bad news from now on out, I know him, honest to God, Dwight"—and I realized it was Dwight he was talking to now not me—"I don't know why you do it. If it was me I would just let somebody plow him under."

Dwight says, "Well it ain't you. Thanks for the drink." He looks at me and he thanks me too. I said I'll go along with him. Sometimes when these things happen they are not finished where they start and you get jumped outside. Dwight said he didn't think so this time and neither did I but I went anyway. We kind of collected Joey one on each side walking out. He went right along with it, he held back only a second at the door to look back where a couple of guys was helping Sleepy onto his feet, and then he looked at Dwight, and then he laughed at him. He didn't pay no attention to me at all. I mean he was a very creepy little guy.

I went along with them and I will tell you why. I have seen a lot in a lot of places, and there is one thing that always hooks me and that is when I see somebody taking care of somebody, because to tell you the truth I just cannot understand it. Why a guy throws his self on a grenade to save other guys. Why some stranger runs into a burning house to get someone out. How it is you can call somebody up in the middle of the night and he will run out to get some other guy out of trouble. You can say all you want about heroes and survival of the race and sacrifice and all like that, and I say bullshit. Maybe you want to believe that stuff but what I believe is that people is either wolves or wolverines when they are not tapeworms or sheep, and that is that.

All the same I keep looking, I really don't know why. I look very hard and I don't like it. I mean it's like I don't want to find out even once that anyone would really and truly take care of someone else without he got something out of it. It's like I'm scared to find it out, like my whole world would get shook upside down if I ever did, but I keep looking.

The first thing happened when we left the Ramble Inn was Joey pulled away from us and run straight out into the street. There was cars coming and a truck and a bus and Joey just did not seem to give a damn. There was a lot of honking and screeching and cussing right away and Dwight, he was still rocking from that powerhouse punch, but all the same he dove out into that traffic and got to Joey and throwed both arms around him and rassled him to the dotted line between lanes and held him there until the traffic opened up and he could shove him back to the sidewalk. He was cussing him out too, and he meant it. Joey just laughed. Dwight told him to get the hell home before somebody killed him, and I think he really meant himself, him, Dwight, was the somebody. Joey just said Nope. He still did not pay any attention to me.

Dwight turned the little guy loose and he started to amble down the street, and Dwight walked slow behind him. He kept his eyes on him almost every second. He said to me well, thanks for what you done in there, it was like good-bye, beat it. But I walked along with him. So after a while Dwight said he could handle things all right. He said, "He gets like this every once in a while, wants to go out and drink. It is not too hard as long as you keep your eye on him and head him off from the big ones." I don't think he meant big guys, I think he meant big trouble.

I said if he didn't mind me asking, when a guy is so eager to get his self killed, why not just let him do it? because he sure is asking for it. And Dwight said "No he's not." He said that positive, I mean like he *knew*.

So there was Joey walking along in the middle of the night like he wasn't going no place in particular and didn't much care, and the two of us following along a little way behind watching him and talking a little once in a while. When I kept on sticking around, Dwight quit saying thanks-and-goodnight things. I found out they were not related, they did not come from the same town, they did not live together or work in the same company or even in the same line. Dwight was a shop foreman, I think in some kind of printing place, he was a pretty educated guy, I mean you got the idea he could go a lot farther if something wasn't holding him back. Joey was a sheet metal man in an auto body place. Also they were not queer. The more I found out about them the more worried I got that here was somebody who was ready to lay it on the line for somebody else without any payoff, none at all. I mean, I don't think they even liked each other.

So I finally asked him right out, why? and all he said was, "There's some things you just got to do."

Then Joey began to run.

You wouldn't believe a spindly little guy like that could take off that way, one second ambling along looking into store windows, the next scooting like a squirted apple seed. I heard that same tired O God from Dwight, and then voom he's off after the little guy. I thought well hell, and went after them.

Joey went straight for three blocks widening the gap all the way. I right away dug that Dwight was not in good shape at all because when I passed him in the first half-block he was already wheezing for breath. So I did not bother with him but made it my business to round up that Joey and nail him down good. It was not easy.

He turned right into an alley and if I had not really been pushing myself I would not of seen him turn right again into a dead-end loading area behind a big warehouse. It was dark in there but not altogether. All the same I could not see him any place.

I backed away looking every place until I was in the alley again so Dwight would see me when he come by, and he did. He was so pooped and tuckered and winded out he could not talk at all, and when I told him which way Joey had went he just nodded his head and hung on to a brick wall gasping and coughing a little once in a while until he was put together again. Then he said, "We got to stop him now. He got something wrong with his heart muscle, he shouldn't run like that. He knows that but he does it every once in a while anyway the dirty rotten little son of a bitch." So now I knew it wasn't just not liking each other, Dwight, he hated that little guy.

He went back into the loading area and looked all around.

Somebody told me once that if you ever want to hide, don't go down or behind, go up. Guys looking for something will always look down or under or behind things, never up unless something attracts them. I remembered that and so started looking up, and sure enough.

I hit on Dwight's arm and pointed. There was a fire escape that went clear up to the roof and about sixty feet up there was a black blob kind of weaving back and forth. If you looked real careful you could see it was Joey, and after a while you could see he was on one of the landings of the steel stairway, and when your eyes got really used to it you could see he was at the end of the landing on the wrong side of the railing, hanging on to it and standing on one leg and pivoting back and forth, hanging out over nothing at all.

"O God. I got to get him. He gets dizzy spells." Dwight started to run for the bottom of the ladder. I got to him in two jumps. It was easy, he did not have his breath back even yet. I said how the hell did he think he was going to get to the ladder?

It was one of those swing-down ladders that if you are on the fire escape coming down you get on it and it comes down, otherwise it stays up on the second floor level so burglars can't get to use it. Somebody must of tied it down and Joey found it like that, he sure did not leave it like that. You would have to be a bird or a polevaulter to get to it now. And up there Joey was swinging like a monkey, I heard him laugh.

Dwight got right under the ladder and jumped. It was pathetic. He jumped and jumped, I think he was more than half out of his mind. "We got to get to him," I think he was saying over and over in between those little tired useless jumps—you could not tell he was so out of breath.

There was a smooth six-inch pipe at the corner of the building running from the ground up to the third floor, I don't know why. It passed about four feet away from that second-floor landing of the fire escape where the swing-down ladder was. From the ground it looked like a long way up and a hell of a way from the landing, and a smooth six-inch pipe is not the easiest thing to get hold of but what the hell. I started up it hand over hand. There wasn't nothing feet could do so I just let them hang there and come along for the ride. Down below me Dwight was trying to follow me, he could not even get off the ground.

When I got above the landing I stopped for a couple seconds to get my breath because a couple of seconds was all my hands had left in them. I flipped my feet up and out to get a swing, swung back and then forward and let go, trying to shove at the same time. It was a nice idea but it did not altogether work. I did not get both hands on the guard-rail as I figured; I got one hand on the flat floor-bars. It hurt a whole lot but I could hang on until I stopped swinging and was able to climb to the landing. I had to lay down for quite a time before I was ready to move on.

I guess I could of pushed the ladder down then and let Dwight take over but tell you the truth I never thought of it. I started up after that crazy Joey.

I heard him laughing again.

I went up kind of on all fours. I think he thought it was Dwight, not me. Anyway when I got to the sixth landing he started to scream at me, "You ain't Dwight, you get the hell out of here, you mind your own goddamn business, it's old Dwight'll take care of me." I did not say nothing but kept on coming. He was still over the rail leaning back against his grip. All he had to do was open his fingers and that was it. I came on slow.

Maybe it was all fun for him up to then, I don't know.

Maybe it was getting mad at me like that, that made some difference inside his crazy head. But as I come close I could see in the little bit of stray light his eyes go funny. I mean he stopped screaming and he stopping swinging and his eyes went white, I guess they rolled right on up out of sight. And his knees started to buckle.

I jumped. I reached for him with my right hand because I am right-handed and because I did not have no time to think. It was the same hand I caught myself with when I swung off the pipe and it was bloody and skinned. It hurt a whole lot but that was all right—it just wouldn't work very good. It landed into his armpit as he fell, which is a hell of a way to catch anybody, and got hold of a bunch of shirt and skin. I fell down and slid forward and he would of pulled me right off after him but I arched my back and caught the underside of the rail with my heels. As long as I could keep my knees bent my heels made a sort of half-ass hook that at least stopped the sliding. I got my other hand on him. He was no help, he was dead weight, he was out cold. I remember thinking to myself for just one second, oh the hell with it, I've done enough. But I did not listen to that and I hung on, and after a minute I found the strength to pull him up high enough to bend his chest onto the deck bars and press back and fall full length on them and pull him all the way in.

Way down below in the dark Dwight was yelling and yelling something. He was yelling, "Don't hit him. For God's sake don't hit him."

I think if he had not passed out like that I would of hit him. Like I said I know a lot of tricks but there are some I know I never got to try yet and I would of liked to try some of them out. But there wasn't any need, and after I rested I hung him on my shoulder and walked down the fire escape with him. The swinging ladder went down without no trouble and I got to the ground and it swung up again with a clang and I put Joey down on the ground.

Dwight jumped on him and felt him all over and put his ear on Joey's mouth and lit a match and rolled back an eyelid and then he hunkered down and pulled a deep sigh. "He's going to be all right."

I said that was a damn shame.

Dwight said he would lay like this for a half hour or so and then come to, and he would take him home. He said then he probably would not pull anything like this again for two, three weeks.

I think I got a little bit mad then and I called him a number of names all meaning Stupid. I said to waste his time looking out for a crazy ugly little fart like that Joey, he should have his head candled.

He hunkered there by Joey and looked up at me and let me run down and then he said well, he guessed I had the right to hear the whole story.

He said there's always one kid in any crowd that is the goat for everybody—the little fat boy. Or sometimes the little skinny boy or the one boy with curly hair. He said the more everybody jumps on that one kid the more you get to hate him, and sometimes it does you good to get him alone and beat the hell out of him just because he is there to beat the hell out of. So Joey was that kid, see, and one day Dwight got him alone and beat the hell out of him, and Joey got up off the ground and hit him. Maybe it was just he was not ready, but he went over like tall timber and banged his head into some broken bottles and was knocked out and cut some, and when he came to in a minute or so Joey was trying to wipe away the blood off his head. Somehow that made him like crazy, and he jumped up and beat Joey and knocked him down and tromped him till he was tired. Then he went home. When they found Joey they thought he was dead and for months in the hospital they thought he was not going to make it. But he made it kind of.

He had something wrong with his spleen and his central nervous system that made him walk a little funny and in his head where the skull fracture had squeezed his brains. Also a broken rib done something to his heart. And according to the state law, a death resulting from an assault was murder even if it happened a long time after.

With all that, any punch or fall was liable to take Joey right off. Dwight knew that and Joey knew that. If ever they found Joey dead the chances were that whatever killed him would not of killed him without he was so messed up, and any coroner would be able to tell. So all Dwight could do was try to see to it that Joey did not get into trouble.

"Every once in a while he gets to brooding about he will never get married or go to college or be like other people, and he goes out and drinks and tries to get himself clobbered so maybe I will wind up in the chair, and also he likes to see me doing all I have to do to take care of him." He looked down at Joey for a long time and then up at me. "He moved from home to Philadelphia and then to Macon and Cleveland, Ohio and now here, and I had to go along too." He looked down at Joey again and said, "I never went to college either and I never got to marry anybody or have kids, I guess I never will. It's twenty-two years now."

I said, "Well, you have just made me feel one hell of a lot better." I said, "I been looking all my life for somebody who does things for other people without he gets anything for it and if I ever found one I believe it would blow my mind." I said, "All the dogs eating all the dogs, I can understand that and I can see how the whole thing works, but if ever you show me one guy who will do big things for other people just because they need doing, I will freak out." And I said, "What the hell are you laughing at?"

He said, "You're one."

I said, "No I ain't." I ran away saying, No I ain't. I don't want to be like that, I don't want anyone to be like that, if anyone was like that, I wouldn't understand how things work.

Story Notes

By Paul Williams

The stories collected in this volume were written between 1957 and 1970. Sturgeon's writing output during this period began to decrease, and he turned to writing for TV and movies for income. During the period from 1965 to 1966, while his relationship with his third wife, Marion, was unraveling, he traveled back and forth between Woodstock, NY and Los Angeles. On the West Coast, he worked with the creators and writers involved in the first *Star Trek* TV series. The first episode of *Star Trek,* "The Man-Trap," which aired on September 8, 1966, mentions him obliquely. In his honor, the first crewman killed by the "salt monster" of the story was satirically named "Sturgeon." Sturgeon's first *Star Trek* episode, "Shore Leave," aired in December 1966, and the second one, "Amok Time," aired in September 1967. This last episode is well-known in *Star Trek* lore for its introduction of the Vulcan hand salute, Spock's sex life, and elements of Vulcan culture.

In the spring of 1966, Sturgeon began to make Los Angeles his permanent home, first living for a period with the writer Harlan Ellison, and then in Sherman Oaks. In the spring of 1969, he met and began living with his fourth long-term companion, Wina. They moved to a house in Echo Park and in January 1970, they had a son, Andros.

"Ride in, Ride Out" by Theodore Sturgeon and Don Ward; first published in *Sturgeon's West,* (Doubleday, 1973). Probably written in 1957 (judging from a mention in Sturgeon's correspondence of stories he was trying unsuccessfully to sell). In 1956, Sturgeon described the process of his collaboration with Ward: *Don dreams 'em up and I write 'em my way and submit them without his seeing them.* Ward, who was editor of the short story magazine *Zane Grey's Western (ZGW),* describes *ZGW* as "one of the last Western magazines to fall before the rising challenge of the TV horse opera." "The market for Western short stories vanished," he reports in his introduction to *Sturgeon's West,* reminding us that the existence of genre fiction, including most of Theodore Sturgeon's opus, depends on the existence of a paying market for such particular types of story.

The epigram "Beware the fury of a patient man" is also quoted in the story "Extrapolation" in the 1964 anthology *Sturgeon in Orbit* (first published under the title "Beware the Fury" in *Fantastic Stories* magazine in 1954).

"Assault and Little Sister": first published in *Mike Shayne Mystery Magazine,* July 1961. Editor's blurb from the original magazine appeared as "A TERRIFYING STORY OF SUSPENSE: THE AUTHOR OF THIS UNUSUAL AND CHILLING MYSTERY STORY SHARES WITH RAY BRADBURY THE DISTINCTION OF BEING ONE OF THE TWO OR THREE OUTSTANDING FANTASY WRITERS OF OUR DAY. WE THINK YOU'LL AGREE THAT HE HAS MORE THAN ONE STRING TO HIS BOW."

"When You Care, When You Love": first published in *The Magazine of Fantasy and Science Fiction (F&SF),* September, 1962; probably written in the first months of 1962. This was identified by Sturgeon bibliographers Benson and Stephenson-Payne as the long-awaited first installment of a Sturgeon novel called *The Unbegotten Man,* which was originally announced in the back pages of the 1950 Greenberg Publishers' hardcover edition of *The Dreaming Jewels.* That means that as far back as 1950, Sturgeon was already developing the novel that he ultimately contracted to write in the early 1960s in which "When You Care, When You Love" became the out-of-sequence opening section, as "Baby Is Three" had been in *More than Human.* As I indicated in the notes to the first volume of this *Complete Stories* series, Sturgeon's interest in pursuing this theme began with his story "Accidentally on Porpoise" in 1938.

The novel-length expansion of "When You Care" that Sturgeon contracted with a publisher to write in the 1960s was to be called *The Tulip Tree.* A large file folder containing notes for this novel can be found among the papers belonging to the Sturgeon Literary Trust. In an introductory feature of a special Sturgeon issue, Editor Avram Davidson of *F&SF* wrote, "There is, of course, the new Theodore Sturgeon story, the first of three, which, when finished, will be published as one book; plus Judith Merril's 'personality' article on the Guest of Honor [while the magazine was on sale, Sturgeon was Guest of Honor at the annual World Science Fiction Convention, held in 1962 in Chicago]; plus James Blish's cameo-like critique of Sturgeon as literary craftsman; plus Sam Moskowitz's Sturgeon bibliography—and, for lagniappe, a short excursion into extraterrestrial zoology by Robin Sturgeon, penultimate child to Theodore."

The editor's introduction to Robin's half-page piece reveals that he is ten years old and that "this article ["Martian Mouse"] was originally written as a school composition."

Blish's article describes Sturgeon, in a much-quoted line, as "the finest conscious artist science fiction has ever had.

Davidson's introduction in *F&SF* read:

"Among the paradoxes of the kingdom of nature is this: that the golden-throated nightingale is drab, while the splendid peacock has a harsh scream for a voice. 'Paradox,' in the sense of 'a seeming contradiction'—but of course really no contradiction at all. The splendor of song is sufficient for the nightingale. The peacock's plumage is glory enough for him. Nature, there, is neither niggardly nor lavish past measure. We have writers who sing sweetly as nightingales, writers who are gorgeous as peacocks. It is a flat fact that Theodore Sturgeon is both. As someone put it to us recently, he 'has an aura.' His flashing eyes, his floating hair, Pan-like beard, continually sparkling wit, his alchemist's fingers, and his ardent pen. . . . It is around us that the circle is thrice-woven; it is we who feed on honeydew and drink the milk of paradise. Much have we traveled in the realms of gold, who have read much (or even little) of his work. It seems only right, somehow, that, with all this, Theodore Sturgeon should have a beautiful wife and beautiful children as well. It seems, anyhow, not right that we can find (after long searching) nothing fresher to say at this point than this: We are proud to publish this newest story by Theodore Sturgeon. It will form (though complete in itself) part of a book, and he has promised us the privilege of publishing the other parts as they are written. The tale has its beginnings with the long, deep thoughts of Captain Gamaliel Wyke, crouching by the winter fire in his four great grey shawls, near the tolling breakers and the creaking gulls. Thus it begins. There is time enough before we consider its ending."

"Hold-up à la Carte": first published in *Ellery Queen's Mystery Magazine*, February, 1964. Editor's blurb from the first page of the original magazine appearance: "Once upon a time (in September, 1962, to be exact),

Theodore Sturgeon had occasion to look through his old files for the carbon copy of an early short story—when lo and behold, out popped another short story, one that had never been published and which Mr. Sturgeon had completely forgotten. This original manuscript was resting in peace under (to quote Mr. Sturgeon) some layers of peat moss in the bottom of an old box.... Now, Mr. Sturgeon could not remember how long ago he had written this newly discovered story—he judged he had done it for some demanding editor back in the 16th or 17th Century....

Well, the interesting thing about this previously unpublished Sturgeon is simply this: it is a genuine 'period piece'—a story that will remind you of 'the good old days' of Street and Smith's *Detective Story Magazine*—the 'dear, dead days' of Herman Landon's *The Gray Phantom,* and of Johnston (*The Mark of Zorro*) McCulley's Thubway Tham; ah, remember? This new-old Sturgeon is the kind of story that was sedately popular in the 1920s, the accepted detective fare of its time (when the hard-boiled experiment was just beginning). It is the kind of story that, we judge, could have been written early in the same decade that saw the birth of Dorothy Sayers' Lord Peter Wimsey, Earl Derr Bigger's Charlie Chan, S.S. van Dine's Philo Vance, and E.Q.'s Ellery Queen.

"How to Forget Baseball": first published in *Sports Illustrated,* December 21, 1964. In the introduction to the tenth anniversary issue of *Sports Illustrated,* the editors described the special feature on "The Future of Sport" as "a practical look at what to expect in the next decade," "the sporting miracles of tomorrow, in color today," and "a chilling glimpse of a game of the far future" (the Sturgeon story). In introducing the special issue, the publisher, Sidney L. James, writes, among other things: "Beyond the practical side of the future is the fanciful. Ours is a science fiction sports story by Theodore Sturgeon, one of the two or three writers who emerged as giants in the field when science fiction moved out of pulp country after the atom bomb made impossibilities valid subjects for serious speculation. Sturgeon's grim, sardonic and somewhat Orwellian view of how sport and society may evolve is one that we are far from sharing, but we do feel that his story—which effectively demonstrates the high level of writing skill in this genre—is a contribution to thinking about sport. And sport is to be thought about as well as enjoyed."

On the title page of the story: OUT OF A FANTASTIC SOMEDAY WORLD WHIRLS A DEMONIAC FLACK IN A FORMLESS CAR TO

SHOW A POOR PRIMITIVE FROM AN ALL-BUT-VANISHED SOCIETY THE NEW NATIONAL GAME, QUOIT. ONE OF THE COUNTRY'S MOST DISTINGUISHED SCIENCE FICTION WRITERS TELLS HOW THE PRIMITIVE IS AT FIRST CONFUSED, THEN HORRIFIED, FASCINATED AND—IN THE END—ENTRAPPED BY A THING HE ABHORS.

"The Nail and the Oracle": first published in *Playboy,* Oct. 1965.

"If All Men Were Brothers, Would You Let One Marry Your Sister?": first published in Harlan Ellison, ed., *Dangerous Visions,* in 1967. In *Dangerous Visions,* each story was bookended by an introduction by the book's editor and an afterword or epilogue by the story's author. Sturgeon, consistent with his use of the auctorial voice (in the style of British novelist Henry Fielding) as part of his stories from the beginning of his writing career, made the afterword part of his story. He used a shortened, rewritten version of the afterword (when he first published the story outside of Harlan's anthology—in *Case and the Dreamer,* a Sturgeon collection of three short novels published in 1974) to conclude themes raised in auctorial asides earlier in the story. So the afterword appears in that shortened form as part of the story, as in *Case and the Dreamer.* It's a letter to the story's reader, parallel to the letter from TS to Harlan quoted in Ellison's introduction.

Finally, for the reader's enjoyment, this is a letter Sturgeon wrote to his wife Marion and their children in Woodstock, New York, dated July 15, 1966, and thus during the period he was staying with Harlan and writing some of the stories in this volume:

Dear Dear Everybody:

This is just a short note to let you know I love you all, each and every single one, and love you well; and that I miss you and will appreciate any tiny word from any of you about what you are doing and what you are thinking about, no matter how trivial you might think it is; it's important to me. Also I want you to know that I am working very hard on my two television shows, The Invaders and Star Trek, and although it is very hard, and coming too slowly, it is going well, and if I work very hard I will be able to be back in Woodstock before the second week in August.

I will tell you about one adventure and one wonderful surprise. The other night Harlan had the wild and sudden impulse to go to a huge dis-

count store called Akron—kind of a Big Scot. Harlan's little bronze Austin-Healey only has two seats, and Norman Spinrad, the writer, is here, and Harlan's girlfriend Sherri, so we took my car, which is a little brown Volkswagen I rented, and off we went. As soon as we got there Harlan dived into the clothing section and I disappeared into Hardware and Tools and Sherri began to look at hats and sweaters and Norman sort of got lost.

After quite a long time, Harlan found me looking at some lumber thoughtfully, and zeroed in on something stacked next to the lumber. "Just what we need," he said, in that superpositive Harlan Ellison way, pointing at a twelve-foot stepladder. "What on earth for?" says I. Says he: "To clean the inside of the skylight." "But Harlan!" "Come on," says he. "Let's take it over to the checkout." "But Harlan," I said gently, knocking him down and putting my knee to his chest, "don't you think it's too big?" "Oh no. It'll just reach," says he. Says I, patiently, "I don't mean for the skylight, Harlan, I mean for the Volkswagen, Harlan: that stepladder is TWELVE FEET LONG.*" Says he, a great light dawning: "Oh." So we went to the check-out to pick up the other things he had bought.*

He had bought the way nobody else in the world buys: hot plate trivets, some Italian knit dickies, some stationery, kitchen stuff, some electrical fixtures, an ebony and wicker settle about the size of our piano bench, and FOUR THIRTY-QUART GARBAGE CANS. *We loaded everything into the garbage cans and carried them out to the Volks. We put them down on the sidewalk. We looked at each other and at the car, which somehow looked very much smaller than it had before we went in. Spinrad, who at the best of times is an Eeyore, immediately sent up a wail of total despair and impossibility. Sherri, who is usually a very self-contained girl, began to laugh uncontrollably. Harlan took out his glasses and put them on, and uttering small sounds of purpose and reassurance, began attacking the problem of loading the car. "See? No sweat! Told you. Now the other garbage can? Just give it a good shove there. Right. What do you mean you can't get the door shut?" and so on. Norman began to get really persuasive with his Eeyorisms.*

The store was now closed and we wouldn't be able to return the merchandise. If the police saw the car loaded like that they'd make us take half of it out, probably miles out on a freeway. And besides it looked as if it were going to rain. About this time Harlan got the last of our purchases into the car and got both doors and the trunk lid closed. 'I told you!' he said triumphantly. The trunk was full and the back seat was full and the seat-backs were tipped forward, the right one against the windshield and the left one smack against the steering wheel. 'Harlan,' I said. 'Where are we going to put the people?' 'Yeah,' he acknowledged, wrenched the door open and started to pull everything out again. The self-contained Sherri staggered backwards across the sidewalk and clung to the building front to keep from collapsing; I don't think I have ever seen anyone laugh so hard. Norman, on the other hand, seemed about to dissolve in tears. Harlan got everything back out on the sidewalk, took off his glasses, polished them, put them back on again and began loading things in a different way. (Do you know how big a thirty-quart garbage can is? Big enough for one of me, or two of Harlan, to hide in with the cover on. . . .) Well—he did it.

And all four of us got into the front seat. We went to a place which serves nothing but pancakes—Swedish and German and French and flaming and with sausages and sour cream and six kinds of syrup and lots more. We ate so many pancakes that we came this close to being too fat to get back in the car. And all the while I was chewing on the knobby thought that Harlan had already bought the garbage cans and that settle when he came back to where I was and started lusting after a twelve-foot stepladder.

"Runesmith": by Theodore Sturgeon and Harlan Ellison; first published in*F&SF*, May 1970. Harlan Ellison's introduction to this story, in his 1983 book *Partners in Wonder:*

"Sturgeon and I go back many years. No words by me are needed to add to the luster and familiarity of his reputation and his writings. Of his personal warmth and understanding of people I've written at length in Dangerous Visions and elsewhere, as I have written of his many kindnesses to me.

Ted came out to the Coast about five years ago and stayed with me for a while, and we got to know each other almost better than we wanted to. (Picture this, if you will: Ted has a penchant for running around in the buff; that's cool; I do it myself a lot of the time. But I make these tiny concessions to propriety when I know nice people with easily blown minds are coming to the house; I wear a towel. After the first few incidents—a cookie-peddling Brownie ran screaming, an Avon lady had an orgasm on my front stoop, a gentleman of undetermined sexual orientation started frothing—I suggested to Ted that while he had one of the truly imposing physiques of the Western World, and while we all loved him sufficiently to overlook the vice squad pigs who came to the door at the request of the Brownie's den momma, that he would make me much happier if he would for Christ's sake put something on. So he wandered around wearing these outrageous little red bikini underpants.) For his part, Ted had to put up with my quixotic morality, which flails wildly between degenerate and Puritan. I would catch him, from time to time, when I'd done something either terribly one or the other with a look on his face usually reserved for Salvation Army musicians who find their street corner is occupied by a nasty drunk lying in the gutter.

But we managed to be roommates without too much travail, and during that period I suggested to Ted that we do a story that we could dedicate to the memory of Dr. Paul Linebarger, who wrote speculative fiction of the highest order under the name Cordwainer Smith. Ted thought that was a pretty fair idea, so I typed out the title "Runesmith" and sat down—I type titles standing—and did the first section, up to the sentence, Smith, alone. Then!

Then, the dumb motherfucker pulled one of those wretched tricks only a basically evil person can conceive. He decided in between paragraphs that he didn't care for the way the story was going and he wrote the section beginning with 'Alone' and ending—without hope of linking or continuing—at the sentence that begins, 'The final sound of the fall was soft . . .'

'Now what the hell is that supposed to be?' I demanded, really pissed off. Sturgeon just smiled. 'How do you expect me to proceed from there, you clown? Everybody knows the plot has to start emerging in the first 1500 words, and you've tied me off like a gangrenous leg!' Sturgeon just smiled. I suppose you think that's funny, dump the hero into a pit, he can't get out, the lions are gnawing at his head. You think that's really funny. Dumb is what it is, Ted, it is dumb!" Sturgeon just smiled.

I threw my hands in the air, dumped the six pages of the story in a file for a week, and didn't get back to it till I'd calmed down. Then I went on and wrote—struggling to smooth the break between my first and second sections and that gibberish of his—the section running from Smith backed to the wall of the landing to the section where he returns to his former lodgings, where the mistake was first made. (But much of what you now find in that longish section came in rewrite. It was only three pages of typescript originally.)

Then I gave it to Ted. Twenty-six months passed. Finally, I called him—he was long since gone from my house, where it was possible to get an armlock on him—and told him if he wasn't going to get off his ass and finish the story, to return it to me, so I could lift out that demented section he'd written, and complete it myself. Nine months passed.

So I called him and told him I'd trash his damned house, rape his old lady, murder his kids, loot his exchequer, pillage his pantry, burn his silo, slaughter his oxen, pour salt on his fields and in general carry on cranky. Four months passed.

So I had a lady friend call him and tell him I was dying of the Dutch Elm Blight, lying on my death bed and asking, as a last request, for the story. He went to the mountains with his wife and kids for a holiday.

'What is all this nonsense about Sturgeon understanding love?' I screamed, stamping my foot.

Two weeks later Dr. Jekyll waltzed into the house and handed me the completed first draft, smiled, went away. I didn't waste any time. I rewrote it from stem to stern, cackling fiendishly all the while, sent it off, and kept the money!

Now how about that, Sturgeon!"

"Jorry's Gap": first published in *Adam,* October 1968. This was one of the first of the "Wina stories" (a name given by Sturgeon to a burst of new stories that flowed forth from his pen and typewriter shortly after the arrival in his southern California life of a woman named Wina who would become his fourth long-term committed life partner and the mother of his seventh child, Andros). He recounts Wina's positive effect on his life and writing in the introduction to his 1971 collection *Sturgeon Is Alive and Well,* which consists almost entirely of "Wina stories."

These stories were also the product of a special relationship Sturgeon developed with two young editors of "men's magazines," Merrill Miller and Jared Rutter, who agreed to purchase and publish any stories Sturgeon sent them, whether science fiction or not. *One can approach the typewriter with a wonderful sense of wingspread with a market like that,* Sturgeon said in his introduction to *Sturgeon Is Alive and Well.* He went on to say: *Nothing will ever stop me from writing science fiction, but there sure is a plot afoot to keep me from writing anything else, and I won't have it. Perhaps now you can understand why I am so pleased with this collection*